disrespectfully yours
best friends book club

jennifer chipman

Copyright © 2022 Jennifer Chipman

All rights reserved.

To every little girl who fell in love with superheroes when they were growing up. I hope you never hide your nerdy side. Embrace it.

Playlist

1. You're Such A - Hailee Steinfeld
2. Ugly Heart - G.R.L.
3. Gorgeous - Taylor Swift
4. Woman - Harry Styles
5. ...Ready For It? - Taylor Swift
6. Skin - Sabrina Carpenter
7. Dancing with the Devil - Demi Lovato
8. The Enemy - Andrew Belle
9. How You Get The Girl - Taylor Swift
10. Love The Way You Lie - Eminem, Rhianna
11. Into You - Ariana Grande
12. ...Ready For It? - Taylor Swift
13. Burnin' Up - Jonas Brothers
14. Starving - Hailee Steinfeld, Grey, Zedd
15. Delicate - Taylor Swift
16. I Knew You Were Trouble. - Taylor Swift
17. Style - Taylor Swift
18. Every Single Time - Jonas Brothers
19. Dress - Taylor Swift
20. sex - EDEN
21. I Like Me Better - Lauv

22. Are You Bored Yet? - Wallows, Clairo
23. used to you - mxmtoon
24. Skin - Rhianna
25. Video Games - Lana Del Rey
26. I Think He Knows - Taylor Swift
27. You're My Best Friend - Queen
28. Call It What You Want - Taylor Swift
29. I Won't Say (I'm In Love) - Susan Egan
30. Wrong Direction - Hailee Steinfeld
31. Love In The Dark - Adele
32. The Way I Loved You - Taylor Swift
33. i hate u, i love u - Garrett Nash, Olivia O'Brien
34. hoax - Taylor Swift
35. Fade - Lewis Capaldi
36. peace - Taylor Swift
37. Love Me Like You Do - Ellie Goulding
38. Underneath the Tree - Kelly Clarkson
39. New Year's Day - Taylor Swift

Table of Contents

Prologue	1
1. Angelina	5
2. Angelina	14
3. Benjamin	24
4. Angelina	33
5. Benjamin	44
6. Angelina	52
7. Benjamin	61
8. Angelina	69
9. Angelina	82
10. Angelina	92
11. Benjamin	101
12. Benjamin	112
13. Angelina	121
14. Angelina	135
15. Benjamin	145
16. Angelina	154
17. Angelina	162
18. Benjamin	175
19. Angelina	185
20. Benjamin	194
21. Angelina	204
22. Benjamin	213
23. Angelina	226
24. Benjamin	238
25. Angelina	253
26. Benjamin	259
27. Angelina	265
28. Benjamin	275
29. Angelina	284
30. Benjamin	292

31. Angelina	307
32. Angelina	315
33. Benjamin	323
34. Angelina	330
35. Angelina	337
36. Benjamin	345
37. Benjamin	357
Epilogue	366
Extended Epilogue	376
Acknowledgments	383
Also by Jennifer Chipman	385
About the Author	387

Prologue

From: ceo@willamettetech.com
Date: April 13, 2020 at 1:49 PM
To: #WillametteTech
Subject: Welcome to the Company!
Hello Team!
I'd like you all to help me welcome a brand-new hire to the company, Angelina Bradford, who is joining our marketing team from PNW Marketing Co.
Have a great day.
Alexander Larsen

From: ceo@willamettetech.com
Date: August 20, 2020 at 11:33 AM
To: #WillametteTech
Subject: Welcome to the Company!
Good afternoon!
I'm excited to announce another new addition to our team: Benjamin Sullivan, joining us as our Controller. Benjamin has spent his last 5 years working for KPMG and we are happy to have him here.
Welcome, Benjamin!

Alexander Larsen

From: b.sullivan@willamettetech.com
Date: September 16, 2021 at 12:04 PM
To: a.bradford@willamettetech.com
Subject: Information Needed
Miss Bradford,
I was told you oversaw the social media campaigns for the last year. I am emailing to inquire about some additional information on budgets and spending, as I find myself missing key details. I'd love to meet with you at your earliest convenience.
Benjamin Sullivan

From: a.bradford@willamettetech.com
Date: September 16, 2021 at 2:12 PM
To: b.sullivan@willamettetech.com
Subject: RE: Information Needed
Hello Mr. Sullivan,
I attached a document with all of the documents originally submitted, as well as the reports from after the campaigns had finished. I think you will find they are quite thoroughly documented.
Please let me know if you need anything else. I am out of town for the next week at a conference, so I am unable to meet in person but am happy to answer your questions over email.
Angelina

From: b.sullivan@willamettetech.com
Date: May 02, 2022 at 1:38 PM
To: a.bradford@willamettetech.com
Subject: Today's Meeting
Miss Bradford,
I was looking over your report from today's meetings and I noticed a few errors in the document. I highlighted them in red

and have attached them in this email so you can correct them before the document is sent out to the rest of the company.
Benjamin Sullivan

From: a.bradford@willamettetech.com
Date: May 02, 2022 at 1:50 PM
To: b.sullivan@willamettetech.com
Subject: RE: Today's Meeting
Ben—I can call you Ben, right?
I really don't need you to send me corrections on my work. I promise, I am competent and I know what I'm doing.
Regards,
Angelina

From: b.sullivan@willamettetech.com
Date: July 28, 2022 at 9:43 AM
To: a.bradford@willamettetech.com
Subject: Budget Proposal Due
Miss Bradford,
I am writing to let you know the budget proposal for your department is due by tomorrow at the latest. Please get it to me at your earliest convenience.
Thank you,
Benjamin Sullivan

From: a.bradford@willamettetech.com
Date: July 28, 2022 at 4:05 PM
To: b.sullivan@willamettetech.com
Subject: Budget Proposal
Benjamin,
You will find the budget proposal for my department attached to this email.
Please do not hesitate to email me if you have any questions.
Angelina

CHAPTER 1
Angelina

"I hate him," I groaned to my best friend Gabrielle as she sat on my desk, legs swinging out underneath her as she flipped through my most recent ad campaign photoshoot.

"Ang," Gabrielle rolled her eyes at me. "You don't even *know* this guy; might I remind you? You've never even met him in person."

To be fair, she'd been listening to me complaining about him for the last year. Since the damn emails started. The guy knew how to get on my last nerve, that much was obvious. I'd always had a short fuse, easy to temper, but it was like one word from him could ruin my whole day. One. Lousy. Word.

Somehow, all this time I'd managed to avoid going to his office or meeting him for coffee. Whenever he tried to talk about business related projects or expenses, I'd handle it all over emails. Like a mature, professional adult. I was proud of myself for that, because if I got this angry at him over his words, how much worse would it be when I saw his face? I hadn't even let myself picture what he might look like.

Well, that was a half-truth. I liked to picture some hideous man who was so insecure in himself that he had to take it out on others. Either way, talk about a fragile ego. In my experience, the only people who spent all of their time tearing others down were the kind of people who had no self-confidence of their own—which was not the kind of person I wanted to surround myself with.

I huffed, and Gabbi set down the photos. "Okay, but seriously, listen to this," I said, opening the email I'd received from him just a few moments ago and reading it out loud.

From: b.sullivan@willamettetech.com
Date: September 02, 2022 at 3:56 PM
To: a.bradford@willamettetech.com
Subject: Department Budget
Dear Miss Bradford,
The attached budget was denied.
Please be sure to make the appropriate corrections, which can be seen highlighted in red, assure it is in the correct formatting, and then resend it to me.
Yours,
Benjamin Sullivan

"I just don't understand why he won't approve anything I send him! And highlighting all of the changes I need to make in red? Who even does that?"

Gabbi peered at the email as she chewed on her thumbnail. "There must be *some* reason, Angelina."

"Yeah, he's determined to make my life a living hell," I muttered. "Gabbi, seriously. I really think if there was one, I would have found it by now."

She shrugged and played with the stack of sticky notes on my desk. "Why don't you just ask Nicolas? He's Benjamin's boss, after all."

Nicolas was one of my best friends from college and the son of the company's owner. He had his own hopes and aspirations: I knew he wanted to take over when his dad retired. We'd always talked about it, even when we were sitting in business classes together. He was a year ahead of me and had joined the family business when he graduated, working his way up through the ranks because he didn't want his father to just hand him the position he wanted.

Eventually, Nicolas got the promotion to Chief Financial Officer over one (you guessed it) Benjamin Sullivan. I knew because Nic had told me all about it, but it didn't mean that Benjamin had to be such a jerk about everything. We were all adults here, anyway, so what did he get off on, sending me rude emails about my proposals?

Maybe it was some weird form of foreplay for him. *Let's annoy Angelina before I go home and jack off!* He certainly wasn't getting any with this attitude. The thought calmed me down, bringing me back to the present, where Gabbi was giving me her typical I'm-your-best-friend-you-should-listen-to-me stare. She was good at those. And so damn good at reading me.

"Whose side are you on? I've been going back and forth with him on my freaking budget for *weeks* now. Do you really think I'm just going to let Nicolas swoop in and fix my problem?" I sighed in frustration. "No. Absolutely not. I'll figure this out myself."

"Alright. Well, you know where to find me if you change your mind."

I exhaled as Gabbi hopped off my desk and headed back towards her office in the human resources department. Once I was alone again, I steeled myself, focusing on the keyboard in front of me. It was time for another email. I was seriously fed up with this asshole.

From: a.bradford@willamettetech.com
Date: September 02, 2022 at 4:17 PM
To: b.sullivan@willamettetech.com
Subject: RE: Department Budget
Dear Benjamin,
We've been going back and forth on this budget for almost a

month already. I reviewed the highlighted sections and have made sure it is all correct.

Can you just tell me what about it is seemingly not able to be approved since we don't seem to be making any headway here? My department really needs this to be finalized so we can get our marketing campaigns together for the next year. Things like this aren't cheap.

Thanks,
Angelina

I was packing up my bag, getting ready to head home for the day when his response came in a few minutes later.

From: b.sullivan@willamettetech.com
Date: September 02, 2022 at 4:21 PM
To: a.bradford@willamettetech.com
Subject: RE: Department Budget
Dear Miss Bradford,
We're recommending that all departments cut their budgets by 20% for the next year. Please adjust accordingly.
I've attached a template so the formatting is correct.
Yours,
Benjamin Sullivan

Seriously? I wondered where the hell this was coming from, because I knew our bottom line wasn't suffering. In fact, it was quite the opposite. Our software systems and applications were flourishing, and we had a great team of designers and programmers who were constantly coming up with new and innovative ideas to keep us expanding. We didn't just focus on software for consumers or businesses, we had departments for both. Either way, I needed this budget so we could *actually* sell them. No matter how good a product is, you can't sell it if no one knows about it. Grumbling, I typed out another quick response before shutting my computer off.

From: a.bradford@willamettetech.com
Date: September 02, 2022 at 4:30 PM
To: b.sullivan@willamettetech.com
Subject: RE: Department Budget
Dear Benjamin,
20%, really?
You'd think the company is going under. We're a high-profiting software company, and we're not going to stay on top by cutting costs that much.
However ridiculous I find that to be, though, I will work on making the necessary changes. The new budget will be attached on Monday.
You will be pleased to know that I'll make sure the formatting is correct.
Always,
Angelina

    I hadn't even gotten out of my office when my work phone pinged. Even though it was way later than I wanted to be here, on a *Friday*, when most people left early (citing the need for a good work/life balance), I glanced down. There was a notification for another email.
    "Geez, does this guy have anything better to do than respond to my emails?" I murmured to myself. I decided to pull it open anyway, just to see if he gave me another snarky response like my grammar being incorrect or using the wrong punctuation.

From: b.sullivan@willamettetech.com
Date: September 02, 2022 at 4:45 PM
To: a.bradford@willamettetech.com
Subject: RE: Department Budget
Dear Miss Bradford,
Thank you.
Benjamin

Thank you? That's it? Dealing with this guy was nothing less than incredibly aggravating. I was not going to let him ruin my night, though. Gabbi, Nicolas, and I had plans to hit the bar; the three of us were going out for the first time in a long time, and Benjamin Sullivan's arrogance would remain confined to the office.

But I had to release my frustration in some way, so I typed out an email that unfortunately would have to stay in my drafts.

From: a.bradford@willamettetech.com
Date: September 02, 2022 at 4:47 PM
To: b.sullivan@willamettetech.com
Subject: RE: Department Budget (DRAFT)
You're an ass.
Disrespectfully Yours,
Angelina.

∽

"So," I started, bringing the glass of beer up to my lips as we sat around a high-top table in the middle of the crowded bar. Gabbi hadn't arrived yet—she'd texted saying she'd be a little late, so Nicolas and I were catching up as we waited for her. Normally we would have come together, but she had been working on something in her room when I told her I was leaving and said to go without her.

Nicolas raised an eyebrow. "*So?*"

"Anything new?" I asked him, setting the glass down and crossing my arms on the table.

"With *me?*" He sounded astonished, as if there was no way there could be anything going on in his life that I didn't already know about. Okay, he had me there, because I knew he was probably too busy with work to have any updates on life.

I didn't want to ask him about Benjamin Sullivan and why he was such an asshole, although it was killing me inside. No point in making Nicolas think I was interested in him, or anything crazy like that.

"Well." He leaned back in his chair. "I got a new assistant. Dad's hoping I can keep this one without scaring her off." We both laughed at that.

Nicolas was a flirt, and I knew several of his assistants had quit because they couldn't take his self-centered personality. I also suspected some of them were a little too into trying to sleep with the CEO's son. And Nicolas might have been happy to share about his conquests, but there was no way he'd risk sleeping with his assistant.

"Also, Dad's planned some sort of company retreat. I think he has some big announcement to make." He scratched his head. "Not that he'll tell me what it is, of course, but I have my hunch."

"Company retreat?" I resisted the urge to groan as I focused on that very specific detail. "Where they make us do stupid things like brainstorming ideas and trust falls?"

Nic stared at me. "Yeah, Ang. He wants to rent out an idyllic mountainside resort so we can do silly little team building exercises." He snorted, but I didn't think he was kidding. In fact, I was pretty sure that was exactly what Alexander Larsen had in mind.

"Oh." I was serious when I said I thought they were stupid. "I'm just saying, half the time people want to do these things when we could accomplish more over email." Especially Benjamin Sullivan. "And anyway, when is this even supposed to happen? It's going to start getting cold soon, and I *definitely* don't want to be out there in the snow."

"Sometime this month, I think?" Nicolas shrugged. "He's ironing all the details out over the weekend. I'm supposed to go help him scout the final location and make sure everything is perfect. It'll be during the week, so don't worry about being gone on the weekend."

"Is everyone going to go? Like the whole company?" Surely it would be better if Gabbi was there too, but he shook his head, crushing my hopes.

"Just department and team heads, I think. It's based on the top percentage of the company. Dad hasn't told me how many yet, though."

I pouted. "So, no Gabbi." She wasn't the head of her HR team yet. Damn. I could have used my best friend for moral support.

"Probably not."

"No Gabbi what?"

Nicolas grinned sheepishly as we both turned towards Gabbi approaching our table. "Hi, Gabrielle. Dad's planning a company retreat, but it's just department heads and up. So I don't think you'll get to go."

"Oh." Gabbi didn't seem fazed, tossing her curled brown hair over one shoulder. "That's okay. I don't particularly love those kinds of things anyway. Having to spend time with a bunch of suits? No thanks. I'd much prefer to spend time with a book." Then she turned to me, nudging me with her elbow. "Hey, think your email buddy will be there?"

"Gabbi," I warned, but it was enough to spark Nic's curiosity.

"Email buddy?"

"Yes," Gabbi said, ignoring my glare. "Benjamin Sullivan has been emailing back and forth with her all day. For months, really."

I felt my cheeks grow hot at the implications of her comment. "About the *budget*," I added quickly, noticing Nicolas's rapt interest. "I've never even met the guy. We've only ever emailed about work stuff. And to be honest, he's kind of an ass." I grimaced, thinking about his less-than-friendly demeanor over our online correspondence.

"Well, I guess you can meet him in a few weeks," Nicolas laughed. "I'm sure he'll be there. He's pretty much a shoo-in for my job whenever I take over as CEO. I'm sure he's still annoyed that he got passed up the first time."

Oh boy. This was going to be a fun company retreat. *Not.*

"Well, I'm starving," Gabbi said, pulling out the menu and

scanning it. "Anyone else want pretzel bites? I'm going to go order a beer."

"Get me another one," I said, finishing the last dregs of mine with a final gulp. If I was going to be forced to spend a week near the devil who was making my working life miserable, I'd need a lot more alcohol than this.

CHAPTER 2
Angelina

The girls were all gathered around the kitchen table in my and Gabbi's apartment, a rare occasion where we didn't meet at a coffee shop or a restaurant for dinner. We had all been friends since college, and we still tried to hang out at least once a week. Our weekly dates were some of my favorite moments, and I always looked forward to seeing them.

This week, Gabbi was griping about the fact that I was going to be leaving her alone. "I can't believe you're going to be gone a whole week," she whined.

"I can't believe that you don't get to go," I sighed, dejected.

"What am I going to do without you for a whole week?"

Charlotte and Noelle eyed us like we were both a little off our rockers. Maybe we were, but there was something about spending every day with your best friend—working together, living together—that made the idea of being separated, even for a measly five days, absolutely horrible.

"I'm sure you'll make do," I laughed. And she would—I knew her. She always had something going on, though it had been significantly less since her last relationship had ended. "If not, there's always books."

Some people hated their roommates, and some people

couldn't live with their best friends. We weren't either of those people. I was glad we had such a close friendship and lived together. Gabbi and I would come home from work, open a bottle of wine, and vent about our days as we took turns making dinner. Or ordering takeout. All bets were off when we pulled out the ice cream.

Our friendship started Freshman year of college when I walked into my dorm room to find Gabrielle sitting on the floor, unpacking a box of books onto her bookshelf.

"I only brought my favorites," she'd said sheepishly, even though there were about twenty books around her. That collection only grew over the year, but that was when I first discovered my love of romance novels. She'd share her favorites with me, and I'd devour them, and then we'd both read them again. It was a good system.

"Hi," I said. "I'm Angelina. Your roommate."

She grabbed my outstretched hand and shook it. "I'm Gabrielle. But you can call me Gabbi. Or Gabs. No one ever really calls me my full name." She'd wrinkled her nose a little, making me laugh.

"I know the feeling. Most people call me Ang, or Lina."

From then on, we were inseparable. That same day, we met the girls who shared the room directly across the hall from us, and then the four of us did everything together. We lived in the dorms for two years before moving out into a house off-campus for our last two. Despite being different majors, we bonded over books and movies and shared everything with each other. We always did. Even when we graduated and started our first jobs, we always kept up constant contact.

We lost Noelle for a bit there, when she moved to New York for a year with her then-boyfriend. Once she got back, though, we started our weekly books and coffee dates and we'd never missed one since. Charlotte and Gabbi, our resident I-burn-through-books girls, would give us recommendations while Noelle and I tried to keep up with our book per week.

Noelle started a new job this summer after graduating with her master's and was now working at our Alma Mater as a Student Advisor. She loved it, as much as she loved her professor boyfriend, Matthew. I was happy she was happy. We had all watched her fight her attraction—and her feelings—towards him, but thankfully, everything worked out, and now the two of them were more in love than ever. They were living together, working at the university, and torturing the rest of us with their sweetness.

As for me? Well, I was still trying to fight my way up to the top, working towards my end goal: Chief Marketing Officer. After college, I had started out working at a marketing agency in Portland, but after two years, Nicolas got me an interview for the Marketing team of the tech firm he and Gabbi worked at, and the rest was history. Now I was the head of my department, working directly under the CMO. And yes, I was very much coveting her job, to the point where I would do absolutely anything to make my boss happy. Like working a ton of overtime even though I was definitely overworked.

I might have issues saying no. It may have also been the reason I was perpetually single, since I had no time or energy to even try to start anything resembling a relationship. Sure, I had a few flings here and there, but nothing that was remotely worth committing to.

There hadn't been a guy I had ever looked at and wanted more with. It wasn't like I was craving cuddles or even sex. I could take care of myself, after all.

"Don't forget we have to figure out plans for my birthday later this month," Charlotte said, knocking me out of my train of thought.

"I'm still recovering from Gabbi's party," Noelle groaned. We celebrated her birthday last weekend and we all may have drunk a *bit* too much. So what if we were twenty-six? We'd had fun.

Charlotte laughed. "I don't need anything *that* intense, I promise. I was just thinking like pedicures, and we could go to a winery or something? Noelle, you can bring Matthew if you want." She paused. "Since, um, Daniel will probably come." We all eyed her suspiciously, thinking the same thing.

Daniel was my brother, a year older than us. He had befriended Charlotte during our Freshman year of college. Sometimes it still surprised me, knowing my brother could be a quiet, awkward Engineer, that he and Charlotte had become so close. She was bubbly, constantly talking, and always wore a shade of pink. I had laughed to myself more than once watching him walk her home from class in her ballet leotard.

They went to dinner—just the two of them—all the time, Charlotte would drag him around town, and they spent most of their free time together, but they had never dated. Or kissed. Nothing had ever happened between them. Not once, in eight years of friendship, had they ever indicated they were interested in something more with each other.

According to Charlotte, at least. But I trusted her, and I knew that if anything happened between them, she would tell us right away. Especially because we all made fun of her more times than I could count. Even my mom had asked me why the two of them weren't together yet. It was one of the brief times I'd actually talked to her on the phone these last few years, but still. She was too busy for me, and I'd accepted that a long time ago.

"Sure," Noelle said, breaking the tension. "I'm always down to bring Matthew. If that's okay with you two?" Noelle looked at Gabbi and me.

"It's fine. You guys know I don't date."

She rolled her eyes. "I remember when *I* said that. It didn't really work out for me."

"Your boyfriend is cool," Gabbi shrugged. "I don't mind."

"Alright. Then it's settled." Charlotte grinned. "Birthday weekend is a go!"

We spent the rest of the night chatting, laughing, and theorizing about our favorite book series, which was always a highlight. I liked that we had gotten each other into the same books, and that we had an endless supply of conversations.

Noelle had brought the book she was working on, asking us for help making sure it wasn't too bad—the girl was an incredible writer, but she had impostor syndrome like no one's business—and we all reassured her that it was going to be great and we'd give her all the feedback she needed. I believed in her wholeheartedly. Plus, her little blush when she confessed that her boyfriend had read some of it—namely, the sex scenes—was the cutest thing on the planet.

I was so grateful to have these women as my best friends.

I BRUSHED my hair over my shoulder, then closed the door to my car before walking to the main lodge of the mountainside retreat to check in. I'd go back for my bags after getting the room keys, not wanting to lug my suitcase around in the gravel twice.

In terms of locations they could have chosen for a week of corporate bonding, I had to admit, this wasn't bad at all. The place was beautiful. Unfortunately, it was completely off the grid too, with no cell phone reception. Something I found out as soon as I pulled up to the main lodge and tried to text the girls to tell them I'd made it safely. So. That was a no-go. Which, I supposed at the age of twenty-six, it wasn't like I needed to report my every movement to my best friends. But I liked someone knowing where I was, especially since I rarely talked to my parents these days.

The main building had a large wrap-around porch with a dozen rocker chairs scattered around, and I could see it went around towards the back, too, where the lake was supposed to be. I had only done a *little* bit of research since finding out where they were sending us. And by a little, itty bitty, tiny bit, I meant that I had hyper-focused on reading the website about the property: all of the different housing options they had (specifically, the small cabins where we would be staying), the activities we would be doing, and of course, what amenities were offered.

Here's the thing. I grew up in Oregon—I was born and raised in Milwaukie—but I was *not* a camping girl. Or a glamping girl. Not really an *outdoorsy* girl period, which meant that this little company retreat that I was attending was quite literally near the bottom of the activities I would have chosen for myself. Despite claiming that she would have hated it, Gabrielle would have fit in perfectly here. She would have loved to go for hikes, take photos, and breathe in the fresh mountain air. She even had the clothes to match it. My wardrobe was seriously lacking in comparison: I didn't own flannel shirts or puffy vests. Not that I would be caught dead in either. I'd decided a long time ago what kind of style I was going to rock: tailored suits and business dresses in the office, and something less formal but still presentable at all other times. Very rarely, I'd dress a little edgy. A leather jacket, sexy bustier, and some tight jeans accompanied by heeled boots normally did the trick to make me feel hot. But this? The only clothes I owned that were worthy of getting dirty were my workout clothes, which now, of course, occupied about fifty percent of my suitcase. I had thrown in some casual flowy dresses, too, because I didn't want to dress like a slob at dinner, and I figured they'd come in handy.

Twiddling my necklace with my fingers, I opened the door to the lodge, taking a deep breath of the scent of the pines around me before stepping inside. At least there was one thing I liked about this so far: the air felt fresher up here. I could breathe clean air, unlike living and working in the city. Even in Portland, sometimes it felt suffocating.

I was marveling at the high beams and the architecture, taking in the warmth of the dark wooden design of the building, when I crashed into something. The force was enough to knock me backwards. I braced myself for impact, shutting my eyes, but it never came.

It turned out, that something was a chest. Somebody's chest. A chest belonging to a man who'd seemingly caught me by the waist before I could fall on my ass.

I let my eyes drift up from his chest—a very lovely, firm, definitely not flabby chest—to his blue collared shirt, up to his face. It was a very nice face. Dark brown hair, lighter than mine, and warm brown eyes that stared back at me blankly. I was wondering if I was ever going to utter another word when he finally righted me, stepped back, and shoved his hands in his pockets.

"You're welcome," he said as I kept gaping at him. "The correct response in this situation is thank you, you know."

I blinked. "What?"

"I caught you from falling. Therefore, proper etiquette dictates that you should thank me. You know, for saving you from a giant bruise on your ass." He leaned down to my ear conspiratorially. "And imminent embarrassment."

I frowned, stopping myself from saying *what* again, just because I had the feeling he was going to tease me over that, too. Instead, I gave him my best glower. "I would have been just fine if you hadn't been standing here blocking the way."

"Oh, yeah?" He chuckled. "Well, I'm sorry for being in your way, *Princess*."

"I'm not—" I sighed. I wasn't a selfish, spoiled brat like he was implying with his annoyingly sarcastic tone. I just didn't expect anyone to be standing in my way. "Whatever. I'm sorry. Thank you for your help." It was almost painful to say the words, the way he was so cocky and sneering at my own awkward experience. I grit my teeth, expecting another equally snarky response, but instead, a different voice called from across the room.

"Sullivan!" A guy came up to him, patting the irritating man on the back.

Wait. Sullivan? As in...

"Benjamin Sullivan?" My jaw was probably on the floor, but I couldn't help it. *This* was Benjamin Sullivan? The asshole I had been exchanging emails with for the past year...

Oh.

Oh *no*.

God dammit, he was hot. It wasn't just his height and how

many inches he had on me—an impressive feat, considering my leggy five foot ten inches. It wasn't even the swoop of his hair or the depth of his eyes. It was just... everything. His presence was massive, and he was simply, unfortunately, gorgeous.

Fuck me. The asshole standing in front of me was my workplace nemesis. The one who could never resist pointing out when I made a mistake. The man I hated, who I'd called Satan behind his back several hundred times.

It took me a moment to realize that he was looking at me skeptically, with a curious frown. I hadn't told him who I was. Did I have to? I didn't like this man. Was sure that after I told him my name, he would realize he didn't like me either. My entire week would be filled with one awkward interaction with him after another, wouldn't it?

Any moment now, Nicolas would get here, which would make the situation even more unpleasant. No matter the smaller percentage of employees present at the company's retreat, word would spread, and soon everyone would find out about how I had crashed into our Controller. Way to make a great first impression.

"Angelina," I finally choked out. "I'm Angelina Bradford."

A flash of something went through his face. Disdain? Annoyance? I wasn't sure, but I narrowed my eyes as he stared back at me. "I see," he said, sticking out his hand. I must have stared at it for a beat too long because he leaned over again and whispered, "You're supposed to shake it."

"I know that."

"Do you?"

Was it possible to escape this plight without wanting to bury myself in a hole? Here I was, finally seeing this man in person for the first time, and what was I doing? Acting like an idiot. I took his hand and shook it.

"Now, that wasn't so hard, was it?"

I changed my mind. He might *look* like an angel, but he was still the devil underneath all those muscles, and I had to remind myself how vehemently I hated him.

I gave him a grimace, and he returned his attention to the other guys in the lobby as I walked to the desk to get my cabin information. I groaned to myself before approaching the counter. The sooner I got my key, the sooner I could flee this nightmare, including—but not limited to—Benjamin's much-too-beautiful face.

The receptionist gave me a look, but I handed her all my information, and she was quick to gather my packet, a key, and a map. "You're in cabin 13," she said, drawing a circle to its location. "Please don't lose your key since we don't have any copies. If you need any extra towels or toiletries, feel free to stop by up here, as well as if you need any additional information about recreational activities this week." She gave me a small smile. "Breakfast, lunch, and dinner will be provided in the lodge every day between the hours listed on the pamphlet, and there's also a schedule of events your company has organized inside. Let me know if we can help you with anything else."

I thanked her and waved her goodbye, and then I was on the way back to my car, fetching my suitcase, duffel bag, and a large purse. I trudged through the dirt path to the small cabin, grateful it hadn't rained today so I didn't have to traipse through any mud. Knowing my luck, though, and the Pacific Northwest, I was sure I wouldn't avoid it forever.

The ground sloped a little as I got closer, and I caught myself from stumbling, looking around to make sure no one saw me. I wasn't normally so clumsy, so why did I feel like such a klutz today? Luckily, no one was around, and then there was my cabin in all its moss-covered glory. Ah, just Pacific Northwest things.

The buildings were small, but each had a little porch with two chairs in the front, and even though the other cabins were close, the tall trees surrounding me made it feel private. I heaved a sigh; grateful they hadn't forced us to share a room. I'd read enough romance novels that I had no desire to experience the one bed trope in real life. *They'd* be the one sleeping on the floor, not me. Now it was just me, content to curl up in bed all by myself.

Inside sat a queen-sized bed with a woodsy-inspired comforter. I was surprised that I didn't mind the decor: black bears and trees. My sense of style was different: I preferred sleek and modern, black and white with pops of color. But here it worked. And, I realized with a small pang of familiarity, it reminded me of home. Of my mom, who loved black bears and had collected figurines of them as I grew up. I didn't want to think about home now, though.

I collapsed on the bed with a sigh, then peeled off my riding boots. I wore dark jeans and a long-sleeved blouse on the drive up—more casual than I would have worn to the office, but less casual than the mountains seemed to warrant. Luckily, the drive had only been about an hour and a half, so I didn't have to leave at the crack of dawn to arrive on time.

My eyes drifted over the schedule as I heard voices from outside. I peeked out the window, wondering who could possibly be making that much noise, and my stomach plummeted. Of all people in the world. Satan himself was walking in the cabin next to mine.

I groaned, flopping back down on the bed. Of course, he was my neighbor for the week. I still couldn't believe I had (quite literally) run into Benjamin Sullivan first thing upon arriving. It was like the universe was determined to punish me for something—and I didn't even know what I had done wrong.

Well, I wasn't going to let him ruin what was supposed to be a week of *corporate bonding*, as Nicolas had called it, but also my much-needed break from the fifty or sixty-hour workweeks I'd been chugging through lately.

I was simply going to pretend he didn't exist.

CHAPTER 3
Benjamin

Chuckling to myself, I watched her figure disappear from the room. She faded from the edges of my vision in a cloud of fragrant sweetness, almost like vanilla, with just a hint of something spicy. I didn't like the way the scent lingered, like it was sticking to me.

"What was that?" Liam elbowed me in the side, bringing me back to reality.

I shook my head. "I don't even know."

To say I was surprised was an understatement. Angelina Bradford, bumping—literally—into me. I was just standing in the lobby, minding my own business, looking at my watch as I waited for my boss—who was younger than me and had gotten the job because he was the CEO's son, much to my annoyance—to arrive when she came crashing in. Crashing into *me*. By the time I realized where she was headed, I was already catching her. She couldn't get out of there fast enough the moment she realized who I was; she'd gotten her cabin key and high-tailed it out of the building.

Her reaction amused me. I knew who she was as soon as I looked at her. After all this time, it was hard to miss anything about her. There she was, after almost two years. Angelina Bradford, in the flesh. It had only been once, but I'd seen her before, briefly, right after I started at the company. A fleeting moment, really, yet her dark hair and long legs were embedded in my memory. I was so intrigued I'd even asked the HR girl leading my tour who she was. I couldn't explain my captivation, but when we started talking over email, she wasn't at all what I had expected. Even with all our daily correspondence, I still didn't know her. We'd been emailing back and forth for a long time, and yet I found myself stunned into silence when she'd looked up at me with that flustered expression.

Of course I recognized her instantly. It wasn't just the way she looked or how she carried herself. Angelina was taller than most girls, with that cherry-red lipstick and her silky-smooth black hair. And if she couldn't be more full of herself, her hair was perfectly styled even on a retreat to the mountains. She was so put together, so focused on her appearance and everything being impeccable. Maybe that's why I liked to annoy her, to rile her up, to see her perfect facade start to crack—why I got a kick out of pointing out when she was wrong.

I couldn't get over how she'd looked completely taken aback to see me today. With only a few floors separating our offices and an internal company database, somehow she still didn't know what I looked like. And I didn't miss the slight look of disappointment on her face before she narrowed her eyes at me.

How was I going to make it through a week of us hating each other in person? A work conflict certainly wouldn't look good when I was trying to vie for a promotion. This was going terribly already.

I stood there like an idiot, frowning at the door where Angelina had exited. Of all the people in the universe fate could decide to deliver to me, it had to be the stubborn girl I'd decided to hate. The woman that, somewhere in between our email feud, her refusal to meet with me or even discuss anything with me in person, and her being hellbent on contradicting me, I had come to resent. Although it seemed to me that she was determined to hate me too. Well, two could play that game.

I had to come up with an all-new game plan now. I needed to get rid of the hostility in her eyes. Even if all I wanted was to drive her crazy and piss her off, I needed to fake it and play civil with her. At the office, I liked imagining her face when she read my responses, making her resend proposals or budgets a few more times than necessary because I liked fucking with her. Barely suppressed rage was clear in her words and never failed to make a grin spread across my face. But if she hated me, would she sabotage my chances for a promotion? Being the Controller of a big technology company was a big deal, and it was something I had worked my ass off for, but I also wanted the freedom to make more decisions and take that next step.

"Fuck," I cursed to myself, smoothing my hand over my face. I'd never worried about women finding me unappealing. I worked hard on myself, my body and my charm, and it had paid off over the years. And despite Angelina's initial reaction when she saw me, her entire demeanor had changed during our conversation. The look in her eyes? The contempt was evident. I was going to have to fix that. Because having Angelina Bradford ruin my chances for CFO was definitely not on my list of goals for this company retreat.

It didn't matter that I couldn't stand her or that she couldn't stand me. I had one goal this week: to get in the good graces of Nicolas Larsen, my boss and current CFO. This company was his birthright, and his father had been preparing him to take over for years. It was only a matter of time before Alexander Larsen handed his son the role of CEO, and when that happened, I needed to have secured my spot on the executive team. I was under him, even if I hated it, and when he got his father's job, I wanted to make sure that I was going to be the one to take his spot.

And I would do anything to achieve my dream. Including charming the oh-so-lovely Angelina Bradford.

"You good, bro?" Liam asked me.

"Yeah," I nodded, running my fingers through my hair. *Was I though?* I'd been with Willamette Tech for over two years, and yet, sometimes, it still felt like I'd just left Texas and moved back to the Pacific Northwest. Two years, and was I any closer to achieving my goals? I wasn't so sure about that. I barely saw my brother, hadn't gotten the work promotion I'd worked so hard towards—not yet—and where did that leave me? It felt like I could never sit still for long; like I was always searching for the next big thing. I'd been doing it since college, or maybe even high school: chasing the path that I thought would lead me to the greatest rewards. But now... I didn't know where I would go from here. Especially if my goals didn't pan out.

I left the main lodge with Liam and a few of our colleagues, returning to our cars to grab our bags and hauling them to the little buildings we'd be sleeping in for the next week. Despite the lack of access to the Wi-Fi, and thus the inability to do my job, I had to admit that this retreat was a welcome break from my life.

Besides, this place reminded me of my childhood. The mountains, deep within the trees, it all took me back to Boy Scout Camp every summer. Those days when I couldn't wait to get out of the house: away from my kid sister and my parents so I could run free in the wilderness. Even if the other kids would make fun of me for always bringing a book with me. I still remembered carrying Percy Jackson to camp and coming home with it well-worn and a little dirty, but I didn't care. My older brother, Hunter, was always there, too, since he was in the same Troop as me. But he was two years older, so we'd often not see that much of each other all summer. He was also infuriatingly perfect at everything, which annoyed me more than it should have. And now, here I was, fifteen some-odd years after my Scout days, surprisingly ready for a week in the woods. Sure, it wasn't exactly like camp, or even remotely like tent camping, but it felt a little bit like coming home. Maybe this winter I'd have to come back for a weekend to ski. It'd been too long since I'd taken advantage of all the activities Oregon had to offer.

"Meet you back at the main lodge?" I waved goodbye to the other guys as I headed inside my cabin, quickly collapsing on the bed. Despite my more-than-strange encounter with Angelina, I smiled to myself. It was going to be a good week. There were no expectations, no disappointed parents or obsessive ex-girlfriends trying to get back together. I could use a break, a week without a reminder that I somehow managed to destroy every relationship I touched.

It was just me, a colleague who hated me, and the boss I desperately needed to get to like me enough to promote me. No sweat. This week would be fine.

∼

THIS WEEK COULD NOT BE GOING any worse. And it was still just the first afternoon.

After freshening up in the cabin and changing out of my button-up and slacks, I threw on a thermal sweater and jeans and made my way over to the clearing outside the main lodge. We were all gathering to wait for the big boss, for whatever welcome session he had planned. I hoped it included food because I was starving. I quickly found Liam, Noah, and Kevin, grateful for their presence as I sidled up to them in the crowd.

Not everyone from the Portland offices was here, but it still felt like I didn't know most of the people around me. I assumed they worked on different floors and in different departments from mine. Truthfully, I had little reason to interact with most of our company employees; I mostly talked with the department chairs, and even then, my interactions were limited.

Angelina Bradford was the exception. She seemed determined to always get the last word. All my emails, even the shortest ones, would get a response, especially if they were snarky and pretentious.

It amused me, picturing her angrily typing away at her desk, trying to come up with quick-witted responses that wouldn't get her in trouble but would get the point across—which was that she couldn't stand me. I'd dare to say, it was almost a form of stress relief. If anyone else read our emails, they would hardly think anything was amiss. But the subtext was there, underlying, in the little quips and retorts in between a budget reallocation or expense reports. It was *fun*. She was the only colleague I put any effort into talking to.

Still, I rolled my eyes thinking about that delightful dark-haired girl. She was obviously not happy with my presence here, as was evident by her current attitude: Angelina was glaring at me from across the fire pit, and I was pretty sure she tried to move as far away as possible when I reached the clearing. Sure, maybe I deserved it, but it still bothered me. I wasn't a bad guy.

She was standing next to Nicolas—my boss, and her friend. I knew they were close from how he'd mention her in the accounting department during coffee breaks. I wondered if she ever mentioned me to him. She had traded her blouse for a fuzzy sweatshirt and her heeled boots for a pair of gym shoes. I didn't know why it surprised me to see her like that, so casual and laid back, but it did. I couldn't decide if I liked it, and I frowned at the thought. Why was I even thinking about it? It wasn't like I saw her regularly at work to even be able to compare her work attire to her casual one. For all I knew, this was how she dressed every day. And who was I to decide if I liked what she was wearing? She caught my eye, and I turned away quickly, cursing internally.

I didn't want her to think I was staring at her. It wasn't even on purpose—she just intrigued me. Unpleasantly, of course. Liam nudged me, giving me a "What was that?" look, and I mouthed back, "Later." I focused my attention on the man now standing on the small wooden platform that overlooked the lake.

"Welcome, everyone! Welcome to a week of rest, relaxation, and, hopefully, good company," Alexander Larsen announced among everyone's cheers. There was a gathered group of about fifty employees all scattered around a large fire pit. It was still nice outside for September, thankfully, though it would probably get chilly when the sun went down. "We've arranged different team building activities, both within your departments and with others throughout the company. You can also take advantage of the other amenities this resort has to offer, like the hot tub and the gym." You could hear a few excited cheers spread through the crowd at that. "Dinner will be served in the main hall every night. I hope you all take this time to unwind from the stress of the office. I know how hard you all work daily, and this is just another little way to say thank you for your dedication and the amount of revenue we've made in the last year." Everyone cheered, because we'd been working our asses off, and we were all glad when our hard work paid off.

"I'm going to call out the groups for when we have activities; you'll be paired with the same people all week. We've chosen to put people together from all across different departments so you get a chance to intermingle and get to know everyone a little better. Our first activity will be in about an hour, so you have time to grab lunch before heading to meet your team activity leaders." Alexander nodded to the staff and started listing groups and names. The more I didn't hear mine, the more I started having a terrible feeling. "And the last members for group two are Benjamin Sullivan and Angelina Bradford. Group three will be..."

My brain stopped listening to the rest as my eyes found hers. Somehow, her glare intensified by the seconds, and if flames could have poured out of her nose or daggers come out of her eyes, I would have been gone in a heartbeat. I wasn't going to cower before a challenge, though, so I gave her my best smirk in return. She whipped around, hair following in her path as she tried to ignore me once again. As if we wouldn't be stuck together, forced to share each other's company all week. She could hate me all she wanted, but I was determined to win her over, and I *would*.

Game on, Angelina Bradford.

Finally, Alexander finished the rest of his speech, patting his son on the back. Most of the employees scattered towards the lodge and the promised food, though my eyes tracked over to Angelina, who was laughing at whatever Nicolas was saying. I wondered what was so funny that her eyes crinkled with joy, and then I decided I didn't care.

We didn't like each other and we never would. I needed to get my intrigue for her under check. Otherwise, I would go out of my mind trying to puzzle over her every move. My only goal was the promotion, and I couldn't risk it by having the CEO's son's best friend hate me. It was a tricky situation, which left me with only one option.

"Hey," I said, going up to her. "I realize we haven't started off on the right foot, so I was wondering if we could call a truce?" I tried for a smile, hoping that, at the very least, we could be civil for the week. But maybe what I gave her was more of a grimace, because even though she was shorter than me, she somehow managed to look down her nose at me.

"No."

Well, can't say I didn't deserve that. "No? You can't even give me a chance?"

"Why should I? I don't *like* you. You've done nothing but prove to me, over and over, how self-absorbed you are. You have no regard for decency or the consideration of others. So, sorry if I don't want to be your friend." She flared her nostrils, and I couldn't help the frown on my face.

"Look, I know I haven't always been the nicest to you, but can't we just start over? We have to spend a week together, and—"

"Fine," Angelina grit out. "Let's start over. Hi, I'm Angelina Bradford, and I don't want to spend time with you more than is absolutely necessary. Happy? Now leave me alone." She crossed her arms, looking at me pointedly.

"Fine," I huffed back, retreating to the other side of the clearing, back towards Liam and the other guys as they headed inside to grab lunch.

"Rejection stings, huh?" Liam said, rubbing his ginger beard.

"I wasn't rejected." I rolled my eyes at his deadpan look. "She refuses to talk to me. I just wanted to apologize."

"You're an idiot," Kevin shook his head.

"Yeah, yeah. I shouldn't have kept emailing her just to entertain myself. I know. It was stupid."

"Did you even know who you were emailing?" Noah asked. "Because you may have picked the most gorgeous *and* the coldest woman at the office. The only person she ever seems to be happy around is Nicolas or that best friend of hers—the one in HR."

She was gorgeous alright. Not that it changed anything. "Yeah, well, apparently she's decided she's going to hate me no matter what, so that's how this week is going to go."

Liam groaned. "What is this, childhood summer camp all over again? I never would have guessed two adults could be so petty—"

"Shut up." I shoved him, causing him to almost lose his balance before catching himself on the railing. "I'm going to win her over, and then this is all going to be fine."

"And how, exactly, are you going to do that? If you haven't noticed, she won't even talk to you."

I smirked at that. "I have a plan."

I hope you know what you're doing, a little voice inside my head whispered.

I hoped so too.

CHAPTER 4
Angelina

"Welcome to our first series of team bonding activities!" the lodge activities coordinator, Ian, announced to our group. After lunch, all the groups assembled outside so we could each rotate through the different ropes courses and challenges.

I was, unfortunately, at the complete misfortune of having *him* in my group.

I didn't think it was punishment, per se, because there was absolutely no way Nicolas's dad knew how much I detested Benjamin Sullivan. Especially with his desire for a truce. God. He was cocky, egotistical, and somehow knew how to get under my skin. Having him around all the time was driving me crazy, like my skin was itching from the inside out. He didn't even seem to realize why I didn't like him, and every time I looked up, I caught him staring at me. If we weren't at a work event, I would have flipped him off so many times already.

It was the fire sign in me, I liked to think. I'd always been easily riled, easy to anger, and first to a fight. I thought of myself as the protector of my friends, but the truth was, I was always the first to stand up for myself too. So why had I let Benjamin Sullivan irritate me for so long? Why had I let him get under my skin without any real pushback? It was disconcerting. As was the fact that the *devil incarnate* was actually hot. Those arms... Clearly, someone up there was testing me.

"Before we get going," Ian said, "and start any of the planned activities, I want to build trust with all of you. So, we're going to start with a series of trust falls. If you can each pair up with a companion, please."

I looked around for a partner, but before I could move toward one of the girls I knew, Benjamin's face filled my vision. My eyes scanned around, frustrated to find that the only other person standing apart from anyone else was him.

I put my hands up. "There's no way I'm partnering up with you."

"Why not?" He smirked, leaning in. "Are you scared, Bradford?"

"No." I wanted to shove him away from me but resorted to acting civil in front of our coworkers. "I just don't want you to drop me."

He looked at me and then at his forearms. "Sweetheart, I don't think you're the one we have to worry about being dropped."

"Asshole," I muttered under my breath. Unfortunately, everyone else was already paired up, so I was stuck with him. I spun on my heels and pointed a finger at his chest. "I swear to God, if you drop me, I will smother you in your sleep with a pillow. Do you hear me, Sullivan?"

"I swear on my honor as a Boy Scout," he started, and gave me the Scout's salute, which I blinked at, "that I will not drop you."

Of course he was a Boy Scout. As if he had been made to be my antithesis: I hated nature, and he loved it. I hated outdoor activities, and he'd probably spent his entire childhood setting up tents and hiking and underwater basket weaving, or something ridiculous like that.

"Okay," the instructor resumed, "whoever is going first, I want you to stand in front of your partner, your back to them, and close your eyes. And when I say go, you're going to fall backwards."

"Ladies first," Benjamin insisted. I turned my back on him, hoping he wasn't leering at me in my workout leggings, and tried to relax. I'd never been very good at trusting people, especially in these kinds of activities.

The instructor gave us the go-ahead, but even with my arms crossed over my chest, I couldn't quite bring myself to do it. What was more embarrassing—not even trying, or falling on my ass in the dirt?

My rigid posture was probably giving away my unease because Benjamin moved closer to me and spoke quietly. "Hey. Breathe. It's fine, I'll catch you."

I closed my eyes, surprised at the sincerity in his voice. I took a deep breath and slowly leaned back, and when his hands caught my sides, I let out a sigh of relief. Then I opened my eyes to find the strangest expression on his face. We looked at each other as he held me for a moment longer than necessary. Finally, he righted me and took a step back, tugging at the collar of his sweater.

Okay, it *definitely* wasn't just me who was affected by this closeness. But no, I couldn't let him affect me like that—or in any way, actually. I scowled as I turned away from him, regaining my composure.

"Alright, now you can switch places." It was Benjamin's turn to stand with his back to me, and I was a little ashamed of the way I was ogling him. Damn those muscles.

"You good back there?" he said, and I could hear the smirk in his voice. Arrogant prick. My response was barely out that he started falling backward, and I quickly realized there was no way I was going to be able to support his weight. Plus, he may have promised not to drop *me*, but I didn't promise anything to *him*.

"What the hell, Bradford!" Benjamin exclaimed as he fell onto the forest floor.

"Oops," I said, batting my eyelashes. "It was an accident, I swear."

"Accident my ass." He glared at me, brushing the dirt off his back and hands. "You did it on purpose, don't even try to deny it."

I just gave him a shrug, and then we were moving on, and our instructor was calling out other activities to do, and by the time we finished, I just wanted to escape Benjamin's constant presence and the remainder of the look in his eyes when he caught me.

They moved us over to one of the several ropes courses they had built in the woods, and I was glad the summer weather hadn't completely departed yet, so little bits of the sun still trickled through the trees. It was cool and damp, but at least I didn't need a jacket.

The objective was to get our entire team through the course, using teamwork and helping each other. It didn't look too hard, I thought, surveying the different levels we'd have to journey through while they clipped us into the harnesses. It wasn't a matter of doing it better than anyone else, the instructor said (although I was determined to do it better than Benjamin Sullivan), but to do it in sync.

When it was my turn, I powered through the first two platforms, pulling myself along and then jumping from hanging platform to platform, but when I moved to the next, moving along two pieces of rope, I slipped. I almost lost my balance, falling off the darn thing, but a hand pulled me back in time and steadied me.

"You good?" the voice behind me called out, and I realized with horror whose hand wrapped around me and pulled me back to my feet, keeping me from falling.

"Um," I breathed, trying to focus on anything else besides his touch. "Yep, all good!" I turned my head slightly. "Thanks." I didn't let myself linger on the way Benjamin Sullivan helped me and pulled myself along to make my way through the rest of the course, thankfully without any more incidents.

Just when I thought maybe our punishment was over, we were taken to the last physical activity of the day, and I wanted to feign sickness to get out of this one. *Maybe if I threw up, they wouldn't make me*—no. I shook my head at myself. I wasn't a coward, and I wasn't going to take the easy way out of this, no matter how much I wanted to.

The tree was huge, and I seriously had no desire to climb to the top of it. My mouth was dry as I stared up at the small boards nailed into the trunk for footholds. At the top was a bar and a pulley system as well as a platform to stand. To jump from.

"Who's first?" our instructor asked, and I peered up at the ladder pounded into the giant tree. Whose idea of fun was this? Certainly not mine. "Everyone has to go eventually, so come on up, don't be shy."

I tried to step backward, but instead found myself somehow nudged to the front of the group, and when the instructor's eyes met mine, I was being harnessed up and sent climbing in the blink of an eye. No chance for me to refuse. No way to get out of this.

It was my worst nightmare. I looked down to the ground, sucking in a breath. I'd never had a problem with heights, and yet this was daunting. A leap of faith. Because there was no one there to catch you. If you missed the bar, you fell—in front of everyone. Which, in this case, was about a dozen coworkers and one very annoying Benjamin Sullivan. Because of course he'd be here to witness my utter humiliation if I failed. I bet he would remind me of this moment for years, too. Maybe I needed to look for a new job, if only to save myself from being made fun of for the rest of my life.

Breathe, I commanded myself as I stood up on the ledge. More than anything, I realized that I was terrified to *jump*. As it turned out, you had to have courage to fall. Falling was scary. Letting go of everything and just do it? That was a whole other level of courage.

I hadn't even realized my eyes were squeezed shut until I heard a voice shouting from the bottom. "Come on, Bradford!" It was him. As if he could annoy me off the ledge, coax me into making the plunge. "You can do it! Just jump."

I shook my head. I *couldn't* do it. It was too tall, too dizzying to even imagine what it would be like to experience the sensation of falling. It didn't matter if I was strapped in, that the people below me held a rope to help belay me down—my heart was beating a hundred miles in my chest, and it was all I could do to clutch the tree. I tried to take a deep breath. *Jump, Angelina,* I told myself.

Just jump.

Jump.

Everyone was chanting my name, and when I finally opened my eyes and took a deep breath, I focused on the bar and let go of everything holding me back.

And I finally jumped.

∽

I COULD ONLY HOPE that day two would go better than day one. Certainly, I'd be more successful avoiding one cocky man this go-around?

The man who caught you when you fell. For no reason, because what benefit did he have to doing it in the first place? And when I'd come down from the tree, the relief evident on his face was… something I needed to *not* be thinking about.

After our first meeting, I hoped I could pretend he didn't exist, but after yesterday, it was painfully obvious that was not going to be possible. Thankfully, I had a reprieve at dinner last night: my table was already full when he got there, so there was no chance for him to sit with us. Our table consisted of me, Nicolas, his newly promoted assistant Zofia—who seemed determinately not excited to be there—and a few other guys I knew from around the office.

Benjamin was forced to sit on the other side of the hall, with some of the guys I had seen him talking to when I'd run into him at check-in. I was happy not to be in his presence, knowing I could breathe a little easier. Not that he stole the oxygen out of my lungs or anything mushy like that; but I was so embarrassed about our first meeting, about how I'd been around him yesterday, that whenever he was too close, I felt on edge, always waiting for the other shoe to drop. And if my breath caught for a moment when our eyes met across the loud room, well, that was between me, myself, and I.

Fuck. This was my worst nightmare. Well, maybe not my *worst*, but I certainly never imagined I'd be thrown smack dab in the middle of a work retreat with my mortal enemy. Office rival. Whatever.

Every time I felt his gaze on me, whether it was devoid of any emotion or a shit-eating grin, it unnerved me. I wasn't going to analyze that, wasn't going to try to get to the bottom of the ridiculous pull I felt towards the man, because when it came down to it, I still couldn't stand him or his personality. He only cared about himself, and he made that obvious from the way he communicated with me over emails, like he was so high and mighty that I should drop anything I was doing for him.

Well, I thought as I swallowed a mouthful of delicious steak, I had a perfect plan to survive (and possibly enjoy) this retreat with no more incidents: I was going to do my best to avoid the hell out of Benjamin Sullivan, get through this week, and then go back to real life and pretend I didn't have an *oh-shit-he's-hot* moment with the guy I wanted to hit over the head with a baseball bat.

Unfortunately, I didn't own one. I wasn't a sports girl. Sure, I went to the gym and worked out regularly, but I'd never been one of those people who had time to get involved with sports or make attachments to any local teams. None of my friends were, which was one of the reasons why we got along so well. Noelle was only just now getting into basketball, because her boyfriend's friends were on the team, and I knew Gabbi's family was into hockey, but that was about it. Daniel had never been either; he was a runner, but not an athlete. Charlotte knew even less about sports than I did, and that was after we girls read dozens of sport romance books. I liked to think that my sports knowledge being entirely from romance novels was alright—that was as much as I needed to know.

The next morning, I rose with the determination that today was going to be a new day, and that meant continuing to avoid the hell out of Benjamin. We'd had enough close encounters for a lifetime. *Fat chance of that,* I sighed to myself. Why'd we have to be on the same schedule and stuck together?

I was an early riser, so after thirty minutes of tossing, I finally got up. The sun hadn't come up yet, but I grabbed a book and wandered in the direction of the main lodge, hoping I could find caffeine and a bit of quiet before the day began. And for a while, I did. The coffee was perfect, and I found a spot on one of the big chairs on the porch where I could enjoy the sunrise and my warm beverage. Until the universe decided I'd had enough peace for the day—a whole ten minutes without *him.*

Benjamin freaking Sullivan was stripping down by the lake.

He was about 500 feet or so from the lodge, so I could see his muscles tensing and pulling as he stretched his limbs. I may or may not have made a choked sound when he bent down. Thank *God* I seemed to be the only morning person here besides him. Of course, while I loved to wake up early to enjoy the peace and quiet, the birds chirping as the sky changed colors, and some light reading, he clearly got out of bed for a very different purpose. One I was trying very hard not to enjoy.

Sue me, his body was gorgeous. Muscular, but not too burly, tall and toned. I could have watched him doing laps back and forth in the lake for hours. His arms cutting through the water, his legs kicking behind him as he swam out and back, out and back. It was beautiful. I was transfixed.

I wished I had my sketchpad. I wanted to draw it all—the sun rising over the water, the lake rippling around Benjamin, a mix of blues and oranges. By the time he got out, I was still sitting there, my book forgotten and drink cooled, eyes taking in the surroundings as Benjamin padded up the steps.

"Enjoying the view, Bradford?"

"You wish."

He smirked at me, the bastard. His hair was dripping onto the towel he slung over his shoulders after he'd pulled a long-sleeved tee on. "Sure looked like you were to me."

"You're delusional."

"Am I? It's okay if you were, you know."

"What?"

"It was a nice sunrise."

I wished I could punch him. I hated his stupid grin, the way he looked at me as if he knew exactly what I was thinking, and somehow twisting my words around. "It was," I finally said, nodding nonchalantly and taking another sip of my cold coffee.

He slipped inside the lodge, and I turned my attention back to the scenery in front of me. Had he really seen me staring? He had his back to me at the beginning, and then he was so focused on his strokes that I couldn't imagine him noticing me like I'd noticed him.

I shook my head and closed my book, sighing deeply. It wasn't like I was going to get any more reading done now. I could go inside and eat something, since breakfast would be served soon. Or I could go back to my cabin and avoid one very annoying brunette man. I scowled, thinking once again about our emails. As much as I wanted to, though, I knew I'd be hungry later, so I put my figurative big girl pants on and marched in to find a bite to eat; I could probably grab an omelet and run out of there before he saw me.

As my luck would have it, when I entered, Benjamin Sullivan was absent, and after scooping up some breakfast and refilling my coffee mug, I went to sit next to Zofia, Nicolas's assistant.

"Hey," I greeted with a smile, now and then watching the doorway lest my evil nemesis decided to sneak in when I wasn't looking.

"Oh, hi, Angelina," Zofia said, perking up. Her curly dark brown hair was left loose this morning, complimenting the collared T-shirt she wore.

"How's it going with Nic?" He was currently holding a conversation across the room, while the hall filled with more people.

She sighed. "Sometimes I'm not sure what I signed up for accepting this job."

"It can't be easy at the beginning. But you like it?"

"It's... Well, you know how Nicolas is."

I nodded, going for a comforting look. "He's a handful."

"He's like a giant puppy," Zofia chuckled. "I'm constantly having to track him down and drag him back to the task at hand." It was true. Nicolas was good, a hard worker, but sometimes he had the attention span of a gnat.

"To be honest with you, after his last few assistants quit... I wasn't sure he'd find someone who was up for the task."

"Well, he practically begged me." She rolled her eyes lightheartedly. "I couldn't find it in me to say no. Besides, it was a substantial pay raise and an even better opportunity. Even if I don't want to be an Executive Assistant forever, I'm certainly doing more than I was in HR."

"Yeah. Gabbi misses you, by the way."

She smiled at me. "I miss her too."

I gave her a little nudge. "What's on the agenda for the day? Anything fun?"

"Oh no," Zofia laughed. "You get to find out like everyone else." She made a zipping motion over her lips. "I'm not spilling."

I pouted, but before I could try to bribe her, we were interrupted.

"Is this seat taken?" I was about to say no, but then I looked up at the man standing beside our table. God, not this again.

"Yes."

"By who?"

"Anyone whose name is not Benjamin Sullivan," I said, pointedly, sipping on my coffee instead of making eye contact with him.

Zofia gave me a look, and I knew I wasn't being professional.

Drat. I could have used a friend's advice on how to handle him. The girls had always been better people pleasers than me, while I'd usually ask for forgiveness rather than permission, charging forward and only thinking about the consequences later.

All I wanted was to escape this day, this retreat, and this man who seemed to hate me so much that he riled me up every chance he got. I wanted to talk to Gabbi, and I couldn't, because there was no reception up here and we weren't supposed to use phones or laptops this week anyway. It seemed like a punishment instead of a reward. All of this was a punishment, honestly. If I never had to spray myself with bug spray again, it would be too soon.

"Come on, Bradford." He frowned, like he was the victim here. Unbelievable. "Are you going to punish me forever for a few harmless emails?"

"Harmless?" I scoffed, trying not to raise my voice as Zofia remained next to me, pretending not to be listening in. "I'd hardly call those harmless. Do you have any idea how…" I cut myself off with a huff. "You know what, it's not worth it. Go ahead and sit, I'm going to head back to my cabin before we get started for the day anyway. See you later, Zo."

"Where's my goodbye?" He had the gall to fake-pout at me.

"You'll get a proper goodbye from me when you earn it."

"How long will that take?" he called after me as I walked away.

"Eternity!"

I had no intention of forgiving Benjamin Sullivan or giving him a chance to prove me wrong. He had dug his grave—now he could lie in it.

CHAPTER 5
Benjamin

Angelina Bradford was a puzzle I couldn't quite figure out. She was frustrating, stuck-up, and full of herself, but it was more than that. She detested me, and for what? Some innocent banter, some harmless fun—and she hated me for it. It wasn't like she didn't give me as good as she got. I never would've imagined I could manage to get under her skin like that, but somehow, knowing I did was satisfying. Especially after seeing it up close, here at the lodge.

Yesterday, during the trust falls, there had been no one else to pair up with. People grouped together so fast. I'd been a little apprehensive about being paired with her, but mostly because of her disdain for me. My worry seemed to be well-placed when she purposefully didn't catch me. No matter. I could survive a few falls to the ground.

Today, our first activity of the day was a series of presentations, which wasn't that surprising for the company to want us to come away with some new insights, even on a retreat.

I quietly slid into the seat next to Angelina, letting my lips tilt only slightly upon realizing that her eyes were closed. After a short introduction, the speaker started prattling on about leadership styles. Interesting, sure, but nothing I hadn't learned before.

Angelina had chosen a seat in the back row, and it was almost too perfect that the seat next to her was still free. Because after she dropped me yesterday, I was even more determined to annoy the hell out of her.

"Bradford," I whispered, nudging her to see if she was asleep. "You're not supposed to sleep through these things, you know."

Angelina opened one eye, saw it was me, and then shut it again and crossed her arms over her chest. "I'm just resting my eyes. Go away."

"No." She gave a little huff of displeasure before finally giving her attention to the woman on the podium. "Come on. You can't ignore me forever."

"Sure, I can." She narrowed her eyes. "It's very simple. If I don't talk to you, you'll eventually give up and go bother some other poor, unsuspecting woman."

"And what, Miss Bradford, gives you the idea that I'm going to give up?" I cocked one eyebrow at her, and then settled even further into my chair when she didn't deign me with a response.

"You're annoying."

"I prefer charming."

She shoved at my arm, and I gasped, pretending that it hurt.

"Shhh," someone hushed us from the row in front of ours, and I gave a small, sheepish wave.

Angelina glared at me one more time before I decided to relent until the lecturer stopped speaking. I wasn't actually listening to the presentation. My eyes were on the stage, but my mind and body were attuned to the woman next to me.

I waited until the presentation wrapped up and everyone was filing out of the room before turning back to her. "Angelina."

She made a shushing noise, looking around furtively before glaring at me. "Don't talk to me, someone might think we're friends."

I raised an eyebrow. "Because that would be the worst thing in the world?"

"Yes."

"Why?"

"You don't even like me. Why are you suddenly unable to leave me alone?"

I shrugged. I didn't have an explanation, not really. "You're fun to tease," I said instead. The wrong answer, from how she scowled at me, stood and left without another word. But if she thought I was going to give up, she had another thing coming.

I was going to annoy her *into* liking me.

∼

AFTER LUNCH, I was surprised when I left the main lodge and found Angelina sitting on a rock, staring up at the craftsman-style building.

"What are you doing?"

"What am *I* doing?"

"Yes."

"What does it look like I'm doing, Sullivan?" she said, raising a pad of paper.

"I don't think the company is paying you to sit out here by yourself, Bradford."

"And I don't think they're paying you to be over here annoying me either, but here we both are."

So we were playing it like that, weren't we? I didn't know what it was about this girl that snuck into every single corner of my brain and made me want to mess with her, but I couldn't help it. I moved around behind her so I could look at what she was doing—what had captivated her attention enough for her to be out here, drawing it. On the page was a rough sketch of the lodge with the mountains in the background.

"You have an eye for that," I nodded to it over her shoulder.

"What?" she said with shock, blinking up at me.

I shrugged. "What, a guy can't recognize good art when he sees it?"

"Sure. Nice, respectful guys can." Angelina let the silence fill the rest of the sentence.

"I'm not so devious that I don't know how to compliment people." And she deserved the compliment—I was sincere about that. She was talented.

"I'm not so sure about that," she frowned.

I chuckled. "Alright, fair enough. Maybe I deserve that."

"Leave out the maybe."

"I promise you, I'm not a complete asshole." I placed my hand over my chest in what felt like it should be a heartfelt gesture, but maybe just came off like something a jerk would say. God knew I'd been one to her on more than one occasion. I was trying to make up for it, though.

"Speaking of asses…" She gave me a knowing smirk. "How's yours?" She totally did drop me on purpose yesterday, dammit.

It was my turn to glare at her. "Sore, no thanks to you."

"That'll teach you to partner with me again," Angelina said in what felt like the sweetest, fakest voice she could muster, before focusing back on her sketch.

"If you think that'll deter me, you're sorely mistaken."

"It was worth a shot."

I couldn't get over her fake smile and how much I wished it was a real one. What could I do to show this girl I was not a real asshole? I liked bickering—and flirting—with her, but I needed her to realize that I wasn't the enemy here.

It probably made me a pathetic idiot, just trying to win this woman over so she would stop hating me. I didn't have any ulterior motive—it wasn't like I wanted to date her. My history with women was less than impressive, given that none of my relationships lasted more than a year, so I had no intention to pursue anything with Angelina.

All I wanted was for her to smile at me, the way she did when we first met here.

I sighed loudly as I walked away from her, but I stopped a few paces away, hoping she'd get the hint.

"What do you want, Sullivan?"

"Care to accompany me on a walk?"

"No."

I resisted the urge to pull the notebook out of her hands only because it wouldn't get me any points. "Come on. Nothing too crazy, I promise. Just down to the main lodge. I heard they put out brownies."

"I don't want to go anywhere with you," she huffed, but then —finally—closed her sketchbook. Angelina rubbed her hands on her pants before standing up and giving me another glare. I raised an eyebrow in question. "Let me make one thing clear. I'm not getting up to walk *with* you. I just so happen to want a brownie."

"Right. Absolutely." I nodded, barely stopping myself from grinning from ear to ear. "So, do you draw often?" I asked her as we set off, wondering if she carried the sketchbook everywhere with her.

She regarded me with a wary expression. "Why do you want to know? You don't like me."

I brushed the pang of dejection aside. "Come on, I think it's cool. Is paper your main medium of choice?"

"If you must know," Angelina said, exhaling a big gust of air, "I prefer painting. But I couldn't exactly bring out a whole painting kit for a week in the mountains."

"Any other fun drawings in there I could see?"

"Uh. No," she quickly shook her head.

"Hey, I promise I won't make fun of it. You're talented."

She hid the sketchbook behind her back. "Nope."

"Fine," I pouted. "But I'm going to wear you down and win you over. Just you watch."

Angelina snorted. "I've already told you, Sullivan. Never gonna happen. I don't like you and I don't intend on forgiving you, so we're not going to be friends. And after this work retreat, I'm going to go back to pretending you don't exist."

Could she, that easily? Because I'd been trying for two years to forget what she looked like. That fleeting moment at the office had been stuck with me this whole time. And now, the image of her so intent on her drawing while she chewed on the eraser at the end of her pencil was ingrained in my brain.

We rounded the corner, coming back in view of the lodge, and I gestured for her to go. "Ladies first."

"If this is some play to get me to go in front of you so you can stare at my ass, I'm sorry, but that's not going to work."

"Angelina." It was my turn to narrow my eyes. "Is that what you think of me? Besides, if I wanted to stare at your ass, I could have done that yesterday." I *did*, actually, but I thought this might be a bad time to admit that to her. "What if this is just you trying to stare at *my* ass?"

She scoffed. "Hardly. Now shut up so I can go enjoy my brownie in peace."

I didn't know why—maybe it was because they ended up being heavenly brownies, but for once, I obliged.

∽

ANGELINA GLARED at me when I slid into the seat next to her. There was a free chair at the table where Liam and the rest of my buddies sat for dinner, but I ignored it. My mission here was to talk to Angelina, to understand the things that made her tick. She'd shown me little glimpses, here and there, of her strong personality, and I wanted to know more.

"Don't sit next to me."

"Why?" I whispered in her ear as I flashed her a cocky grin. "Afraid you'll like me?"

"No." She rolled her eyes. "I'm just worried your massive ego is going to take over the entire table."

I smirked, making myself comfortable despite her protests. "Princess, how could it? You're here."

After getting tired of staring me down, Angelina turned to Nicolas and his assistant. "How was your day? I feel like I hardly saw either of you."

Nicolas sighed. "My dad had us running around doing errands for him all day. I feel like this is the first time I'm sitting down and relaxing." He looked over at me. "How was your day, Sullivan?"

Nicolas and I had always been cordial to each other, but never really friends. Now I had the opportunity to strengthen our relationship, to make sure I got on his good side. Because when he got his promotion, I needed to have my spot secured as well.

"It was great, thank you," I said, grinning at Angelina.

Nicolas gave her a look, but let it go. "Have you met Harper Young yet?" he asked, indicating to the light-brown-haired girl sitting across the table. "She's the new head for the Graphic Design team."

"I haven't." I nodded to her in greeting. "Nice to meet you. I'm Benjamin Sullivan."

"Oh, I know," Harper said.

"You do?"

"I'm afraid your reputation precedes you, Mr. Sullivan." I glanced at Angelina, but she ignored me, pushing around the salad on her plate with her fork. "Oh, it's not all bad, I assure you," Harper added with a toothy grin.

What had Angelina told her about me? I raised an eyebrow in question, but she quickly changed the subject. "How's your brother, Harper?"

I could recognize a lost battle when I saw one. I continued to give Angelina little quips throughout dinner anyway and did my best to stay present in the conversation—even when I had no idea what everyone was talking about. I suspected Angelina was doing that on purpose, to try to make me uncomfortable or make me want to leave, but it honestly didn't bother me. I'd just nod along and pretend like I knew what was going on. Fake it till you make it. A lesson that had been driven into me since childhood.

After dinner, Liam caught up with me, an insufferable smirk on his face.

"What?"

"You know, I've never seen you like this," he said as I watched Angelina leave the main lobby area.

"Like what?"

"I don't know. Entranced? Captivated? Like you can't keep your eyes off her, dude."

"I have no idea what you're talking about."

"Sure," Liam snorted.

"We can't stand each other."

"Whatever you tell yourself to get by, man."

I frowned. "I'm serious."

"Sure. And I'm serious that you *like* her."

"I like *annoying* her. Not the same thing."

He patted me on the back, not arguing with me further as he just shook his head and headed off into the night.

What was with him, anyway? Sure, Angelina was intriguing, and I was trying to get into her head. But to imply I was enchanted at all with her, that I might want something more than to get on her nerves... That was ridiculous.

"I need a drink," I muttered, setting off towards the bar. My plan was turning out to be more difficult than I'd anticipated.

CHAPTER 6
Angelina

"Can I get a cosmo?" I found myself very grateful that this lodge contained access to alcohol, especially after the day I had. I plopped down on a stool, needing a moment to myself. After a long day of group activities and being *pestered* by a certain man, I needed a drink. I groaned to myself, thinking about how he had to sit next to me at dinner as if he was determined to needle me. Like if he kept poking at me, I might... what? He had already succeeded at making me hate him. I didn't think it could possibly get any worse than that, but maybe I was wrong. As far as I was concerned, he was the absolute *worst*, and I had no desire to get to know him to prove myself right on that front.

I kept pondering, running a finger over the rim of my martini glass, enjoying the solitude. The bar was fairly empty, tucked inside the lodge next to the dining room.

"Is this seat taken?"

Of course. I didn't have the energy to argue anymore, so I just shrugged and got ready to ignore another Benjamin Sullivan attack. He didn't get enough out of tormenting me for the past two days—the past year, really—that he had to ruin my night, too?

I was convinced this was a punishment from the universe or something. The way he always managed to find me and tease me, and worst of all, how he found a way to get under my skin. Now more than ever. Those inquiring eyes of his were a problem: it felt like he was searching for something. I didn't like it one bit.

I still wasn't sure why he had insisted on keeping up our weird email battle for as long as he had; maybe it *was* some form of weird foreplay for him. I couldn't count the number of unsent drafts in my email folder, which included notes such as *I loathe you*, *I hope you fall down the stairs*, and *I'm going to get Nicolas to fire you*. They were, admittedly, not my proudest moments. I'd even started including stupid little snarks on my email signatures just to piss him off. Respectfully yours? Pfft. More like *Disrespectfully yours*.

"Sure," I said finally, before taking another sip of my drink. He sat on the stool next to me before waiving the bartender over to order his own drink. "Whiskey? Really?"

"Not what you expected from me, Bradford?" I watched him as he sipped slowly, with that stupid upturned corner of his lips. What *had* I expected? I didn't even know him. Was I being a bitch, making assumptions about him?

I shrugged. "I feel like most Oregonian men I've met order craft beers. Especially in a place like this." I waved a hand around at the lodge. It really did have that feel to it. The entire space just oozed Pacific Northwest. And I couldn't think of anything that screamed Portland more than microbreweries.

"Well," he said, taking another sip before looking over at me with those captivating brown eyes. "Maybe I'm not most men."

I rolled my eyes and turned my attention back to my glass. "No, you're certainly not," I muttered under my breath. *Most men wouldn't keep up a digital email sparring for a year.*

I finished my drink in a deep gulp, savoring the sweet and tangy flavor. I needed another one if I had to deal with Benjamin Sullivan. A strong one, something that would allow the heat I felt from his body mere inches from mine to flee my brain. I didn't even like the guy, so I was determined not to feel anything other than animosity towards him.

I ordered a second cosmopolitan and tried to divert my eyes from his fingers strumming along the wood of the bar.

"Why do you hate me?" His sudden closeness made my heart skip a beat, his voice a caress over my skin.

"W-what?" I stuttered. I never stuttered. Damn him.

"What did I do to make you hate me?"

I looked up into his eyes to see if this was another one of his teasing jokes, but all I found was sincerity. How could he not know? "The real question is what did I do to you."

"Angelina." He put a hand on the bar, swiveling his stool towards me. "I'm serious."

"So am I. You seriously don't know?" I said, frowning. I couldn't figure him out. He was an asshole to me over our email correspondence, but here, in person, all he seemed to want to do was get close to me. It didn't make sense. "Why do you care anyway?" I asked instead, not giving him an answer.

At that, he looked miffed. Almost... hurt. But that couldn't be. "I don't," he said, taking another sip of his drink. "Hate me all you want."

I narrowed my eyes at him. "Why did you sit next to me tonight? At dinner, and here."

"Maybe I just wanted good company."

I laughed at that. "And I'm good company? A girl you can't stand?"

"What makes you think I can't stand you?"

I stared at him for a moment before finishing my second drink. I wouldn't let him do *that*.

"Can I get another one?" I called out to the bartender. Apparently, I was dealing with this by consuming alcohol. Thankfully, I knew my limits, and while I had no intention of getting drunk tonight, I certainly needed to be at least a little tipsy to endure whatever Benjamin Sullivan was putting me through. "So, what else do you like to do besides harassing innocent women?"

There was a devilish twinkle in his eye when I finally deigned to look at him. His knee knocked against mine as he practically purred, "I don't think you're innocent at all."

I almost spit out my drink. Struggling to regain my composure, I glared at him. "Wouldn't you like to know?" I wanted to wipe that unnerving smirk from his face. And ruffle his stupid, perfectly combed hair. Why did he have to be so handsome again?

"Maybe I would."

I sighed. Maybe a truce wasn't such a bad idea. Sure, he annoyed me, but he hadn't done anything to hurt or mock me since we'd been here. He didn't seem to do anything with malicious intent. Maybe if we got to know each other a little better, he would at least leave me alone.

"So, who is the real Benjamin Sullivan? Turns out, your reputation precedes you," I said, thinking about what Harper said at dinner. We talked often enough since we worked together, but I'd never mentioned the emails feud to her—I mostly complained to Gabbi and Nic. So, what *else* could she have been talking about?

Benjamin exhaled, hanging his head. "Apparently, I've gotten quite the reputation as a player around the company." He spoke quietly, skimming the rim of his glass with his thumb. "Which isn't true—really. I promise I'm not like that." He glanced at me with earnest eyes, as if he needed me to believe him. *Why*, I couldn't fathom.

"Why would everyone assume you were?"

He shrugged. "I don't date."

"Ah."

"What about you?"

"What about me?" Should I tell him that I didn't date either? But instead of people thinking I was a player for it, they thought I was uptight, shrewd, or simply a slut if I slept with more than one guy in a month? Maybe we were both being judged for things that weren't fair. I knew how everyone liked to gossip.

"Are there any preconceived notions about you that everyone is wrong about?"

"Everyone calls me a bitch. Ice-cold, emotionless."

"And you're not?"

I snorted. "No, I am."

"I find that hard to believe. Don't give me that look. Underneath all of that..." He gestured to my hair and makeup, perfectly styled despite our setting. "I think you're a nice person. A *good* person."

"Well, my best friends would appreciate that, but you'd be the first."

He laughed. "Maybe no one else really sees you, hm?"

Silence hung between us for a moment. Maybe it *was* hard to really see me if you didn't want to try; to see through the front I presented to the world and wonder about who I was. But now, Benjamin... It sounded like he wanted to. Still.

"You don't know me."

"You're right. I don't." He finished the rest of his drink and looked at me. "So, tell me then. Who *is* Angelina Bradford?"

Who was I? Sometimes I felt like I still didn't know. I held his stare for a minute before shaking my head.

"Can we start over?" He didn't let me reply before adding, "Please."

God, I knew I would end up regretting this the moment I said the word, "Yes."

His demeanor shifted, as if his body sagged in relief. "Hi. I'm Benjamin Sullivan." He grinned, sticking out his hand to me.

"Hello, Benjamin. I'm Angelina Bradford." I took his hand, giving it a firm shake.

"Angelina," he said, like he was tasting my name on his tongue. I banned a very unbecoming thought from my mind as soon as it formed. "It's very nice to meet you. I'm always very impressed with your work."

An awkward sound came from my throat. "You are? But—You're always..."

"Always what?"

I realized Benjamin's palm was still in mine, so I dropped his hand and looked away from his questioning stare. "Never mind." I shook my head. "Enchanté." *Nice to meet you.* It felt like a little piece of myself I was offering up to him.

"French, huh?" I smiled into my glass to block him from the view. "That's surprising."

"Is it?"

"Yeah. Most people take Spanish these days."

"Oh. Well, I've always loved France." I wasn't going to tell him the extent to which I loved it—the reason why I'd started learning the language in the first place, but at least I'd shared something with him.

"I always wanted to learn Japanese when I was younger."

That piqued my interest. "Really?"

"Yeah. I had this big, grand idea that I was going to move there."

"And how's that going for you?" I grinned.

He chuckled. "Turns out some dreams panned out better than others."

It might have been the alcohol, but we kept chatting about the most random things, and somehow, all night, the thought had never occurred to me that I could have just gotten up and left. Could have simply removed myself from the bar, gone back to my cabin, and not sat next to Benjamin Sullivan at all.

But I didn't. Because sometime after my third drink, I'd started to enjoy myself. And when he looked at me, with emotions hidden behind those deviously handsome eyes, I knew I was *screwed*, because I wanted to know what they had to say. Wanted to explore the secrets inside his mind. Wanted to know why he was so persistent and determined to annoy me when we could be just like this.

The bar closed about an hour later, and I didn't want the night to end. So, it wasn't really a surprise when Benjamin held out his hand to me and said, "Do you want to get out of here?"

∼

I WAS GIGGLING. Me, Angelina Bradford—I was giggling, because I was having *fun*. With Benjamin Sullivan. As we ran across the dirt outside under the starry night.

I'd worn a light, long-sleeved cotton wrap dress to dinner; nothing too fancy, but now that we were out in the dark, I could feel the dampness settling into my skin. But I didn't mind—not with the alcohol and the exhilaration of being out here with him warming my blood.

After kicking my shoes off, I buried my toes in the grass and tilted my head up to look at the stars. "It's so beautiful out here."

"Yeah," he said, his voice low and close, though when I peered at him, his eyes weren't on the stars or the scenery at all. "Come dance with me," he said suddenly. I raised an eyebrow, but he stretched out a hand. "Come on," Benjamin pleaded, nodding towards the dock. "Dance with me."

I couldn't have explained why I took his hand. Even later, when I was sober again, it was the one decision of the night I was trying to understand more than anything else. Maybe I'd given up on my resolve to hate him, but I certainly didn't *like* him, and yet... There was no hesitation. I placed my palm in his and let him guide me over to the little dock on the lake.

"How are we going to dance if there is no music?"

The dock had little twinkling lights looped around the railing, which lit it up in a beautiful glow. It took my breath away, and I couldn't believe there was a sight more captivating than the lake in the morning mist with steam rising from it. A sight I had enjoyed before one broad-shouldered man had disturbed it with his strokes through the water. Though maybe he'd made it even better. Although I would never admit that out loud.

"Who said there's no music?" He gave me a sly expression as he pulled his phone out of his pocket and opened Spotify. A slow song started playing, quiet and soulful. I looked up at him and I shocked myself a little bit when I placed my hand in his. He pulled me close, settling his other hand on my waist.

I was slow dancing with the man I'd hated up until two hours ago. And I had no intention of stopping. Was I insane? Most likely. There was no other logical explanation. It was either that or the alcohol. Though I'd never made reckless choices before, not even when I was drunk with my friends. Still, I blamed it on the drinks instead of analyzing the situation any further.

I didn't stop, didn't drop his hand or pull away from him, and we kept dancing. Even as we rocked in a slow circle with our hands clasped between us and my other hand resting on his shoulder. Even when the first song ended and another one began. We were closer than we ought to be—closer than had any reason to feel this right.

I shouldn't have been feeling this way in his arms. Good. Content. I shouldn't have rested my head against his chest as we moved to the rhythm. Shouldn't have let myself inhale the scent of him, something like bergamot and musk. Even as the music faded into the night, and I lost count of how long we swayed there, saying nothing, I didn't move from his arms. Wasn't sure I wanted to. I tilted my head up to look at him, and that's when I caught his eyes reflecting into mine.

I wasn't the type of girl to blush often—but there was something in his gaze that made my body feel warmer. Lighter. Perhaps almost cherished. And I wasn't quite sure of what I was supposed to do with all of that. I avoided that by saying nothing, settling my cheek on his chest as we swayed in the darkness of the night, long past my bedtime.

When I eventually pulled away, I felt frozen on the spot watching Benjamin's eyes track over my face, my lips. The hand that had been resting on my waist moved to brush my cheek—his thumb rubbing over my jawbone like he had with the rim of his glass earlier.

And damn everything, damn him and me and this retreat, but at that moment, all I wanted was for him to kiss me.

He didn't.

Time passed and he stood there, holding my face, looking like he was in a trance, hypnotized from my very presence. I wondered if he knew that he was affecting me the same way. If I was looking at him the way he was looking at me, well...

I closed my eyes, soaking the moment in, knowing I would never again experience such a blissful understanding where no words were exchanged.

Eventually, it was Benjamin who broke the moment. "We should go to sleep," he said quietly, creating some distance between our bodies.

"Right," I murmured back, hoping the heat from his touch would stop lingering. That the desire to feel his lips against mine wouldn't torment me for days, because I didn't know what I would do if I was forced to be close to him and *couldn't* act on it.

I followed him off the dock, back to dry ground, not missing the way he put his hand on the small of my back to steady me, guide me. As if he was still worried about me being a klutz like I'd been yesterday. Okay, I was a little worried, too, but not because I couldn't walk in my shoes, or because the dock was a little shaky. I was just feeling all out of sorts with Benjamin standing so close to me; he was the one making me feel unsteady. Unmoored. Like if I had stayed there, staring into his eyes, I would have drifted away.

And there was one thing I knew for sure: I did not want to get lost in Benjamin Sullivan or his eyes.

CHAPTER 7
Benjamin

I hadn't planned for any of it—the bar, the dancing, or how right she would feel in my arms. I could have stayed there forever, just moving to the rhythm of the music, but when she looked at me with those bright blue eyes... I almost lost it right then and there.

I *wanted* to kiss her. I thought maybe she wanted it too, but just a few hours before she'd told me she hated me, and I couldn't bring myself to do it knowing she might regret it. So I pulled away, forcing myself to put some distance between us so that I wouldn't fuck it up even more.

When I told her that people thought I was a player, I'd wanted her to know the truth. That I *wasn't*. I wasn't some guy who slept around or flirted with women to try to get into their pants. That had never been me. Sure, I could enjoy a moment of passion, a lust-filled encounter that didn't leave me wanting, but that was consensual, a mutual understanding that neither party required anything more from the other.

Though it had been a long time since I'd even enjoyed that. I couldn't explain why it was so important to me that Angelina knew I wasn't some fuckboy, but it was. It wasn't that I wanted to get to know her to sleep with her—sure, she was beautiful beyond belief, there was no use denying that; but it was the look in her eyes when she told me that everyone thought she was an icy, unfeeling bitch that had sunk into my heart.

And it really seemed like she believed that about herself. But I had seen through her glacial exterior, and I felt like I was slowly but surely discovering the truth—Angelina Bradford wasn't a bitch. She was just a scared woman who used her outer strength as a barrier to keep people at arm's length. It was what she was doing with me. But if she thought that I was going to treat her like that, like she was nothing but a pretty face, I needed to make her change her mind and see how brilliant and talented she was.

We should go to sleep, I said last night. It had broken whatever spell was between us. It succeeded in its goal, even though it was the last thing I'd wanted.

∾

I WISHED I could say I slept in. That knowing we didn't have anything planned until lunchtime, I stayed in bed or read a book or did something to relax. But no. At six AM on the dot, I woke up to the sun's rays streaming into my cabin, and that was it. I was awake. I could have gone for another morning swim, but knowing how Angelina had watched me from the porch of the main lodge yesterday as I did laps in the lake... It had unsettled me, how her gaze almost seeped into my bones. Why? I couldn't explain it.

Yet I had all this pent-up energy I had to expel somehow, which made an idea crept into my mind. It was crazy, a scheme to get closer to her, but I couldn't resist.

So I rolled out of bed, made myself presentable, grabbed a backpack, and headed towards the main lodge to get fuel and snacks for the day. If I could snag some fruit and granola bars, we would be good, but I found myself wondering what Angelina's favorite snacks were, what kinds of things might make her happy.

The lodge staff called out a welcome as I entered the breakfast room, which thankfully was currently empty. Even though breakfast wouldn't be ready for a bit yet, there was a whole spread of snack foods out for the taking. I was glad I'd noticed them yesterday—it made it easier to put my plan into motion. I was able to nab some trail mix and applesauce as well as other snacks, and after a quick goodbye to the staff, I went back to my cabin to pack the rest of my things.

∼

Angelina

I AWOKE the next morning to an insistent knocking on my cabin door. Even though I was an early riser, I hadn't expected the wake-up call. I certainly hadn't expected Benjamin Sullivan to be standing there, leaning against one of the wooden posts on the porch and wearing a pair of hiking boots with an eager look on his face. Just like that, any hope I had of a morning of peace flew out the window.

"Sullivan," I said, addressing him as I tightened my robe.

"Come hiking with me."

I raised an eyebrow. "What gives you the idea that I would want to do that? And have you heard of that magic little word?"

He sighed, running a hand over his forehead and through the longer-on-top strands of his hair. "Look, it'll be..." He bit his lip like he was trying to force the words out. Gritting his teeth, he finished his sentence. "*Fun.*" I didn't miss how frustrated he looked, and it made me want to laugh. Like I was tormenting him or something, and not the other way around.

"You're not doing a very good job at convincing me. That was mediocre at best."

"Fine, Bradford. Don't come." He rolled his eyes, before fixing a devilish grin on his face. "Just FYI though, if I get eaten by a bear, the company thinks we're out together, so you'll be to blame." He gave me a little wink as I felt my blood boil.

"You signed us up—*together*?!" I barely restrained myself from screaming at him. God, what was it about this man that made my professionalism fly out the window? I needed to get myself under control. "What the hell makes you think I would want to spend time with you? Especially on a hike?" I hissed.

Last night, that little voice in my head said. *Last night indicates that you most definitely want to spend more time with him.*

"Come on," Benjamin pleaded. "I'm not so bad once you get to know me."

He had me there. After last night, I might have seen a new side of him. That didn't mean I wanted to see any more, though. Just that, maybe, I could hate him a little less.

"I don't even have the right shoes." I hadn't expected all the activities the company was making us do. Sure, I'd brought my sneakers, but they weren't suitable for a hike in the woods. Still, no words left my mouth when he fished a brand-new pair of women's boots from his backpack. "You... brought me shoes?" My mouth opened and closed more than once without any sound coming out. Great. "How do you even know what size I wear?"

"Ten, right?" He sighed. "Look, Angelina, you don't have to make something out of it that it's not. Just take the boots and join me."

"Well, apparently since I don't have a choice," I grumbled, taking them from his hands and moving to go back into my cabin. "Give me five minutes."

This was really going to be the longest week of my life. I pinched the bridge of my nose. I quickly washed up, then I fixed my hair into a ponytail and put on a pair of athletic leggings and a workout top. When I pulled the door open, Benjamin was sitting on the porch steps, and he stood with a grin.

"Almost ready now, Bradford?" He looked me up and down as if appraising my outfit choice before eying my socks.

"Yeah," I said, sitting on the porch chair to pull on the boots, hoping my thick wool socks would be enough to prevent any blisters.

Benjamin swooped in before I could tie the laces. "Let me," he said, patting his leg to indicate I should put my foot there. "Too tight?" he asked after he finished the first one, and I shook my head. He placed my foot down and picked up the other one, repeating the process, looping the laces through the little medal hooks before tying them perfectly—not too loose, but I didn't feel like my foot was being squeezed, either.

I was still amazed he'd managed to find the right size, especially considering the only person I was close with at this retreat was Nicolas, and I doubted he'd ever paid attention to my shoe size.

"Alright." I stood up, running my hands down my leggings as I looked at him. "I think that's it."

"Is that all you need?" He raised an eyebrow. I looked at myself.

"Yeah, I guess."

"You don't want a water bottle? Or a light jacket in case it rains?"

"Oh." I should have thought of that. "Right. Come in a sec while I grab them." He followed in behind me, watching as I pulled things out of my bag and shoved them into a small drawstring backpack.

"Have you ever been hiking before?"

I shook my head. "Not an outdoorsy girl. I like to avoid the bugs and the dirt, if possible."

"She really is a princess," he said to himself, and I glared at him.

"Sorry that we didn't all grow up with parents who took us camping and hiking all the time."

For the briefest moment, his jaw seemed to clench, and I wondered what the distant look in his eyes meant. "Right."

"Yeah. Well." My parents hadn't been big on vacations when we were younger. There were things we did as a family—movies, Disneyland, summer trips to the coast—but the older we got, the less we did things all together. And when my parents divorced, it was always two of everything. But vacations, those slipped quietly away, like a dream we couldn't quite reach.

So maybe I resented Benjamin a little, with his perfect life and his perfect family. I was sure, with all his money, that he'd never had to work a day for anything in his life. I bet they'd doted on him from the time he was a kid. He probably didn't even need this job, this success—not like I did.

"Alright," I said, gesturing to the path. "Lead the way, Boy Scout."

Benjamin muttered something under his breath before starting along the path, heading into a denser part of the forest, with only a narrow trail to show we were heading in the right direction.

The direction of what, I had no idea. I was just along for the ride, forced against my will to traipse through nature. I just hoped I would make it through the day without twisting my ankle—or worse, falling on my ass in front of Benjamin. He would get way too much pleasure out of that, and I wasn't going to give him the satisfaction.

Along the hike, I stumbled through the giant roots of the trees several times, trying not to fall flat on my face. Luckily, these boots he gave me provided a much better grip than my gym shoes would have, and I was very grateful for my good balance and posture for helping me stay upright. Still, it was nothing like the walking I was used to.

"Where are we going?" I groaned, gulping down water from my bottle.

"You'll see. Not much farther."

Reluctant to sound like a broken record or the kid who constantly asked, *"Are we there yet?"* on a road trip, I kept my mouth shut as we moved further into the forest. I hoped he was as good of a hiker as he was a swimmer and that we weren't going to get ourselves lost.

Luckily, I was pretty sure I could easily follow the path back if he abandoned me, or if this was all just one elaborate prank to get on my good side and then say *surprise, bitch!*

"You know, I think you're deranged. You actually *like* doing this?" I huffed, already thirsty again after barely ten minutes. "You're fucking crazy."

"Here," he said, holding out his bottle of water to me. I took it without thanks, because I had emptied mine a bit back, and I was out of breath as I slumped down on a rock, panting heavily.

"Are you sure you're not trying to kill me? Because this feels like a punishment worse than death."

"God, you're dramatic," Benjamin rolled his eyes, taking the bottle back to take a big gulp himself. Eyes closed, he tilted his head back, exposing his neck and Adam's apple. Gulp, gulp, *gulp*. I wondered what he'd look like if he poured the rest of the water down his—I blinked. *Woah*. Where had that thought come from? I didn't actually want to… see him shirtless, did I?

Okay. *Maybe* I did. His arms were finely sculpted, perfectly in theme with the mountains we were climbing, and the way his muscles flexed under his checkered shirt… I kind of wanted to feel him up a bit. Yeah, I needed to get laid. Get my head out of the gutter. Forget about all of this, go to bed early tonight, read my favorite book, and get these vile (and very horny) thoughts out of my system, forbidding them to overrun my brain.

"If I'm dramatic, I don't want to know what you're classified as," I chirped back.

"Some would say…" He wiggled his eyebrows. "A charmer. Or a flirt. Take your choice."

"You're a maniac."

He laughed. "We're almost there, I promise. I think you'll like this."

Luckily, he wasn't lying, and after we rounded another bend of the trail, a beautiful lake came into view: it must have been deep, because it was a dark blue color, and the mountains that towered over it took my breath away.

"Wow," I said, looking around. "This is gorgeous."

"You like it?" He sounded satisfied with himself.

"Yeah," I nodded. I wished I could have lied and told him no—but the truth was, I was in awe of this place.

"After I saw your sketchbook yesterday..." Benjamin tried to act casual by scratching his head, but I could tell the meaning behind his gesture. "I just thought you might like to see it. And, you know, draw it."

I did want to draw it—so badly, my fingers were twitching. But... "I left my sketchbook back in my cabin."

He shook his head. "No, you didn't."

"What?"

"Check your backpack."

I frowned, then opened the bag, and—he must have snuck extra stuff in it while I went to grab my windbreaker. It was full of snacks and my sketchbook, that he'd tucked into the back where it wouldn't get ruined, along with my set of pencils.

"I... I don't know what to say."

"This is where normal people usually say *thank you*, Bradford."

I laughed, then stuck my tongue out at him. "You'll get a thank you when you deliver me safely back to my cabin."

A beat passed. "You know I'd never let you get hurt, right? You're safe with me."

Benjamin unpacked a picnic blanket from his bag and other supplies; pulled out some breakfast goodies, and we munched on the food with hardly a word spoken between us, enjoying the scenery, surrounded by the rustling of the trees and the chirping of birds.

Once we were done, he stripped his shirt off and went to take a swim in the lake while I drew the mesmerizing, enchanting sight in front of me. Only after that, eraser shavings dusted off the page, did I finally start drawing.

"Benjamin?" I said once we were on the road back. I waited for him to look at me. "I know."

CHAPTER 8
Angelina

My feet, while not plagued with blisters, were *sore*, and while there was nothing I wanted more than a bubble bath and a glass of wine, that was not in the cards for me tonight. For one—I only had a shower, and for two—I was stuck, once again, sitting next to Benjamin Sullivan at dinner after the rest of the events of the day concluded.

"So, we're doing this again?" I muttered to him through clenched teeth, trying to appear like I was smiling even as the man who frustrated me to no end (for more than one reason, unfortunately) sat next to me like nothing was wrong.

"Doing what again?" He acted all innocent, as if he hadn't dragged me on a multi-mile hike earlier when all I wanted to do was stay asleep until lunchtime.

I rolled my eyes. "Never mind."

Why was he so insistent to stick to my side like glue? Was this some sort of a bet to get me to talk to him, to like him? To wear me down slowly, annoy me till I wanted to jump off the nearest mountain?

He looked at me with a question in his eyes, but I looked away. We were sitting with different people tonight, and Harper gave me a look when I caught her eye at the table next to me. I gave her a shrug in response. I didn't have an explanation for why Benjamin and I were sitting together again. I didn't have an explanation for *anything* that had happened today, really.

"So, Benjamin," someone asked him across the table, "was your hike a success?"

"Oh, yes, I think it was." He smirked at me, which earned him a glare. "I'm not sure my hiking partner enjoyed it very much though."

"Oh?" The red-headed man at the table raised an eyebrow before turning to look at me. "I'm Liam, by the way."

"Angelina." I gave him a friendly nod. "Pleasure to meet you."

"Oh, the pleasure is all mine," Liam grinned. I had a strange impression that if we had been standing, he would have taken my hand and kissed it. He looked like a gentleman—very much the opposite of the man at my side, who for some reason was scowling at his friend.

"Wine, ma'am?" The server asked, and I nodded.

"Yes, please."

"Would you like red or white?" He held up the selections in his hand, and I went with the red. As far as I was concerned, if Benjamin Sullivan was going to be around me in this close of proximity, I deserved a glass of wine (or two).

"So, how was the hike, Angelina?" Noah, one of the other guys, asked.

"The lake was breathtaking." And if I had to be honest, the company hadn't been half bad either. It seemed like more fun not to give Benjamin the satisfaction of saying that, though.

"Oh, the lake, huh?" Liam chuckled, and I narrowed my eyes.

"Yes, the *lake*," I said, stressing the words while stabbing at my salad with a fork. What was up with these guys? Benjamin was now openly glaring at his friends, and I wondered what had crawled up his butt and put him in such a bad mood. I chuckled to myself at the thought, causing Benjamin to look over at me with an odd expression that I promptly ignored.

The rest of the dinner went smoothly, but when most

employees gathered around the campfire afterwards, I didn't feel like joining them. Instead, I brought a glass of wine outside with me and leaned over the railing, staring at the way the sunset was reflecting on the lake's surface.

I detected his presence without looking over, and I didn't even have to say anything. It was like he was just as aware of me as I was of him.

"Did you really not like the hike earlier?"

I hummed to myself. "Can't let your buddies think I enjoyed myself, can we?" I looked at him as I took a sip of wine. "I have a reputation to maintain, after all."

He sighed. "Angelina..."

"Should we sit?" I asked, and he nodded, "After you." I grazed my thumb over the edge of the wine glass as we sat on the chairs on the patio outside the lodge. It was a chilly night, but I could barely feel it, thanks to the wine warming my body, and maybe, just maybe, the closeness of one Benjamin Sullivan.

I told myself to stop staring at his lips, but I couldn't help it. I wondered what they'd feel like on mine. When I'd drawn the profile of his face earlier, there was something about his cheeks and those full, desirable lips that made my heart flutter.

Dammit, I didn't want my heart to flutter around him. I didn't want to feel *any* of it, but there was something about this man that made me... reckless, and careless; so much so that I almost wanted to let go of my qualms and just live in this moment.

"Benjamin, I—"

"Why do you hate me?" he said, cutting me off. "You still hate me." It wasn't a question. "I just want to figure out why." He fixed his eyes on me, before averting them and running a hand over his face and through his hair. "If I know why you hate me, I can fix it."

"Are you that dense, or just that much of an asshole?" He wasn't, though—dense. And I was suspecting he wasn't much of an asshole either, not after he'd made sure I had everything I needed for the hike today. Sure, he had basically forced me to go on it, but if I hadn't, I never would have seen that beautiful lake. I never would have been able to sketch those things I was now so desperate to paint. I wished, not for the first time this week, that I had my brushes.

"Please, Angelina," he said. My name sounded melodious dripping from his lips. I sighed internally. Despite how much this man infuriated me, I didn't really hate him. "What can I do to fix it?"

Maybe he wasn't purely trying to annoy me anymore. Maybe... Maybe this was something else entirely. Still, I wasn't sure I could give him anything more than what I knew. "Boy Scout, I think you should be able to figure this one out."

"I'm going to wear you down one day, you know."

I did know. The more time we spent together, the closer my long-standing barriers crumbled. "You're delusional," I said instead. "Why do you want to spend time with me this much?"

"Come on, Princess, are you telling me you actually haven't enjoyed my company?"

I couldn't exactly deny it, so I just stared at him, wondering how the hell I had gotten myself in this situation. He looked at me, a now empty wine glass forgotten on the table next to me, and then to the lake. "I have an idea."

"Oh, no. If it has anything to do with that water, that's a hard pass from me."

"Let's go for a swim," Benjamin said, extending out a hand to me. When I hesitated, he raised an eyebrow. "Or are you scared?"

"Scared? Of a little late-night dip in the lake? Never."

I wasn't scared, more just apprehensive—it was too many things: the dirty lake water, the proximity to him, how crazy it was that we were even here in the first place, talking like old friends...

His hand was still hanging in midair. A beat passed before I finally slipped my palm into his, a little shiver going through me as the warmth of his hand spread to mine.

We were holding hands. Me. Holding hands with Benjamin

Sullivan. My mortal enemy. My hot-as-fuck workplace *nemesis*. The bane of my existence. And maybe none of that was true anymore, but what were we doing, anyway? I might not have answered any of his questions, but he hadn't answered mine either.

And here we were, going on a late-night swim. Sure, everyone else had left the campfire and the main lodge area, but... I peeked over at him. This was crazy, wasn't it? That I was placing so much trust in him, a man that I barely knew and insisted I couldn't stand?

Yeah. This was madness.

∽

Benjamin

We approached the dock, Angelina's hand wrapped firmly in mine. Holding her felt strangely steading; important, somehow. It felt like every little moment we'd shared the past few days had been leading us here. I'd never expected anything like this to happen, let alone with her. A weird feeling spread through my chest whenever she was near me. It made me giddy, but also content; peaceful.

I liked bothering her, but after three days of persistently nagging her, I realized that I'd come to enjoy spending time with her, too.

On the porch, she'd looked at me with those big blue eyes filled with an emotion I knew wasn't hate or disdain, and when she'd let her gaze drop to my lips, I almost lost my restraint. Because I wanted to kiss her. And to stop myself from doing it (*again*, since I seemed to like punishing myself), I asked her to come with me down to the lake. It was late, no sounds left surrounding us but the occasional cricket chirping, rustle of branches from the wind, and the gentle lull of the water lapping at the shore.

I dropped her hand when we reached the dock, and I started to unbutton my shirt.

"What are you doing?" she squealed, her voice catching in her throat.

"Surely you don't expect us to swim in our clothes?" I removed the last button from its hole and then stripped the garment from my body.

"No." She shook her head and then narrowed her eyes at me. I watched her walls go back up in an instant. "What's your play here, Sullivan?"

"There's no play, Bradford. I promise. Scout's honor. Just swim with me." I pushed the slacks off my legs and stood there, just in my boxer briefs as Angelina stared at me, fully clothed.

Finally, with a frustrated sigh, she reached back and unzipped her flowing green dress, letting it slide to the ground. Illuminated in the moonlight, my eyes wandered down the length of her body.

She was quick to snap her fingers. "Eyes up here, mister."

I smirked. "It's dark, I can't see much anyway."

"I still don't want you staring at me, so stop that."

"Okay," I said, stepping closer to her until our chests almost touched. I brushed her curls away from her cheek, all the while keeping my eyes on her stubborn expression. "This good?"

Her breath caught as my hand started a pattern down her body. Her neck, her shoulder, her arm. Her skin was warm, soft. In the dark, I couldn't see every detail, but what I saw was enough for this moment to plague my dreams for the rest of the week. The lace of her black bra, the hint of her cleavage, the dip of her hip. The way her tongue wetted her lips. I knew I wouldn't be able to forget one bit of it.

"I..." Her voice was quiet, less feisty than the girl I'd gotten used to fighting me every moment of the day.

I stepped back and moved to the edge of the dock, facing away from her. I pushed my boxers down and flung them on top of my clothes. I looked over my shoulder at Angelina, shamelessly tracing the curves of her body, before giving her a smirk and jumping into the lake.

The cold rush of the water hit me, harsh and freezing. I quickly came up for air and brushed strands of hair off my forehead, watching Angelina as she stood on the dock. "Well? Are you coming?"

She must have mumbled something—a curse against me, most likely—but then turned around, before quickly turning back. "Don't look," she ordered, then waited for me to cover my eyes. I could still see her in my mind, turning her back to me, unclasping her bra and gently placing it on top of her dress. A deep breath, and then her underwear was off, added to the pile. Finally, she plunged into the deep waters.

When she reemerged, I was transfixed by her beauty. Before me was a beautiful moonlit goddess, wet curls framing her face and forming patterns on her skin.

"Angel." Mine was a wordless plea, a helpless instinct. "You're..." I cleared my throat. Shook my head, because words were failing me.

She quirked an eyebrow. "I'm what?"

I held out a hand in a silent question, and this time she came to me with no hesitation. I pulled her into my arms, and she let me. I wrapped my hands around her waist, and she sighed. I leaned into her ear and said on a reverent breath, "You're so fucking beautiful."

She laughed and brought one hand up to cup my face. "Have you looked in the mirror lately?" She poked at my cheek.

"Who are you and what have you done to Angelina Bradford?" Angelina pushed off me, kicking her legs to swim away. "Oh, is *that* how you want to do it?" Her laughter was a siren's song in the night. "I knew you were attracted to me!" I swam after her and enjoyed our game of cat and mouse as I chased her through the lake. It was like she *knew*—knew what would happen if we let ourselves touch each other again. Could feel the same things pulsing through her veins that I could. But could we give in?

"Keep telling yourself that!" she shouted back.

Could we? No. She was just playing with me. I was still an arrogant asshole to her. But then, why did she look at me like *that*? Why did she say, "Aren't you going to catch me, Sullivan?" Why, when I finally used the full strength of my arms, the body I had so finely tuned from hours in the pool, did she let me catch her from behind, lift her, and spin her around in the water before bringing her against me?

When our bodies touched this time, each inch of her bare skin was flush against mine. Her breasts pressed against my chest, my arms around her back and hers on my shoulders. Our lips were only a breath apart.

"Tell me," I gasped against her mouth.

"What? That you're beautiful? I don't think your ego needs any more boosting." The joke fell flat. She was as affected as I was. I couldn't help myself from tucking strands of her hair behind her ears.

"Tell me," I said again, onto the skin of her cheek. Barely a whisper, but it was so much more. It was a plea, a prayer, a benediction upon her lips. "Tell me that I can kiss you." It was a burning need. And I would respect her telling me *no*, but, God, I needed to know what she tasted like. Needed to feel her lips against mine. I needed her to know that I would make it good for her.

"If you don't," Angelina said, lips touching mine. A caress, not a kiss. "I think I might dunk you in this filthy lake water."

I didn't care how big my grin was. That was the most Angelina Bradford thing she could have said, and I fucking adored it. I adored *her*. I bumped her nose once, twice, before finally—finally—my lips were on hers, and the chill of the water was gone, as well as everything else surrounding us. Her arms wound around my neck, her fingers intertwined in my hair, and her lips parted for me.

It was blissful heaven as my tongue explored her mouth, as my lips tasted the sweetness of her lips. It was the first kiss I would have waited a lifetime for.

Angelina tugged my hair and pulled me even closer, and I didn't want to stop kissing her—couldn't have, because every fiber of my being was screaming at me that this was right, this was right, *this was right*.

When we were forced to separate to take a breath, lips swollen and Angelina's eyes lidded with lust, I placed one more kiss on her mouth before she buried her face in my neck.

"Fuck. That was some kiss, Princess."

She hummed in agreement, rubbing her nose against my throat.

I pulled her back in for another kiss, suddenly very aware of our nakedness and how close we were pressed against each other. "Angelina?" I breathed, knowing that if we stayed here, tangled up in each other any longer, we were both going to do something we might regret. Well, that she might regret. Because the only thing I would ever regret with Angelina Bradford was making her hate me in the first place.

"Hmm?"

"Should we get out?" It took everything in me to get the words out, with her hands roaming my body.

"Oh." She suddenly stopped and pulled away, and I knew then that I had broken the spell. Whatever magic the moonlight had brought us, whatever heat had been between us, it was gone. But I had to do this, I didn't want her to regret this. Regretting *me*. "Right." She gave me a brief nod and floated away from me, moving around in the dark water.

I swam back to the dock and pulled myself up, then quickly got dressed. "I'm going to turn around now," I informed her, "if you want to get out."

I could hear her as she lifted herself onto the platform, and then there was the sound of water dripping on the dock, the pitter-patter of the little droplets hitting the wooden surface.

"Okay," she finally said, touching me on the shoulder to indicate she was dressed.

I offered her an arm, only a little surprised when she took it without argument, leaning on my shoulder as we walked back, shoes in hand.

"I think I'll need to take a scalding hot shower to get the smell of lake water off of me." She frowned, sniffing her hair.

I laughed. "Story of my life at camp every year."

Angelina shivered a little as we neared the main lodge, quiet and completely dark after everyone else had gone off to sleep. I kind of liked that it felt like we were sneaking around. Like two horny high school kids that secretly went for a swim. It made me feel alive.

We sat on the big rocking bench on the deck, looking out at the way the moon reflected on the lake. I went and grabbed us towels to dry off with, so we didn't shiver out there in our wet clothes. I didn't want to ruin the moment so soon. Who knew what would happen tomorrow.

"It's so peaceful," she murmured. The chair moved slowly back and forth as we curled up on one side of the seat. "Was your childhood like this?"

"This calm and serene? No." I sighed, reminiscing past summer nights. "Imagine this place full of rowdy, annoying teenage boys and then multiply that by about a hundred, and that's about what my Boy Scout camp experience was like every summer. Besides," I added, giving her a lazy grin as I drew circles on her shoulder, "there were never any girls this pretty to look at." I was rewarded with a shoulder punch.

"You're an idiot." Still, she snuggled closer to me. I almost puffed up my chest at the satisfaction I felt over that.

"Tell me about your summers?" I really didn't want to talk about mine. How my parents used to send us off to camp for almost the entire summer because they were too busy to entertain us when we didn't have school. How at least I had Hunter, even if we rarely saw each other, but I'd always felt bad for Em, who had to go alone.

Angelina pulled away slightly before laying her head down on my lap, her wet hair fanning over my legs. I held my breath for a moment, almost pinching myself, because this? It didn't feel real. She adjusted a bit and then closed her eyes with a sigh. I wondered if she'd punch me again if I tangled my fingers in her hair.

"There isn't that much to talk about," she started. "We used to take a family vacation once a year. Normally it was to Disneyland. That was about the only time I remember all of us being happy and getting along." The feisty, fierce woman I was slowly getting to know looked dejected, a sad smile on her face, and I decided that maybe she could use a comforting touch after all. "Besides that, well, I was constantly trying to get out of the house. My parents... They fought a lot. I went to a lot of art camps, spent a lot of time in the studio."

"Is that how you got so good?"

She laughed as I ran my fingers through her hair, gently massaging her scalp. "Maybe. I like getting lost in it. Finding something so beautiful to paint that it's all you can focus on until it's done."

"And painting... You said that's your favorite, right?"

"Yeah. But I tried all sorts of things. Oil painting, acrylics, and watercolor, of course, but then there was my year of ceramics, trying to make things on the pottery wheel, and my adventures in knitting, cross-stitching... You name it, I've probably tried it. But it always came back to drawing and painting for me."

"I wish I could have had a cool hobby like yours."

"Come on, Boy Scout, you didn't do anything fun? No underwater basket weaving?" She laughed, and I liked the way her eyes lit up a little bit, and I wondered if a sound had ever been so beautiful.

Underwater basket weaving. It was a running joke between Scouts: an exceptionally useless skill and worthless merit badge—because when were you ever going to put it to use in reality?

I chuckled. "My parents were so focused on us getting into good colleges that I think by the time I was old enough to decide what I liked to do, I was out of chess club and piano lessons and into academic decathlons, volunteer work, and studying for SATs."

"There wasn't anything you loved to do?" She looked up at me with a frown, but for the first time, it wasn't *at* me. It was *for* me. Like she was sorry for young Benjamin, who didn't get the chance to really be a kid. I'd always been too busy chasing the future my parents had planned for me.

"Sure. When I escaped my parents, I'd normally just read." Comic books and sci-fi novels, yes, but she didn't need to know that. I tended to hide that part of me. Girls had made fun of it before, so I was going to protect myself the best way I knew how.

"Reading has always been a big escape for me, too," she said with a yawn.

"Really?"

"Mm-hmm. My best friends and I even have a book club."

"What're you reading right now?"

She giggled. "It's a book about fairies and a girl falling in love with her enemy, who turns out to be her soulmate."

"Fairies? Like *Tinkerbell*?"

"No. They're Fae. Like, elves but with magic."

"Mm, so pointy-eared men get you going, huh?"

"Oh, shut up," she said, but made a little happy noise as I kept up my massage of her head. "I like it. And the main character—she paints too. Kind of like a kindred spirit."

"And is that who you're most like?" I asked, wondering if book characters meant as much to her as they did to me. I was beginning to suspect the answer was yes. But I wasn't going to tell her how thirteen-year-old me had found a bit of himself in a dark-haired demigod who loved the water and all things blue. Blue had always been my favorite color, but suddenly it wasn't just blue. It was the exact hue of her eyes.

Angelina yawned, stretching her arms as she responded, "No. I'm more like her older sister. The one everyone calls a bitch."

I frowned. It wasn't the first time she'd said something to that effect about herself. I was afraid she really believed that about herself and I didn't like it; even after a few short days, I could see how much life she had in her. Sure, she tended to be closed-off and intense, but that didn't make her a bitch. Not in any sense of the word.

I must have been lost in my thoughts for longer than a few moments, because I didn't notice Angelina nodding off on me. Her lips were curled into the tiniest smile when I looked at her.

"Princess." I nudged her shoulder softly. "Are you awake?"

When she didn't stir, I slipped my arms under her legs and back, lifting her up. Slowly and quietly, I stood from the chair and carried her to her cabin, knowing she would rather sleep in her bed than out here among bugs and mosquitoes. Not to mention we were still damp, and God knows what would happen if she caught a cold because of me.

After some artful maneuvering to find the key in her backpack, I got in and set Angelina on the bed, tucking her in. I took a moment to look at her, sleeping peacefully.

"Goodnight, Angel," I whispered as I shut the lights off and closed the door behind me.

CHAPTER 9
Angelina

I kissed him. And I *liked* it. Did I like him? I didn't think so. Benjamin was handsome, there was no use denying that to myself, but that was it. It was his body that I liked; that caused a reaction in me. That made me want to pull him against the nearest tree and have my way with him. Which was inconvenient, since usually I was excellent at keeping my most primal thoughts at bay and letting my brain rule my actions.

I stayed in bed longer than usual that morning, trying to process how this guy had gone from my sworn enemy to someone with who I was sort of enjoying spending time within just a few days. By all accounts, it didn't make sense. Normally it took me forever to warm up to someone, and yet I agreed to go hiking with him, I danced with him, even took my clothes off in front of him. Sure, it was dark, and he'd covered his eyes, but that still didn't explain how I was able to completely let go and just... be in the moment.

Sometimes I had a hard time doing that even with my best friends. My mind was always overthinking, overanalyzing, endlessly running in circles. But I'd fallen asleep on his lap, and he'd carried me to bed. I remembered waking up, feeling warm and safe in his arms, and I didn't make a sound, shocked as I was to find myself cradled by the man who kept asking why I hated him.

By the time I pulled myself out of bed, I groaned thinking about going to whatever activity or group exercise they had planned for the day. No matter what it was, I was just going to be thinking about last night the whole time. Still, breakfast time was almost over, and as much as I wanted to go back to sleep, I would be cranky if I didn't eat something, so I took a quick shower and then trudged down towards the main lodge.

Someone else had the same idea, because the first time I saw Benjamin today, he was plopping down in the seat next to me, eating a bagel sandwich topped with ham, cheese, and eggs.

I shoveled another forkful of eggs into mine.

"Hi," he said after he swallowed another bite.

"Hey."

"Did you sleep okay?"

I nodded. I felt self-conscious all of a sudden, but I tried to shake it off. "Yeah. You?"

He gave a little tilt of his head before focusing back on his plate. After we both scarfed down our food, eager to finish before we were kicked out, Benjamin looked at me.

"What?" I asked, taking another sip of my coffee. I needed the caffeine to give me the strength to deal with him. At least that was what I kept telling myself.

"Meet me in an hour by the cabins." So. We weren't going to talk about what happened last night, apparently.

"O...kay? Don't we have some activity we're supposed to go to?"

He gave me that devilish grin and leaned in. "We're playing hooky. Wear something you can get wet in."

I scoffed. "If you're hoping for round two in the lake, let me stop you right now. Skinny dipping is limited to late-night adventures only. No repeats allowed."

"Oh no," he shook his head. "You're not getting off that easily."

"Getting off with what?"

His smirk grew bigger, and in the second it took me to realize the double meaning I unintentionally implied, he stole a strawberry off my plate and popped it in his mouth, before standing up and striding out of the room.

What. The. Fuck.

I couldn't figure him out and it drew me crazy. Even more perplexing was the fact that I wanted to. I was tired of being caught off guard by him.

Nicolas sat next to me after Benjamin left, and I hoped I didn't look as much like the deer in the headlights that I felt.

"You two seem to be getting closer."

"Do we?" I muttered. "Huh."

He cocked his head, a very doglike mannerism that seemed to fit him just perfectly. "What's with that look?"

"Nothing. I'm just finding that he's not at all what I expected. Maybe I judged him too prematurely."

"You know, I think someone's been trying to tell you that for the last year."

I groaned. "Gabbi is so going to give me the *I told you so* speech when I get home, isn't she?"

"Oh, most definitely."

"I tried to hate him, you know," I said, letting out a sigh. "But apparently that's impossible. Like, this guy is just *impossible* to hate. I hate that I *can't* hate him. Why are you looking at me like that?"

Nicolas took a moment before replying. "I've never seen you like this before. Not even in college."

"Like what? And if you say enamored or some other bullshit..." I warned, scowling at him.

He laughed. "None of *that*, don't worry. Just... challenged. It's fun, to see someone who can go toe to toe with you. Who doesn't run away at the first hint that something is hard."

"So?"

"That's a *good* thing, Angelina. Maybe... I dunno, try having some fun with him?"

"Who are you, and what have you done with my friend?" I crossed my arms over my chest. "You were supposed to be on my side here. Solidarity and all."

Nicolas shook his head, chuckling. "I am on your side, Ang. It's just... Do you know when the last time you looked really, truly happy was?"

I shrugged. I hated when people asked me that as if I was supposed to be able to pinpoint one specific memory. Like I could pull something up and just be like, '*Yes! Here is the last time I was happy!*' The truth is, the answer was no. Really, truly happy? I didn't know. I was happy with my friends, of course, spending time with them was the best part of my life. But was that enough?

Was Nicolas right, that maybe Benjamin was someone I could have fun with? I liked to imagine we could have all sorts of *fun*, especially after our kiss last night, but would Nicolas still think that if he knew? I certainly wasn't going to tell him now. Admitting that maybe I hadn't let myself be happy in a long time was hard enough.

"Just think about it," he said, before grabbing his peanut butter covered bagel and banana and standing up from the table. "Let yourself be happy, Ang. You deserve it."

He was gone before I could say anything, presumably off on some errand for his father or to find Zofia. I didn't envy all the things he had to do as CEO-in-training and his father's son, but he seemed to be doing pretty okay for himself.

Was he happy? Nicolas had always been so positive, joyful, and full of life. Sometimes it used to annoy me, how damn bubbly and full of energy he was, but I became friends with him anyway. Not that I had much of a choice—once Nicolas decided that he was friends with someone, he didn't take no for an answer. And so, I had somehow ended up with the world's biggest golden retriever man bouncing around me whenever possible. Damn. Maybe I was the only person not really living.

It made me think about Noelle. How closed off she'd been after returning from New York and before meeting Matthew. It'd been hard to encourage her to open her heart to him, to allow herself to have a future with him. Was I doing the same thing with my life? Discarding every chance at a different future because I was too focused on protecting myself?

Maybe I needed to make a change.

I headed back to my cabin, ready to clear my head and try stepping into the ice-cold waters of my future. Hopefully, I wouldn't *actually* plunge into the icy waters of the lake with Benjamin, but I put on my swimsuit as requested just in case, before layering on more clothes.

This man really was determined to get me wet, wasn't he?

~

Benjamin

"What are we doing?" Angelina asked as we trudged through the wilderness towards my surprise. I wanted her to relax, to lean into her hidden adventurous side a little bit more. I could tell she didn't often leave her comfort zone, and for some reason, I wanted her to experience what life had to offer outside the office walls. With me.

"You'll see," I said, trying not to smirk too much. I didn't want to rile her up, not today at least. I wanted her to enjoy this.

Pushing back some branches so she could enter the clearing, I waved her over to where I had tied up the canoe to a small pier. Despite myself, anticipation hadn't left me all morning, ever since I'd woken up with a stupid grin on my face. Not only because of the kiss—okay, mainly for the kiss, but I also wanted to spend the day with Angelina, regardless of what would happen between us. And maybe I wanted to surprise her a little, and that's why I organized this outing, along with a few more surprises up my sleeves.

"We're going canoeing? You've got to be kidding me."

"What? You wore your swimsuit as I instructed, didn't you?"

She rolled her eyes. "Yes, Sullivan. I wore a swimsuit."

"Good. Because like the sign says, you may get wet." I never denied being a cheeky asshole. Thankfully, she just glared at me.

"There's no sign, Boy Scout."

"Okay, so this isn't Splash Mountain. Just go with it."

"You seem to want me to go along with a lot of your schemes lately."

"Think about it, Princess. Would you rather be out here with me, or listen to a seminar about sexual harassment in the workplace?" Sure, we'd have to make it up later, but this was worth it.

"Maybe you should sit through it," she deadpanned. "You don't seem to be able to take no for an answer."

"I didn't hear you saying no last night. Or any other attempt at stopping me, for that matter."

Angelina rolled her eyes, shoving me away with her hand, but it lacked her usual bite. She placed her hands on her hips, looking between me and the canoe. "So, are we doing this?"

"Get in," I said, untying the boat after she was seated and pushing it into the water before hopping in myself. We each took an oar, paddling towards the middle of the lake, and I couldn't stop smiling as I sat across from her.

"What now?" she asked, catching my eye.

"Nothing."

"Sullivan," she laughed after a minute. The sound was music to my ears. "I think we're just paddling in circles."

"Hm?" I looked around. "I guess we are. Where do you want to go?"

Angelina looked across the lake and then narrowed her eyes at me. "Didn't you map out our course? You're the resident wilderness expert here."

"I did, but that was before all of your bad paddling got us to the middle of nowhere." I grinned, and Angelina pulled her oar out of the water towards me, splashing me.

"Hey!" I splashed her back, and she shrieked. "I told you that you might get wet."

Finally getting our paddling in sync, we managed to move upstream. After paddling for a while in silence, I found a nice-looking shore so we steered the canoe over to take a break.

"I have to say, I definitely took living here for granted," Angelina said, stretching her arms before kneeling at the river's edge. My stomach rumbled, and she startled, looking up at me. "Should we go back for lunch, or...?"

I shook my head. "What part of playing hooky did you miss? I brought food." I held up the bag with our lunch packed inside, and we sat on the rocky beach one next to the other.

"Maybe you aren't completely worthless, after all."

"I'm good for a lot of things."

She stuck out her tongue as I handed her a sandwich and a bag of barbeque chips. The silence fell upon us while we ate, but it was a comfortable one. It'd been happening a lot, us enjoying the quiet without needing to fill it with small talk or awkward conversations.

Once we were satisfied with our full stomachs, we resumed our journey and paddled farther up the river to another lake. At some point, Angelina started to move.

"Can you hand me my bag?" She stood up, leaning forward to reach for it.

"Hold on, don't—"

"Just give me—"

I tried stopping her, but I miscalculated our weights, and that's when disaster struck. The canoe lurched, causing Angelina to lose her footing and tumble over the side. When she resurfaced from the cold, murky lake water, *murder* was written all over her face.

"Shit," I cursed, offering her a hand to help her back onto the canoe. "Here, I'll—" But I couldn't finish my sentence, nor was I able to pull her up, because Angelina wrapped her hand around mine and tugged me in after her.

This woman.

Of course, we were both still fully clothed. My T-shirt and flannel were stuck to my chest and my pants were uncomfortably heavy; Angelina didn't seem to fare any better. We were both treading water, the canoe only a foot or so away.

Slowly, a grin spread over Angelina's face before she dove her hand into the water and sent a splash my way, making me gasp in indignation. I splashed her back, and we didn't stop until we were both screaming and laughing. Completely soaked to the bone, keeping ourselves afloat as we stared at each other, it was the most fun I'd had in a long time.

"Hi," I smiled.

Angelina swam closer to me, her legs wrapping around my waist as she pulled her sweatshirt off her body. The T-shirt was next, and finally, I could see her swimsuit: a little black polka-dotted bikini.

"Hi," she whispered back, palms coming to rest on my chest. "Looks like we're all wet." She scrunched up her nose, and I laughed.

"What do you say we head back and go dry ourselves off?"

"Or," she said, with a delightful twinkle in her eye, "you can peel off your clothes and come swimming with me, Sullivan."

"Trying to get me naked again, are you? You like my body that much, Angel?"

She tsked, but those pretty red cheeks let me know what I didn't need to hear. Angelina tried to pull away from me, but I wrapped my arms around her back, forcing us closer together, and the remaining wet garments did little to hide the planes and curves of our bodies.

We were in dangerous territory here. I knew what her mouth tasted like, and it was all I wanted to have again.

"Angelina..." I warned in a low voice as she tugged at my shirt. I wanted it off more than anything, but I felt like I needed to keep some sort of barrier between us, or that line we'd silently agreed to draw was going to be blurred forever, in a way we couldn't come back from.

"Just let it happen," she breathed against my mouth, before pulling the shirt over my head. And then her lips were on mine, her hands tangled in the hair at the nape of my neck.

There were no slow, teasing kisses this time. I tried to pace myself, but desperation struck us both like lightning. How could I end this when I was so hungry for her? When her legs squeezed my waist, her nails scratched my scalp, and her teeth bit my lips like she was punishing me for something and all I wanted to say was, "*Again*. Do it again."

When we came up for air, panting heavily and my heart racing a hundred miles an hour, the heat in her eyes was unmistakable. "Damn, Bradford. If I'd known you could kiss like that, I would have stopped being an asshole a lot sooner," I said, resting my forehead against hers.

She snorted, shoving at my shoulder. "Jerk. Like I would have let you."

I nipped at her ear, and her giggle inflated my ego more than any compliment or good performance evaluation on the job. "Should we go back?"

"Is it bad that I don't want to?"

"Only if you're going to admit that you actually like spending time with me."

"Hmm..." She pretended to think about it, the little she-devil. "Nope."

I flicked her nose. "Guess that means no dessert."

"Dessert? You brought dessert?"

"Oh, that got your attention, didn't it?"

She poked me in the chest. "You can't torment a girl with sweets like that. It's just rude." She huffed. "If you did that to Noelle, it would be World War Three."

I smirked. "Don't worry, Angel, I'm not going to withhold the strawberry angel food cake from you." I gave her a little wink. "Name's a coincidence."

Angelina shivered then, looking down between us before peering at me from under her lashes. "Maybe we should..."

I nodded, swimming us back over to the canoe. After we were both sitting safely inside, I pulled out the towels from my backpack. She snuggled into the material, warm from the sun, and I hid a smile as I dried my face, thankful now more than ever that Angelina decided to give me a second chance.

CHAPTER 10
Angelina

Still wrapped in our towels, Benjamin and I began paddling back towards the cabins and warm, dry clothes.

I didn't want to leave—the moment, our bubble, that insane pull I felt towards him whenever his body was close—but it was the smart thing to do. Especially when he decided to pull out the mason jars full of strawberries, angel food cake, and whipped cream.

"Oh, this is heavenly," I moaned. I may or may not have made a few extra unnecessary sounds, but he'd affected me more than I thought was possible when we were in the water, and I wanted to give him a dose of his own medicine. It'd been all I could do to resist rubbing up against him, desperate for friction as he claimed my mouth like a man possessed. *Fuck,* I really needed to stop thinking about it.

Luckily, dessert had led to different (and safer) conversations, and here we were now, sitting along the bank of the lake that was our starting point, neither of us wanting to break this—whatever it was—between us.

We constantly teased each other, but I had so many questions about who he really was, the kind of man he was, and they were begging to burst out of me.

"So. Mr. Outdoors. Tell me." He raised an eyebrow, and I continued. "How'd you get this good with all of this?" I waved a hand around, gesturing to the canoe, but also thinking about our hike yesterday.

"It's like you said. I camped a lot when I was younger. And being a Boy Scout didn't hurt."

"Did you like it?" I was still surprised that the businessman I emailed and the outdoorsy man sitting next to me were the same person.

He shrugged. "Sometimes. It wasn't all sunshine and rainbows."

I was hesitant to ask him the next question, but I decided to go with it. "What about your family?"

"My brother and I... He was always the one who excelled at all this stuff. I tried to be good at it just to be able to relate to him." Benjamin took a deep breath, and I wondered what was going on in that head of his. I hadn't noticed before, but the more we spent time together, the more I could see that he often retreated into his head. He was cocky, confident, and could be downright conceited, but there was this look on his face sometimes that I couldn't ignore. "We're not close. Or we haven't been in years."

I moved a bit closer until our arms brushed against each other. He didn't say anything about it, continuing to stare at the sun setting over the lake. "What happened? If it's not too personal to ask."

"It's fine. It's the same thing that happens to most people, I guess. We grew apart as we got older. To be honest, I resented him a little bit." He sighed. "Hunter was always our parents' favorite. He was the one who went to medical school, following in their footsteps. And Em, my little sister... Well, she got a pass as the only daughter. Daddy's little girl," he chuckled, fondness apparent in his voice. "When she said she wanted to be a fashion blogger, it felt like they would have gone along with whatever she wanted, no matter what."

I let his words settle over me for a moment. Then I said

quietly, "Parents do a great job of fucking us up, don't they?" I didn't want to talk about my parents, about the divorce that had wrecked our home. Despite it all, at least I'd always had my brother by my side. He'd been something like my best friend growing up, especially in high school when making friends was difficult for me and I never really knew who I could trust.

That was one thing about being popular I realized a long time ago. Even if everyone thought you were cool, with your designer handbags and expensive shoes, you were still just as much of a loser as the kid that got slammed into a locker every day. People just decided one day who to idolize and who to hate, for no reason whatsoever.

When all the glitter and the magic was gone—the popularity, the money, the perfect parents, all that was left was me and my brother.

"Hey." Benjamin nudged me slightly, pulling me from my memories. "They didn't fuck you up. You're kind of perfect, you know?"

I scoffed, shaking my head, but I couldn't rein in the small smile that curved my lips. "I'm not," I murmured, a quiet confession into the murky waters of the lake. It was serene out here, peaceful and beautiful. Maybe that was why I wanted to share more with him. And maybe that was why he felt inclined to share more with me, too.

"I moved here to be closer to him."

"Your brother?"

He nodded. "I took the job here knowing it was close to the hospital he was working at. And even then, in the last two years, I've barely reached out," he chuckled self-deprecatingly. "It's stupid, but I feel bad interrupting his shiny, perfect life."

I frowned. "He's your brother, Benjamin. I'm sure he would make time for you."

"Maybe." He shrugged before asking, "What about you? Your family?"

"My brother and I were best friends growing up. Even went to the same college. If I ever needed someone, he was always there." Even when I didn't have my parents, I always had Daniel. "It was great."

"And now?" If he noticed I didn't bring up my parents, he didn't mention it.

"I'm pretty sure he's in love with one of my best friends, even though he won't admit it." Benjamin's eyes widened in genuine surprise. "It's the dumbest thing because *everyone* can see it, but the two of them insist they don't think about each other like that." I rolled my eyes. Two idiots, really.

"It'd be nice to have someone like that," Benjamin said.

"Like what? Hopelessly pining over you?"

"No." He bopped my nose. "A best friend. Someone you want to be with because you can't imagine anything else. I don't know. Something easy, I guess."

I laughed. "Love isn't easy."

"Isn't it?"

I wished I could say that it was. That I believed in love. That the girl who sat around reading romance novels and watching romantic comedies just to feel something truly believed that someone was going to swoop in, sweep her off her feet, and she'd live happily ever after. But I hadn't believed that in a long time. So I shrugged, reluctant to share something so personal.

We were both quiet for a while until I heard him humming.

"What?"

A beat. "I wish I'd gotten to know you sooner."

I punched him in the arm. "Stop saying such nice things like that."

He winced. "You know, I do think you're going to give me a bruise if you keep hitting me in the same spot."

"Such a shame that you deserve it."

"Oh, do I?"

I barely had the time to nod that Benjamin stood up and, in a quick move, picked me up over one shoulder, my towel falling onto the ground as he ran towards the lake among my squeals.

"Benjamin!" I shrieked. "Put me down right now! Don't you dare!" I was underwater before I could utter another word.

I changed my mind. I *did* hate him. Even more so when I came up for air and he took my breath away all over again by kissing me.

∽

MY HAIR WAS STILL WET, braided in double Dutch braids, when we finally entered the lodge for dinner, after hours of kissing and laughing and talking about things I never would've imagined sharing with him. We only took a break to have a quick shower in our respective cabins and change into more proper clothes. It'd been the perfect day, I had to admit. And maybe we had skipped out on the work stuff, but I had *fun*. For the first time in a long time, I had laughed so hard my stomach hurt.

"You two looked awfully cozy," Nicolas remarked as I sat next to him at the bar to get a drink.

"No, we didn't." But I thought back to our canoe session and the ensuing talk on the dock. I didn't even realize that someone might see us. Shit.

"It's okay, Ang," Nicolas smiled. "I won't tell anyone about your secret crush."

"I don't like him like that," I groaned. "He works under you. You know what a jerk he was to me. Why would I *like* him?"

Nicolas shrugged, giving me a delighted little grin, earning himself a little shove. "Ouch. What was that for?"

"For being annoying."

"Is that any way you treat one of your longest friends?"

Sometimes I still didn't understand how I befriended the biggest goofball on the planet. Sure, he was a good businessman, serious when he had to be, but Nicolas Larsen was basically a golden retriever in human form. He had a huge heart, and from the moment I sat next to him in my Financial Accounting class, it was like he adopted me into his little pack of friends. I didn't really mind, because I mostly just had the girls, and sometimes it was nice to enjoy the simplicity of a friendship with a guy.

Especially one who never had any interest in me romantically. That had never stopped him from trying to introduce me to all his single friends, though. I'd never been interested in any of them, but even when I told him I didn't have time for dating, he kept it up. I thought it was kind of sweet.

But for all his matchmaking attempts, Nicolas had never found the girl for him either. I knew that his hopeless romantic heart was just waiting for the right girl to walk into his life. I thought back to the way he and Zofia had shared a whispered conversation at dinner last night, and I wondered if maybe...

I shrugged off that line of thought and threw an arm around him. "You're just lucky I can stand you."

He gave me a little puppy dog face as we ordered our drinks, and we left the bar once we got them. "What would I do without my grumpy friend to bring me back down to earth?"

"Float helplessly into space?"

He laughed. "Come on, I heard there's a make-your-own pizza bar for dinner tonight."

"Fancy."

"I mean, it's not steak and potatoes, but I think it'll do."

"Dude, you need to let that go."

"Never."

"See you later?" I spotted Benjamin standing at the high-top table, waiting for me.

Nicolas nodded, looking over towards Zofia. "Yup. Have fun with your man."

"He's not—" I started, but he set off before I could even finish, and I huffed as I joined Benjamin.

Sure, we'd kissed. A few times. And it was good, great even. The man knew how to kiss, sue me. It didn't make him *mine*. Not by a long shot.

"Hey." I held up the drink I had fetched for him.

"Wow, what service," he said with a smirk, and I gave him my best glower.

"Drink it before I change my mind, Sullivan."

He chuckled. "Thank you for the drink, Angelina." A little bit of warmth rushed through me at his sincerity. At his using my name like that, without a hint of sarcasm or dislike.

"You're welcome."

We enjoyed our drinks in silence, and I used the time to take him in. I couldn't believe I'd kissed him. That this gorgeous man might be interested in me. Was it just me, or did he look even better tonight? His hair had dried a little curly around his forehead, and he looked so nice in his blue button-up shirt and dark denim jeans. My mouth went a little dry as I watched him, peering at him over my glass.

He leaned over the table to whisper, "Are you going to complain if I sit next to you at dinner?" I shook my head. "No?"

"No."

He grinned. "Did I finally win you over?"

I wanted to deny it, even though my heart was leaping out of my throat just at his proximity. After the lake—everything felt different.

His hands holding me up, clinging to my back... I wanted them everywhere. Dammit, I should have brought a vibrator with me, because I needed to let out all this pent-up frustration. I needed to not look at Benjamin Sullivan and want to jump his bones. That was out of the question. Absolutely forbidden.

Still, I couldn't say that to him. It'd mean admitting defeat, and I was one sore loser. "You're alright."

"Just alright, huh?"

I took another sip of wine. "Come on, let's go find a table."

Dinner was torture of the worst invention. My skin was itching, crawling like it only wanted one thing. I was so incredibly aware of his body heat, his thigh next to mine. His magnetic presence lured me to him.

And then, while everyone was involved in a conversation

about some activity that must have happened today, I felt his hand brush my leg under the table and it was all I could do to stop myself from jumping at the scorching touch. I tried to keep my breathing under control, but as he inched closer and closer to where I wanted him to touch me the most, I hissed, "Stop it."

Don't tease me, when this is all I want and everything I can't have.

He didn't move any further, but he didn't take his hand away, either. Instead, he drew circles on my skin beneath the edge of my dress, up and down my thigh and along the inner part of it.

I wanted to growl in frustration or yell at him (or possibly push back my chair and position myself on his lap), but we were at dinner, and I had no intention of making the whole company aware of what was going on between us. I didn't need them to know how desperately I wanted Benjamin Sullivan.

As soon as our meal ended—which I'd barely picked at, despite the pizza being delicious—I stood from the table, ready to run out of there.

"Oh, leaving already, Angelina?" a colleague asked.

I nodded. I was too turned on from his touches, burning up at my core, and I couldn't take it anymore. "Yeah, I'm not feeling well," I murmured, pulling my cardigan tighter around my shoulders and excusing myself. I didn't need to look at Benjamin to know that he had a shit-eating grin on his stupid face.

It was chilly outside, which gave me some much-needed relief. I leaned against the railing, tilting my head up to breathe in the fresh air, letting the cool mountain air bring my body temperature down.

For a moment I wondered if he'd catch my drift.

He did. Of course, he did.

"I hate you," I breathed as soon as I felt his body cover mine from behind.

"No, you don't," Benjamin said, his nose nuzzling my neck.

"Yes, I do."

He pressed a kiss to the sensitive skin right under my jaw, making me shiver. "You're such a bad liar."

"Am not."

"Are too. It's okay, though. I like the way you lie."

I moaned as he bit me before soothing the redness with his tongue. I wanted to push him off, just to know that I could, but then he took my earlobe in his mouth and all my logic seemed to vanish. All I wanted was him. "Ben…" I whimpered. "Not here. Someone might see."

"Everyone is still inside," he whispered. "It's fine."

I shook my head. I didn't want him to mark me, and I didn't want us to get caught. Knowing our bosses were just inside and could come out at any moment to find us this close together was too much.

"I need you," I panted, rocking my hips back against him. I didn't miss his gasp, the sharp intake of air as he planted his hands on either side of me on the railing, caging me in.

I needed him, and the truth terrified me.

CHAPTER 11
Benjamin

I need you. Did she even know what those words did to me? She was gorgeous in that long-sleeved maroon wrap dress; the bodice pushed her breasts up in a perfect way while the gown left her ankles bare. Even those little pearl studs she was wearing and the double braids she'd done. She had no idea, did she?

"Should we go to my cabin?" Angelina replied by pushing her back against me. "You're killing me, babe," I groaned in her ear as I tried to adjust myself, not wanting to walk around with a massive bulge in my jeans.

She turned, looking up at me with those beautiful blue eyes, and I almost kissed her right there. Where anyone could have seen.

The feeling of her body flush with mine hadn't left my mind since our swim in the lake that morning. It was too bad, because now I couldn't resist touching her anymore, and the only way to do that without anyone noticing was to stroke her leg under the table at dinner. I'd teased her with slow movements, but the truth is, I was tormenting myself even more.

"I thought you hated me," I murmured, tilting her chin up.

"Yeah, well, things change."

"You can just say it, you know."

"What?"

"That you like me," I whispered like a secret.

She scoffed. "I don't."

"You're so cute when you try to deny the obvious." That earned me a glare. "You can admit it out loud, you know. It's okay. It's just you and me here."

Angelina shook her head, crossing her arms. "Never gonna happen." I wondered if that was true, but in this moment, I didn't care. I wanted her and she wanted me, and that was enough.

She pushed away from the railing and tugged at the lapel of my shirt, lust clear in her eyes. "Take me to your place?"

I laced my fingers with hers and pulled her off the patio, setting off towards the cabins. Once we were far enough from the main lodge, I brought our joined hands up to my lips and kissed the back of her hand.

"Do you know how beautiful you look tonight?" I said, wondering if anyone's beauty had ever captivated me like Angelina Bradford's had.

"No." She grinned. "Tell me."

I hummed, pretending to think about it while pulling her against me as we approached my cabin. I squeezed her hand, and with the other I traced an invisible line along her neckline. "This dress has been tempting me all night."

"Is that so?"

"And these..." I let my fingers brush over her cleavage. Angelina let out a tiny gasp that went directly to my boner. "These have been driving me crazy since I saw you in that bikini of yours."

"What about," she said, voice heavy with desire, "when you saw me in *nothing*?"

"I think you might need to jog my memory, Princess. I can't quite remember." She bit her lip and pressed herself against me before raking her teeth against my jaw, making me hiss. "I can't get you out of my goddamn mind, no matter how hard I try."

"I'm just waiting for you to do something about it, Sullivan."

∼

I SLAMMED the door to my cabin behind me as we finally disentangled ourselves from each other.

"I think we just need to—get it out of our systems," Angelina said, panting roughly and pulling at my shirt.

"Baby, do you really think once is going to be enough with me?" It sure as hell wouldn't be enough for me. I wanted to do a case study of her body and kiss every inch of her skin.

"Well, once is all we've got, so we gotta make it count."

"Why, think you'll get addicted to me?" I pulled my tie the rest of the way from my neck.

"No. I just don't do relationships." Angelina looked at me as we stood, a breath apart, and I couldn't take it anymore. We had one thing in common at least.

"Come here," I said, before spinning her around and pushing her up against the door, my mouth roughly claiming her.

She moaned as my tongue slipped past her lips, our mouths connecting in passion. I could have stayed like that all night, coaxing her soft lips open, watching her eyes lidded with desire, letting her tug on my hair as we kissed until we were breathless. But I wanted more.

My whole body was burning for this woman. This woman who rarely showed me a smile, but when she did, it felt like winning the lottery. This woman who had fearlessly stripped on the dock and joined me in the lake at night, even though every instinct inside of her seemed to be screaming to do the opposite. Ever since I'd felt her wet body pressed against mine, her breasts against my chest, this moment had felt inevitable.

"Benjamin..." Angelina started, but trailed off in a whimper when I kissed her jaw, down to her neck and collarbone. I mouthed the neckline of her dress, and all I could think about was that I wanted it off.

I wove my fingers into her hair, pulling apart her braids, and brought our mouths together again, kissing her deeply. Fiercely. Giving her a taste of how good I would make it for her if she let me. Words might fail me, but our tongues, our lips, the way she gasped when I nipped at her—it all spoke louder than any speech I could give.

I slid my hand down the side of her body, cupping her breasts in my descent; I stroked over her hips until I reached her thigh, where I fisted her dress and bunched it up to expose her.

"Am I going to find your cunt dripping for me, Angelina?" I said against her mouth.

"N-no," she protested weakly as I started drawing circles across her inner thigh before pushing my thumb against the lacy fabric that covered her center.

"These seem like pretty sexy underwear to bring to a work retreat." I grinned as I pressed on her clit and Angelina jerked in my arms. I tugged her dress up to her waist and looked at her for confirmation. When she nodded, I looped a finger through the black lace. "They look good on you, but I think they'll look better on the floor," and I dragged them off, leaving her bare before me.

Angelina let out the loveliest moan when I pushed my fingers inside her, finding it warm and wet. Eyes flickering shut and head tilted back, she was a vision. I wished I could immortalize her face at this moment; I never wanted to forget the way she looked when I was the one to give her pleasure.

"Please," she breathed.

"Please what? I want to hear you say the words."

Her fingers tightened around my shoulder when I bumped her clit. "Please, stop teasing me and *touch me*. I think I might actually kill you if you don't."

"Your wish is my command," I said with a smile before dropping to my knees. I wanted to taste her, to devour her before I even thought about fucking her. I could wait, no matter how much my aching cock disagreed. If we only had one night, I was damn sure taking my time with her.

The first swipe of my tongue over her pussy was like heaven. I toyed with her, swirling my tongue around the sweet bud and up and down her folds until Angelina was making adorable mewling sounds and burying her fingers in my hair, pushing me closer into her.

"Fuck, Angel," I growled as I feasted on her. "You taste divine." I kept it up relentlessly until her cries became more and more desperate, until her chest was heaving and her body shaking with the need to come. She gasped when I sucked her clit. "Is this what you need?"

"Harder," was all she said, and I gave it to her.

When Angelina came with the sweetest cry, I swallowed her juices and kept licking her all over, waiting for her to come down from her high. I was almost positive that I was in heaven now; that I had died, and *this* was my reward. My Angel. Getting to know this woman's body, getting acquainted with her taste, every inch of her skin.

Once her breath evened out, I stood up and placed a kiss on her cheek. "Turn around," I instructed, and she did without arguing. I slowly slid the zipper open, placing kisses on her back as I did so. I tugged down the dress, delicately pulling the sleeves off her arms, and let the gown fall to the floor. Angelina stepped out of it and turned to me, left only in her black pushup bra.

"You're a fucking vision." I didn't think I had any breath left as Angelina reached around and undid her bra, leaving her completely bare. She was perfect. I took in every inch of her greedily, grateful that she let me. I didn't know how much time had passed, but when my gaze met hers again, Angelina was eyeing me with a feral glint in her eyes, and I knew I was overdressed.

"Your turn," she said, stepping close to me, tempting me with all that naked flesh, but I'd let her have this. She slowly undid the buttons of my shirt, pushing each one out, like she was determined to draw this out. To torture me.

Finally, after pushing the shirt off my shoulders, Angelina ran her hands down my arms and then up again from my stomach to my chest, over the finely sculpted muscles that had come from a lifetime of working out, running, and swimming.

Slowly, her fingers trailed down until she cupped me through my jeans, and just that one touch—*Fuck*. First the button, then the zipper, she slowly pushed the denim off my body. I kicked the garment out of the way before standing tall in front of her.

A moment passed. Then another.

This woman, who was such a pain in the ass, who always wanted the last word on everything, was dumbstruck. At a loss for words. Eyes trained on my briefs and the erection underneath them, Angelina's cheeks turned a beautiful shade of red.

"Do you…" She gulped.

"Speechless, Princess?"

She shook her head and seemed to collect herself before narrowing her eyes at me. "No. There's nothing to be impressed with." *That's my girl.* Just a little bit of teasing brought out the fire in her.

"I don't think you'll be saying that once I'm inside of you, sweetheart."

"Whatever." She tried to look displeased, but I knew she was just putting on an act for me. I could see how turned on she was. How much she wanted this. I had tasted it on her, I had marks on my skin to prove it. "Do you have…" Angelina bit her lip. "I didn't bring any condoms."

I nodded, taking her hand. She kissed me slowly and pushed me towards the bed, where we collapsed in a mess of limbs. With a hand, I reached into the nightstand and tossed the foil wrapper on the bed.

We kissed, explored each other's bodies, and kissed some more. I could have stayed like that forever.

Just as I was leaving kisses down her breastbone, Angelina pulled away for a moment. "This… We…" She shook her head as if she was trying to find the words amid the haze in her head. "This isn't a relationship. No strings. Just sex. Okay?"

I licked her nipple before surging forward to kiss her again. "Just sex."

"Good."

"Now shut up, Princess." Angelina's scowl was terrifying even when she was naked under me. "The only sounds I want to hear from you is *yes, please, more*. Got it?"

"What about *stop*?"

"If you need to," I conceded. "But trust me, you're not going to be asking me to stop, Angel." Because I was going to make it good for her—I would treat her right.

She huffed as I peeled the underwear from my body, freeing my erection. I was more than well-endowed down there, and I could see Angelina's eyes widen as she took all of me in.

"You can say it," I smirked. "You are impressed." I puffed up my chest as I loomed over her, restraining my urge to take her hard and fast in the way I knew would make this end much too soon. I had plans to make it last all night long.

"I'll never admit that," she breathed. Her eyes said it all, though.

After rolling the condom on and giving Angelina a sweet kiss on the mouth, I lined up my cock with her entrance and slowly pushed the tip inside, causing her to inhale deeply. I stopped and held myself there, one hand gripping her thigh and the other cupping her face.

We were both panting heavily, looking into each other's eyes. It took me a moment before I remembered what this was, what this was *not*. I kissed her again, deep and dirty, until she was breathless and squirming for more under me. I wanted her begging, but I needed her to say the words first.

"Please, Ben," she finally gasped.

"Use your words, Angel. What do you want?"

"Fuck me," she groaned out, "please, just—ah!" I slid all the way to the hilt, making little fireworks go off behind my eyelids. "God, *yes*. You feel so good."

She was right—and I was wrong before. *This* was heaven.

Heaven was Angelina Bradford's pussy, warm and tight around my cock. Holy shit. I let her adjust to my size for a minute before I pulled out, and Angelina's arms circled my back, her fingers digging into my ass as if she could push me into her even further, deeper.

"Tell me you hate me," I whispered against her ear as I thrust into her again.

"I hate you."

"Again." I lifted her leg between us, changing the angle, and she cried out.

"I hate you. I hate you, I hate you, *I hate you.*"

I moved in and out in punishing thrusts as Angelina fisted my hair tightly and rocked against me. Every little moan she gave was rewarded with another push. I leaned down to close my mouth around one of her nipples, running my tongue over it before sucking; all the while, I made sure to squeeze and rub the other one, intending to make her lose her mind.

She was close, if the way she was writhing and emitting little delicious sounds was anything to go by. When her eyes fluttered shut, I gave her a harsh thrust, making her gasp.

"Eyes open." I wanted her to look at me when we came.

And I wasn't going to last much longer. Not like this. Not with her eyes on me. Not when her lying about hating me made me want to swat her cute little butt and then massage it to soothe her. But we'd have time for that later. Maybe when I got her on top of me.

I reached down to her clit, giving her enough pressure that she sobbed as I rubbed circles over it. "Good girl," I hummed. "Now come for me."

"I hate you—*oh*, God!" Angelina screamed as she reached her climax, her body spasming all around me as I kept fucking her through it.

"That's it," I groaned, chasing my own release. "Fuck. I'm gonna come, baby."

Angelina crossed her ankles over my back, pushing me against her. "I want to feel you when you come," she said, nipping at my ear. "Come inside me, Benjamin."

That was all it took. The pressure, her words—I was spilling inside of her, filling the condom as Angelina moaned into my lips.

∼

ANGELINA

I couldn't believe how good it felt. How *right*. Of all the sex I'd experienced in my life (admittedly, a decent amount, especially considering my hookups in college), it was never like this. Benjamin was rough, in all the right ways, but he'd made sure I was taken care of. Prioritized my pleasure over his own.

Somehow, he knew exactly what I needed, even when I didn't. And I liked the way he ordered me around in bed, pushed me around, treated me like I *needed* to be commanded. From anyone else I probably wouldn't have taken it, but from him... I loved the way he took control. Like he knew I needed to let go of it.

Benjamin got up to clean himself off, I used the bathroom, and now we were lying in bed quietly after I rested my head on his chest. I didn't know whether to kiss him, ask him to fuck again, or cuddle up into his side.

The last option... Where did that even come from? This wasn't a relationship, and I didn't need comfort. We were just sleeping together to get it out of our systems. I had said as much to him.

Except, looking at him, his muscles relaxed in the low cabin light, his hand absentmindedly trailing over my shoulder, I could feel my arousal growing again—and maybe something else, too, but I pushed that thought to the back of my mind, untouchable. Maybe once wasn't enough for this demon inside of me to be sated. I didn't know what Benjamin was doing to me but *fuck* if I didn't want to ride him all night, to relish the soreness between my legs from the burn of him. Revel in how he stretched me and filled me sublimely.

I pressed a kiss on his chest, right above a nipple. He groaned, and I resisted the urge to lick him all over, wondering how he would sound with my tongue on his body. On... other places. "I know we said once, but technically, the night isn't over yet... right?" I gave him a devilish grin. I kissed his perfectly defined jaw, like it was sculpted by a God. I hated how damn beautiful he was.

It wasn't fair. If he wasn't so good-looking, maybe I could still hate him. I tried to shake off the thought, though, because it wasn't true anyway. He'd shown me that it was so much more than that. I actually... and I loathed to admit it, even to myself, but I *did* like him. I liked his smile when he joked with Liam and his other friends. I liked his confidence when it came to all things outdoors. I liked how he was always kind to the lodge staff and a gentleman to our female coworkers.

I liked the way he treated me. Yes, he was insufferable. But somehow, it seemed like he perked up a little every time I found myself having fun with him on his crazy adventures. He kept doing all these little things for me, and I wasn't sure what to make of them.

"Are you saying you want to go for round two, Bradford?" I hummed, looking at him while deciding my best plan of attack.

"Ask nicely, Princess."

I pushed against his shoulder and pinned him on the bed. "Oh, Your Majesty, Master of the Fine Dick, will you please fuck me again?"

His laugh echoed in the small space. Then he grinned at me, and I thought he looked like the devil—a really hot one, but still. "I thought you'd never ask." He was already hard again and ready to go. It was almost electrifying, how intoxicated I was just from the feeling. From the thrill that rushed through my body. How many guys had I been with that were spent after only one round, or left me unsatisfied entirely? Meanwhile, Benjamin had made sure I came twice before he did.

I was definitely going to miss this after our one night was over.

Benjamin reached over to grab another condom from the nightstand, and once he was ready, I straddled him. "This time," I said, leaning down to flick my tongue against his earlobe, "I'm going to be on top."

"Oh, I'm going to enjoy this," he purred. "Take what you need from me, m'lady."

I intended to. I planted both my hands on his chest and rode him, and the new angle was *heavenly*. I closed my eyes and gave myself into the pleasure, wondering if there would ever be anything better than this.

CHAPTER 12
Benjamin

Waking up with a warm feeling of contentment spreading through my body wasn't something I was used to, but it happened that morning. Unfortunately, it lasted for a whole whopping five seconds. When I opened my eyes and rolled over, expecting to find Angelina next to me, I was met with cold sheets and a disappointing silence. Well, *shit*.

"You sure have been spending a lot of time with that girl, haven't you?" was Liam's first thing he said to me at breakfast. I gave him a noncommittal hum as my eyes trailed over to where Angelina was sitting with Nicolas and his assistant. They were laughing about something, and I resisted getting up and going over there.

After last night... Maybe she needed some space. I didn't want any space though. What I wanted was to wake up and find her in my arms, but apparently, she had other ideas. She'd snuck out and gone back to her cabin as soon as I fell asleep—like I was a dirty little secret.

Angelina stole a glance at me, and I almost raised my hand in a little wave. God, I was pathetic. A girl didn't want to spend the night, so what? It's not like she regretted it, at least I didn't think so. Not after the second time. Or the third. After we collapsed on the bed, sweaty and exhausted, she let me take her in my arms, so, no, I didn't think regret was an emotion going through either one of our heads.

But she did say it was just sex. And we had hardly gotten any sleep last night, too busy losing ourselves in each other, so I supposed I could blame that on my current mood.

"Dude," Noah said, snapping me out of my trance. "What's with you?"

"I'm fine. All good. Nothing new to report here."

"Sure," Kevin said, shaking his head, but I knew where they were all looking. Who they were looking at.

I'd been too obvious in my pursuit of her the last few days, in my desire to get her to like me. And it had worked... But it also *hadn't*. Angelina still wouldn't admit she liked me, even though she had essentially begged me to fuck her. Not that she needed to beg. Even if she wanted me, she didn't really want *me*. Just my body. It kind of made me feel a little gross, but mostly just used. I had to get over it.

What I couldn't get over was the feeling of being with her. I slept with my fair share of women in life—in college, girls were throwing themselves at me, because they knew I was well-off and had rich parents, and I didn't exactly stop them. Same as when I started working and frequenting more expensive bars. But it had never been like this, felt like this. I'd never had sex with someone where all I wanted was to focus on her pleasure and nothing more. Even when it'd been hard and fast with Angelina, it'd also been... sinfully slow, and wickedly good.

Fuck. I would have a hard time finding another woman without comparing her to Angelina.

"What's on the docket for today, guys?" I asked them, trying to distract myself.

"We're supposed to be taking the chair lift up to the top of the mountain," Liam said, sipping his orange juice.

Noah smiled, closing his eyes. "This has been a good week. I didn't realize how relaxing it would be to be up here."

His definition of relaxing and mine were two completely different things, I feared. But I looked forward to the rest of it. I wanted to savor every moment before we had to go back to reality.

∽

ANGELINA

I LOOKED AROUND, hoping to join Nicolas, but he and Zofia were already at the front of the line, about to board the chair lift to the top.

Damn this company. Of course, they had to plan out the events so well that part of this retreat included taking us up to the top of the mountain. They were serving us lunch at the little lodge up there, and plenty of people intended to go hiking and explore the trails.

I'd been here before in the winter, plus a few times in college when the university had done cosmic tubing—the girls and I had loved that—but I'd never been in the summer. Had never sat on a chair lift when there wasn't snow under me. Looking around, at all the green grass, the trees, and the little wildflowers that were in bloom, it felt like a whole different world than it did in the winter.

My turn was getting closer and closer, though I was still without a riding partner. I was lost in thought, figuring I'd probably end up getting squished between two strange guys, when his voice tickled my ear. "Riding solo, Bradford?"

I glanced at him as he slid in next to me in line, trying not to picture him naked. Thankfully, there wasn't his usual smirk on his face, his eyes full of warmth and light.

"Sullivan." Why did I think once would be enough with him again? He was a vision in that light blue sweater, stretched across his chest. And that stubble... Mouthwatering, really.

"You were gone when I woke up," he whispered, leaning in.

I glanced around at the people near us. I didn't want them to overhear or think we were acting differently, even though we definitely were. And it was all on me being awkward.

After our last round, when Benjamin had fallen asleep, I didn't know what to do with myself. I couldn't fall asleep, feeling him breathing next to me, and panic started to rise in me, so I slid out of the covers, pulled on my dress, and hightailed it out of there like some sleazy one-night stand.

But that's what it was, wasn't it? Just one night. I had insisted on that. I didn't do relationships, and he didn't date, so what was the point of committing ourselves to any more nights? Yet now...

"Can we talk about this later?" I whispered back. He frowned but agreed. Thankfully, he seemed to be accommodating, even if only for now.

We were up next for the lift. I was happy to have him riding beside me, but I was also holding my breath just watching the small chairs ascend from the ground. Why did it look like an even further distance up without the snow?

Once we were settled in and the metal bar was closed over us, I closed my fingers around it, grateful for something to stabilize me. *You're not going to fall,* I tried to reassure myself. *You're not going to fall. You're not going to fall.*

"Are you scared of heights, Angel?" I couldn't look over at Benjamin. Couldn't bear to see whatever emotion was in his eyes. I knew he wouldn't make fun of me, but after last night and the way I snuck out, it was harder to hold his gaze.

"No," I said, barely shaking my head, but I couldn't help the way my breath hitched as we raised higher and higher. I tried to calm down, to remind myself that I wasn't going to fall out, that there was a bar holding me in place, but it was more terrifying without all the snow that always looked like it would cushion you just in case. A lot more terrifying.

I wasn't afraid of heights, not *really*. I was afraid of falling. Slipping through this metal bar and plummeting to the ground. Where was the giant white blanket of snow when I needed it?

That tree the other day had only reminded me how much I hated the feeling. A fall from this height... I shut my eyes tight, willing myself not to look down.

"Hey," Benjamin said, taking my hand off the bar and squeezing it tight. "I've got you. Just look at me." His voice was calming—soothing, even, and when I opened my eyes, it was to his hand cupping my cheek, his thumb brushing over my knuckles. I slowly felt the panic melting away from me.

Our eyes locked, and the moment felt comforting, almost intimate, instead of scary. I somehow managed to forget I was dangling more than thirty feet above the ground.

"I won't let anything happen to you." And it was the sincerity in his words that made me swallow my pride.

"I'm sorry," I said quietly.

"For what?"

"Last night." Hurt flashed in his eyes, so I was quick to specify. "For leaving."

"You didn't have to."

I bit my lip. "I just..."

"It's okay," he said. "You don't have to tell me. Just be here, with me."

"I can do that."

He kissed my hand. "Good."

When we got off, Benjamin dropped my hand, and we moved towards the little log cabin building where we'd find our lunch. I was desperately in need of food, but even more than that, desperately in need of putting some distance between the two of us. If he kept looking at and touching me like that, I couldn't be held responsible for my actions much longer.

I ordered a grilled cheese and seasoned fries, while Benjamin got a bacon cheeseburger. It was delicious, but the meal was over much too fast, leaving us back outside to ourselves, and the thoughts I was sure were running a thousand miles a minute through his head.

But he didn't ask why I left. I suspected he knew I needed the time to open up to him about my shit. Like whatever plagued me... He could sense it, and he was giving me the space to share on my terms.

I liked that—feeling that way. I never felt rushed or uncomfortable around Benjamin, and maybe that was why I was still willingly spending time with him.

We leaned over the railing, and I stared out at the surroundings. The mountaintops, the trees, the little streams running down the sides of the mountains that would run into the lake below.

"Wow," I said, not wanting to take my eyes off it for even a moment. "It's beautiful up here." I felt like a broken record. How many times had I said that this weekend? But it was true. Portland with all its greenery was stunning, but this mountain was even more so.

"Yes," he agreed, "It is beautiful." But when I turned to look at him, he wasn't looking at the view or the mountains. He was looking at me.

I cleared my throat. "It's crazy how different it looks without all the snow."

Benjamin hummed in agreement and rested his hand over mine on the railing. I wanted so badly to lean on him, to stay in this moment for as long as I wanted to. But I couldn't, so I did what I've always done best. Bounced back. Changed course, and then onward.

"You aren't going to make me hike again, are you?" I asked, frowning as I looked down at my attire. Okay, so *maybe* I wore the boots he'd given me, as well as a pair of black leggings and a flowy tee, with a three-quarter zip sweater tied around my waist, but that was just me being practical.

I had yet to figure out how he knew my shoe size, or where he bought the boots in the first place. We hadn't even known each other before I ran into him in the lobby, so there was no way he would have brought them here randomly. And if he asked one of the other women to try and find a pair of shoes for me... I didn't want to think about what the gesture meant.

But luckily, despite being new, the boots were way better than my gym shoes. And I was wearing my thick wool socks, preventing any blisters from forming. Hopefully.

"Come on, Angelina, do you see this place? We can't be up here and not explore it. Maybe we'll even find a bear."

"I can say with absolute, one hundred percent certainty, that we do *not* want to find a bear up here."

"What about cougars? Wolves? Elk? Wolverines?"

"Maybe we should just hope to see some cute little deer, Boy Scout," I said, patting him on the shoulder. "I would personally like to not get eaten alive by wildlife today."

"You're no fun," he pouted.

What we did see? Chipmunks. Lots and lots of chipmunks. I would have been happy to see an otter in the wild one day, or maybe a cute little rabbit, but not something with big claws or teeth.

Benjamin guided me along the loop he'd chosen in silence, only stopping to comment about a plant species or tree every now and then. It was farther than some of the other hiking trails, which meant no one else was trekking near us and we had the path to ourselves.

"Boy Scout, are you sure you aren't getting us lost?" I asked as I leaned down to readjust the tongue of my boot.

"Positive." He gave me a reassuring grin. "We're not going too much further ahead."

I groaned, "Last time you said that we still had like a mile to walk."

Finally, after too many grumbles (from me), a lot of encouragement (from Benjamin), and way too much mutual banter, we stumbled upon a waterfall at the top of the trailhead.

"Oh. Wow," I breathed. It ended in a shallow pool—not quite deep enough to submerge in—before it continued down the side of the mountain. As the snow melted in the warm months, it would find its way down the mountain before it filled the lakes and rivers in the valleys. It was why the water was so chilly, but also such a beautiful color. It was clear mountain runoff, after all.

"Too bad we can't swim in it," I murmured, and I didn't miss how Benjamin stood closer to me. Close enough for me to lean against his chest.

He kissed the top of my head as I snapped a photo of the sight before slipping my phone back into my pocket. I was so content to just stay like that, but eventually, Benjamin sighed in my ear. "Time to head back?"

"Hmm."

"Want me to carry you?"

The *yes* was on the tip of my tongue, but as I looked at him over my shoulder, the expression on his face was so full of himself that I rolled my eyes and shoved at his arm for good measure. "No, I can walk."

"Shame. Guess I didn't fuck you good enough last night then." I was a little sore, but I wasn't going to tell him that. I glared at him instead. "You can slap me if you want. Or," he gave me a cocky grin, "I could slap you."

Heat rushed to my cheeks as I thought about where exactly he could... spank me.

"Are you blushing, Bradford?"

"No. Shut up." But I buried my head in his sweater. Fuck him, honestly. It'd been forever since someone fazed me like this, and I hated him for it. "Stop making that face," I muttered into his chest.

He tilted my face up. "Why?"

"I'm embarrassed, okay?" Benjamin hummed in amusement, and I tried scowling at him, but I was losing the battle with his eyes.

"Don't look at me like that, Princess."

"Why?"

"Because I'm trying really hard not to kiss you senseless right now."

"Oh." I breathed, or maybe I didn't—I wasn't sure. Maybe I had stopped breathing. Maybe I did want him to kiss me in front of this waterfall.

What I wanted, more than anything, was to remember this moment. I pulled out my phone, nuzzling into his chest, and snapped a selfie of us. One where we were looking at the camera, one where he was looking at me—and then... One of us, kissing.

I couldn't explain why.

Looking back at them later, I'd still be lost for words. But I treasured that photo of the look in his eyes before he kissed me like a man with no other goal in life.

Benjamin carried me on his back all the way back to the trailhead.

CHAPTER 13
Angelina

"Today was perfect," I sighed. I couldn't have imagined a better day—except, maybe, one where we didn't have to traipse up and down a mountain. My feet were sore, but after coming back from the mountain, showering, and having a filling dinner, I was feeling blissfully content. Even with Benjamin by my side.

He hummed in agreement. "And you know what the perfect way to end this little wilderness adventure is?" he asked, giving me that cocky grin I'd grown so used to.

"What?" I eyed him skeptically, worried he was about to carry me off somewhere else. I'd had enough adventures for the year, thank you.

He whipped out a bag of marshmallows from behind his back. "S'mores."

"Oh, are we five years old now?" I snorted.

Benjamin gave me a little pouty face. "Bradford, s'mores are the *quintessential* camping experience. Live a little."

"Okay, first, we're not camping, we're literally staying at a four-star wilderness *retreat*. And second, I do live, thank you very much. I can just live without burnt marshmallows and chocolate on graham crackers."

"No, no, no." He shook his head passionately. "You've been doing it all wrong. You have to try the *s'mores à la Sullivan*. Boy Scout, remember? I have perfected my technique to make the ultimate s'more."

"Alright, *MasterChef*," I shrugged, figuring I might at least get some entertainment out of this. "Lead the way."

We wandered over to the campfire and I plopped down on one of the logs that served as seats while Benjamin unpacked the contents of his bag.

"Where'd you get all of this stuff, anyway?" I asked as he shoved a marshmallow onto a stick.

"A gentleman never reveals his secrets." He winked.

"Sure, sure. It's just... The closest store is down the mountain, and there's no way you actually brought all of this with you, right?"

"Never underestimate the value of a good s'more, Bradford."

"You're so ridiculous." I pushed his shoulder.

"You like it."

"Definitely not."

"Come on, just admit you like me."

"What is this, the seventh grade? I don't like you." I scowled. "Now make me a s'more before I get bored of you." I snapped my fingers, pointing at the white, uncooked marshmallow.

"As the Princess commands." He stuck the pole over the fire, and I watched him for a few moments, elbows on my knees as I studied his technique—and then his face, the happiness that lit up in his eyes as he stared into the fire.

"You really like doing this, huh?"

He nodded. "I told you my family used to go camping when I was younger. It was some of the only times we were all together as a family. Me, my brother Hunter, and my sister Emily... My parents always pushed us hard. Normally, they'd just send us off to camp for the summer, but when we were out on camping trips, in places like Yellowstone or the Grand Tetons, none of that mattered and we were just a *family*. We'd crowd around a campfire and laugh for hours. Hunter would always burn his marshmallows and Emily would always make me roast hers for her. I never minded, though." His smile never wavered as he poked at the marshmallow to test it.

"I know what you mean," I nodded as I took one of the poles from him. "I have all these good memories of my family when I was younger. Before..." I bit my lip, deciding that no harm could come from sharing a little bit more about myself. "Before my parents divorced. When we were all happy and together. And now those moments are almost—sacred? If that makes sense. Family vacations, movie nights..." I closed my eyes, thinking about all those times before my parents turned into two people who couldn't stand to be in the same room. Before the fighting tore our family apart. "It's nice to have something like that, I guess. But sometimes I miss the old us."

I pushed a marshmallow onto the sharp end of my stick before holding it above the coals of the fire, letting it sit evenly in the warmth as I rotated it little by little, careful not to let it burn. When it was done, I held it out to Benjamin.

"And so the student becomes the teacher," he grinned, smushing my perfectly golden marshmallow between the chocolate and graham cracker goodness. "Here you go," he said, handing me the finished product and setting my pole over the fire pit.

"You know, this just looks like a regular s'more," I laughed. But truthfully, it *was* kind of special, because we'd made it together.

"Shut up and eat it, Bradford," he said, squishing his own, and when I took the first bite I had to admit—it was *good*.

"Oh," I moaned. "I've missed these."

"Ha! You like it. I win."

"Never underestimate the power of a good s'more," I said, smiling at him. Benjamin took another bite of his, but I could see the way his eyes trailed over my face. "What?" I asked him, frowning. "Do I have something on my face?"

"No," he shook his head. "It's just... Your smile."

"What about it?"

"You don't smile that much. And it's... You have a beautiful smile, Angelina."

"Oh." I averted my eyes, feeling the blush creep up my neck. Yes, we had slept together last night, and we had spent almost every moment of this retreat together, but still, this compliment? It almost warmed my heart. My very cold, very bitchy heart.

"I can't believe this is the last night already," I said, changing the subject. Emboldened by his words, I leaned against Benjamin's shoulder, loving feeling like we'd been transported to another world. Between the campfire, the sliver of the moon, and the lights strung on the dock, it was almost magical out here. Like anything could happen.

Maybe something already had.

Even if I didn't want a relationship, I'd always have these memories. My camera roll was full of the things we'd done over the last few days. Without Benjamin, I probably wouldn't have been pulled out of my comfort zone enough to have done any of those outdoorsy things—hiking, canoeing, even making s'mores tonight. I would have been content to sit on a chair and read or draw and miss out on all the beauty surrounding us. And even if I still hated the bugs, the smell of bug spray, and the dirt, I was glad that I let myself do all those things.

"Thank you, Benjamin," I whispered, low enough that I doubted anyone else nearby could hear. If Nicolas had noticed anything different between Benjamin and me since yesterday, he didn't mention it, and no one else seemed to spare a glance at us either.

"For what?" asked Benjamin.

I looked around us. "For all of this. For making me do things I didn't want to do. For *this*." I wanted to snuggle in closer to him, to relish the last few hours together, but we were still outside, in the main view of the lobby. And despite being pushed out of my comfort zone this week, there were still things I didn't want my coworkers to see.

I knew how the office rumor mill worked, and I didn't want everyone to be focusing on my love life instead of how hard I worked to succeed at the company. Especially when I wasn't even *in* a relationship. It wasn't like I was thinking about the future. I loved my job. I loved my life. And I was okay with it the way it was—even if I never found a partner, I was okay with that.

Benjamin's kiss on my forehead brought me back to reality and out of the musings of my mind as he gave me a soft, "You're welcome."

I had misjudged him so much. Sure, he was a sarcastic asshole at times, and he never failed to get on my nerves, but he was also caring. He wanted me to have a good time. As much as I insisted that this friendship was impossible, I had to admit defeat and declare it a success on his part. Damn it.

"Do you want to call it a night?" I said in a low voice, eyes focused on the flickering fire in front of me so I didn't have to look at the tenderness in his eyes.

"What do you want?" he whispered back.

For this week not to end. For life to be this simple all the time. For you to hold me in your arms one last time. Although there was only one answer that wanted to tumble out insistently, one that I forced back deep inside and locked away. *You.*

"Your bed," I said instead. In a few days, everything would go back to normal. I'd go back to hating him, he'd go back to sending an email correcting me every time I used a comma wrong, and life would be back to how it was supposed to be.

"You know, there is one thing that wasn't perfect about today," Benjamin said, curling his finger around the end of my ponytail.

"And what's that?"

"You not being in my bed when I woke up." His words were a seductive whisper down my body, igniting a dormant fire in my bones.

"I've just... I've never woken up in bed next to someone before." It was the first time I'd ever said the words out loud. I wasn't ashamed of it, but it was something very personal. Benjamin deserved to know it didn't have anything to do with him or what we'd done.

I'd slept with people before, but there was an intimacy in sharing a bed with someone that I'd never been ready to let myself have. Letting them hold you as you slept, letting them see you first thing in the morning, it all was too much.

All Benjamin said in response was, "Hmm."

"I know it's not the answer you expected. Do you think it's weird?"

"Didn't you have sleepovers as a kid?"

"Yeah, but—"

"It's just a sleepover, Sullivan."

I shook my head. "Is it though?"

"Come on, then," he said, offering me a hand up. "Let's go to sleep."

"Sleep?" I squealed. "Just *sleep*?" No. Just—no. What? The best course of action was for me to say goodnight. Retreat to my cabin, alone. That would prepare me for when I'd be back in the city without the temptation from the devil himself. One night was enough between us. It would have to be.

And yet... I still took his hand and let him guide me along the path back to our cabins. What a weak, weak woman.

I was still deep in thought when Benjamin leaned in, burying his head in my hair as he nuzzled against me while we walked.

"I smell like campfire," I said with a snort after sniffing my shirt. "You can't possibly find this sexy." I didn't feel particularly attractive right now either, between the makeup that was surely running from sweat on my face and my hair, frizzing despite the ponytail.

"And what would you possibly know about what I find sexy?" Benjamin wiggled his eyebrows, and I pushed him off the path, hoping he'd trip on a root and break his ankle. Okay, maybe not quite that, but it would be vindicating to watch him eat shit.

"Right, I forgot, Boy Scout over here gets a raging boner from square knots and camping in the woods." My voice was dripping with sarcasm, but he still gave me that goofy smirk.

"More like the girl with the venomous tongue is the most attractive vision on the planet."

We stood one before the other when we got to the split between our two cabins, not quite touching, staring at each other. There were things left unsaid, questions left unasked. I was still reeling over my earlier omissions. Benjamin was the first to speak.

"If it wasn't clear before, I think you're the most beautiful woman, Angelina. I like your sharp wit and the way you make me earn my place next to you." His Adam's apple bobbed in his throat. "I... I think I've had more fun with you this week than I have in a long time."

I didn't know what to say, but then again, maybe I didn't need to say anything. Maybe the only words that needed to come out from my lips were a whispered, "Me too." Because it was true. Sure, I'd been glaring and scowling at him every five minutes, but when was the last time I laughed so much?

And, suddenly, I knew that I didn't want the night to end just yet. I opened my mouth, ready to tell him I didn't want to just sleep, but Benjamin beat me to it.

"You know, I lost my key today," he said, grinning. "Do you think I can share your bed for the night?"

That made me pause. I couldn't stop thinking about getting his hands on me, but this? A whole night in his arms? He was going to ruin me. I didn't know everything, as much as I tried to make it appear that I did, but I knew that much.

Benjamin Sullivan was not the kind of man you could spend more than one night with without something catastrophic happening.

I had survived thus far without any life-altering collisions but running into him on the first day of the retreat was proving to be its own kind of momentous crash. A cosmic realigning of the stars, forcing me into everything I stayed away from all my life.

"But I don't..." I swallowed. "I can't—I don't... do that."

"Do what, Angel?" He gently tilted my chin up to force my eyes to meet his. "What are you scared of?"

Good question. "I..." I just shook my head. What was I scared of? Everything. Letting myself get close to someone wasn't in the cards. Not right now, and maybe not ever. But I really, really wanted a repeat of last night.

"Okay, what about this? We'll try, and if you really don't want me to stay the night, I'll find an excuse and ring up Liam, and I'll be out of your way. What do you say?" Benjamin grabbed my hand and squeezed it, soothing my worries. I could work with that. "Besides," he added with a grin, "after tonight, you can go back to hating me and pretending I don't exist."

"I can't pretend you don't exist," I scowled. "You're like a rat who found his way into my walls and curled up there and d—" He placed a finger over my lips. I drifted my eyes up from his torso and, fuck, it was too easy to get lost in his eyes. He always did that—got me out of my head, made me stop talking and focus on him. "I don't want to," I whispered.

"One more one night, Bradford?"

"On one condition."

"Anything."

"No feelings. This is still just sex."

"Just sex," he confirmed, tugging at my ponytail before bringing our mouths together.

∽

WE WERE a mess of hands and a flurry of fabric as soon as the door closed behind us, and before I knew it, I was stripped down to my underwear. Apparently, Benjamin was committed to getting me out of my clothes as soon as possible.

He didn't waste any time before cupping my center and

pushing two fingers inside, filling me deliciously.

"Benjamin," I panted, eyes squeezing shut as he crooked those long fingers like he knew exactly what spots would make me see stars. He wrapped his hand around my ponytail, tugging on it lightly. "I still smell like smoke. And I'm sweaty," I said, knowing I wasn't going to be able to focus on anything else till I got clean.

Benjamin simply licked up my throat in response before I gathered my strength and dragged him to the walk-in shower. Luckily, it would fit both of us quite well. I turned on the water, and Benjamin had that glint in his eye when I asked, "Coming in?"

"Oh, I wouldn't miss it," he grinned as he shut the glass door, pulling me back into his arms and taking my mouth in another deep kiss. The hot water running down our bodies felt amazing, and we both relished in it for a moment before Benjamin grabbed my shampoo bottle from the little ledge.

"Turn around," he said, and I was happy to comply. If he wanted to wash my hair, well—who was I to complain about that? "Let me take care of you." He soaped up my scalp, giving it a light massage, and oh did that feel good. I tried not to, but the moan escaped anyway. "Angelina, if you keep that up, we're not going to make it out of the shower."

"Sorry," I giggled, but I wasn't sorry at all. That sounded just fine to me.

After rinsing out the shampoo, Benjamin grabbed the conditioner bottle and gently rubbed it onto my lengths, slowly massaging the back of my neck too. "Oh, that feels nice," I sighed, closing my eyes.

He let the conditioner sink in, which made me wonder how many girls' hair he'd washed to know that. He then soaped up his hands with my body wash and rubbed it all over me, making sure I was rid of the fire smell. It was small touches at first—his hands down my back, across my shoulders, my arms. And then those big, dedicated hands moved over my breasts, rubbing my nipples in circles, and I swear I could have come right there just from that.

"God, your hands…"

He kept moving them down my body, stroking my stomach, my sides, and then down to my thighs.

I was dripping wet in more ways than one, and all I knew was this little shower session was going to drive me out of my mind soon. He was turned on, too, if his dick had anything to say about that. It was standing straight up, so glorious, nestled against my lower back. I let Benjamin rinse me off, and then I turned around, wrapping my hand around his length before giving him my best smirk.

"Your turn."

"Angelina," he rumbled, eyes almost black with lust. I rubbed his chest and arms with one hand full of body wash as I kept the other one pumping him up and down. After I determined he was appropriately clean and soap-free, I dropped to my knees.

"I want to taste you," I breathed. I didn't even care that the stone tiles of the shower were pressing into my skin, because as I fisted his length and watched his eyes squeeze shut from the pleasure, I felt like the most powerful woman on the planet.

"Oh, fuck," he groaned when I put my mouth on him, closing over the tip. "Your mouth feels so good, baby."

I looked up at him as I licked around the head, giving it a light suck before turning my attention back to his shaft. I ran my tongue along its length as I explored with my hand, squeezing his balls lightly. He moaned more, and I decided I liked his tortured sounds. I was getting wet from just seeing him come undone like this.

Still, I wondered if I could take all of him in my mouth. I'd never deep-throated anyone before; I'd never tried—never felt comfortable enough with a man where the thought of sucking him off turned me on. Until now.

One hand still firmly wrapped around him, I brought the other one to my entrance, gathering the wetness there before rubbing my clit. *Yes.* I needed the friction, something to take the edge off the throbbing I felt between my legs.

Benjamin made a choked sound as I moaned around him and slid onto him further, relishing the feel of him against the back of my throat, before he slowly pulled me off. "I don't want to come down your pretty throat, Princess. Not this time, at least."

I wiped my lips with the back of my hand. "So, are you going to fuck me or what, Sullivan?"

He smirked and tossed me over his shoulder, dripping wet and all, his hand on my ass as he wrenched open the shower door. For a second, I wasn't sure if we were even going to dry off before going at it, but then he was setting me down, wrapping a towel around me, and drying me off reverently. There was so much care in the action that I didn't know how to handle it.

"Mmm. That's nice," I grinned.

He growled something as I tried to dry off my hair, and I let him take over, watching in the mirror as he rubbed over my tresses, getting most of the wetness out but leaving it damp. Once he dried himself off, too, I was once again back over his shoulder, and he smacked my ass as I squirmed to get down.

"Benjamin," I cried as he walked us into the bedroom. "I need—"

"Shh, I know what you need, Princess." He rubbed my ass, easing the light sting. I felt like putty under his hands.

He dropped me on the bed, pulled a condom from his discarded pants, and was on top of me faster than I could blink.

"On your hands and knees," he ordered, and I quickly scrambled up to obey him. I heard the crinkle of the foil as he unwrapped the condom and rolled it on himself, but he didn't push into me yet. He fondled my ass, squeezing like he was memorizing the way it felt in his hands.

"Please," I whimpered as he finally lowered his mouth, licking a line down my entrance.

"You taste so good," he said. "Fuck." He sucked my clit, and I thought I was going to melt from how good it felt, his hands still massaging me as his tongue played with me. Benjamin gave me a few more long licks before the bed creaked as he shifted position.

"But I want to feel you around me when you come." I felt his tip nudging my entrance as he ran it up and down through my wetness, and when he finally pushed inside of me, I cried out.

God, even after last night, the stretch from his size was insane. He gave me a moment to adjust before one of his hands wrapped around my throat as the other gripped my hip so tight that I might bruise, and I couldn't have stopped the noises I made as he rutted into me even if I'd wanted to.

And fuck. At this angle, taking me from behind? I didn't want to.

All I could feel was him, him, *him*, flooding my senses and fucking me into submission.

I would have done anything he asked, I realized, as he gave me over to that pleasure, drilling his cock into me. Because it'd never been this good before—not with anyone—and all I wanted to do was chase this feeling. Chase the high.

"Scream for me, Angel," Benjamin groaned, thrusting harder, more relentlessly. "Just for me."

I shut my eyes as I clutched at the sheets. His hand on my throat squeezed tighter, but he always seemed to know where the line was; he didn't hurt me or made me uncomfortable. He was giving me just the right amount of pressure to make me see stars.

And see stars I did. His commanding words made me fall apart, screaming as he combined his punishing rhythm with his thumb rubbing at my clit, and I almost lost consciousness when I came—harder than I ever had, with his name on my lips as I barreled into ecstasy.

Benjamin slowed his pace as I rode out the aftershocks of my orgasm. I knew he was close, but it surprised me when he pulled me up against him, my back to his front, sitting me in his lap as he thrust up into me.

"Oh my god," I gasped. "I can't—"

"You can," he reassured me, kissing my neck as he continued, and I wondered if I'd ever find another man who could fuck me this good and still be so caring.

He turned my chin to kiss me, claiming my lips like he was claiming every inch of my body, and I felt his release as I opened up to him. He groaned, muttering sweet nothings into my neck.

And as the sounds of *"feels so good"* and *"good to me"* settled over me, I gave myself over to the feeling, letting another orgasm wreck through my body, gentler this time but just as powerful.

Once we had both regained our breath, Benjamin slowly pulled out of me and went to the bathroom. I needed to pee, even though all I wanted was to stay in our sweaty sex cocoon a little longer.

After coming back and flipping out the lights, I climbed into bed. I was only a little relieved when the first thing Benjamin did was pull me into his arms, wrapping his body around mine. Spooning me.

Another thing to check off my *I'm-a-chicken-and-scared-of-intimacy* list. Yup. Cuddling had always seemed like too much for me, so I'd never really done it. But with him... I relaxed in his arms.

He leaned down, kissed the spot behind my ear, and then murmured, "I only had the one condom."

The force of my laugh surprised me. "I think my brain might explode if we went for round two now."

A beat. "Did I hurt you?"

"What?" I looked at him and saw he was eyeing my neck with an angry frown, his jaw set. I didn't realize I was absentmindedly rubbing there. "No." I pulled my hand away, wanting to reassure him. It didn't hurt, it... "It felt good," I mumbled, embarrassed to admit it. By how much I liked him taking over, commanding my every move. It felt freeing—like I could finally shut my brain off. I didn't have to think, I could just give myself to him, trusting him to make me feel good. "I liked it."

He relaxed at once, pressing a kiss to my neck. "Good." Then he covered us up with the sheets and settled down, his limbs intertwined with mine.

I listened to his breathing slow down as he crept closer to

sleep. It would make sense after going that hard that I'd be tired enough to fall asleep immediately, except I was wide awake. Even in his arms, curled into his warm body, I couldn't seem to turn off my brain.

"Angelina," he muttered, as I stared ahead at the wall.

"Hmm?"

"What's going on with you? I can almost feel the way your brain is running a hundred miles an hour."

I rolled over in his arms to look at him. "I told you I've never done this. This is why. My brain won't shut off, and then I can't stop thinking about it. About having someone in my bed. About... everything."

He kissed my forehead before pulling me to his side. We hadn't bothered to put our clothes on, so being skin to skin like this, without any other intentions except comfort? It was strange. But... nice.

"Do you need me to turn your brain off?"

"Not... like that." I shook my head. I didn't need more sex to sleep. That might have the opposite of the intended effect. "And we don't have any more condoms, anyway."

"There are other ways. And that's not what I meant anyway, you dirty girl." In my well-fucked stupor, I flushed red a little, grateful he couldn't see the way my body reacted in my embarrassment. "We could talk."

"About what?"

"Anything."

I thought about it. I knew a little bit about his family, and what he liked, but how much did I really know about *him*?

He took my hand, lacing our fingers together, and placed it on his chest, where I could feel his heartbeat.

"Tell me something about yourself that you've never told anyone."

We might have talked for an hour or it could have been five minutes, I couldn't tell. But my last thought before I fell asleep was that, maybe... maybe this wasn't so bad.

CHAPTER 14
Angelina

I awoke to a face smiling at me, drawing circles on my skin as the morning light seeped into the cabin.

"Hi," I whispered, feeling totally out of my element but, strangely enough, I didn't hate it. I didn't mind finding Benjamin in my bed. That was possibly the weirdest revelation of the whole week.

"Hey." He gave me one of those cocky grins before stretching, causing my eyes to follow the flexing of his arms.

"We have to pack," I said, wishing I didn't have to ruin this perfect sleepy bubble. He hummed in agreement but rolled over and pulled me against him, burying his head in my neck. "Sullivan," I laughed, and then gasped when his lips connected with my skin. "We don't have time," I grit out as I attempted to push him off me, but he just kept placing kisses on that sensitive spot.

"Just let me savor this," he mumbled.

"Wait. How are you going to get your stuff if you can't get into your cabin?" I narrowed my eyes at him, but the flash of guilt in his eyes gave him away. "You had your key the whole time, didn't you?"

He sat up and flicked my nose. "A good magician never reveals his secrets."

"You could have just asked to stay over."

"You would have said no."

"You're right, I would have."

"And nothing's going to beat the memory of waking up next to you. So, I'm not sorry. Unless you hate me for it," he added after a moment, and I thought he was joking but his face was serious when he looked at me.

I pushed at his bare chest, rolling my eyes. I couldn't find it in myself to care, either. It was for the best.

Benjamin slid out from under the covers, and I instantly missed his warm presence. I watched him tug his clothes from last night back on, content not to move from my sheet-wrapped cocoon yet.

"Meet you at the lodge for breakfast?"

I gave him a hesitant smile. "Sure."

And then he was gone. Not a goodbye, no kiss on the cheek, or even one last lingering glance. Which was... disappointing. Because despite all my resistance, this man had shown me—with small gestures during the past week—how it felt to be cherished. And I didn't know what to do with that.

Once alone, I resigned myself to my fate and got up, showered, and threw on a loose sundress and light sweater before pulling my hair into a side braid and applying a thin layer of makeup. It was one of those days where I didn't feel like I needed the boldness of heavy makeup or red lipstick to feel like myself, so I finished it off with a pink shade.

It was strange, because it was me in the mirror, but a different version: a little sun-kissed, with just the right amount of tan giving a beautiful glow to my skin, and there was a light in my eyes that hadn't been there in a long time.

"When was the last time I was truly happy?" I pondered out loud to myself, reflecting on the sentiment Nicolas had asked me the other day. But I shook it off and finished packing my bag.

I was looking forward to getting back to civilization, back to my apartment and my friends, but part of me would miss the girl

I'd found here. The one who laughed more freely, who let herself be dragged on adventures, who appreciated the little moments because she knew they'd be gone in the blink of an eye.

I lugged my stuff out of the cabin, huffing every time the gravel got caught in the wheels, but then I was finally back at the main lodge and there was an arrogant and unfortunately very sexy man standing at the railing, waiting for me.

Benjamin was wearing a loose button-up and khaki pants, looking as casual as ever. He nodded at my bags. "Want me to put those in your car, Princess?"

I shook my head. "I figured I'd throw them in after eating something." I didn't want to walk all the way there right now. Somehow it felt too final.

"Ravenous this morning. Must have worked up quite the appetite last night, hm?" He gave me a little wink.

"I—"

He laughed at my furious blush. "You don't have to answer that. Come on." He grabbed my bag, pulling it up the stairs. But he didn't offer me his hand, nor did he place his hand on my back to guide me into the building. It was probably a good thing, I decided. Because this wasn't something that was going to continue, so I shouldn't have gotten so comfortable with his touches.

Breakfast mainly consisted of French toast, and we both happily piled a few pieces on our plates. There was also sausage and bacon, and we each took some before sitting down at a table.

Benjamin eyed my bowl. "What's that for?"

"To dunk my French toast in," I said, cutting it into chunks and dipping them individually. "I don't like when it gets super soggy."

"But that's the best." He frowned. "The bread absorbs all the syrup, and then it's extra delicious."

I snorted, glancing at his plate drenched in syrup. "Sure."

My eyes drifted around the room, at all sorts of groups chatting and smiling. Somehow, I'd spent most of my time here with the man sitting next to me, and I wondered if I made a mistake by not engaging with the rest of the company's employees. I couldn't bring myself to care too much, though.

Once breakfast was over, Alexander Larsen stepped to the front of the room and cleared his throat to get everyone's attention.

"I hope you all had a great week—and hopefully you learned a little bit about yourselves and each other throughout the activities as well. I know I enjoyed the hot tub and sauna." We laughed, and he continued. "We're gearing up for another busy few months at Willamette Tech, so I hope you're all ready to get back to work next week!" A few people groaned, which made him chuckle. "Well, that's all from me. A big thank you to the staff here who were so incredible and especially the culinary team, who made all this delicious food. A big round of applause of thank you for all of them, and then we'll see you all on Monday!" Everyone cheered, thanking the lodge staff, as well as Alexander himself.

I caught Nicolas's eye as I went to put my plate in the dirty dishes bin.

"Hey," he said, running his hands through his floppy blonde hair.

"Hello to you too, Mr. Big Shot. Crazy to think that you'll be the one running these kinds of things someday, huh?"

He gave me a bashful grin. "Don't remind me. My dad does that enough." I laughed, and Nicolas looked at me, those hazel eyes impossibly bright. "Did you have a good week?"

I glanced towards Benjamin, who was talking to his friends, and there was no other answer in my mind except for, "Yeah. I really did."

Nicolas gave me a small smile and patted me on the shoulder. "Good. See you Monday then?"

I nodded. "Have a good weekend."

"You too."

After I'd said my goodbyes to everyone else, including Zofia and Harper, I knew what was coming, and yet I still dreaded it even as Benjamin carried my bags down the stairs and, once we were out of view of the lodge, took my hand in his. It felt right. As much as a goodbye could feel right.

My bags were all loaded in the car, and I still didn't know what to say. I just stared at the ground, digging my shoes into the gravel as I gnawed on my lip.

"So, uh... I'll see you around?" Benjamin said, closing the trunk of his car—a blue sports car, which didn't surprise me in the slightest—and turning around to face me.

Did I want to see him again? If you had asked me that at the beginning of the retreat, I would have said no, of course. But that was five days ago, which felt like an eternity. The number of revelations, the things we'd learned about each other, it all felt too enormous to shove back into a box. But I didn't know how I was feeling, so I simply shrugged and went with, "At the office? Sure."

He shrugged. "Maybe."

I raised an eyebrow. "Where else would you see me?" I crossed my arms, frowning. "I'm not inviting you to my apartment. We had an agreement. Mutual satisfaction, just for a night." He opened his mouth, but I beat him to it. "Two nights. Whatever. But that's it."

"Sure," Benjamin nodded. But instead of saying goodbye and getting in his car like I thought—hoped he would, he took a step closer to me. Exhaled once and pulled me into his arms.

He buried his head in my hair like he did in bed this morning. "Do you still hate me?" he whispered it against my neck, causing a shiver to shoot down my spine.

It would be so easy to say *yes*. To go back to the place where we had been before—bickering, hating each other. Not being able to stand being in each other's presence.

But I shook my head.

"I want to hear it, Princess."

"I don't hate you," I mumbled under my breath.

He hooked his finger under my chin and tilted it up to look me in the eyes. "What was that?"

"I don't hate you," I said, louder this time.

He grinned. "Good." I was sure he was going to kiss me. I'd always been confident in my looks and my abilities, and at this moment, I was so sure that I was kissable. And the way he was looking at me...

But Benjamin Sullivan was always one to surprise me, and he stepped back, out of my grasp. Gave me another one of his sexy little smirks—I hated what those did to me—and then walked to his car, pulling the door open.

"Goodbye, Bradford," he said, addressing me as if nothing happened between us. If he was playing the long game, trying to make me want him, well, he had another thing coming.

Sure, he had made the first move here, but I wasn't going to be the one to make it next. As far as I was concerned, there was no move to make whatsoever. Our non-relationship ended here and now. Still, I watched him drive away, wondering if this was the last chapter in a story I hadn't even realized I'd been reading.

"Bye," I whispered to no one. The air, the trees, the leaves blowing in the wind.

If this was over, if it was the end, shouldn't I feel something... lesser? Sad, or regretful maybe? Instead, all I felt was the warmth that was thrumming in my veins, the feeling of contentment as I drove away from the lodge where I had somehow found some missing piece of myself. A girl who could have fun, who could live in the moment and enjoy herself. A girl who knew what she wanted and went for it.

A girl who had the best sex of her life with the *worst* person possible to have sex with.

Even if I wanted to sleep with him again, I didn't even have his phone number. What would I do with it, anyway? Booty call him after a few hours apart? We spent a whole year sending stupid snarky emails back and forth without the need to get to know each other. We could go back to that, and it would be okay.

"Honey, I'm home!" I called out, entering the apartment. It'd been a long week without my best friend, and I was glad to be home.

"Hey!" Gabbi came into the living room as I wheeled my bag through the door. "How was it?"

"Eh," I shrugged, feigning disinterest. "Typical corporate retreat, I think."

She raised an eyebrow. "That's it? That's all I get? Nothing exciting happened at all? The office is *always* full of drama," she huffed in disappointment.

"Well, how was the office this week?"

"Quiet. I almost came back and worked from home, honestly. I thought I was going to go crazy."

"But you didn't!" I tried to fake my enthusiasm because I knew, sooner or later, she was going to look at my face more closely and interrogate me about the one topic I didn't want to talk about.

When I packed up my car and said goodbye to Benjamin Sullivan, asshole extraordinaire, I also said goodbye to what had been the best sex of my life. And I was having a hard time coming to terms with that.

"What's that look on your face?" Gabbi poked me on the shoulder as I collapsed on the couch with her. Like clockwork.

"Ah. It's nothing." She raised an eyebrow at my grimace. "Okay, maybe not nothing. It's just..." I bit my lip. "I might have... hooked up with someone while we were out there."

"You did what?!" Gabbi squealed in excitement, well aware of how infrequently I let myself go out with men. Being so busy meant I hardly went on dates—hardly ever got laid.

"I know, it's surprising to me, too. But, *damn*, Gabs. It was the best sex of my life," I groaned.

"And who might this mystery hookup man be? Are you going to see him again?"

I snorted. "I doubt it. We said goodbye, and that was that."

"Angelina." She glared at me. "You're not even going to try to see if it could go anywhere? This could be your chance."

"Unlikely."

"Why not?" Gabbi frowned at me.

"Because... It's Benjamin Sullivan."

Her mouth opened and closed multiple times with no sound coming out. "*The* Benjamin Sullivan? The one who loves sending you emails for his little foreplay game? I thought you hated him!"

"I did! I did hate him, it's just..." I looked up at the ceiling, trying and failing to put my thoughts into words. "I don't know, Gabs. He's not the person I thought he was."

"So, you don't hate him anymore?"

I shrugged. "Maybe I never hated him. Not really. He just has this very irritating ability to get on my nerves, you know? But I think I might have judged him too soon."

"Of course you did," my best friend sighed.

"Don't be like this," I frowned. "Don't give me that I-told-you-so speech. It's still not happening. We don't get along." A lie, but I could only accept so many revelations in one day.

"But you said the sex—"

"The sex *was* great. But there's not going to be any sort of long-term relationship here. I don't have time for it. This was easy because we were stuck together in the mountains, but now we're back to reality."

"Did you even ask him if he would want to?"

"Of course not."

"Then—"

"Then nothing! It's not like I'm going to waltz into his office on Monday and ask him if he wants to keep having sex with me. And there's absolutely no way he's going to agree to a friends-with-benefits thing."

"So, you're friends now?"

"What? No."

"Mhm."

"Gabs. Don't—" I stopped when I heard a noise in the apartment. "What's that?"

"What?"

"That noise."

A small sound came from Gabbi's room. Like a chirp. Or...

I glared at her as the sound continued to get louder. "Do you have anything you want to tell me?"

Gabbi smiled at me, then crossed the living room to open the door to her bedroom, pulling a tiny bundle of black fur up into her arms as it meowed again. "I might have, you know... adopted a kitten."

"You what?! I leave you alone for a week and you get a cat?"

"Kitten. And come on, look how cute she is!" Gabbi gave me her best pout, holding up the little paws.

"I wish you had included me in this," I frowned. "You know I love cats."

Gabbi laughed. "Well, you can borrow her, but you can't steal her. She's mine."

I moved over so I could scratch the kitten under her chin. "What'd you name her?"

"Don't laugh. Her name is Toothless." She grinned, but I raised an eyebrow in question. "Like the dragon from *How to Train Your Dragon*! She reminds me of him."

"That's cute," I chuckled. I kept scratching her kitten's little head, the black fur so soft under my fingers.

"Seriously, though, Ang," Gabbi said, "I think you should talk to him again."

I sighed. "We agreed it was just a fling. When in the woods, right? Like, when in Vegas, except less glamorous. Anyway, I'm sure if we hadn't been sequestered with a hundred other people, he wouldn't have even looked at me."

"You're kidding, right? Do you not know what a smokin' hot bod you have, girl?" Gabbi gestured to me. "Those legs! They go on for miles!" I gave her a look, and she gave me one of her best smiles. "I'm serious, though. Any guy would be lucky to have you.

If he doesn't see that, he's an *idiot*. Besides, I've told you before I thought he had a crush on you."

"Thanks for the pep talk. But I'm serious too. One, this isn't elementary school where you bully the girl you like. That's toxic as fuck. Two, I don't have time for a relationship. Not if I want to keep moving up with the company, and not if I'm going to stay focused on the future."

"Plenty of people have successful careers and relationships."

"Maybe. But I can't deal with someone being all clingy and needy for my time. What I need is someone who will be there for me when I need them and leave me alone when I need space."

"You're ridiculous if you think someone who cares about you wouldn't do that."

I rolled my eyes. "I may be ridiculous, but you're stuck with me."

"Yeah, yeah. Love you too." Gabbi left a kiss on my cheek before taking the kitten back to her room, nuzzling the little ball of fur with her face.

CHAPTER 15
Benjamin

The worst part of the retreat being over was that I no longer got to see Angelina every day. In just a week, we had gone from sending veiled insults via email, to bickering every time we were near each other, to spending every minute together, talking, laughing, and sleeping together.

And then it just ended.

I wasn't sure how to feel about that. Of course, her office was only a floor below mine, so it wasn't like I'd never see her again, but our parting felt... final. I didn't know if she'd want to see me. And I certainly didn't want to pressure her into anything, even if all I wanted was to talk to her again. To get one of those rare smiles, maybe make her laugh. It was the best sound on the planet, her laugh, and I didn't even know if she'd ever grace me with it again.

But I was going to have to move on, accept the fact that Angelina Bradford wanted nothing to do with me. The consequences of my actions, really. I just needed to find someone else and get over it. That would help me focus again—on work, on the promotion I was desperate to secure.

So, when I walked into my office on Monday morning, it was

with the acceptance of my fate, that two nights were all we would have together. To get it out of our systems. *Fuck,* I wished that was enough to get her out of my system. She probably had. I could picture her entering the office today, with her tight ponytail and a bright red pantsuit, ready to take on the world without sparing her hookup a second thought.

I sighed, giving up on my spreadsheet and instead pulling out my phone to text Liam, seeing if he wanted to get lunch together. I needed to distract myself with thoughts other than of her.

When he texted back to meet him at our favorite brewery around the corner at noon, I exhaled deeply before steeling myself to finish some of the work that had piled up on my desk.

∽

THE RECEPTIONIST STOPPED me when I got back, letting me know that I had someone waiting to meet with me in my office. Strange. I hadn't scheduled any meetings, nor had I had something on my calendar today. I wouldn't have taken so long at lunch with Liam otherwise.

But when I rounded the corner, sitting in the chair in front of my desk was a dark-haired woman, playing with the strands from her ponytail. I blinked. Crossed my office door, and her vanilla-and-spice perfume invaded my nostrils.

"Angelina. What are you doing here?" I finally managed to say as I took my place on my desk chair, studying her face.

"I've been wrestling with the idea in my mind all day," she announced with no preamble. "Coming up here. Seeing you. I know we said we would just get it out of our systems, but..."

"But?"

"But I had to see you."

I let her words sink in for a moment. It'd only been two days since we had seen each other, yet I yearned for her. "Maybe we should keep seeing each other."

Angelina was fidgeting with the rings on her fingers, smoothing out her pencil skirt, but stopped when she realized what I'd said. I caught sight of her black pumps and felt myself growing hard. Fuck, she was beautiful at the lake retreat, but here, in her perfectly polished element? She was the hottest woman I'd ever laid my eyes on.

"Yeah? Can't get enough of me, Sullivan?"

"We can pretend it's not the other way around," I smirked. "But yes, I could spend an eternity worshipping your body and not get tired of it, Princess."

She looked at me thoughtfully, crossing her legs. "You wanna be fuck buddies then?"

"Are you saying you want to be friends with benefits, Angelina?"

"No. Not friends. I don't *like* you, remember?" Sure, she didn't. But I knew the truth. She didn't hate me anymore, no matter what she said; she wouldn't be here if she didn't like me at least a little bit. But I'd let her pretend, let her try to keep whatever self-preservation she thought she had. "But we need ground rules."

"Rules?"

She nodded her head. "Yeah. So that we can keep things casual."

I could do casual. I was *great* at casual. I could do without a clingy girlfriend who was upset when I wasn't at home because I was busy with work. I needed someone who would understand my way of life, and who was better than Angelina, who practically lived at the office? "What are you thinking in terms of these rules?"

She held up her index finger as she counted them off. "One. No sleepovers. We get what we need, and then we leave."

"Okay." Waking up next to her in the cabin had been blissfully perfect, but I knew how much the intimacy had freaked her out. "What else?"

"We can't see each other more than three nights a week. Otherwise, you'll get attached." I snorted, but I understood what she was saying. If we were spending every night together, we'd essentially be in a relationship. Which wouldn't be casual at all. "No dates." I frowned at that, and she explained. "I'm not looking for romance. I don't have time for dinner and…" she waved her hands around, "all of that." *Shame.* Even if we were going to be casual, I still wanted to be a gentleman. I would have done those things for her just because I wanted to take care of her.

"Okay. Anything else?"

She listed them off again. "No sleepovers, no dates… No cuddling." She bit her lip. "No gifts. And no feelings."

"Alright." I nodded, unable to contain the smirk that spread over my face.

"Don't you have anything to add?"

"Hm. You'll need a safe word, of course."

Angelina's jaw dropped. "I—what?"

I breezed right past her surprise. "Do you want me to write all of these down, like a contract?"

"That's—not a bad idea actually."

I laughed. "Angelina, we're not signing a contract for our no-strings-attached relationship."

"Well, it wouldn't hurt, you know. Just to keep us from blurring the lines."

"No lines to blur here," I about purred. "We're *not* in a relationship, after all."

"Right. And don't think this is because I like you."

"Well, sweetheart, don't go and fall in love with me. That's the final rule."

"As if," she huffed. Then stood from the chair and started towards the door. "So, I'll see you tonight?"

"Hold on. There's no rules about where, right?" I smirked at her, then glanced at the blinds that covered the office door and windows. It took her only a second to catch up.

"We can't—"

"Come on, live a little, Bradford." I stood and stepped closer to her, close enough to whisper in her ear, "And get on my desk."

I could hear the hitch in her breathing, see the arousal that filled her deep blue eyes, and it spurred me on. I snapped the blinds shut, whirling around to find her sitting in my chair, amusement clear in her eyes.

"Hmm... I think I said the desk, did I not?"

"I don't take orders from men," Angelina said, her lips twitching.

"Maybe not." I moved the contents on my desk aside, into neat, orderly piles. "But something tells me that if you want to be a good girl, you'll listen to me."

"What if I don't want to be a *good girl*?" Minx. All I wanted was to get my hands on her, but I leaned against my desk instead, like an animal on the prowl. Angelina stood too, leaning into me. "Perhaps I'd like to find out what you do to bad girls," she crooned.

Oh, she had no idea. I wanted to tie her up and spank her until she screamed my name, but that would have to wait. Even with the door locked and the blinds shut, we were still in the office, and there was no way I was risking that here.

"Next time," I promised her, breath rough against her ear. I'd tie her up and give her what she wanted—next time. "For now..." I rounded the desk and lifted her up in a quick movement, placing her on the free surface. "I want to taste you again. But you're going to have to be quiet, Angel."

I kneeled in front of her, hands already moving underneath the tight black skirt to pull her silky panties off. "Already so wet for me," I murmured, caressing her folds.

"You look good on your knees for me," Angelina breathed with a smirk. "But don't expect me to return the favor. I don't kneel for most men."

"Ah, baby," I said, lips only an inch from her bare skin. "I'm not most men, am I?"

She began to protest, but I wiped the smirk off her face with a long lick of my tongue up her slit. I didn't stop there, though, not pausing my ministrations for even a second. I lapped at her clit, alternating between sucking it and scraping my teeth against it—giving her what I knew she loved. What I'd learned she craved, after our two nights together. Hard, rough, relentless pursuit of her body, her pleasure.

I could have gone on like that for hours, just feasting on her and her juices, but my erection was becoming unbearable against the zipper of my slacks—aching to be buried inside her.

"Sullivan," she panted roughly as I pulled my mouth from her. "Please."

"What do you want, Princess? Use your words."

"Make me come, please."

No one could have wiped the smug look from my face. "My fingers or my cock?" She glared at me. "What do you want to come on, Angel? It's up to you."

Angelina's answering scowl only made my erection stand further at attention, until finally she gave in. "Your cock."

I surged forward to kiss her deeply, our lips parting for each other, and I could taste dark chocolate and coffee on her tongue.

"Wise choice. You have no idea how badly I want to be inside of you again," I panted, pulling a condom out of my briefcase. Not so gentlemanly perhaps, but better safe than sorry. Everywhere.

"Good," she said, spreading her legs, that pencil skirt shimmied up her thighs, and underwear blissfully discarded on the floor. "Then hurry up and fuck me," Angelina rasped against my ear.

I was still fully clothed and hadn't even bothered to loosen my tie or unbutton my shirt because I was so damn focused on the girl in front of me. She unzipped my pants for me, pushing my briefs down, allowing my dick to spring free, and before I could even roll the condom on, Angelina was licking down my length, stroking it. "Angel," I grit out. "If you do that, I'm not going to last."

Her only response was a wicked grin, before taking the wrapper from my hands, opening it, and rolling it down my cock. Slowly, like she had all the intentions of torturing me. Once I was ready, Angelina guided me to her entrance as I gripped her ass—digging into her soft, luscious skin with my fingers.

I nudged my way inside of her, barely past the tip before I swore. "Fuck, you feel so good." I shut my eyes, willing myself not to come just from this.

Angelina wrapped her legs around my waist as her long red fingernails dug into the dark wood of my desk. I let her adjust for a moment, and then I thrust all the way inside, making her cry out.

"Shhh, Bradford," I said as I pulled out before thrusting in again. "They might not be able to see us, but if you're going to be that loud, someone will certainly hear you."

"Shut up and fuck me harder," Angelina hissed as I picked up that punishing pace that I knew she loved.

She threw her head back, some of her locks escaping the ponytail as she tried to keep in her moans. The breathy noises that she emitted instead spurred me on even more.

"Your pussy is so perfect," I groaned, and I couldn't hold back anymore. Knew that if I kept up this pace, it was going to be over too soon. So I pulled her off the desk, still joined, and sat on my chair. "Ride me. Get yourself off."

"Oh," she gasped, and I knew that the angle, this new position, allowed me to push even deeper. "Goddamn it, Boy Scout. You feel so good inside of me."

And then she was rocking over me, chasing her orgasm, rolling her hips to get the friction she so badly needed on her clit.

"Good girl." I praised her, and then I started playing with her clit, eliciting a choked sound, causing her to grip my shoulders tightly.

"I'm—I'm getting close," she panted in my ear.

"I want you to come for me, Angel."

She nodded frantically, biting her lip as I rubbed circles

against her sweet nub and moved my hips in time with hers. One, two, three more, and Angelina cried out, coming around my cock in the middle of the day in my office. God, I would never get the sight of my head. I gripped her waist and chased my release, needing to come inside of her, to spill into the condom as her pussy continued to flutter around me.

I buried my moans against her neck when I came, wrapping my arms around her body.

"Fuck," I muttered as she climbed off me. I cleaned myself up and disposed of the condom.

"Maybe," she said, still a little breathless, "we shouldn't do it at the office next time."

"Why? Don't feel like being a naughty girl again?"

She hummed, her breath warm on my neck as I took her in my arms again. "I'd rather scream your name in bed."

This girl—constantly surprising me. "Well, then. Next time, I'll fuck you so hard you won't *remember* your name."

"I'm counting on it." Angelina picked up my phone off my desk, and after I unlocked it with my face ID, she typed in her number and sent herself a text to have mine. "There. I'll text you."

How had we not exchanged numbers before? I knew our phones didn't work at the lodge, but the thought of not having had her number until now was strange. She handed me her phone, and I read the contact name she'd saved me with: *Boy Scout*. Cheeky woman. I wished I had one of those selfies she had snapped of us during the retreat. Back when things seemed so much easier, when we didn't have to deal with the realities of real life.

She pulled her panties back on before fixing her suit and remaking a perfect ponytail. "Thanks for the orgasm. See you." And with a wink, Angelina was out of my office, her long stride carrying her back towards her own.

I had to marvel over the fact that somehow, I had managed not to rip her clothes off. We were so desperate for each other, for this release, that we'd fucked with our clothes on. In my office. At work.

Oh, I was screwed. Because Angelina Bradford had walked into my life, and it seemed, had no intention of walking out of it.

And I had no intention of letting her.

CHAPTER 16
Angelina

"How was your day?" Gabrielle asked as I collapsed on the couch, wrapping myself up in one of our giant blankets.

I tried not to smile, but it was hard to keep my lips from moving involuntarily. "It was good."

"Oh?" She gave me one of those wicked little grins, and I had to roll my eyes at that. "Any updates on the situation with one Mr. Sullivan?"

I wrinkled my nose. "Don't call him that."

"Why? Because you're on a first-name basis with him now?"

"No. It just makes him sound old. Or like a client I'm just trying to land."

"Well, you are trying to *land* him, aren't you?"

"Gabrielle," I groaned. "I am not trying to get anything with him." Except for *under* him. Alright—she didn't need to know that. My best friend would probably figure it out herself, with her excellent detective skills. Usually, I loved that about her, but not when it came to my sex life. "Actually," I said, happily petting Toothless when she scratched at the couch and mowed for attention, "I had a meeting with Alexander Larsen this morning."

Gabrielle's eyes went wide. "Is everything okay? Did something happen?"

"Nothing like that. Everything is great." I grinned at her confused gaze. "I'm in the running for the Chief Marketing Officer position."

"Oh my god! Angelina, that's great! We'll have to get drinks to celebrate soon."

"Hey now, let's not celebrate too prematurely. I don't have the job yet. It sounds like Fiona's not going to retire until the end of the year."

"But you will," Gabbi beamed. "Because once Angelina Bradford sets her mind to something, she doesn't give up."

Sometimes it was overwhelming how much my best friend supported and believed in me. "You're right."

"I know I am," she said, patting me on the shoulder. "You just need a reminder every now and then of how great I am."

"You're ridiculous."

"I know that too, but that's why you love me."

"Mmm," I echoed, and Gabbi swooped in next to the couch and swept Toothless into her arms. "Hey!"

"No cuddling with my cat until you tell me you love me."

"I love you," I said, truly meaning it. "You're my best friend. Now gimme the fluff back." I stuck out my hands, giving her my best pouty face. "Please."

"Oh, fine," she sighed, going back to the kitchen where she was making dinner. "Any other updates?"

"I have a work dinner tomorrow night."

"Do you know if he'll be there?"

"No. Seriously, do you think I keep tabs on his schedule?"

"I don't know. How else did you manage to avoid him for so long?"

"Well. Mostly, I didn't have this position yet, so I didn't get called into any of the big meetings. The rest..." I shrugged. "I guess I got lucky." I heard her mumbling something. "What?"

"Nothing. Now, you're sure there's *nothing* else you want to talk to me about?" Gabrielle batted her eyelashes at me from the threshold.

I laughed. "Fine. You win. I saw him today."

"And?"

"And his desk is a perfectly comfortable place to sit," I said, stoically.

"You did *not*!" She gasped. "You naughty girl, I can't believe you. Was it good?"

"My lips are sealed."

"Are you going to see him again?" I shot her a glare. "Oh, you *are*!" Gabbi exclaimed. "Are you dating him now?"

"Woah there, don't get too excited. It's nothing like that. Just casual."

"Just casual, mind-blowing sex, and you're saying it's *nothing*!? You are crazy."

"What about that girl you went out with last? What was her name… Hannah?" I decided to divert the conversation. "When are you seeing her next?"

"I don't know. I can't tell if she actually likes me or not and it's stressing me out," she sighed. "I might break it off."

"Gabs…" I frowned. It seemed like every time Gabbi put herself out there and met someone, she'd find all the things wrong with them and end it. I knew she wanted someone to love, someone to care about her, but dating apps were the worst. That's why I'd never even tried them. Being a hopeless romantic with the highest standards on earth was the worst. That's what books and book boyfriends were for.

"It's fine!" She plopped down on the couch next to me, setting a plate on my lap as well as a bottle of ketchup.

"Chicken nuggets?" I asked, raising an eyebrow.

"Shut up. You know it's my comfort food."

My phone buzzed on the coffee table, and somehow, I knew who it was as soon as my eyes met Gabbi's.

BOY SCOUT
Is texting you against the rules?

"Not serious, huh?" Gabrielle muttered under her breath, but I ignored her to type a reply.

ANGELINA
The jury's still out on that one. As long as you're not texting things like "in bed, thinking about you, good night xx" we'll be okay.

You're insane.

I would never.

Good, because you'd make me not like you even more than I do now.

Keep telling yourself that, Angel.

～

DINNER the next night was at one of the nicer restaurants in Downtown Portland, and everyone was dressed to impress as we all assembled in a private back room. I was glad I had at least gotten a day's notice to figure out what to wear, because I wouldn't have wanted to embarrass myself by showing up in a simple work outfit. I'd been torn between two dresses, but ultimately, I chose a black fitted one with an asymmetrical hem and a jeweled collar. Looking around the room, I decided that was the right choice. My other option (bright red) would have stood out too much.

I sighed in relief as I glanced at the rest of the guests. All the company's employees were already here, and it would be a pleasant night.

The door chimed open, and when I looked up, my breath caught in my throat. Fuck. There was absolutely no reason for my heart to start racing the moment I saw him walk into the room. We hadn't seen each other in two days, and even though I now knew what his body looked and felt like, seeing him like this, all dressed up in a three-piece suit... It did something to me.

Something that I abhorred, because that cocky smirk on his face said that he saw me, recognized the heat in my gaze, and liked it. Shit. How did he keep getting the upper hand over me? In our game of hate and war—as much as I was the one who made the rules—I was losing. I kept caving the minute he touched me, which is why I needed to be strong, and stick to the ground rules. My body might crave his, but that didn't mean I wanted him. It was just hormones and sexual compatibility, and that was all there was between us.

Even if he felt like a drug I couldn't get enough of.

"Fancy seeing you here, Bradford," Benjamin said as came to stand next to me at the bar.

"Sullivan." I raised my glass of red wine as a greeting. "Didn't know they'd let just anyone in here." Never mind that I only got invited yesterday.

"Ha. Funny." His eyes swept from my silver pumps up to my eyes, trailing over my body. "I like this dress on you," he breathed against my ear, leaning in a bit too close. "Think you might let me strip it off of you later?"

I subtly pushed him away to maintain some distance between us. "Absolutely not. And don't do that here." I gave him a pointed stare. "This is a work dinner, and we're professionals."

He cocked his head. "Professionals, huh? We had a very professional work meeting the other day, didn't we, Angelina?"

"Shut up," I muttered, though I knew he was right. Nothing about this—us—would ever be professional. Which was why we needed to keep it separate from work. I wasn't risking my promotion by doing something as stupid as flirting with Benjamin Sullivan at a company dinner.

"Ms. Bradford." I looked up to see Benjamin's ginger friend from the retreat, Liam, standing behind us. "How nice to see you again." He'd let his stubble grow out, and now was sporting a well-groomed ginger beard. Huh. He looked handsome like that.

"Hello," I smiled. "How've you been?"

"Oh, great. You know, just catching up on work from last week." He slid in between us, ordering an old fashioned.

I nodded. "I feel like I need a week's vacation after that week."

Benjamin scowled at me as Liam raised an eyebrow. "That exhausting, huh?"

I bit my lip trying to avoid Benjamin's eyes. "Mhm."

"It was nice to see you, Angelina," he said once he got his drink, touching my arm lightly. "Don't be a stranger, okay?" He gave me a little wink as he walked away, and I didn't miss how Benjamin scooted his barstool closer to mine, leaving our thighs touching.

"What?" I looked up at him, feigning innocence as I sipped my wine.

His voice was low when he finally responded, "If you bite your lip one more time, I'm going to do it for you."

Why was he all worked up now? All I did was be nice to his friend. Unless... "Oh my god. Are you jealous?" I laughed at the expression on his face.

"Of course I'm not *jealous*. Of Liam? Why are you smiling about this?" he scowled. "I just don't like the way he looked at you."

"That's cute."

"What?" he hissed.

"It's cute that you think I'm yours to be possessive over."

He narrowed his eyes but didn't say anything, just took a sip of his drink.

The grin didn't leave my face for a long time, his annoyance fueling my pleasure. I'd never seen him so put out over anything, and maybe that's what amused me the most: I found a way to get under his skin.

"Come on, let's go sit at our table and we'll see who else I can flirt with," I waggled my eyebrows at him.

"Angelina—" He huffed.

Not that I was going to. I kind of liked our arrangement, even if it hadn't really begun yet. I didn't have any plans to let someone else get mixed up in it. Benjamin was enough of a time commitment.

"Do you really think I'm going to prowl around looking for someone else to fuck when I have you, Sullivan?" I whispered under my breath. "Relax. I don't plan on finding another man. For now," I added with a wink.

He was still frowning, but at least some of his grumpiness seemed to disappear at those words, which made me relax. Because I was the grumpy one here, and I'd come to rely on his sarcastic personality to break the tension.

Goodness knows sometimes I needed that.

As it turned out, we weren't even seated next to each other, and as I took my seat, I switched back to work mode. Mergers, acquisitions, brand campaigns, what I thought about the current social media campaign, the graphics department—you name it, we discussed it. My favorite part of the evening was sitting next to Naomi Moore—one of our software engineers, who was rocking a sleek, cropped bob and wore a short leather jacket in place of a blazer. She was half Vietnamese and I loved hearing her talk about her family, her girlfriend, and how she'd gotten to Willamette Tech.

It was a reminder of how we all got here. How, even as a medium-sized, growing company, we were still small enough to get to know the people in other departments, because we cared about that. And maybe, I realized, I hadn't been doing a good enough job of that lately. Because Naomi—fun, edgy, sophisticated Naomi—was brilliant, and exactly the kind of person our social media should have been featuring. The person who should be plastered on the marketing campaigns because she was incredible. A breath of fresh air. Genuine and free-spirited. I made a mental note to myself to go and talk to her tomorrow, because I knew we could create something beautiful together.

The rest of the night passed in a blur of light chatter and laughter, and when I got home, I was happy to make myself a big cup of hot chocolate and curl up with a new romance novel on the couch. Just what the doctor ordered. Peace and quiet.

And if I didn't ask a certain brunette to come home with me, well, he didn't ask me either.

CHAPTER 17
Angelina

"Happy Birthday!" I flung my arms around Charlotte upon arriving at Powell's to celebrate. It was one of our favorite spots to explore in Downtown Portland, since our college days, but it'd been a while since the girls and I had all gone together, victims as we were of our busy schedules. It was a huge place, taking up an entire city block, with multiple floors and most genres having an entire room to themselves.

I loved getting lost in the books, forgetting about life problems and work worries and just immersing myself in rows of pages.

Charlotte gave me a big grin, spinning around in a pink corduroy overall dress that she had layered with a white turtleneck underneath and a pair of beige heeled booties. It was so her, to be all pastels even in the middle of autumn.

Her birthday was actually tomorrow, Sunday, but we were celebrating early since we knew we'd need the day to sleep off the party.

"How are you feeling? Ready to turn the big two-six?"

Charlotte groaned. "When did I get so old? I don't like this."

Noelle laughed. "Join the club, babe."

"So, what are the plans for today?" I asked our red-headed leader, who was wearing her favorite pumpkin-colored knit sweater and a tan skirt.

I loved that we all had such different senses of style, because we all stood out in our own way. If Charlotte was girly and Noelle was preppy, Gabbi was sportier and more casual versus my elegant, classic style, though I'd just as often rock a leather jacket and skinny jeans. We weren't all cookie-cutter duplicates of each other and never had been. I'd dealt with that enough in high school—the popular, mean girls who tried to make themselves feel better by wearing expensive clothes and looking down on you if you repeated an outfit; luckily, when I got to college I realized people just didn't care. And these girls—my best friends—we all accepted each other wholeheartedly, never being anything but the biggest cheerleaders for each other.

"I planned a little book hunt for us." Noelle's rosy cheeks brightened as she smiled.

"A scavenger hunt?" I raised an eyebrow. "Really?"

"Come on. It'll be fun!" Noelle was flushed with excitement as she pulled pieces of paper out of her tote bag and handed them to us. "Whoever finds the most *unique* book wins." She waggled her eyebrows, and I really didn't want to know what she meant by that.

Gabbi grinned. "And what do we win, exactly?"

Noelle bit her lip. "Bragging rights?" A little giggle escaped from her lips. "I don't have any actual prizes…"

I laughed as I looked over the prompts. "Okay, I'm a little skeptical, but this does look fun."

The list was printed on a notecard-sized piece of paper, and each category had a little box next to it to check off.

1. A Book in Your Favorite Color
2. A Book with A Cartoon Cover

3. A Fantasy Book
4. Your Favorite Author
5. Book You Haven't Heard Of
6. Has Been Made into a Movie
7. You Can't Wait to Read
8. Has an Animal on the Cover
9. Book You've Read More than Once
10. Wild Card

"And we have how long to find them all?" Charlotte asked.

Noelle glanced down at her watch. "Eh... Do we think thirty minutes is enough?" I made a face. For ten books? We could take two hours to go through here on a normal day. "Maybe an hour?" The rest of us nodded. "We can meet in the coffee room when we're done." Each room at Powell's was assigned a color, but there was also the coffee room on the first floor with a little café and lots of tables.

"Sounds perfect to me." The Birthday Girl gave us two big thumbs up.

I looked around. "It really has been forever since I've been here. Reminds me of our college days when we'd spend all day curled up in the aisles, reading books."

"Life was so much simpler then," Gabbi sighed.

I nudged her with my elbow. "You make it sound like we're *old*. We're only twenty-six."

Charlotte scrunched up her nose. "Next thing you know, we're all going to be thirty."

"And hopefully I'm not the only one in a relationship by then!" Noelle looked at the three of us with a glint in her eyes. Gabbi gave me a subtle nudge and I rolled my eyes.

Benjamin and I weren't in a relationship, not by a long shot, and even though the sex was great, I doubted it would work out long-term. And I certainly wasn't going to go out of my way to find someone after our friends-with-benefits arrangement ended. I wouldn't have the time."

Charlotte smiled. "Hopefully. You know, I've always dreamed about the four of us living in the same neighborhood and raising our kids together one day." That girl was so baby crazy, I was pretty sure her ovaries cried every time she saw little kids.

"I don't know if I want to have kids," I said. I'd been thinking about it a lot more recently, for whatever reason. About what the future would look like once I'd gotten my promotion and the job I'd always dreamed of.

Gabbi nodded. "I've always thought... You know, if I have one, that'll probably be it. But only if I really love my partner." She wrinkled her nose. "If they're not helping, I'm not having their kid."

"Okay, back on track!" Noelle urged us. "We only have a few hours and I think this will be fun for all of us. Also," she said, her smile lighting up her freckled face, "I made us matching tote bags to put our book hauls in." She pulled them out of her bag and passed them to us. Each one was screen printed, featuring an open book with a heart in the middle, a different color on each of ours, with the words *best friends book club* in cursive at the top. We all gave her grief about naming us that, but the bags were cute, and the heart on mine was red—my signature color.

"You did not," Gabbi laughed. "I love it."

"I've been saying I wanted to make us book club gear," Noelle grinned. "I had to come up with a sneaky way to get away with it. Figured this way, you'd be forced to use them."

Charlotte held hers up, detailed with a light pink heart. "It's adorable, and you know I can always use a new tote to take to dance." I was sure she loved having her kiddos at the dance studio comment on whatever she was currently carrying.

"Alright, now shoo!" Noelle said. "Meet you all back at the coffee shop in a bit!"

And with that, the four of us all took off in different directions through the store—which was easy, considering there were eight different rooms of books, not including the coffee shop. Some of them were sections we hardly ever shopped in, sure, but I loved wandering through all of them anyway.

I'd spent many hours as a teenager here, when my mom would drop my brother and me off. Sometimes, after I finished wandering the aisles or moved on from the YA section, I would sit in the travel section and read book after book about France. It had been my dream to go there when I was little, and while my shy, quiet brother was wandering the sci-fi or the games section, I would be flipping through books about Paris, imagining what it would be like when I saw the Eiffel Tower in person.

Then my parents got divorced, and any hope of convincing them to go on a European trip was quickly destroyed, but I didn't stop praying for the day I'd get to go.

It finally happened in college. I was offered the opportunity to study abroad in London for a summer, and I spent a glorious three days exploring the city I had always read about in books. I'd been dreaming about going back ever since.

Being at Powell's always brought back memories like that. The happy ones, where getting lost in a book meant getting lost in a new place. Reading still did that for me, when I needed to shut off my brain, but I'd long since stopped reading travel books and started reading romance, where everything made sense. Sure, the main characters usually had obstacles to face, but at the end of the day, it was Happily Ever After for them. I liked that—liked that everything wrapped up in neat little bows. That even the characters who had seemed so broken and joyless at the beginning could find the person they were meant to be with.

Unfortunately, it was fiction, and that wasn't how real life worked. Maybe it did for Noelle, swept off her feet by her gorgeous Professor boyfriend, but it wasn't how it worked for most of us. It wasn't how it worked for me.

Men had always thought I was too much. Too independent,

too high maintenance, and too focused on my career goals. Too tall even, which was absurd. And my personal favorite—too much of a bitch. So, I was independent and wanted to be able to take care of myself—was that really that ridiculous of a notion?

I ran my fingers over the spines as I wandered down the romance aisles, looking at the list from Noelle. There were so many options I had for the categories, but I wanted to try to find ones I didn't already own or hadn't read, so I could add to the floor-to-ceiling bookshelves at home. Gabbi and I had been doing our best to fill them, though my favorite was when Noelle would come over and by the time she left, she'd have completely reorganized them. It took up the extra room in our three-bedroom apartment, but it was worth it to have our own library.

I might not have as much time to read as my friends did—and in some ways, I only had myself to blame for that—but I still found myself picking up new books when I wanted to relax on the weekends, or when I had a moment to myself after work. Usually, with a glass of wine—it helped me unwind.

Especially when I'd been bickering with Benjamin over emails. Now, after the explosive nights we'd shared at the retreat and that day in his office, all of those little things that used to piss me off seemed like they had simmered down in my mind—and then completely evaporated away.

I snorted to myself in the middle of the aisle. It seemed like so long ago when we hated each other. Everything was different now. We'd gone from enemies to something that resembled friends (with a few extra benefits), and I was surprised at how much I enjoyed spending time with him.

He still got on my nerves like no one else did, and now I was pretty sure that tormenting me got him going, but the more time we spent together, the more I found that I didn't mind his sarcasm or his quick wit. And it was kind of fun, flirting with him.

Even if it was just sex. I used my knowledge of the romance

genre to lay down the rules: if we didn't sleep next to each other, there wouldn't be any moments of intimacy in the morning. If we didn't go on dates, we wouldn't keep revealing more about ourselves to each other. If we didn't act like a couple, we wouldn't risk falling for each other.

I'd never let myself rely on anyone; I'd always taken care of myself and put myself first. Yet now, despite all those rules, I was surprised to realize how much I was enjoying being with another person with no complications. There were no strings, no attachments, and no feelings, but it was comfortable. A comfort I'd never shared with anyone else, even the few flings I'd had in college or the short-lived relationships I'd had since then.

By the time I wandered into the coffee room, tote and an arm full of books and mind full of thoughts of Benjamin, Paris, and romance plots, all three of the girls were already sitting there, waiting for me.

"Sorry if I kept you waiting," I said, smoothing a strand of hair behind my ear as I slid into a chair at the table they had chosen.

"You didn't!" Charlotte said with a smile. "We pretty much all got here in the last five or ten minutes."

Noelle looked proudly at our stacks of books.

"So how do you want to do this?" Gabrielle asked, eyeing the forty books we now had sitting on the table. It looked a little ridiculous when they were all laid out like that. "One prompt at a time?"

"That works," Noelle nodded, shuffling her stack around. "We can just go in order down the list, and when we get to the end, if anyone wants to swap books before we check out, we could do that."

"Oooh, that's smart. Stealing books from each other," Gabbi remarked.

Charlotte looked at her pile hesitantly. "I don't..."

"I think we can all agree no unauthorized stealing is allowed," I said. "Birthday Girl wants to share hers first?"

She nodded, giddy to reveal each of her picks. We went around the table, swapping book titles and reading off the backs. It was fun, because even though we all had a billion books to read —to-be-read lists a mile long—we found books no one had heard of before. I was surprised by how few duplicates there were between the four of us.

Gabbi and I *had* managed to pick up the same fantasy book (*"Enemies to lovers! With dragons!"* she exclaimed) and I knew this called for a binge-reading day on the couch, feet to feet with Toothless cuddled up between us. We'd always loved buddy reading, and I'd been so busy with work lately that maybe I had neglected our friendship more than I realized.

"This was so fun," Charlotte smiled. "Thanks for the surprise, Noelle."

"Of course! I loved planning it. This is something I feel like my students would have loved when I was a Hall Director. Probably a shorter version, but still." Noelle had given up her Hall Director job after graduating with her master's in Student Affairs but still worked for our alma mater as a Student Advisor. She loved working with the undergrads, and the amount of passion she had for them was clear in the way her eyes lit up when she talked about them.

"Hey!" I protested when Gabbi stole a book from my pile. "That's mine."

"I'm not stealing it, silly. Just looking."

I stuck out my tongue. "What time do we need to start getting ready to make it to dinner on time?"

Charlotte looked at her watch. "I'm good heading back now if you all are? Unless we want to wander a bit more."

We'd all finished our drinks and goodies from the cafe, so all we had left to do was check out at the register with our stacks of books.

"One last loop through the romance section wouldn't hurt, right?" Noelle said, and we all laughed.

After our very successful bookstore shopping trip, we headed back to my and Gabbi's apartment to get ready for dinner. We were meeting the guys at the restaurant, and I was kind of glad it would just be a quiet night with our friends. Charlotte had a few other close friends at the dance studio where she worked part-time, but she'd told us that they were going to celebrate another day. It was just our little gang going to the winery together for food and drinks, and Char couldn't have been happier.

I was glad that just being surrounded by the people she loved was enough to make her happy. We'd all snuck our gifts to Noelle before today so that we could surprise Charlotte with them when Matthew showed up; knowing all she expected was our presence made surprising her even more worth it. She was the baby of our group, always the last to celebrate her birthday, and we all took extra special care of her because of that.

Noelle was wearing a glitzy champagne wrap dress that hugged her body and showed off her beautiful curves, while Gabrielle chose a one-shoulder emerald green dress that made her eyes pop; Charlotte—being Charlotte—was in a baby pink tulle dress with a full skirt and bows on each shoulder. She looked beautiful. I ditched the black for once, going for a silver dress with long sleeves, a deep plunging neckline, and an asymmetrical hem. I liked to think it made my legs look longer—something the girls groaned over as we were getting ready. I was already the tallest one, so they hated when I wore heels and towered over them even more.

Once we were all glammed up, our hair curled and styled with our makeup done to perfection, we piled into Gabbi's Mazda and drove to the restaurant.

"He's going to completely flip out over you," Charlotte was gushing to Noelle in the backseat, who blushed as she tucked a curl behind her ear.

"I'm counting on it," Noelle giggled. "God, you should see the way he's obsessed with my curves. It's like—"

"We get it, lovebird," I laughed from the passenger seat, effectively preventing her from going on and on about the love of her life. I was happy for her, truly, but I wasn't always in the mood to hear her gushing about how much Matthew adored her. And maybe, for the first time, I was regretting the armor I'd built up around my heart.

Huh. I was not ready to unpack that yet.

"Oh, look, there's a spot," I said, indicating the street parking that was open. Gabbi quickly pulled in, and I was happy to see that Matthew and Daniel were already waiting inside—awkwardly not saying much to each other, as men were ought to do.

"Matthew!" Noelle waved to her man when we joined them, and his eyes lit up with a warmth I was starting to become all too familiar with and trailed down her body.

"You look stunning, sweetheart." He wrapped his hands around her waist before placing a kiss on her cheek.

"Thank you," she mumbled, and I had to look away. For so long, I'd pushed the thought away—of ever finding someone who would love me, of being happy. And it'd been okay while all of us girls were single. But now, watching Noelle with Matthew, watching how much he loved and cherished her... Would I ever find something like that? And if I did, would I be able to recognize it and open myself to it?

Gabbi rested her head on my shoulder as Daniel and Charlotte chatted with the seater.

"They'd make a good couple," Matthew muttered under his breath.

I sighed. "We've all been saying that for years."

"What are you guys talking about?" Charlotte asked, popping back up, her curls bouncing as she gave a curious smile.

"Nothing," Gabbi waved her off.

"Charlotte, party of six?"

"That's us!"

We were led to a table in the corner of the restaurant. Gabbi, Daniel, and I sat on one side, while Matthew, Noelle, and Charlotte took the other.

I turned to my brother. "How've you been?"

He shrugged. "Alright."

"Just alright? That's it?"

Daniel lowered his voice. "Have you talked to Mom lately?"

"Not in a few weeks, why?"

He hesitated, like he was trying to decide if he should talk about it here, but ultimately decided against it. "Later. I don't want to ruin Char's day."

"Okay," I frowned, but didn't have time to think too much about it because our waiter came over and we ordered a few bottles of wine for the table, as well as appetizers. Charlotte went with her favorite white wine: Moscato. She was nothing if not consistent, after all. I was about to take a drink from my wine glass when I heard an all too familiar voice from behind me.

"Fancy seeing you here, Bradford."

Oh no. Not here. I looked up and Benjamin's eyes met mine. "Oh." I might have squeaked it, but I was too shocked to see him here. Suddenly, I was very thankful that there was no free chair at the table. I wasn't sure what I would do if he invited himself to the party—which I wouldn't put past him to do, shameless as he was.

Yes, you do know, said that little voice in my head that was always encouraging me to do the most reckless things when it came to the man who stood at my back with a stupid grin on his face. *You'd go home with him and jump his bones.*

Right.

"What are you doing here?" I finally choked out.

"Dinner with some old friends from college," he said, pointing to a table where two attractive-looking women were sitting, as well as a handsome man in a suit. "What about you?"

"Celebrating," I said simply. He raised an eyebrow, so I added, "It's Charlotte's birthday tomorrow." I gestured to the blonde across from me.

The girls all stared at me, waiting for me to introduce him to them. Which made me realize—except for Gabbi, they had no idea who Benjamin was. And I was about to introduce my brother to the man I was sleeping with. Fuck me.

"Everyone, this is Benjamin Sullivan." Noelle and Charlotte's jaws dropped open, just a little bit, while Matthew looked confused. "We, uh... work together. Benjamin, these are my best friends, Charlotte, and Noelle, and you might remember Gabbi?" I pointed each one out to him. "This one's my brother, Daniel. And that's Matthew, Noelle's boyfriend." I didn't think I missed the relief on his face when he realized neither of the guys were there with me.

He gave them all a dazzling smile, and I could feel the butterflies in my stomach just watching it bloom over his face. Oh, for the love of God. "It's great to meet Angelina's friends." He nodded to Daniel. "And her brother."

Daniel mumbled something back, and I was eager to get Benjamin out of there before everyone started asking more questions. "Yes, well, very nice to see you. You should probably get back to your, erm, friends." I tried to push him away, but it was hard from the current angle, what with him standing and towering over me as I sat.

Benjamin bent down, close enough that he could whisper in my ear, "I'm not going to be able to get the sight of you in that dress out of my mind, Angel. Damn."

He quickly stood with a wink, leaving me feeling very glad I was sitting down. He waved goodbye to my friends, and I watched him walk back to his table, wondering if he was going to take one of those women home with him. What was going to prevent him from sleeping with someone else while we had our little arrangement? Nothing.

The thought lingered in the back of my mind all night, even

as I enjoyed the company of my best friends, as we all cheered for Charlotte and sang Happy Birthday while she blew out her candles.

I'd told him I wasn't going to sleep with anyone else. But was he?

CHAPTER 18
Benjamin

> **BENJAMIN**
> Are you home?

> **ANGEL**
> Just getting back now, yeah.

> I can't stop picturing you in that dress, Princess. Can't stop thinking about all the things I'd love to do to you...

> Is that an invitation, Sullivan?

> Always.

> Be there soon.

> Keep the dress on.

> And the heels.

Of course she responded with an eye-roll emoji. I sent her my address, eager to see her again. Despite our agreement, we hadn't properly seen each other since Monday, and I was going crazy with want. I thought about texting her several times, but I didn't want to seem overeager.

We'd exchanged numbers, but she said she would text me. She didn't. Maybe she didn't want to see me so soon after our first encounter, or maybe she wanted to keep some distance between us. Either way, my patience had run off.

When I opened the door to my apartment thirty minutes later, she was still wearing that glitzy, glittery silver dress and the black strappy heels.

"Hey." I stepped aside, leaning on the door as she walked in.

"Nice place," she said appraisingly. It was a penthouse apartment in one of the high rises on the South Waterfront. The city looked beautiful, sprawled beneath me, from outside the huge windows in the living room. It was one of my favorite things about living here—that, and the close commute to work.

"Thanks. Just wait until you see the bedroom." I gave her a wink, and I waited for her to roll her eyes, but she just stared at me. "Fuck, you're so pretty," I said, dragging a hand down my face.

"You know..." She stepped towards me and grabbed my tie, slowly pulling me closer. "What you said to me tonight was very unfair, Sullivan."

"Was it now?"

She nodded, tightening her grip. Our bodies were flush against each other. "So, you're going to have to take responsibility."

"Responsibility for what, Angel?" I asked, but my hand was already moving to the bottom of her dress—and somehow, I wasn't surprised to find that she had ditched her underwear already. My fingers danced on her inner thigh for a moment before stroking her core. Deliciously wet. Had my comment turned her on that much? Or had she sat there, at dinner with her friends all night, thinking about me? "Did I do this to you, baby?"

"Mhm," she groaned as I swiped one finger over her clit.

"You're such a naughty girl, coming here dripping wet for me. Aren't you?"

Angelina whimpered. "Please," she breathed, pushing against me, wanting more than just light touches.

"Not yet," I said, pulling my hand away and guiding her over to the couch. I sat down and tugged her onto my lap, making her straddle me. "You know..."

"Hmm?" Her eyes were glazed over with lust, and I loved seeing her like this. My girl. Even if it was only like this, I was the one who got to see her face so open and vulnerable. I knew she wasn't this unrestrained with anyone else.

"You still haven't picked a safe word."

She huffed before realizing I was serious. "Oh." She blinked. "You were serious about that?"

"Yes, Princess, I was serious about that. If you ever want to stop, we'll stop. If you don't like something, you tell me. I'm never going to force you to do anything."

"So are we talking like..." She swallowed, and then looked at me from under her lashes. "Whips and chains, or...?" God, I had to stop myself from pushing her onto the couch and have my way with her right then and there.

"No bondage, Angel. Unless you'd like that, then we can discuss that and I could make arrangements accordingly."

She bit her lip. "Um..."

I tilted her chin up to look me in the eyes, tapping her on the nose. "I want to take care of you, Angelina. So I want you to know that I'm never going to do anything you don't like. Do you understand?" Angelina nodded. "Use your words, please."

"Yes. I-I understand."

"Okay. Good. Now, pick a word."

She scrunched up her nose. "Satan."

I couldn't help the laugh I let out. "No."

"No—literally, you are the devil, I swear. Let me think."

I kissed her on the cheek. "I'm just teasing you. You say stop, I'll stop. I know what stop means, baby. I never want you to feel uncomfortable because of me."

She nodded, and I realized then, that as much as I wanted to peel her dress off her, I was also coming to enjoy spending time with her like this, talking, just as much. I would have been content to just sit on the couch chatting with her. Learning more about her. What was her favorite flower? Her favorite book? How did she take her tea, what kind of candles did she love?

Angelina got up, moving to look out the windows, to the sparkling lights of the city below. I stepped up behind her, wrapping my arms around her waist, and nestled my head against hers. She relaxed into me.

"Did you have fun with your friends tonight?" I asked. All I'd wanted was to pull up a chair and join them, but I couldn't. Liam's friends from college were visiting, and he asked me to come along. It wasn't like I was remotely interested in those girls, but watching Angelina's expression when she saw them made me chuckle.

"Oh, yeah," she said. "It was great." But there was a sad note in her voice.

"What happened?"

"What?" She looked at me, like she couldn't believe I picked up on the emotions she was trying to hide. "Oh. Just... After the party, my brother told me that my mom is going to get remarried. I don't know how to feel about it, is all."

I knew I couldn't really make her feel better with words, so I stroked her arms. "When was the last time you talked to her?"

"It's been a few months. We're... I don't know. I didn't even know she was dating someone."

"It's okay if you don't know how to feel, Angel. Even as adults, our parents' actions can impact us in ways we don't completely understand."

"It's not like I expected them to get back together. Or even wanted that," she sighed. "It's just... weird."

I nuzzled into her hair, swaying her back and forth gently. It made me smile how a few minutes ago, everything had been so sexually charged, and now we were talking about family and feelings. These moments were precious to me, when Angelina let her guard down and let me in. I knew she was showing me a rare side of herself, and I would never take it for granted.

I ran a hand down her curls. "I like your hair like this," I murmured.

"Down?"

"Yeah," I said, spinning a finger around one of her loose curls. "You always wear it up. It looks nice."

"I didn't think…"

"Didn't think what?"

"That you'd noticed." Angelina spun around in my arms, tilting her head up to look at me.

I tugged on another strand. "I like your ponytails, too, but I feel like you're freer when it's down like this." I wished I could have captured the look in her eyes as she stared up at me with those beautiful, dazzling blue eyes. "Although, you're the most beautiful woman no matter what you're wearing or how you style your hair."

"You're just saying that because we're sleeping together," Angelina mumbled, drawing her eyes away from me.

"No." I cupped her cheek, forcing her to meet my gaze. "I mean every word I've ever said to you, Angelina. I don't care if you're in muddy hiking boots and a layer of bug spray or campfire smoke or dressed up to the nines. You're fucking perfect. Every piece of you."

She gave me a little nod before wrapping her arms around me, tucking her chin into my chest and hugging me tightly. I wanted to kiss her so badly at that moment that I could barely breathe.

"Thank you," she finally breathed out, and if we hadn't been so closely connected, I doubted I'd have heard it at all.

I kissed the top of her head, holding her close for a few more moments. Then I brought her head up to mine and kissed her slowly. The kiss wasn't passionate or hungry. No, I placed sweet kisses against her lips, one after the other, coaxing her open. I could have kissed her all night like that—slow and steady, this quiet exploration of each other's mouths, just basking in the moment.

It reminded me of the chair lift, when she'd shared a little bit of herself with me. When she'd let me comfort her. Whatever her insecurities were, the things she struggled with—I wanted her to know how much I cared for her, as a person, before I ever cared about anything else.

Our slow kissing turned deeper, more desperate, with Angelina's hands scrambling to loosen my tie, but I had other ideas. I waited until she'd undone the knot and then I finished pulling the rest off myself before throwing it behind me on the floor.

"Angel," I whispered. "Turn around now. Hands on the glass. I want to fuck you against the window."

Angelina complied with no hesitation, and I quickly went to grab a condom before I hitched up her dress, not bothering to take off the shimmery material. I unzipped my pants and sheathed myself before leaning over her, caging her against the window.

"You just need someone to take care of you, don't you, baby?" I murmured. "Someone who knows you need to be in control of everything except this. Hmm?"

"Yes," Angelina whimpered. I wanted her to let go, to put her trust in me that I'd give her exactly what she needed. She wasn't fully herself tonight; that much was obvious. The fire that normally burned so bright, her quick wit and easy banter were nowhere in sight, so I wanted to distract her from her worries. I could give her pleasure and help her to forget, at least for tonight.

"You want me to shut your brain off, don't you, Angel? Fuck you so good that there are no thoughts left in that magnificent brain of yours?" I teased her clit, rubbing it with my thumb before pushing two fingers inside of her, stretching her for my cock.

She moaned at the touch and arched her back further, pushing her back into me. "Fuck me, *please*."

I could only obey. I guided myself towards her entrance, just pressing the tip into her, admiring her biteable ass and her beautiful tanned skin against the city lights.

"Sullivan," Angelina grit out. "I'm not breakable. Hurry up and stop teasing me."

Ah, *there* she was. "Yes, Princess."

I slammed into her, enjoying the loud gasp she gave as I gripped her hips, watching her breath fog up the glass. She was warm and snug around me, and I had to shut my eyes from the sheer pleasure of being inside of her. No matter how many times we'd done this, I still couldn't believe how good it felt.

Her hands pressed against the window and the sight was incredibly hot: knowing Angelina was exposed for everyone to see sent shivers down my spine. No one could see us from the street, we were too high, but the buildings around us... "Does this feel good, baby? Being fucked where anyone could see us? See your pretty face as you take my cock?" She moaned louder in response. "Words, Princess," I said, sliding out of her, waiting for her to speak before pushing back in.

"Y-yes!" She shuddered as I reached around, turning her head so I could kiss her roughly as I thrust into her again, all the way to the hilt.

"That's my good girl," I moaned, enjoying the feeling of her tightening around me when I rewarded with praises. "I've been waiting for this all night, since I saw you in that dress."

"Harder," she cried, wriggling against me.

I wouldn't be able to savor this tonight, because the more I rocked into her, the closer I got to my own release. *Fuck* was I glad this was no longer a one-time thing. I rode her hard and fast and Angelina gave me as good as she got, soon screaming and succumbing to her climax. I wasn't far behind her: she squeezed around me and I was a goner, spilling into the condom. My breathing was ragged and uneven as I took her in my arms, still nestled inside of her.

I should have left it there. Should have pulled away and cleaned myself, shown her the bathroom, and then said goodbye.

Instead, I got rid of the condom, sat on the wooden floor, and took Angelina in my lap before taking a blanket from the couch and covering us with it. I kissed her hair, and then I placed a soft kiss on her mouth.

I shouldn't have done it. She'd laid down the rules—I should have been able to respect them. But I didn't want her to leave yet.

"I should go," she murmured after a few minutes.

"A little longer," I whispered back, and she relaxed against me, leaning into the touch. I knew she needed this just as much as I did from her contented little sigh, and that was everything to me.

Eventually, she pulled away, and I brushed the hair back from her face. "I'll see you tomorrow?" I asked, wishing we didn't have to say goodbye, but I knew this was what she wanted. What we'd both agreed on. Because we weren't in a relationship, even if it felt like it in moments like this.

This thing we were doing... It would end one day.

And this infatuation I'd grown over the last two years, only compounded over the last few weeks, it was going to ruin me if I didn't wise up and get smart about this.

If I didn't accept that Angelina Bradford would never really be mine.

∼

"Hunter?"

Ever since those days at the retreat where Angelina and I had started opening up about our pasts, our families, I'd had this nagging feeling in my gut that I couldn't ignore anymore.

I missed my brother. I missed having him in my life. Part of the reason why I'd moved here was because of him, to get closer to him; it was about time I fulfilled my promise to myself.

"Hey, Ben," his voice came through the line. "What's up?"

"Can't I just call my brother without needing something?"

"Sure," Hunter laughed. "But you normally don't."

"I know," I sighed. "But I'm trying to be better. I know things have been... weird between us the last few years. But I want us to be close again."

"I'd like that too," he said quietly after a moment. Relief washed over me. "I always figured you were just too busy with your fancy accounting job."

"Like you aren't crazy busy with your fancy job as a doctor, Hunter."

"Eh, fancy schmancy." I could almost feel him rolling his eyes. Ever the humble man who would never admit that he was doing something incredible. Like saving lives and working with children wasn't one of the most admirable things you could do. Hunter had a big heart, and I knew it was buried deep down underneath the layers he'd built up to protect himself.

"So... Have you talked to Emily lately?"

"Oh, yeah. She texts me a few times a week. She seems pretty happy, even though I think Mom and Dad are furious that she didn't finish college," he chuckled. But he was right—our sister had decided to drop out of private university, paid for entirely by our parents, and had been determined to find her own way in the world. I admired her for going after what she wanted and not caring what our parents thought.

"She's braver than I ever was."

"Nah," Hunter dismissed my thought instantly. "You carved your own path too. Mom and Dad wanted you to be just like them, go to medical school, be a doctor or a surgeon. You were smart enough to do anything you wanted, Ben, but I admire that you chose the career that actually interested you. I'm proud of you, you know that?"

My chest warmed at the admission. "Thank you. At least someone is. You've got it the easiest, being Mom and Dad's golden child, Doctor at a fancy hospital."

"It's not all fun and games, I promise," Hunter said. "And yes, I do love it, but I can't even tell you the last time I took a day off. Or the last time I had fun besides grabbing a beer with colleagues after work."

"Well, we should do something then."

"Yeah. We're definitely long overdue for that."

"My fault, I know. When's your next day off?"

"I think I have two days in a row next week back-to-back. I'll check my schedule, and then I'll text you."

"Sounds good. I'm down for whatever."

"Even a hike?"

"Maybe let's take it slow and start with a drink."

He laughed. "You know... It would be nice to have a hiking partner again."

It would, wouldn't it? Going out with Angelina while we were on the retreat had been fun, but Hunter was different. He'd always been a bigger outdoor man than me, but I had to admit that those hiking trips when we were younger had really bonded us. It was one of the reasons I still enjoyed it, even now.

"I'm sorry for letting us grow apart. For... resenting you all these years, Hunter. You didn't deserve that."

"You can't take all the blame. Maybe I didn't defend you to Mom and Dad as much as I should have. I might not have always been the best older brother."

I shook my head, even though he couldn't see me. "I know it's not going to happen overnight, but I really want to be close again."

"Me too, Ben. Me too."

"Okay. See you soon, then."

"See you."

As the line clicked shut, I couldn't help but smile. It felt like so many things in my life were finally falling into place. I had the girl—kind of. I would soon have my brother again. And the promotion I'd always dreamed of was within arm's reach.

A knock at the door caught my attention and I looked up, hoping it was a certain dark-headed girl. I had to hide the disappointment when it was Liam who entered my office.

CHAPTER 19
Angelina

My computer dinged with an IM from Gabbi.

G.MEYER

Hey! Some of us are getting drinks after work. You in?

A.BRADFORD

Who's going? I'm down.

G.MEYER

I think Harper, Naomi, Nicolas, maybe Zo, and I know there are a few others?

LITTLE DOTS APPEARED on the screen indicating that she was typing, but the next message didn't come through. I just sent the question I knew both of us were thinking.

A.BRADFORD

Is Benjamin going?

> **G.MEYER**
> Not sure, but you can invite your boyfriend if you want.

> **A.BRADFORD**
> We're not dating, Gabs. But sounds good. Text me the address.

I sighed, rubbing my temples. Did I want to invite him? Hang out with him in a setting around other people? Sure, things had been good lately. We'd seen each other a few more nights after Charlotte's birthday dinner, and I wasn't going to get over the way he'd eaten me out on the couch the other day anytime soon... but did I want to invite him to drinks with my work friends?

Being at a bar meant we'd be drinking. And being around him under the influence of alcohol meant I was *definitely* going to pounce on him. Suddenly, I couldn't think of a reason why that was a bad idea.

> **ANGELINA**
> Hey, Boy Scout.

> **BOY SCOUT**
> Yes?

> You busy tonight? A group of work people are getting drinks.

> Wanna come?

> Are you saying you want me there, Bradford?

> No.

> Come if you want. I don't care.

I sent him the address and then went back to the task at hand, focusing on my project as I popped my AirPods in. I needed this to go well if I wanted to get my promotion. I'd already talked to Naomi and she'd agreed to do some photo shoots and social media campaign stuff to represent the brand. I was absolutely stoked to work with her.

Before I knew it, I caught noises from outside my office; I raised my head and noticed it was 5 PM already. Damn. I quickly finished up my work, then glanced at my appearance in the small mirror I kept on my desk, touched up my hair and lipstick, and headed out to meet the others at the bar.

Benjamin had never confirmed whether he was coming or not. Not that it mattered, of course. But I didn't have to wonder for long, because as Gabbi waved at me from the booth, my eyes met Benjamin's. He was sitting at the bar like he was waiting for me before joining the rest of them.

I tilted my head towards the table, and he stood, grabbed his drink, and slid in right next to me in the big, spacious booth.

"Hi," I said, trying not to pay attention to the wide-eyed expressions around the table at Benjamin and I's wordless communication.

"Hey!" Gabbi said, more cheerful than I thought was normal for her.

"Hello," Harper chimed in, and I watched as her gaze lingered on Benjamin. Oh. Did she think he was available? Because I might not be dating him, but I wasn't about to give him up to anyone else either. Benjamin gave a little smile, also greeting the group, and then everyone descended back into their smaller conversations.

"I saw you when I was heading out, but you were so focused I didn't want to interrupt you," Gabrielle told me.

"It's okay. You know me. Ever the perfectionist. And this project... Well, it needs to be perfect."

Her next words were quiet in my ear: "He looked like a lost little puppy sitting at the bar waiting for you."

"What?"

She sighed. "You don't even see it, do you?" I just shrugged, turning my attention to Benjamin.

"Hey, Angel," he said, and I had the oddest desire to lean into him, to let him wrap that arm that was stretched across the back of the booth around me. "Did you have a good day at work?"

I nodded. "It wasn't bad. You?"

"Fine." He took another sip of his drink.

A waiter came by and asked for our orders. Before I could say anything, Benjamin beat me to it. "Hard, or wine?" he asked me, and my jaw closed shut. Was he going to order for me?

"Hard," I mumbled.

"Can I get another one of these?" He lifted his glass of whiskey. "And she'll have a cosmo. Did I do good, Princess?" he added in a whisper while everyone was busy ordering.

I did my best not to look affected, giving him a small shrug. "I suppose it'll do." He remembered what I was drinking from that first night at the bar at the retreat. A warm feeling pooled in my stomach, and I wasn't sure how to evaluate that. This was supposed to be no-strings-attached sex, just friends with benefits, so why did it matter that he remembered what I liked?

His lips tilted up into a satisfied smile, and I gave him a little scowl. I knocked my knee into his under the table, ignoring how comfortable we'd gotten around each other. He bumped his knee against me, and we kept it up until Benjamin put his hand on my thigh, stilling my leg. *Don't look up at him, don't look up at him, don't look up at him,* I chanted in my head. Thankfully, I was saved by the girl across the table.

"Oh!" Naomi's voice was a welcome distraction from Benjamin's warmth seeping into my skin. "How's the marketing campaign planning going so far, Angelina?"

"Good," I confirmed. "I sent in the pitch today. Once I get the all-clear and budget approval, we'll be good to go." I did my best not to look at Benjamin—you know, the man in *charge* of the budget for our company.

"That's great! Sounds like the hardest part is done then." I nodded, and Naomi didn't miss a beat. "There's this super cool new software I've been working on..."

We dived back into conversations about work, and I avoided

acknowledging the man at my side. When I looked over at Gabbi later in the night, she was staring at me, and I raised my eyebrow in question. She shook her head, but I knew what she meant. She'd been eyeing me with a knowing smirk on her face the entire night, and when her eyes drifted downward, I realized the weight of her look: Benjamin's hand was still resting on my thigh.

I never once tried to move it all night.

～

SOMETIMES I LIKED to wallow in self-pity on the couch, and this was one of those nights. Truly, I was miserable, and the last thing I wanted to do was to see anyone or do anything. I was perfectly content hiding under my pile of blankets for the next five days or so. Maybe a week. And a half. Toothless napping at my feet only added to my desire to never leave the fetal position.

Gabbi was out getting drinks with some of the other members of the HR team. It was weird, after so long being best friends, to think that we had any circles that didn't include each other, but then again, I now had my *not*-relationship with Benjamin, so maybe it wasn't so strange anymore. It was all okay, really. In some ways, I was happy to be miserable alone.

I'd come home from work and immediately collapsed into a ball, where I still sat with no intention of moving until bedtime.

"Toothless," I said, addressing the little black ball of fluff curled up with me. "You're lucky you don't have to go through all of this, girl." She purred at the attention, and even though I knew she didn't know what I was saying, her presence was comforting.

My phone buzzed as I scratched her head, and I fumbled to open it.

BOY SCOUT
Want to come over tonight?

ANGELINA
Can't.

> What's going on?

I sighed, adjusting the heating pad over my stomach as I resumed my position. I'd always had terrible periods, and even on birth control, my cramps were awful, especially at the beginning. All I wanted to do was lay there and wallow for a night. I certainly didn't feel sexy, and I definitely wasn't going over to see Benjamin in my current state.

> Nothing. I just don't feel good.

> Are you sick? Do you need anything? I can bring you soup.

> No, you don't have to do that. Really. It's fine, I'm just on my period. I feel bloated and gross and I just want to lay here and die.

> Okay.

Great. I managed to push him away with my cranky mood. I groaned and laid my head on the arm of the couch, pressing the heating pad further into my skin and hoping the warmth would lessen the pain currently wracking its way through my womb.

I closed my eyes for only a moment, and when I reopened them, it was to the sound of a knock at the door. I checked my phone and realized more than thirty minutes had passed. Heaving myself off the couch, I went to answer it.

The person standing on the other side of the peephole wasn't who I expected.

"Oh," I said, speechless as I opened the door to find brown eyes full of concern.

"Hi. I brought ice cream and chocolate." Benjamin held up a bag like an offering, as if to symbolize, *I come in peace.*

"Well, this is a new benefit," I joked. *So much for rules, huh?* But maybe this was operating in a gray area. It wasn't a date, and it wasn't dinner, and if I paid him back later it wouldn't count as a gift. At least, that was what I told myself.

"I just wanted to make sure you were okay."

"I'll be fine." I bit my lip, eyeing the bag in his hand. "Do you... want to come in?" I looked between him and the messy couch, grateful Gabbi wasn't home. "I was thinking about watching a movie."

He nodded and pushed past me, walking to the kitchen. Benjamin didn't even ask before he started going through my cabinets, clearly looking for bowls and utensils. After the fourth door, he finally found them.

"The ice cream scoop is in the one next to the spoons," I said when he opened the silverware drawer. He looked up at me and frowned when he saw I was resting my head against the cool granite island. "What flavor did you get?"

"Coffee."

"How'd you know that was my favorite?"

"I have my ways, Angel," he said with a wink, digging out a few scoops of ice cream before sliding the bowl in front of me.

"Such service," I said with a fake gasp. "How can I get you to wait on me hand and foot like this all the time?"

"Angelina..." His voice was low, serious. "What do you need, baby?"

I swallowed. I tried not to let it show just how much all this was affecting me. I'd never been one of those girls who got giddy from pet names, but somehow, in this instance, it felt like so much more. I curled my hands around the bowl and spoon before taking it back to the couch, back to my heating pad and the nest I wanted to burrow into. Toothless had disappeared, probably back into Gabbi's room to hide, which didn't surprise me with a stranger in the apartment. Even though Benjamin had come over once in the last week after work, she still wasn't used to having a man around.

Benjamin followed me to the couch, still holding the grocery store bag. He cleared his throat. "I got you some dark chocolate, too. It seems like you like the stuff. My sister said that Midol would probably help the best, so I got that too, but if you need anything else—"

"Benjamin." He called his sister to ask about periods? "Why are you here?" He ignored me and lifted my feet so he could sit underneath them, pulling them onto his lap. "We're not dating," I said, point-blank. "This is just sex, so why are you doing this?"

But Benjamin didn't answer. He started massaging my foot instead. "I've been wondering if those heels you're always wearing make your feet hurt," he muttered as he continued rubbing and massaging, from sole to ankle, spending extra time kneading the arch of my foot.

"They're not so bad," I shrugged, taking a bite of ice cream. "I'm used to them. Pain is beauty, you know."

"You're beautiful no matter what you wear."

Wearing no makeup and curled up in my pajamas on the couch, I felt anything but. I couldn't remember the last time a guy had seen me like this—so vulnerable, without anything to cover up the dark circles under my eyes or with my hair undone. Taking off my makeup had always felt like taking off my armor somehow, like everything that made me confident and sure of myself was left at the door, along with my heels.

Those same heels that I was wearing when I had my legs wrapped around his body. My cheeks heated at the thought, at the vulnerability I was displaying now, but if Benjamin noticed my embarrassment, he didn't comment on it. He just kept rubbing my feet.

"What are we watching?"

"Don't laugh at me." I eyed him skeptically, wondering if he'd judge me for the choice, and then thought, what the hell. "I was thinking *Princess Diaries*."

"The one with Anne Hathaway?"

I blinked. "Yeah."

"Sounds good." He tapped my bowl. "Eat it before it melts."

"You're really okay with watching that?"

"Angelina. I have a sister, remember? I used to watch this kind of stuff all the time."

"Right." I shoved my spoon in my mouth before I said something else that was stupid. He wasn't appeasing me to make me happy anyway, he was just used to it because of his sister.

That was what I told myself to not let my chest fill with warm fuzzies, the way it did as I watched one of my comfort movies side by side with my not-boyfriend, slightly-more-than-friends-with-benefits guy.

I needed to get us back to how we were to start. To the place where we were arguing all the time and I couldn't stand near him for more than five minutes, because this—cuddling up to him on the couch with my legs in his lap watching a movie—was too much. Too vulnerable. Too not me.

And I had no intention of ever losing myself to another person, especially not like this.

CHAPTER 20
Benjamin

The next few days flew by with work, and Angelina and I hadn't spent a night together since last Friday. But that wasn't stopping me from doing something nice for her—no expectations. We'd agreed on *just* friends with benefits, and this felt like something on the friend part that I could fulfill.

"You make the popcorn," I instructed, "and I'll queue up the movie."

"Where's it at?"

"Third one on the left," I called out as I rummaged through my DVD collection.

I wasn't quite sure how we'd gotten here or why she'd even agreed to this, something that fundamentally went against every rule Angelina had set for us, but I didn't care to find out. I would simply enjoy our night together, regardless of how it ended. Yes, the sex was great, but after last week, this was starting to feel like something more. It hadn't even been a whole month yet since the retreat, but I was already feeling things shifting between us.

The thing was, I hadn't shown Angelina all of me, not my favorite hobbies, or my dreams and goals. Not to mention my fears. After everything that happened between us, I didn't think she would make fun of or dismiss it. It felt like the opposite, really

—that she wanted me to share myself with her. Wanted me to tell her about the things that defined me, and to give the same in return.

It was so different from any other relationship I'd been in, and yes, we weren't dating, but she was the only woman who had ever taken the time to get to know the guy underneath the suit. I wasn't just some rich kid with a fancy apartment and a perfect job to her. With Angelina, I finally felt like maybe I was just Benjamin. And it felt good.

I looked at the titles in front of me, pondering. I knew some people thought it was weird that I had hung onto my DVD collection with streaming being so popular, but I liked the way it sent me back to my childhood—rare movie nights with my mom and dad, the three of us kids all curled up with them on the couch after we picked our movie of the night. A nice, happy memory, where none of us were fighting or resenting one another.

"You know, I don't know your favorite movie," I said, thumbing through the cases.

Angelina padded over to the living room with a giant bowl of popcorn in her hands. "If I had to pick, I guess it'd be *10 Things I Hate About You*."

"Really?"

"Is that surprising? You know I like romance. We watched *Princess Diaries* last week."

"Not surprising, I guess, just..." I shook my head. I thought it was funny that she picked a movie about a grumpy girl who fell in love with the man she hated.

She narrowed her eyes. "Watch what you say, Sullivan."

"I wasn't going to say anything!" I raised my hands in mock surrender. But it was on the tip of my tongue: she was so anti-relationship that it amused me how much she enjoyed love stories. Sure, that didn't mean she was anti-*love*, but Angelina certainly seemed to have an aversion to being in it herself.

"What's your favorite movie, anyway? Please tell me it's not a stereotypical dumb guy movie."

"Well, that depends," I grinned. "Where does *Back to the Future* fall?"

"Really? I grew up watching those! They were some of my dad's favorites. I've seen them all a dozen times." Her smile was radiant as she set the bowl down and plopped on the couch.

"Oh no," I shook my head. "We aren't watching in here."

"We're not?" She looked at me skeptically, and I picked up the bowl with one hand and held out the other to her. After she reluctantly took it, I steered her to my bedroom, where I'd strung up lights and got a movie ready—along with the rest of our snacks and a fluffy blanket.

Angelina gaped at me. "What's all this?"

"I wanted to do something nice. You know. After last week." She tilted her head at me, and I tried not to panic too much. Did I overdo it? "Is it too much?" I looked around sheepishly, and then at the title card that was frozen on the TV screen. *You've Got Mail*, starring Tom Hanks and Meg Ryan: somehow, it felt like the antithesis of us. They had hated each other in person but fell in love online, versus us, who hated each other over emails and fell into... whatever this was, in person.

"No," she finally said as I climbed onto my bed. "I've just... No one's ever done something like this for me." Angelina bit her lip. "No one's ever treated me the way you do, period."

I ignored whatever happened inside my chest at those words, and I gave her a cocky grin instead. "So, you like it, Princess?"

"Oh, shut up," she said with a roll of her eyes, still standing next to the bed. "You have to ruin everything."

"Come over here," I said, tugging her onto the bed with me.

"You know, this kind of feels like a date."

"You know..." I wiggled my eyebrows. "I don't quite think I care."

"Benjamin, we made rules for a reason—"

"Fuck the rules." I pulled her closer and covered us with the duvet until she reluctantly let herself lean against the pillows. "I just like being with you."

"I just—"

"Now be quiet and watch the movie," I said, pressing play on the remote and placing the bowl of popcorn in between our legs.

"Bossy," she muttered under her breath, and I resisted flicking her ear or giving her another smartass remark when she laid her head on my shoulder. I nuzzled my nose into her hair, inhaling her scent.

If I was being honest, I barely paid attention to the movie. Her body against mine was too distracting. At one point, she shifted, and I stopped myself from wrapping my arms around her and kissing her neck. That would have her scutter away like a scared squirrel.

The worst part about the movie ending was knowing I had to let her go. But the popcorn was long gone, and there was no way I could convince her to stay for another one. Or the night.

"I should go," she whispered in the semi-darkness, then gave me a light kiss before rolling out of bed. "Thank you for tonight. This was nice."

"Or," I said, scared to do the wrong thing, but deciding I didn't care. I hadn't woken up next to her since the last night of the retreat, and it was killing me how much I wanted to again. "You could stay." I hoped it didn't sound as desperate as I felt.

Angelina paused for a moment before shaking her head. "I can't. We..." Her voice got quiet and low. "We can't."

"We're adults, Angel. We can do whatever we want."

"You know what I mean. We have rules for a reason."

"I'm going to wear you down sooner or later."

"About what?"

"Being friends."

She rolled her eyes. "Isn't it enough that I'm sleeping with you, Sullivan? Being your friend... That would be like selling my soul to the devil."

"Mmm... But a very handsome, sexy devil, no?"

"Oh, shut up."

"You like it," I spoke in a singsong, not caring if my tone was more affectionate than normal. "You like *me*."

Angelina crossed her arms. "No."

"You do. And it's killing you to not be honest with yourself."

"Nope."

"Sure."

I knew the line she wanted to keep between us—the line that it felt like was set in concrete—but I was walking in the sand, hoping for the sea to wipe it away. Waking up next to Angelina in the morning was heaven, but this felt like my personal form of torture.

Though I had one small victory tonight. I'd held her in my arms, she had let me cuddle her. And none of it had been about sex. We had enjoyed each other's company with no need for it whatsoever.

And maybe I was trying to prove to myself that I could be good for her—or maybe it was delusion talking.

"Goodnight, Benjamin," Angelina whispered from the door, and it took everything in me not to beg for a kiss.

"Goodbye," I said, watching her go, trying to put together the pieces of my sanity that kept crumbling any time I was around this girl.

∾

"Hey." Angelina stood across my desk, and I looked up to find her in a pair of houndstooth pants, a black turtleneck, and red heels.

"To what do I owe the pleasure, Ms. Bradford?" I asked, arching an eyebrow as I relaxed in my chair. She had a stack of papers in her hand, and I could tell from the expression on her face that she wasn't here for a friendly chat—or a quickie. Which was *fine*, since we'd already decided that we probably shouldn't do it at work again.

"Do you know anything about this?" She plopped the pile on top of my desk, a large REJECTED stamp in red on top of it.

I frowned. "What's this?"

"My budget for the marketing campaign I submitted the other day. Do you know why it got rejected?" She looked at me like she was hurt, and I realized—

"Oh. Shit. Angel, I didn't do this."

She was still glaring at me, but her posture loosened slightly. "Really?"

"Let me look through it, and I can figure out what happened." I resisted the urge to lean over and smooth her hair back, to ease that wrinkle line on her forehead that she got when she worried too much. "I'm not the only one who approves these things, you know."

"I know, it's just—" She sighed. "You've been emailing me and giving me grief for the past year. I figured nothing would change."

"I would never decline your budget just because it was *you*, I promise. Most of those times, we had to reduce costs of the budget overall and, you know..." She raised an eyebrow, silently telling me to continue. "I liked fucking with you," I grinned. "And it got you to reevaluate your priorities, so really, wasn't it a win on both ends?"

"No," she deadpanned. "All that got you was me hating you."

"Oh, but don't you remember? You don't hate me anymore."

Ah, there was my favorite scowl. "There's a high chance I'm going to start again."

"Give me a bit to go over this, and I'll talk to whoever rejected it. Okay?"

"Yeah. This is just... It's really important to me, you know? It has to be perfect." I didn't ask, but my expression must have said it all. "I haven't told many people yet, but I'm sort of in the running for a promotion. And it's my dream job." Her grin was tentative but radiated so much happiness that I found myself wanting to be a part of her success, no matter how small.

"I won't disappoint you."

She exhaled a steadying breath. "Alright. I'll see you in a bit?"

"I'll text you." Never mind that we could have used the company's instant messaging system. I wanted to reassure her that I wouldn't let her down, but I decided it was best to let my actions speak for themselves.

A couple hours later, after talking with a few other members of the accounting department, I finally texted her. Work was almost done for the day anyway, so I figured I could recap her quickly before we left.

BENJAMIN
I figured it out.

ANGEL
I'm just finishing up a few things down here, I'll come up when I'm done?

Sure.

Thirty minutes later, I heard the telltale sign of her high heels clicking against the tile floors, and there she was, giving me an imperceptible, hopeful smile as she opened my office door. Most people wouldn't notice the difference from her usual on-the-job expression, but I'd been studying her face enough to know the smallest of changes.

I pulled out the stack of paper I'd reprinted and held it up for her. The letters stamped on top now read *APPROVED*.

"What'd you do?" She raised an eyebrow at me, but relief radiated from her.

"I moved some things around with the Marketing budget. Turns out there was a pot of unallocated funds sitting around to be used for discretionary projects. This one, well, it seemed to fit the company's needs."

"You did that?" she said after a moment. Her shock stung a bit. I set the pile down, stood up, and grabbed Angelina's hand with both of mine.

"Why does that surprise you so much? That I'd help you." She shrugged, but I knew it was something deeper. I didn't want to pry, but I hated that she thought I would just brush her off or think her job wasn't important. "If you ever need anything, Angel, you can count on me. Okay? Whatever you need."

"I—" Angelina exhaled deeply. "I was worried that I'd overreacted storming in here like that. That you'd just ignore me. Or tell me you'd look into it but wouldn't actually help." A bitter smile took over her features. "I was ready for you to call me a pretentious bitch, like a lot of people have before."

I smoothed her hair over, offering her whatever semblance of support I could with that simple gesture. I didn't have all the right words, but I'd try. "I'm in your corner, don't forget that. I promise. I'll never dismiss you or brush off your request for help." I tilted her chin up to make her look into my eyes, and I went for the kill, selfish bastard that I was. "Come home with me?"

Angelina hesitated for just a moment, then nodded. I turned my computer off while she went to grab her purse and coat. We met at the elevator, and I was glad for the emptiness of the building at this hour. My car was in the underground parking, and once we were seated, I turned to her with a smile. "So, I'm starving. Are you hungry?"

"What?"

"Food. What do you think, Bradford?"

"Well… We could order in when we get to your apartment?"

I sighed, not hiding my exasperation with her *rules*. "We can go and get something without it being a date if that's what you're worried about."

"That's not—I wasn't worried about that."

"Okay. So, let's go get food."

"Alright. Fine." She gave me that grumpy glare again. "But I'm picking the place."

I grinned victoriously. I knew she just needed a little push, even if she never denied me her fire. I'd come to look forward to the little bits of spite in her eyes when I'd taunt her or spur her on. "Of course. Your pick, Your Highness."

We ended up at a cute little Japanese Ramen place, where we ordered shoyu ramen for me, miso ramen for her, and a side of gyoza and edamame to share. I was pleasantly happy with how our night was turning out. Sure, it wasn't a date, but it felt nice to be somewhere different from our respective places with Angelina.

"Ben?" We were talking about plans for the weekend when I heard someone calling my name.

"Hunter. Hey." Our brief hug was more awkward than anything else, but I was glad to see him. "It's good to see you."

"Who's this?" he asked, nodding at Angelina.

"This is Angelina. We work together." Which was an accurate enough description. I doubted she'd want me broadcasting the terms of our arrangement to anyone, let alone my brother. "Angelina, this is my older brother, Hunter."

Her face made that little O shape like it always did when she realized something, but she quickly turned it into a polite smile and offered her hand to him. "I've heard so much about you. It's nice to officially meet you."

My brother looked at me with a mischievous grin on his face, like he knew something I didn't. "You told her about me, huh?"

"Shut up," I said, giving him a light shove. "It's not like that."

"Not like what?" Hunter said, trying to play all coy and innocent.

"We just ordered our food. Want to join us?" Angelina asked him, and even though I was happy to see my brother since we hadn't been able to get drinks yet, I couldn't help but grimace a little.

"I'm sure Hunter's plenty busy and can't stay," I said, hoping he'd take the hint.

"Nonsense, Ben. I can sit down and have a bite with my brother and his girl."

"Oh, no, I'm not—" Angelina started, but she trailed off right away, apparently struggling to define what we were *not*. Hunter just smirked. Bastard.

"We're not together," I clarified. "Just friends."

"I see," he said, but I heard him mutter something under his breath.

"So," Angelina said, and I could tell she was trying to cut through the tension that was running high between us. "Benjamin told me all about how your family used to camp when you were kids. Do you still like doing that, too?"

"When I can," Hunter answered. "Haven't had much time since college between medical school and then residency."

"Oh, that's right. Benjamin told me that you were a doctor."

Just then, the waiter dropped by with our food, and I'd never been so thankful to have something to keep my mouth occupied. It also allowed Hunter to place his order.

Angelina asked him a few more questions about his job—mostly answered with short, one-word responses or grunts, before she held up some of the gyoza, which I hadn't touched yet. "Want one?" she asked, and I nodded.

Whether she forgot Hunter was sitting with us or just didn't care, she dunked it in the sauce before lifting it to my lips with the chopsticks so I could take a bite. Which was... weirdly intimate, and I didn't know how to react to it. I cleared my throat after I swallowed. "Um. Thank you."

"They're good, right?" She popped another one into her mouth, and I just nodded. They were good, but I thought I might internally combust if she tried to feed me again. Hunter raised an eyebrow but kept quiet otherwise.

So much for insisting we were just friends.

CHAPTER 21
Angelina

Despite Benjamin's help the other day with the budget of my newest project, I still came home from work frustrated, trying to jump through hoops and getting pushback after pushback. I was sick and tired of it. And Gabbi was sick and tired of listening to me complain, but I needed at least one outlet for my anger so that I didn't seethe all night. I was used to that about myself now, but I knew it was a lot to handle sometimes.

That it made *me* a lot to handle.

Still, there was one person I wanted to talk to, and I wasn't sure if this was incredibly terrible of me to ask, but I wasn't sure I cared anymore.

ANGELINA

> Listen, I know this sounds super forward and that's totally not my intention, but Gabbi is tired of listening to me and I could really use you right now.

BOY SCOUT

> Okay?

> Like, I know I hate everyone and I also hate you, but Gabbi just rolled her eyes at me and at least I can scream at you and you'll be mildly turned on by it, so can you come over and let me vent?

Woah there, Princess. What's wrong?

> Please.

Oh, you know it's serious when she pulls out the P card.

> ...
>
> That is NOT the P card.

Don't be dirty, now. We're just having a civil conversation.

> Just get over here before I strangle you alive in your sleep.

That would require you to actually sleep over with me, which you won't do, so it sounds like I'm safe.

> You're impossible.

Angel?

> Yeah?

I'll be there in 20.

> Bring wine.

"Is Gabrielle home?" That was the first thing Benjamin asked when I opened the front door.

"No, she's out on a date."

"I didn't realize she was seeing anyone."

I rolled my eyes. "Because you're *so* caught up on office gossip?"

"Well..." Benjamin scratched the back of his head. "No, but..."

"She's just seeing this girl she met online." I tugged on his shirt to pull him into the living room, only then noticing the bag on his arm. "Did you actually bring me wine?"

"Yes," he scowled, "but you're about to lose wine privileges."

I pouted at him as he went into the kitchen, then followed him when he opened the cabinets to take out two glasses.

"I didn't know she liked girls," he said, finding the corkscrew.

"She likes both. But it's not like you know her that well anyway, right?"

"Oh. Sure. I've only met her a few times in passing. Still."

"You're being weird."

He straightened up. "Oh. *No.* I didn't mean it like that," he hurried to say. "That's great. For her. I mean I was just surprised because—"

"Calm down, I know what you meant: office gossip." Benjamin nodded sheepishly as he opened the bottle of wine. "Yeah, Gabs doesn't really like to advertise that she's bi. Some people are really weird around her when they find out. Assholes. But she's happy with herself, and nothing else matters."

Benjamin handed me a glass full of red wine. "So, is it serious?"

"Gabbi and her girlfriend?" I shook my head. "I don't think so. Gabbi gets in her head a lot. Honestly, sometimes I wonder if she's more motivated in seeing me happy than she is herself."

"Hmm."

"What?"

"Maybe she can focus on herself now."

"Why?"

"Because you're happy with me." There was a smirk plastered on his face and yet I felt the weight of his words wash over me.

"So, what upset you so much that you called me over?" Grateful for the excuse to change the subject, I immediately launched into my rant.

I started pacing back and forth, only taking breaks to sip on wine as I wildly gestured with my hands. "And *then*, she had the audacity to tell me that—Why are you smiling?" I frowned, stopping in front of him. Benjamin was leaning against the counter, lips turned up in the slightest of smiles as he swirled his glass of wine. "Is my unhappiness making you happy?" I crossed my arms over my chest and glared at him. Maybe if I stared long enough, he would feel the daggers coming out of my eyes.

Now that would be a sight for sore eyes—a dagger to the throat. Too bad we weren't in a fantasy novel.

Benjamin seemed to do his best to steel his face, drawing it into a neutral expression. I shouldn't get mad at him over this, and I wasn't—not really, but there was something about how quick he was to incite me to anger that always felt like a flip switching inside of me. "No. Definitely not. It's just—"

"Just what?" I sidled up right next to him, my body an inch from his. "I'd be very careful with your next words, Sullivan."

If this was a game of cat and mouse, I was the cat, and I wasn't afraid to pounce. Literally. Even if that meant we consecrated the kitchen. On second thought, I should probably move this discussion to the bedroom.

Benjamin put his lips close to my ear, and his hot breath against my skin had me feeling a little weak in the knees. "I'm smiling because I like that you're comfortable enough around me to complain to me." He placed a kiss on the sensitive skin under my earlobe.

"I'm not—" I had to swallow a whimper. "*I'm not.*"

"You can deny it all you want, Angelina, but I know the truth."

"And what's that?" I said, narrowing my eyes into slits. If I gripped my wine glass any harder, it would probably shatter. But he'd be all sweet and clean up the mess and freak out over me bleeding, which sounded as equally unappealing as this conversation was.

"You like me," he grinned.

I frowned. "No." Benjamin took the glass out of my hand, guided me to the couch, and then sat beside me. I looked him straight in the eyes when he gave me that smirk. "I don't like you."

"Okay, Angel."

His eyes drifted over the coffee table, landing on the ringed book sitting there. Oh no. My sketchbook. I hadn't put it away earlier, and if he looked through it now...

I dove for it, trying to snatch it before he did, but I was too slow. "Don't!" I said, trying to pry it out of his hands before he could open it.

"What's this?"

And there it was. Page after page of sketches of his face. And his back, his shoulders, his chest, beautifully devoid of a shirt after I saw him swimming during the retreat. That I was mortified was an understatement. I opened and closed my mouth like a fish, with no sound coming out. Great.

"Definitely don't like me," Benjamin smirked, flipping through the sketchbook. I wasn't embarrassed that he was seeing the drawings, just—I hated when he was right. I didn't want to admit it, and he knew it. I shook my head, and he laughed. "Come here, baby." He pulled me against his chest, and I relaxed into his hold as he kissed the crown of my head. "You don't have to hide from me. Okay?"

He tilted my chin up so my eyes would meet his, and when I finally nodded, he kissed me, sweet and long, until I was gasping and begging for more.

And then I dragged him to my bedroom and let him help me forget all of my worries.

"Coming June 2023: Angelina Bradford meets her match!" Noelle grinned, holding up a pretend notebook and paper like she was going to write the book.

"You know," Charlotte said, stirring her soda with a straw. "I think there's a book already named something like that."

Noelle laughed. "Whoops. But seriously, I think there's something there."

I hadn't been able to contain it any longer after Gabbi's smug look, so when she mentioned my *mystery man*, the whole story spilled out of me.

Well—most of it. I wasn't divulging the details of our sex life to my friends, especially not the way Benjamin pinned me down and held my wrists while he fucked me last night. Damn. Too hot of a thought for a friends day. I mentally fanned myself.

"I swear, it's just casual—nothing serious."

"I remember when I used to say that too. Look how that turned out for me."

"Shut up," I said, rolling my eyes at Noelle playfully. "Just because you got lucky doesn't mean the rest of us will."

"I don't know, Ang," said Charlotte, who seemed deep in thought. "He's met your brother. That's more than any of your other flings ever got."

I groaned. "This isn't a fling. It's a mutually beneficial transaction. With rules. We have sex and that's it."

"That's it?" Gabbi raised an eyebrow, finally chiming in. She seemed a little out of it today, and I was sure it had something to do with her date last night, but I wasn't going to mention it if she didn't.

"Yes," I reaffirmed. "That's it." We didn't need to talk about the movie date, or the way Benjamin had brought me ice cream when I was on my period with no expected reciprocation whatsoever. Nor was it important to mention that he always made sure I came before he did.

The first time I gave him a blow job, he hadn't even let me

finish before he was pulling me up and throwing me on the bed to have his way with me. I sighed as memories of that night came back to me. When had I gotten so obsessed with sex? It felt like ever since I started having it regularly, it was constantly lurking in my mind.

And I had definitely already broken the no more than three nights a week rule. But we didn't sleep over, and the rest of the rules remained intact. Even if some nights all we did was make out and play around with each other without even having sex.

It was casual. We didn't talk about the future. We weren't making plans, buying each other presents, or giving each other expectations. He didn't make me dinner and expect me to clean up after him. In fact, he didn't cook for me at all. It was takeout or delivery if we did share a meal, and even then, I tried to keep those to a minimum after the disaster at the ramen restaurant. I'd gotten so swept up in his eyes that I literally fed him with my chopsticks, and the way he'd bitten that dumpling—with his eyes focused straight on mine... God. And then he came back for another bite. With his brother sitting there. Like I said, a disaster.

"So, Noelle," I said, diverting the conversation from me and my not-relationship. "How's your first month of school been?"

"*Ohmygod*. So good! I love my students. One of them brought me a bag of peanut butter M&Ms the other day after I said they were my favorite." She sighed contentedly. "This is the best job I could have ever imagined." A little blush spread across her cheeks. "And it doesn't hurt that Matthew's office is only a floor away. We get lunch together almost every day."

"You guys are the cutest," Charlotte said. "I hope I find something like that one day."

"You will," I reassured her.

"You all will," Noelle said fervently. "Seriously. And then we're all going to buy houses next to each other and live our best lives until we're old grandmas playing bingo in our free time."

I huffed. "Can't we be doing something cool? Bingo is so lame."

"Okay," Noelle made a face. "We'll be reading romance novels until we're 95 years old while we sit around drinking lemonade and tea and gossiping about our children's children. Sound better?"

Gabbi laughed. "You're crazy."

"Maybe." Noelle grinned smugly. "But if it happens, you'll be eating your words."

"I hope we're always together," Charlotte said, voice small, and I knew what she meant. I reached over and clasped her hand, giving it a tight squeeze.

"I don't know a lot about the future and how it's going to turn out, but I do know that there's not a chance you guys are leaving me, ever. Sorry to say, you're stuck with me." I smiled, and Charlotte squeezed my hand back.

"Same."

I truly didn't know where I'd be without them in my life. They were as much of a support and lifeline to me as my family had ever been. If I ever needed anything—I knew they'd have my back. If I was acting stupid, I knew they'd call me out on it.

It was why I knew that we'd stand the test of time. We'd been friends for eight years, and nothing would change that.

"Everyone's still free for the Halloween Party in a few weeks, right?" Noelle asked, perking her head up from her phone.

"Oh, yeah!" Gabbi grinned. "I can't believe you guys agreed to host. This is our first time not having it in an apartment since college."

"Matthew's inviting some of his friends as well, so if any of you wants to bring someone, feel free!" she grinned. "The more the merrier. The only requirement is, of course, as tradition dictates—costumes!"

"Oh, hell yes," I said. "Are we doing a group thing again this year, or...?"

"Well..." Noelle turned sheepish. "Matthew and I were kind of talking about doing something with the two of us. But if you three want to do something together, that's okay!"

That's when I realized things were really changing. Of course Noelle would want to dress up with her boyfriend for their first Halloween together. It was to be expected. And it was great.

What was not expected was my sudden desire to have someone to dress up with too.

CHAPTER 22
Benjamin

"Hey. I come bearing food," Angelina said, going straight for the kitchen. She'd gone home after work to change—a loose black one-shoulder sweater and a tight pair of denim jeans that showed off her killer legs: not her usual fancy outfit, but a stunner nonetheless.

"Mmh, smells good."

We'd devolved into a pattern: she came over to my place and we'd eat and talk or watch a movie, get our sexual desires out of our systems, and then she'd go home. Or, if Gabbi wasn't there, I'd go over to Angelina's. The main perk of movie nights at their house was Toothless curled up in my lap: I liked petting her head until she was purring for me. Something Angelina always frowned at: she hated it a little bit how much Toothless loved me.

It was almost infuriating how much she insisted on following her rules, because there was casual, and then there was… whatever we were doing.

Her eyes drifted to the TV, where I was in the middle of playing *The Legend of Zelda: The Wind Waker* for about the five hundredth time. I could have been playing *Breath of the Wild*, but there was just something about the childhood nostalgia of this game that kept me coming back. Angelina flopped on the giant couch. "What are you playing?"

The interest she showed in my hobbies always left a pleasant feeling of warmth in my chest.

"*Zelda*."

"How do you play?" she asked, picking up a controller.

That made me pause. "You want to play with me?" I asked, surprised.

"Sure, why not?" Angelina tossed her hair over her shoulder. "It can't be that hard, can it?"

I snorted. Sure, there were harder games to play, but I had it on Hero mode, which was more difficult than normal. I saved my game so I could turn it off. "Maybe we could play something together instead?" I suggested, and she gave me the smuggest grin I'd ever seen. *I'm going to kick your ass,* it said, *and you're going to like it.* Oh, I certainly would.

I rifled through my two-player games, finally pulling out *Mario Kart*, hoping Angelina would enjoy that. I swapped out the cartridge and then handed her the second player controller.

"We used to play this all the time when I was younger. Emily always complained to our parents that Hunter and I always won, so we'd have to let her win every once in a while, otherwise we'd get it taken away."

Angelina laughed. "Yeah, that sounds about right."

"Want to bring the food over here before we start?" She hopped up to grab it. "I'm starving," I said, admiring the delicious looking Italian food.

"Well, let's dig in."

After we'd both filled up on pasta and I'd cleaned up the dishes, we picked up the controllers. "Ready?"

"Ready to kick your butt."

"We'll see about that." I was the reigning *Mario Kart* champ at my house, and if I wanted to beat her tonight, well... No one could blame me for being competitive. It was in my veins—that's what it was like being the younger brother.

I heard her humming as she studied the controller while I moved us to the character selection screen. Angelina chose Rosalina and I picked Link, which made her chuckle. I quickly flipped through the rest of the settings, setting us up for an easy 4 track race.

I either seriously overestimated my skills, or *majorly* underestimated hers, because at the end of the final course, Angelina had finished first every time.

"You totally hustled me!" I said, jaw dropping open.

Angelina laughed, her brilliant blue eyes sparkling with mischief. "Benjamin, you do remember that I have a brother, right? I've been kicking his ass in Mario Kart for a *long* time." She leaned in a little. "I just wanted to fuck with you."

This woman...

I let a moment pass before I picked her up and tossed her over my shoulder, eliciting a shriek of surprise. "You know," I said, hand on her ass, "I think I know exactly what kind of punishment you should get for that."

"Punishment? But I won!"

"I know. But that doesn't mean you're getting off easy tonight." I dropped her back on the couch, licking my lips as I pinned her down with my body. "Gotcha."

And then I kissed her until she was panting and rolling her hips against me. I wanted to take my sweet time with her.

"You're the worst."

"I think you mean the best," I said, nestling my body between her legs. "I promise it's okay to admit that you like something other than the way I fuck you, Angel." I pulled up her sweater and trailed my lips down the line of her stomach. "I won't hold it against you."

She squirmed underneath me. "Benjamin..."

"Mmh. Should we bring this to my bed, Princess?"

"Uh-uh," Angelina shook her head. "Need you now. Couch works."

I laughed, but I intended to take my time and show her exactly how badly I needed her, too.

Later, when our desires were more than satiated and movie credits were rolling on the screen, Angelina cleared her throat. She was wearing a pair of my flannel pajama bottoms, looking adorable. "You know, we never talked about exclusivity."

"What do you mean?"

"If we were okay with the other sleeping with someone else."

"Are you?" I said after a bit, dreading her response. I knew how I felt—I didn't have the desire to be with anyone else. I hadn't in a long time.

Angelina shook her head. "No."

I gave her a brief nod, relief washing over me. "Good." My hand slid around to the back of her neck, pulling her in closer, almost nose to nose. "I'm not either."

The vulnerability in her eyes was as clear as day as she held my gaze. I knew this was a risky territory for her. "Good," she finally said.

"Okay."

When Angelina slipped out of my apartment like a bat into the night, I stayed awake, wondering what the hell I was doing with her.

∼

ANGEL

How was your day?

And if your response is "great", I will slap you through the phone.

I'm serious. Do not try me, Sullivan. I know where you live.

BENJAMIN

My day was fine. Better now. Did something happen?

> Just overheard some assholes gossiping about me by the water fountain. I've decided I hate all men.
>
> Including you. Sorry. I haven't given up on my Benjamin Sullivan hate crusade.
>
> Anyway, men are trash.
>
> Why aren't you responding??

Open your door.

ANGEL

> There is absolutely no way you haven't seen How to Lose a Guy in 10 Days. It's a classic. WTF??
>
> I'm coming over right now. No sex until the movie is finished. No objections.

BENJAMIN

Do you want Chinese food? I'm thinking about getting some on my way over after work.

ANGEL

> Omg. That sounds heavenly. Please.
>
> Sweet & Sour Chicken and noodles for me, please!
>
> Also—I don't share. Get your own.
>
> Thank you.

Your wish is my command, Princess.

ANGEL

Do you think the concept of While You Were Sleeping is weird? Like, she falls in love with his brother while she's pretending to be with a guy who's in a coma. If that happened with your brother, how would you feel???

BENJAMIN

...

You're not getting out of this. Don't even try ignoring me.

I KNOW WHERE YOU SLEEP

Packing my boxes as we speak. HAH!

brb going to go fall in love with your brother!

You wouldn't dare.

I would.

Answer the question.

Can we just watch the movie together instead?

... be there soon.

ANGEL

So in the book I'm reading, the guy does this thing, with his uh...

sends picture of the page

What do you think?

DISRESPECTFULLY YOURS

BENJAMIN

Are you propositioning me for sex right now? Because I think that's a violation of sexual harassment in the workplace.

I wouldn't know. I skipped the seminar to make out in a canoe.

But I'm sure you wouldn't know anything about that. Going to have to call my canoe boyfriend instead.

… get over here and fuck me, please.

Send me the next page first.

BENJAMIN

Should I get food?

ANGEL

Pizza. Pepperoni, please.

And if you put pineapples on it, I will never speak to you again.

Get garlic knots too. Those are the bomb.

… A double order. Thanks.

Alright, your Highness.

And for the record, I don't like pineapple on pizza either. But I'm glad to know where you stand.

What movie are we watching tonight?

I'm voting Mamma Mia! Exclamation mark necessary. Because it's a great freaking movie.

JENNIFER CHIPMAN

> One of these days I think my man card is going to be revoked from all of these romcoms we're watching.

Pff. You love it.

> I got a new multiplayer game for the Switch. Want to kick my ass again?

I like that you're just admitting now that you're never going to win against me. Hah!

> One of these days I'm going to get you to play an actual game with me.

I mean, if you teach me how to play, sure. I don't mind playing the games you love.

> Huh.

... I'm going to regret saying that, aren't I?

??? BENJAMIN?

> :)

BENJAMIN

> Work is killing me. I have deadlines galore and have to stay late tonight. Raincheck?

ANGEL

No!! How dare they!! We had plans!

> I'm sorry, really...

They're going to pay for this.

Benjamin?

> What?

DISRESPECTFULLY YOURS

> Unlock your office door.

BENJAMIN
> I'm in bed and I can't stop thinking about how gorgeous you looked at the office today. How did we ever hate each other again?

ANGEL
> Speak for yourself, Sullivan.

> I do love it when you lie.

> Also, in the interest of full honesty, I have been using a photo of a cat as your contact icon this whole time. I think I need a new one.

> WTF?? At least tell me it's a cute cat. Or a fierce one. Like a jaguar.

> *sends photo*

> I'm never talking to you again.

> Use this one. *photo attached*

> Wow. I've been blessed with a photo of THE Angelina Bradford. It's a true miracle.

> If you keep it up, THE Angelina Bradford is going to punch you in the arm. In that spot where I know you have a perpetual bruise. HARD.

> I have dark chocolate cake with raspberries?

> Hold that thought.

~

In the blink of an eye, two weeks had passed, and not a day went by that I didn't talk to or see Angelina in some capacity. Strangely enough, I'd come to rely on it.

> **ANGEL**
> Come over tonight?
>
> I need you.

I could never resist her when she said something like that to me. Thinking about being inside her, holding her in my arms, the look of blissful pleasure on her face when she comes... Fuck. I was in too deep with this girl already. Only a month, and Angelina had sneaked into my brain and now she seemed to reside there. I'd gone out for drinks with Hunter, and I couldn't even look at another woman at the bar. At least three girls flirted with me throughout the night, but I couldn't care less.

I knew Hunter noticed I'd been acting strange, especially after that night at the restaurant. I tried to play it off because I hadn't told him about the true nature of my and Angelina's relationship —or lack of one. And what would he say? He was my older brother. I doubted he'd be impressed with a girl who wanted to ride me at any opportunity but had no desire to actually be with me. I didn't want him to be disappointed in me. In my inability to make a woman stay.

Maybe, I thought bitterly, maybe he wouldn't judge me. He was a doctor; did he even have time for a relationship himself? It was more likely than not that there was a doctor or nurse he liked getting freaky with at the hospital. I had my fair share of hookups and failed relationships in high school and college, but so did Hunter.

When I showed up at Angelina's that night, my eyes widened as I took her in. She was wearing a robe tightly wrapped around her waist and her long, black hair was unbound and flowing down her back. Beautiful. *And mine.* Even if it was temporary, she was mine, and I wasn't going to let her forget it.

"You're a fucking goddess," I told her, following her into the apartment.

"Gabbi isn't home." That was all it took for me to pull her into my arms, feeling the need to touch her, to taste her.

"Good," I said, and then I kissed her, deeply, passionately, as I pressed every inch of her body against mine. Neither of us pulled away until we were forced to come up for air, panting roughly; the heat in her gaze was intoxicating as we stood in the living room, staring at each other.

A soft meow came from behind me, and I chuckled. "Should we bring this to your bedroom? I wouldn't want eyes on us."

"Eyes—what?" she said, then followed my gaze to look at the ball of fur on the couch. She scoffed, giving me a playful punch to the shoulder before tugging me into her room. "I hate you."

"No, you don't," I laughed.

"Mhm. Jury's still out." And before I could reply, she pushed me down to a sitting position at the edge of her bed. "I have a surprise for you." Angelina grinned, her black satin robe loosening around her body as she undid the tie.

And let it fall to the floor.

"Fuck, baby," I breathed, eyes scorching a path over her naked skin. I wanted to rip the black lace lingerie off her with my teeth. Wanted to kiss every inch of her skin and show her just how much I longed to worship her. God, I'd do this every fucking night if she let me. But there were rules, and I wasn't allowed to break them. "I don't want anyone else to see you like this but me," I said, gripping the back of her thighs.

She raked her hand through my hair. "Only you."

Fuck if that didn't turn me on even more. I stroked her back, her waist, up to her covered chest. I rubbed my fingers over her hardened nipples, visible through the lace of the bodysuit she wore. It was adorned with pearls and ribbons, and somehow it was so very her. Elegant and sophisticated, yet dirty. "Such a good girl," I praised, reveling in the little gasp she emitted as I pinched her sensitive skin.

"You haven't even seen the best part," Angelina gave me a sly grin, taking one of my hands and guiding my fingers between her thighs to her—Fuck. This fucking thing was crotchless. Holy hell.

She leaned down to kiss my jaw and lick my neck, while her blood-red painted fingernails went to my crotch, palming my erection and making me hiss. The things this woman could do to me... One second she was getting on my nerves, and the next I was getting on my knees for her.

"What am I going to do with you?" Her eyes were lidded with lust as I rubbed my thumb over her clit, pleased to see her breath coming out in short puffs. "Hmm, Princess? Will you tell me what you want?"

"I want you to fuck me."

I hummed. "Beg me for it."

The fire in her gaze burned, and she dropped to her knees in front of me, icy blue eyes never leaving mine. "Please," she moaned, cupping herself. "I need you."

I unzipped my pants, and she licked her lips. "Suck me." That was all I needed to say before she freed my cock and wrapped her lips around me.

"Ah, that's it. Good girl," I groaned as Angelina ran her tongue over my tip, licked and sucked me, alternating between languid exploration and quick movements that made my head spin. God, it was heaven inside her mouth. And her confidence made me want to take this a little further—if she'd let me.

"Angelina. Do you trust me?" I cupped her cheek to make her look at me. There was no hesitation in her nod, so I tilted her chin and slowly plunged deeper in her mouth. "Tap my thigh if it's too much."

The sound of her agreement vibrated around my dick as she took me like the little overachiever she was.

I fisted her hair, tugging on it slightly to get a good grip as Angelina let me slide deeper in her throat. I closed my eyes when she made a soft choking sound. I let her breathe and then tried again. Her hands grasped my pants, and I started fucking her mouth in earnest, with shallow thrusts. The sounds she made around my cock were music to my ears; the saliva pooling in her mouth was making it easier for me to move in and out. I wanted nothing but to spill over her pretty lips, to paint her tongue with my seed, but I needed to be inside her more.

It was an effort to pull away, Angelina rocking back onto her heels before looking up at me. In a split-second decision, I pulled off my tie, snapping it tightly in my hands, and I wrapped it around her eyes, tying it off on the back of her head. "Good?" I asked, holding my breath.

Her voice was barely above a whisper when she said, "Yes." And I laid her down on the bed.

"Good girl," I said against her ear, letting the words dance in the tense air before kissing down her neck, over the lacy fabric that concealed her breasts, and down her stomach until I reached her thighs.

The fact that she had surrendered all control to me made me even more eager to bury myself inside of her, and I didn't even bother to remove my pants before I rolled a condom on and entered her.

"Oh, fuck," I moaned. "Fucking perfect." I pinned her hands to the bed, forcing her to take everything I was giving her and nothing less. She cried out when I placed her leg on my shoulder before thrusting in again, and again, and *again*, until we were both breathless, and I grabbed her neck to claim her lips in a searing kiss.

Nothing had ever felt as good as whatever was between the two of us at that moment. And that's when it hit me, so suddenly that it almost made me double over: I liked Angelina more than just as a friend with benefits. I wanted more with her, I wanted…

I wanted everything.

CHAPTER 23
Angelina

He wrapped his hand around my neck, and my vision almost blacked out.

"You look so pretty with my hand around your throat, baby," Benjamin purred, squeezing lightly on the sides of my neck, not tight enough to bruise or make me feel unsafe, but enough that every sensation was amplified.

I had never done this—given myself to someone so fully, let someone take control like this. But, fuck, I liked it. Reason flew out of my mind and all I could feel was the pounding of my heart and the pleasure engulfing my body. There was nothing I loved more than Benjamin taking control, blocking out everything that wasn't him. It was a high I'd never get tired of.

"Benjamin," I cried out, his other hand keeping a firm hold of my waist as he rutted into me relentlessly. "I'm gonna—"

"That's it," he said. "Come for me, Angel."

His words, combined with the rough way he was treating me, sent me over the edge, and I tumbled into bliss as my fingers fisted the sheets and my toes curled. It was pure ecstasy, and I didn't hold back the moans as he continued fucking me through it.

His silky tie was still covering my eyes, so I couldn't see him. I could only feel his hands on my body, his lips kissing me—always in unexpected places, always hungry for me.

Benjamin grunted, letting me know he was close, and I couldn't help the way my legs wound around him, locking him in. He loosened his grip around my neck, and then his thumbs dug cruelly into my hips as he came with a loud cry. Even though I couldn't see his dilated pupils or the sweat on his forehead, I'd memorized his face enough that I could picture it all.

I was catching my breath when he leaned his forehead against mine, and a moment later I was pulled up, sitting on his lap with him still inside of me. We both groaned at the change of angle.

His hands stroked my arms gently, then untied the makeshift blindfold, allowing me to see just how undone he was. I didn't want to know what I looked like after he'd fucked me so roughly —not at all the perfect, polished Angelina I liked to present to the world. But I didn't care anymore. Not with him.

"We should..." I said, pulling away, but he shook his head and buried his face in between my breasts.

"Let's just—" His shuddering breath make my skin erupt in goosebumps. "Stay like this. For a minute. Please."

"Okay," I relented, bringing my hands to his hair, a complete role reversal of what we'd done mere minutes ago. I let my fingers dance over his shoulder blades, the back of his neck, down to his collarbones, content to just touch him. I went down further, unbuttoning the rest of his shirt and pushing it off, wanting to feel his skin. It was inebriating to know he was so taken with me that he didn't even bother to take his work clothes off. To know he lost control because of me.

"Angelina," he bit out, "if you keep doing that..."

Oh. I couldn't keep the satisfied grin on my face when I felt him hardening inside of me again—already. I ran my hands over his arms, appreciating his muscles, before I started placing kisses on his collarbones, down his pecs, and his beautifully sculpted chest. One of these days I needed to go with him to the gym, just so I could sit and watch him work out. I was pretty sure it would reduce my panties to a sopping mess, but the view would be worth it.

Plus, maybe I could get him to fuck me in the shower afterward. I moaned out loud at the thought, and Benjamin squirmed under me. "Angel," he warned.

I laughed. "Sorry, I can't help it. I'm obsessed with your body."

He smirked, kissing me on the lips before finally pulling out of me. I already missed him, but I knew it wouldn't be long before he was back and ready to go again.

I wrapped the sheet around my body as he padded into the bathroom. "You," he said, leaning against the doorframe after he finished, "are insatiable." He'd also stripped his pants off, leaving that wonderful erection free to the air, and his naked body made me foam at the mouth.

I did my best to give him a sultry smile. "I can't help it when I have you."

"Mmm." He came back to bed—crawled, really; pulled the sheet off of me and then proceeded to push each of the straps of my bodysuit down to bare my chest. "I'm going to take my time now. Taste every inch of you."

"Oh god," I moaned as he licked one nipple and then lightly bit it. I brought my hand to my clit, needing the friction. I knew he'd get me close to climaxing and then pull away, and I was going to die if he didn't let me come soon. But he grabbed my wrists and pinned them behind my back.

"Uh-huh." He made a tsk sound with his tongue. "You're not allowed to touch yourself. Now, are you going to be a good girl or do I need to tie you up?"

"Benjamin," I pleaded as he continued to hold my wrists, licking and kissing all over my chest.

"You'd like that, wouldn't you?" I couldn't help rolling my hips into him. "Tying you up it is, then." A moment later, I was on my back and my hands were tied together and to the bed frame.

There was the telltale sound of a condom wrapper, and my own voice crying out when Benjamin pushed into me, all the way to the hilt. And then he did take his time, lighting my body on fire with every touch, with every stroke, with every languid thrust. He left me panting and crying for a release as he brought me to the edge repeatedly, but never quite let me tumble over.

"Stop teasing me," I cried the umpteenth time I felt my orgasm slip away.

"Say please, pretty girl," he cooed, and I was lost in his eyes as he rocked into me.

"Please," I begged, uncaring of how pathetic I sounded. "Please, please, please, *please*—ah!" Stars clouded my vision when he finally let me come, the sweetest rush of adrenaline coursing through my body.

I didn't know how long it took me to come back, but when I did, my hands were free and Benjamin was massaging them. I hummed, still feeling like jelly. "I guess I do like being tied up after all." I closed my eyes and smiled when he laughed.

Minutes later, we were lying in bed, refreshed and cleaned up. I looked over at him, watching his chest as it rose and fell in time with his calm breathing.

"That was…" I ran my fingers over my neck, tracing where his fingers had been, then I did the same with my wrists. I was glad we were fully in the fall season, with most days cold and wet; that way, I could cover up any mark Benjamin left on me and no one would be the wiser. I did love to look at them, though. The visual representation of his possessiveness.

He hummed in agreement, nuzzling his head against my breasts. I wasn't going to admit it to him, but I liked being like this—curled up against each other, skin to skin.

There were a lot of things I'd been thinking of lately that I hadn't told him. How much I enjoyed spending time with him. How much I enjoyed our text message conversations. When he'd bring food over after work and we'd just sit, cuddled up in front of the TV on the couch at his place or mine, and go through my list of rom-com movies.

We watched *Back to the Future* the other day. I liked watching his favorite movies with him, too.

What I didn't like was finding myself *wanting* to go with him to Noelle and Matthew's Halloween party. October 31st was getting close, so tonight was as good as any to ask him. Better to rip the band-aid off right away.

"So, I know this may sound a little weird, but Noelle is hosting a Halloween party next week. And... I was wondering if you might want to go with me?"

I held my breath for what felt like the longest minute of my life.

"Hmm," Benjamin mused. "That depends. Are costumes involved?"

I snickered. "That's your make-or-break requirement? Costumes?"

"I think it's fun. Sue me."

I stuck my tongue out at him. "Well, *yeah*. It is a costume party. Or, at least, they are highly encouraged. It's Noelle's favorite holiday, so she goes all out."

"Then yeah. I'm in." He pulled me on top of him, grinning like the Cheshire Cat. "Do you get to pick what we wear, or do I?"

"I'm going to regret this, aren't I?" I smoothed down the one strand of hair that always seemed to fall onto his face.

"Oh, most definitely."

"Bring it on, Benjamin Sullivan. Do your worst." I liked to think I'd known him long enough to trust he wouldn't put me in something too stupid or too embarrassing, so I wasn't too worried about submitting control to him in this. Goodness knows I loved it enough in the bedroom.

Benjamin closed his eyes and relaxed, holding me tight. I poked him in the arm after a minute. "You have to go," I said, looking at the door.

He pouted before opening his eyes. "What if I stayed?"

I sighed. "You know how this works. This isn't a thing. If you stay over, you're going to get attached, and I can't deal with a clingy man who won't leave me alone." I stared at him, hoping he'd understand how serious I was about this. "I won't."

"You're so worried I'm going to get attached to you. But what if you get attached to me?"

"Not going to happen."

"Why not?"

"Because I don't like you."

"Nice try. Wanna go again?"

I huffed and lifted myself up on my knees. "I told you; I don't do relationships. I don't have time for it, so if you're looking for anything more than just a fuck buddy, the door is over there." I crossed my arms after pointing towards the hall.

Never mind that he was right. I *was* getting attached to him, and that was exactly why I couldn't budge on this. I couldn't risk it. I needed to guard myself. My rules were already crumbling all around us, but I had to stay firm on this one. My heart was on the line.

For a moment I thought he would insist more—his eyes were screaming something I didn't want to read. But then he only let out a sigh and shook his head, giving up on it. He pecked me on the cheek before rolling out of bed and silently getting dressed.

I fought every instinct to take my words back, to ask him to come back to bed, to hold me until I fell asleep. I watched him go, and when he murmured, "I'll text you tomorrow," before disappearing out the door, all I could think about was how much longer I could keep this up without it breaking me apart.

～

IT TURNED OUT I DID, in fact, regret letting him pick our costumes. Not because I didn't look hot in my suit, but because it was skin-tight leather, which wasn't the most comfortable piece of clothing. Luckily, Portland Halloweens were generally cold and rainy, so I hoped I wouldn't sweat to death at Noelle and Matthew's house.

I raised my eyebrow as Benjamin walked out of his bedroom in his costume. "You totally already had that, didn't you?"

"I'll never tell," he said, but the smirk gave him away.

He stood closer to me, tugging at my hair that I had curled and left down. "I like it when you wear your hair like this." I couldn't ignore the way he looked at me, with so much heat and passion in his eyes that I constantly found myself lost in them. "But..." Benjamin eyed me from head to toe: my leather bodysuit, the heeled boots, the gloves in my hand with little claws on the end, the utility belt clipped around my waist that held a fake jeweled necklace in one of its pouches. I'd even gotten a whip—though I had no intention of using it. "I think you're missing something."

"What's that?" I fluttered my eyelashes at him. He wasn't wearing his cowl yet, but he'd already done his makeup: his eyes were smudged with black. It made me giggle, seeing him like that, but he looked good.

Benjamin revealed something from behind his back and placed it in my hands.

"Where'd you find this?" I gasped. It was a replica of Anne Hathaway's headpiece when she played Selina Kyle—Catwoman—in *The Dark Knight Rises*. It was beautiful and stunningly made. I'd found a few 3-D printed ones, but nothing with this level of detail. "I looked for one all week, but I couldn't find anything that would get here in time." My suit wasn't a perfect replica of hers—nothing like Benjamin's Batman suit—but this would tie the whole outfit together. And, I had to admit, it looked so freaking *cool*.

"I did." Benjamin grabbed it from my hands and slipped it in my hair before smoothing a few strands down and pulling the front zipper of my suit just an inch. "Perfect," he whispered, and even though I'd just applied my bright red lipstick, I wouldn't have cared at that moment if he had kissed me and messed it all up.

We might not have been dating, but Benjamin and I were friends now. Our hookups had turned into something more. I didn't know what it meant that we spent more of our nights together than apart—even without sleeping over—but if I was being honest... I liked this. Liked having someone that I found myself relying on, a little bit more every day.

"Ready to go, Batboy?" I asked, patting his chest where his bat symbol sat.

He scowled. "It's Bat*man*."

"I know, silly," I laughed, and Benjamin smacked my ass before pushing me out the door of his apartment. "Hey!" I rubbed my butt, easing the stinging sensation. "Don't do that."

"But you like it when—" I placed my hand over his mouth, eager to keep the words from spilling out where anyone could hear. I didn't need his neighbors to know my sexual preferences, thank you very much.

"Benjamin!" I shrieked when he licked my hand. "Gross."

"My tongue has been in your mouth but that's gross?"

"I know where your mouth's been, but do you know where my hand has been?"

"You washed your hands ten minutes ago. Right after you used them to—" I kissed him to shut him up.

"Careful, sweetheart," I purred against his lips, tracing my fingers across his chest. I hadn't put the gloves on yet, but I had gotten a special manicure for the occasion: black stiletto nails, longer than usual, that in themselves looked like the perfect Catwoman claws. I was a little obsessed with them. "I bite."

"Mmm," Benjamin said, wrapping an arm around me. "Oh, Kitty-cat, I hope you do."

"Better be on your best behavior then," I said with a wink.

When we parked the car in front of Noelle and Matthew's house, my jaw dropped. I was absolutely floored. Because Noelle had always loved Halloween, had always decorated her dorm and then our shared house junior and senior year, but *this*? This was a whole new level. The entire front yard was decorated, and when we went in, the inside was decked out as well. Fake cobwebs dusted cabinets and couches, and everywhere I looked was something Halloween themed: pumpkins, skeletons, ghosts, you name it. There wasn't a surface free of knickknacks.

We wandered towards the back of the house where we could hear voices. The guests were mostly adults, since very few of our friends had kids yet. Two of them were Matthew's best friend and his wife, Bryan and Elizabeth, whose son Theo was running around dressed in a dinosaur costume onesie. They were dressed as dinosaur trainers from Jurassic Park. It was so cute.

"Angelina!" Noelle exclaimed, a smile so big it overtook her rosy cheeks. Her hair was styled in two braids to go with her costume: Anna from *Frozen*.

"You look amazing!" I said as she pulled me into a hug.

"And you look hot, damn!" Noelle appraised me before giving me a thumbs up. Matthew entered the dining room with their dog close behind. Snowball looked adorable with a pair of antlers —she was Sven, while Matthew was dressed as Kristoff. Truly, he was perfect, especially now that he let his hair grow long.

"Thank you," I laughed. "Noelle, shouldn't Snowball be Olaf? You know, since he's white?"

"Oh." She looked at Matthew, who just scrunched his nose. "Well. Matthew doesn't really like Olaf, plus we thought she'd be cuter with her little antlers. And look! Her collar has bells on it!" That explained the noise—though I wasn't convinced that Matthew's costume didn't also contain bells.

Just then, Charlotte came into the room, dragging my brother along. Her hair looked like it'd been spray-painted pink, and she was wearing pink leggings as well as a pink leotard, decorated in orange stripes. I pieced together what they were supposed to be when I saw Daniel wearing a Shark costume: Sharkboy and Lavagirl.

I almost squeaked from the adorableness of it all. Although I had no idea how she convinced him to dress in a couple's costume while I could never even get him to dress up for Halloween with me. One year during college, he had—very begrudgingly—agreed to go as the Dipper Pines to match with my Mabel costume from *Gravity Falls*, but after that, we were back to a resounding no any time I asked.

"Oh my god," I whispered to myself. "This is hilarious."

Benjamin leaned down to say in my ear, "Do you think they remember me?" Oh—right. I forgot for a moment there. I had spent so much of the last month with him, but he hadn't spent time with any of my friends yet. He'd only met them all briefly during Charlotte's birthday dinner, but I'd sent him away before he could really introduce himself. And now... Everything felt different than it did a month ago.

He nudged my arm, prompting me to introduce him, properly this time. I pulled him to my side, looping my arm through his, and cleared my throat to get their attention. "Everyone, I think you remember Benjamin. My..." *My Benjamin,* that's what he was. I looked at him, and even though I couldn't see his eyebrow through his mask, I could almost feel his questioning stare as he glanced back at me. "Friend," I settled on. And finally, the term sounded right—although incomplete.

Noelle gave him a big grin and greeted him affectionately, looking positively glowing with Matthew's hands on her waist. It was funny, because Noelle had never really been a small girl—and goodness knows she loved her curves—but next to Matthew, she looked tiny. "So nice to see you again!"

Benjamin shook their hands. "Thank you for letting me come. I appreciate it," he said. Then greeted my brother next. "Daniel, good to see you. And Charlotte." Charlotte turned a little red, probably at being mentioned in the same sentence with Daniel, but it didn't faze my brother one bit.

I'd told Benjamin about their dynamic: best friends, never dated, stuck on their "not attracted to each other" pantomime. No matter how hard we girls had tried to convince Charlotte to give it a shot, she wouldn't budge. She said there was no way she'd risk their friendship *for something that wouldn't work out anyway.* I used to wonder if Daniel had stayed away from Charlotte in college because of her friendship with me, but lately I'd been more and more convinced they were simply scared. And idiots. The two of them were made for each other.

"Where's Gabbi?" I asked, not seeing my roommate around. Not that I'd been at our apartment a lot these past two weeks. I'd been at Benjamin's more nights than not. Under him, over him, on the couch, on his bed, the kitchen counter... Let's just say I was thoroughly enjoying having a place all to ourselves.

"Oh, I think she's just running late," Noelle shrugged. "She texted that she was on her way."

"Ah, okay," I nodded, then turned to Benjamin. He took the cowl off, leaving his hair sticking up in funny directions; but after seeing him all polished in a suit every day, with perfectly styled hair, combed back or gelled, I almost preferred it this way. It looked similar to when I ruffled it with my hands or tugged on it during sex.

"I'm here!" A voice called from the living room, and there was Gabbi, huffing as she readjusted her skirt and the tote bag under her arm.

Charlotte giggled. "Please tell me you did not bring a stack of books to the party."

"Well..." Gabbi acted all innocent. "They are part of the costume."

"Sexy librarian?" I asked, raising my eyebrows. "Did you bring Hannah?"

"Nah. That's over." She shrugged. "Also," she pointed at her outfit, "not a sexy librarian. Just a regular librarian who enjoys a good romance book." She brushed her hair away from her face and gave me a smile.

"So, basically you on an average day?"

"Shut up," she huffed, shoving at my shoulder lightheartedly.

"Everyone else had someone to match with. I didn't have any good solo ideas."

"It's okay, Gabs," I said, slipping my arm through hers. "Let's get a drink and plot out how we're going to find someone for you."

"No no no. I'm perfectly fine by myself."

After glancing at Benjamin to make sure he'd be okay without me as a buffer, I steered Gabrielle into the kitchen. She needed a drink—and so did I if I was going to get through the night without jumping my 6'2 *not-boyfriend* in his stupidly nerdy and stupidly hot Batman costume.

CHAPTER 24
Benjamin

Being surrounded by Angelina's friends was surprisingly... normal. In the best way. It didn't feel awkward or boring at all. Besides, I loved watching her light up as she talked to them. Right now, Angelina and Noelle were discussing the book that the latter had been writing over the last few months, and I found out Angelina had drawn the artwork for the cover. I resisted the urge to wrap my arm around her shoulder and kiss her to let her know how proud of her I was.

She was different with them than with me; more open, warm. Affectionate. But I liked that. She was a multifaceted woman, and I was glad that she had so many people she cared about—and that cared about her. But I secretly loved to know I had a side of Angelina that no one else got to see. There was a lot I still didn't know about her, but tonight made me even more eager to peel off every layer, discover every hidden corner of her personality.

Matthew, his best friend Bryan, and I gathered in the kitchen as the girls congregated in the living room.

"So, when are you going to propose?" Bryan asked.

I watched Matthew's face brighten with joy, and he looked over into the living room, to the group of giggling girls. "I want to, but... Not yet. We're both enjoying this, living together and spending as much time as we can together. Plus, she's got her new job. There's no reason to rush it."

Bryan chuckled. "No reason to rush marriage and kids?" He looked over at his wife, who was holding their infant son. "Man, all I know is they're the best thing that ever happened to me." His eyes shone with happiness, and it made me smile.

I had thought about marriage before, but never about what it really meant to have a family. I could picture my own, maybe, someday: a little boy running around in a Robin onesie, or a daughter dressed as Batgirl. I wouldn't care, but I would make sure they knew that I was proud of them no matter what path they chose in life. And always, always, knew they were loved.

My parents had done their best, in the way they could, but they had worked so much, missed so much when they left us with a nanny or babysitter. I didn't know what my future would look like, if I'd ever get married or have kids, but I knew that if I did, I would make sure to be home. To be a home to them.

Daniel came back from wherever he had wandered off to and joined my side after grabbing another beer from the fridge. "So, you and my sister, huh?" he said, raising his beer so we could clink the bottles together. Height ran in the family, that much was obvious. And even though he was younger than me, Daniel gave me that look—one that said, *if you hurt my sister, you're dead.*

I would do no less for Emily, so I understood. "We're not—"

"Fucking?" I clenched my jaw. I didn't like talking about Angelina like that. "I can tell by the way my sister looks at you that you're more than just friends." I almost laughed, thinking of the way she always insisted we weren't even that. "We went to college together. I don't know what you are to each other, but I'll tell you one thing: Angelina never let me meet her flings. Not a single one."

I washed down a lump in my throat with a big sip of beer. I couldn't think about what that meant or how it made me feel, not right now. But I couldn't help my next words: "She's special. Your sister."

Daniel nodded. "She is. And most guys don't take the time to figure that out. They only see what's on the surface."

She'd confided that to me. People called her awful things—the person I saw as a brilliant, strong, independent woman, so many others had chosen to tear down, simply because she hadn't needed them to succeed. She didn't talk much about her past relationships, but I could fill in the blanks enough to figure out why she didn't want to be in another one.

I did have an experience with something like that, didn't I? Girls who wanted more from me than I was ready—or willing—to give. Girls who saw who my parents were, the size of my trust fund or bank account, and wanted nothing but the perfect life money could provide. And as I grew more and more distant, they would tell me things I already knew: that I was bad at relationships. That I was impossible to love.

And fuck—maybe Angelina and I were both screwed up in our own ways. But I saw her, and I liked her for who she was. Sharp edges and all.

"What about you and Charlotte?" I said, nodding in the direction of the blonde, whose face was lit up with excitement as she laughed with the girls. "Angelina told me you've been friends since college. You never...?"

Daniel shook his head, chuckling. "I have residency in the friend zone, man. Besides, she'd never see me like that." I didn't miss the way his eyes trailed over Charlotte wistfully, and I wondered if Angelina was right, if there was something more between them. But even if there was—what right did I have to tell him to confess his feelings when I was sleeping with his sister because I was so messed up from my past relationships that I was too scared to try and have more with her?

"Hunter!" I shouted over the music, waving my brother over when I saw him in the entryway. He walked over, a scowl clouding his face. "Hey, why so glum?"

"I just got off work at the hospital. Thirty-six hours." He was still wearing his scrubs, stethoscope and all.

"You sure you're okay?"

He grunted, and after I got a drink in his hand, I dragged him over to Angelina and her best friend. "Where are we going?" he asked, crossing his arms over his chest.

"Just come with me," I said, hoping he'd bear with me. Our little sister might have been the best at pouty faces, but I still knew how to make my older brother cave. He gave another grunt that I took as approval to continue—not that I would've stopped if he'd said no. "Hunter," I started once we joined the girls. "You remember Angelina." I tried not to ogle her, but she looked absolutely delectable in her leather getup. "And this is her best friend and roommate, Gabrielle." I motioned to the brunette, who was looking at my brother with an interested glint in her eyes. "Angelina, Gabrielle, this is my brother, Hunter."

"You didn't tell me your brother was coming," Angelina said. "It's nice to see you again, Hunter."

Hunter's rigid posture loosened up a bit, and he smiled. "I didn't know if I was going to make it until the last minute. I just got off work."

"Gabrielle," I said. "Do you mind if I steal Angelina away for a moment?" Her friend gave me the thumbs up of approval, and I placed my hand on the small of Angelina's back to steer her towards a quiet corner of the house.

"Who are you supposed to be?" I heard Hunter ask Gabrielle, and I turned to look at them once we rounded the corner of the hall. He crossed his arms over his chest.

Gabrielle gave a deadpan look at my brother as she lifted the book in her hands. "A librarian." She was wearing a skirt, white button up, and a cardigan as well as a pair of glasses to complete the look. Hunter snorted. *Oh boy.* "What?"

"Nothing."

"Are you making fun of my costume when you picked the most basic thing of all time?" Gabrielle laughed. Angelina looked at me and had to clamp a hand over her mouth, lest she burst out laughing. Now, *this* was something I didn't anticipate.

"Is this even real, anyway?" Gabrielle grabbed the stethoscope from around Hunter's neck, popping it in his ears before tapping on the diaphragm.

Hunter grunted, clearly put out by the brunette's forwardness, but didn't take back the tool like I was sure he would. Instead, he covered Gabbi's hand with his own and placed the diaphragm on her chest as their hands remained connected. "That's how it's supposed to be used."

Gabbi blinked up at him, surprised by the gesture.

"Is she blushing?" Angelina gasped next to me.

I could only shake my head, incredulous at what was happening before my eyes. My brother kept his gaze on Gabbi, until he said one word: "Strong."

"W-what?"

"Your heart."

Her mouth opened and closed as my brother forced out a sigh. "Dr. Hunter Sullivan. It's nice to meet you, miss..."

"Oh. Gabrielle Meyer." A beat passed before Hunter removed his hand from her chest and placed the stethoscope back around his neck. "But my friends call me Gabbi. Or Gabs. I always thought Elle would be a nice nickname, too, but I could never quite get that one to stick."

"I work at OHSU. Just got off."

Gabrielle bit her lip guiltily. "I'm sorry—I didn't mean to imply..."

"That I wasn't actually a doctor?" Hunter almost chuckled, the corners of his mouth tilting up in the closest thing to a smile he did all night. "It's alright. I won't take it personally."

"Does she normally babble like that?" I asked Angelina.

"No. Never. Did you do that on purpose? Trying to set them up?"

"What?" I laughed, deciding we had intruded enough and

guiding her into the coat closet. "No. I was just trying to get you all to myself. My little cat burglar keeps disappearing on me." I kissed her lips, softly, and she responded by kissing me back, harder.

A devilish grin spread across her face, her eyes alight with humor under her mask. "Maybe I'm stealing the family jewels," she purred. "You should probably tie me up to make sure I don't do anything else that's bad, Batman." Angelina fluttered her eyelashes. "Have a pair of handcuffs handy?"

I pulled her flush against me and kissed her again. "While I'd love to tie you up, Kittycat," I said, voice tight, "I don't think now is the time or place."

She hummed, stroking down my chest. "You're right, Batboy. Later. Besides, I'm hungry. Want to see if there's snacks?"

"Let's go." I took her hand, lacing our gloved fingers together, and even though I couldn't feel her skin against mine, a little rush went through me.

"Noelle always makes the best desserts," Angelina gushed as we went back to the kitchen. "She's obsessed with sweets, so her spreads never disappoint." And she didn't. There were bloody red velvet cupcakes, spiderweb brownies, pudding with Oreo crumbs on top and pumpkins to look like dirt, and shaped cookies, and that was just the tip of the iceberg.

"Damn," I whistled. "This is quite the selection."

"Yeah. Don't expect this much from me though. When I host stuff, I normally just order pizza and chips."

I stole a quick kiss to her temple. "You're perfect, Angel. I wouldn't want you to do anything different."

Angelina looked up at me, her blue eyes somehow standing out even brighter with her makeup and cat mask. "Thank you," she mouthed, squeezing my hand once, before grabbing a plate and piling up goodies in it.

Noelle's desserts were some of the tastiest things I'd ever had. I wondered why she didn't open a bakery and do it full time, but she was happy with her new job at the university from what Angelina had told me, and that's what mattered.

After we ate, Angelina pulled me to a large room that appeared to be the designated dancing floor. I let her guide me in the middle of it, looping one hand around her waist as we swayed together to the slow song that was playing.

"Thank you for inviting me tonight," I said, and I hoped she knew how much I meant it. "It's nice seeing this side of you."

She tilted her head. "What side?"

"The carefree, happy side. I don't get to see it often, you know." She bit her lip. I wanted to kiss away that habit of hers. "Stop that," I whispered, leaning closer.

"Stop what?"

"Making me want to kiss you."

She hummed, standing on her tiptoes to reach the last inch and bring our faces level with each other. "Maybe that was my goal, Batboy."

I didn't care that we were at her friends' house, among friends and strangers alike—I brought my hand up to her face, cupping her cheek. "Don't tempt me, Kittycat."

"It's you and me. The bat and the cat," she murmured.

I nuzzled my nose down her throat, the crook of her neck. "No. It's you and me, Angelina and Benjamin. Just us."

"You know what they say: a kiss can be even deadlier... if you mean it." She winked, and I picked her up and twirled her around. Her laugh filled me with joy and excitement and something else I didn't dare name. When I put her down, I cupped her cheek, tracing her bottom lip with my thumb. She opened her mouth then, the tip of her tongue brushing my finger, and I stopped caring about everything. About the other people in the room, about her friends or her brother or my brother, I stopped caring about her rules—all I cared about was feeling her lips against mine. So I kissed her, and I didn't stop until Angelina pulled away, flushed and breathless.

"Take me home, Benjamin."

~

I HAD NEVER DRIVEN HOME FASTER, both my hands on the steering wheel. Heat was simmering between us in the small space, but I couldn't look over at her—if I did, there was a hundred percent chance I'd crash the car, and that would not do. But we'd been sharing those stupid flirty remarks all night and I was going to snap as soon as I could put my hands on her.

"You knew what you were doing, ordering this damn suit, didn't you?" I pushed her against the front door as soon as I closed it behind us. I let my fingers brush her exposed collarbone, toying with the zipper pull in the front. The leather was skin-tight, clinging to every gorgeous curve of her body, and it'd been driving me crazy all night.

I couldn't believe she had agreed to dress up with me, or that she had invited me to her best friend's Halloween Party at all. And after what her brother told me—it felt like something had changed between us, and I intended to show her just how good things could be between us if we just gave it a chance.

Angelina blinked at me, acting all innocent as she ran her tongue over her lip. "You're the one who picked the costume, big guy." She patted my chest. "Or did you want something less flattering?"

I growled and kissed her before grabbing the zipper pull with my teeth and sliding it down over her chest. "Gorgeous," I breathed, fondling her breasts.

Her hands were roaming under my cape, getting frustrated with it. "How the hell do I get this off of you?"

I laughed. I'd had this costume for several years—back when I used to go to comic book conventions—but I'd certainly never tried to have sex with a girl while I was wearing it before. "Hold on," I muttered, placing a kiss on her lips before I reached behind me, undid the clasps and unzipped the suit, taking it off—leaving me in my undershirt and briefs.

"That's better," Angelina purred, and I focused my attention back on her, pushing the leather material off her shoulders and crouching down to finish unzipping it to her waist. She unbuckled the belt and wiggled the rest of the suit down her legs, leaving her just in a black pushup bra and a thong. My cock stirred to attention.

"Much, much better."

Angelina reached her hand up, brushing a thumb under my eyes. And then—she laughed. "You know, I can't take you seriously with the eye makeup on."

"Oh, really? Do you want me to fuck you or not, Kittycat?"

"Yes. But first..." She slipped out of my arms, wandered over to the bathroom, and came back with a cotton round covered in solution. "Close your eyes."

I did as she asked, and I felt her sweeping the soft cotton over my eye area, delicately rubbing the makeup off. She kept going like that until she finally whispered, "Done."

When I opened my eyes, I couldn't take it anymore. I pulled her in my arms and kissed her deeply. "You don't even know how crazy you make me."

"I think I have an idea," she said, giving me a little smirk as she snuck a hand inside the waistband of my boxer briefs. I took the opportunity to get rid of my undershirt, and then I cupped her ass, digging my fingers into her skin.

"I just can't help myself around you. I've never been able to."

"Is that why you liked pissing me off so much?" She gasped when I pushed my erection against her.

"Absolutely. Fighting with you turns me on."

"Hmm." Angelina wrapped her arms around my neck, staring up at me with a strange look.

"What?"

"Just wondering what I've done to deserve you."

I kissed her jaw, once on each side, before placing another on her lips. "Is this you admitting you like me?"

"Maybe."

"Oh." I blinked, not expecting her response, but I quickly recovered. "Good," I said, and hoisted her in my arms, reveling in the feeling of her body all around me when she wrapped her legs around my back; the only thing separating us a measly layer of fabric. "Guess that means we're officially friends now, huh?" I wiggled my eyebrows, and Angelina smacked my chest.

"Don't make me take it back."

"Oh, you're never taking that back. It's set in stone now. Angelina Bradford is officially Benjamin Sullivan's friend. I'm afraid you're stuck with me for life."

She rolled her eyes. "Remind me why I put up with you again?"

"Because the sex is great?" And I rocked into her, letting her feel just how much she was affecting me. "Because I fuck you right, baby. And because you like me."

"Yeah." She pressed a kiss on my lips. "I do."

"That cost you something to admit, didn't it?" I asked, holding onto her glorious ass, wondering how long I could resist before I couldn't hold back anymore.

"I thought it would..." Angelina bit her lip as she threaded her fingers through my hair. Her eyes shut, and she breathed out. "But it wasn't as hard as I thought it would be."

"That's my girl," I said, and I meant it in more ways than one. When she opened her eyes, they were full of fire, and I knew it was all for me.

"So," she rolled her hips. "What was that about fucking me right?"

"Oh? You want some of this?" I ground against her, and she moaned loudly when I hit the perfect spot.

"More," she said, a little breathy. "Please."

"Anything, Princess. Anything for you." *I'd do anything to make you happy*, I thought. *If only you knew.*

I carried her to my bedroom, dropping her down on the bed before unclasping her bra and sliding off her thong. I pulled my underwear off as well, and then I was pulling her on top of me, ready to slide in home—

"Condom," Angelina groaned

Shit. How had I almost forgotten? I was always so careful, and I wasn't about to stop now. I reached across her, pulling one out of the bedside table and sheathing myself.

As soon as I pushed inside, we both let out a moan, and I knew I wasn't going to last long.

"You good?" I asked, pushing a hair off her face. I didn't want to move too fast, even though she was aroused and wet—I still stretched her, every time.

"Yeah," she said breathlessly, her tits bouncing as she slid up and down my length before bending down to kiss me. While my tongue was in her mouth, relishing her taste, I thrust up my hips, filling her body completely, and I could feel Angelina's gasp on my lips.

Between the feeling of her warm heat and the pent-up tension of the night, I couldn't hold back. I immediately picked up the rhythm, holding her waist to help her bounce on me, fucking her at a fast pace.

"Y-yes," she cried out. "Right there. Oh *god*. Keep doing that." Her eyes rolled in the back of her head, and I couldn't have stopped even if I wanted to.

I was mesmerized, watching her get herself off on top of me. It was amazing seeing her like this, so completely in the throes of pleasure. So completely *mine*.

Angelina's long black nails—more similar to claws, honestly —moved along my chest, running down my muscles, as I kept up my punishing pace, over and over until she threw her head back.

"Eyes open, Angel," I instructed. "Look at me when you come."

Her pussy tightened around me, her muscles contracting as I rutted into her, and I was right on the edge with her. I leaned up, sucking her nipple into my mouth, giving it a little bite when she moaned. *Fuck.* It was too good like this. I needed more. I always needed more with her.

Angelina leaned forward, holding onto my shoulders as I tightened my grip around her hip dips. "Stay the night tonight?" It came out suddenly and out of the blue, but I needed her to say yes. I needed her to stay. "Angelina," I breathed against her cheek.

A prayer on her skin.

Her breath stuttered, and she looked like a goddess when she came, digging her nails into my skin and leaving marks behind. "Yes," she said, and I felt something fundamentally shift inside of me as my orgasm shook through my body.

A streak of possessiveness rushed through me and all I could think about was that I needed this woman. I needed her glares and her fighting, her smiles and her laughter, and every inch of her fiery spirit.

Because she felt like...

She felt like *mine*.

∽

"BENJAMIN?" Angelina padded into the kitchen, finding me sipping a glass of bourbon.

I couldn't sleep. Having her sleeping in my bed, all cuddled up to my chest, was fucking with my head.

"Hey." She sat on the barstool next to me and leaned her head against my arm. She was wearing one of my T-shirts—it wasn't too big on her, reaching mid-thigh. I had to look away. "Everything okay?"

I nodded, setting the glass down so I could bury my nose in her hair, inhaling the sweet scent of her shampoo. We'd showered after we had sex—she insisted I still had residual eyeshadow on my face, and I knew she hated feeling dirty. We'd soaped each other and bathed in silence. It was almost like back at the cabin, but softer. More emotionally charged, somehow.

There wasn't a hint of fire, or heat, just us: two people who cared for each other, taking care of each other. I rubbed at my chest, thinking about how much that action meant to me.

"I want to show you something," I said, taking her hand and guiding her to the room with the door I kept always closed. I opened it and held my breath.

As soon as Angelina's eyes landed on what was inside, I felt the heat creeping up my neck, and all my instincts told me to slam the door shut and find a way to make her forget what she just saw.

"What is all this?"

My office. The room that contained, or rather, that was quite literally the culmination of all the things I enjoyed the most. Fandom things. On full display for Angelina to see. "It's, um..."

She spun around to face me. Of all the expressions I expected to see on her face, exhilaration was not one of them. "You're totally a *nerd*, aren't you, Sullivan?"

"Well..." I scratched my head, feeling my heart rate skyrocketing. I was trying to keep up with the cocky and self-assured persona I so carefully curated all the time, but the fear of Angelina seeing me as nothing but a loser was winning out.

"It's adorable." She gave me an ecstatic smile, and I wondered at the implications of that. How easy had become for her to give it to me—how easy it was for her to accept this. Accept me. She started exploring the room, her eyes cataloging every piece of my years-long collection. Her fingers drifted over the comics, as if she was mesmerized. "This is why you picked our costumes. Why you had that Catwoman mask when I couldn't find one anywhere."

I nodded sheepishly. "You don't... think it's weird?"

She sounded genuinely confused when she asked, "Why would I?"

"Because most women think it's weird for a grown man to still like all of this stuff."

Her gaze softened. "Boy Scout. I almost had sex with you in my costume, and you think I'd find it weird that you like nerdy shit?" I shrugged self-consciously. I lost count of how many women had made fun of me for it. "It's as much of a hobby as everything else. Besides," her voice grew lower, "I think it's sexy as hell, Sullivan."

"Y-you do?" I blinked at her, speechless. Her acceptance of me, fuck, it was the best feeling in the world. I hadn't realized how much I needed it until now. And her flirting, her teasing—all it did was turn me on.

Angelina came and stood in front of me, and I loved that gorgeous smirk that spread over her face, with one side of her mouth curved up just so. "Mm-hmm. And you can feel free to tie me up any time with those cuffs of yours." Her fingers trailed up my chest, a spark of amusement and arousal lighting up her face.

"Don't tempt me, Princess," I murmured. "I want to do nothing more than keep you tied to my bed and feast on you all day."

She leaned up, her nose running over the line of my jaw. "And what's stopping you?"

I nipped at her bottom lip, kissing her as she opened up for me. "If you keep being this fucking perfect, I'll—"

"You'll what?"

Have to keep you forever.

I felt the truth of those words hitting me with the force of a thousand bricks. Fuck. *Fuck.* Saying the words was out of the question. I'd only begun to admit it to myself—admitting it to her would ruin me, simple as that. She'd push me away and disappear from my life, and I couldn't let her. I couldn't allow myself to lose her. I needed to keep her in the only way I could.

"Come on." I grabbed her hand, pulling her out of the room. "Now that I've revealed my deepest, most embarrassing secret, let's go to bed."

"You're not going to disappear on me again, right?"

I kissed the back of her hand. "Nope. As long as you promise not to disappear before I wake up."

She shook her head, and I steered us toward the bedroom. She yawned, her eyes fluttering closed as she let me cocoon her against my chest.

"Goodnight, Angel."

"Goodnight, Ben."

I kissed her head, and the last thought I remembered having before succumbing to sleep, was that I'd left the door to my office open.

CHAPTER 25
Angelina

November was in full swing, and though I was sad to see the pumpkin decorations go, the cold drizzle this month brought with it meant we were one step closer to Christmas and every little kid's dream: snow. While we didn't always have a White Christmas in Portland, I was always hopeful for it, and I couldn't explain the joy that filled me when I'd run to the window and see a dusting on the ground. Sure, we had to get through a whole bunch of work things first—and Thanksgiving—but it felt like Christmas was just around the corner.

"Where are we going?"

"Just trust me." That was the thing—I *did*. Benjamin had proved to me, over and over, that I could trust him. I was holding his hand as he pulled me down the street. We entered a well-lit and bright shop, decorated with superheroes all over the walls. I raised an eyebrow at him.

"What are we doing here, Sullivan?"

"I've never..." He swallowed, giving me another glimpse into his vulnerable side. "I've never brought someone here before. Never shown this part of myself. But I—"

"Like comics? I sort of gathered as much after Halloween," I smiled softly, giving a little squeeze to his hand.

"No. Well, yes. It's just... Every girl I've ever been with made fun of me when I showed them this," he said, opening his arms. "The side of me that wasn't the cocky, confident businessman. So, I guess I just shoved it down and stopped letting other people into this part of my life. But you..."

My breath caught at the look in his eyes. When did we become this to each other? Someone the other could count on, rely on. Someone we could share our secrets with and confide in. Had it happened in the last couple of weeks, or had it always been there, since the days at the retreat? I stared at him, silently willing him to continue. I needed to hear it, wondering why *this*, holding Benjamin Sullivan's hand in a comic book shop, was the one thing that made me feel right in my life.

"You're different."

You are too, I wanted to say. "Well, Batboy," I said instead, shaking off the too-warm feeling settling in my chest. "Want to show me your favorites?"

It was his turn to gape at me. "You *want* to hear about comics?"

"Of course. But only if Batman and Catwoman comics are included," I batted my eyelashes at him. I liked them for us—the bat and the cat. I liked the playfulness that came out between us when we were in costume at the party, amplifying our usual teasing banter.

Most of all, I wanted to reassure him that I was here, and I saw him, and I liked every part of him. And, *okay*, maybe I wanted to lick him a little bit as well. I couldn't help it when he looked all shy and bashful. Seriously, though, I couldn't remember the last time I looked at him and didn't feel a mix of emotions swirling in my head. All I wanted to do was show Benjamin how special he was, and how stupid those other girls were to make fun of him— to let him go. He didn't talk much about past relationships, but I had the sense that somewhere along the lines, someone (or *someones*) had fucked him up.

We weren't even together, and I could tell that Benjamin

Sullivan as a boyfriend would top the charts. There'd be no competition, not with how he took care of the people important to him. And somehow, I had become one of those people, and it made me want to thank him every minute of every day for his sarcastic ass trying to find ways to make me smile.

"Lead the way," I told him, gesturing to the store. He grinned at me, pulling me to a specific shelf in the last aisle, and talked my ear off about his favorite Batman comics.

There wasn't one single moment where I wished I was somewhere else, or with someone else. Even when Benjamin picked out an issue and brought it to the register, presenting it to me like it was a box of chocolates or a bouquet of roses. It wasn't either, but it was better.

Because this was us, and I was starting to think we would be good together. Real good.

"Want to go anywhere else before we head home?"

"Dinner?"

It didn't occur to me until later, that when he'd called it home —his place, where I'd spent so many evenings, and now was spending the night—it really felt like it.

～

NOTHING in my life made sense anymore. The worst part? I was enjoying every second of it. Every broken rule, every derailed plan, every yes that should have been a firm no. All because of one spectacular tall-dark-and-handsome man.

One day, we just sat in silence on the couch, my legs over his lap as he rubbed my ankles and I read a particularly filthy period romance about a duke who loved to ravish his lady. (And, yes, the evening ended with ravishment of my own, of course.)

Another night, Benjamin fell asleep while watching a movie, and I spent the rest of it sketching his face, admiring the lines of his body. He was perfect, and he was—*not mine*. Maybe that was the problem. I was spending more time with my not-boyfriend, the man that I insisted I was not in a relationship with, than I was spending with my best friends.

The one rule I kept clinging to for dear life was the no-dates rule. But Benjamin taking me to his favorite comic book shop and then out to dinner felt like nothing but a date. What else was left to hold onto my sense of control?

I kept telling myself that, as long as neither of us caught feelings, we'd be fine. As if the reassurance would make it true.

Saturday brought with it our friends' coffee date, and while I was happy to see the girls, it was the first time we had all gotten together since the Halloween party, which means I could see a thousand questions under their barely contained curious gazes. They were practically bubbling with them, about to explode really.

"Alright," I sighed, ready for an attack from all sides. "Let me have it." It'd been a long time coming, after all.

"Oh my god, you're *totally* dating him!" Noelle exclaimed.

There it was. This felt a little bit like karma for how much we teased Noelle. At the time, we had pushed her because we knew how much she wanted to be with Matthew and to reassure her that she was ready to date again. Completely different from whatever they all thought they were going to accomplish with me.

"No, we're not dating," I said in a calm tone. Benjamin and I were just friends. Friends with some great benefits, sure, but we had firmly settled into the *friends* camp. There were no feelings involved whatsoever.

No matter how tenderly he'd put my mask on at Halloween, or how it'd felt when he showed up unannounced with the latest release from my favorite author. Or a thousand other instances where I had to force down emotions that I wasn't allowed to feel with him.

"Come on, Ang," Noelle insisted in her sweet voice. "You spend how many nights a week with him? That's basically a relationship."

"A relationship requires *feelings*, of which there are none.

Therefore, we cannot be in one." I glared at her, willing Charlotte or Gabrielle to speak up and defend me, but the two of them stayed silent and avoided eye contact.

"I'm just saying. That sounds a lot like what Matthew and I were doing before we labeled it."

"No, this is completely different. I don't even like Ben in that sense." *Don't you?* Shut up. "We're just hooking up, that's all. No strings attached."

"Sure, sure." Noelle sipped her coffee, hiding her smirk behind the mug. "I would believe you if you hadn't shown up to the Halloween party in matching costumes."

"So did those two!" I jabbed a finger at Charlotte, because she and Daniel were just as coordinated as we were.

"That's not fair," Charlotte argued. "We're best friends. We've been doing matching costumes for years."

I scoffed, but before I could reply, Gabbi chimed in. "He also brought his brother along." Traitor. She thought that was a point against me, but I'd seen the two of them talk for hours. I needed to investigate *that* ASAP.

"What's your point? Benjamin is trying to reconnect with his brother. So what if he invited him along?"

"Angelina..." Gabbi sighed.

"I know you guys think I need to find someone to be complete. That I need to let love into my life or some bullshit like that. But I don't. I don't have time to love someone or deal with all of its complications. I'm perfectly content to climb the corporate ladder by day and read romance novels by night. And live vicariously through you." The words had always rang true before, but somehow, now they felt a little hollow.

Like there was a little voice in the back of my head saying, *but what if you're already in deep and are just scared?* Maybe that was the problem—I had spent so long on my own, that I didn't know how to handle being loved.

"Well, at least you found a guy you can stand to be around," Charlotte said. "I can't even find anyone I like enough to go on more than one date with." My heart clenched for her. It was hard to watch your best friends struggle. Charlotte wanted to get married and have a family more than any of us, and I worried about what would happen if she couldn't have it.

Or if she wouldn't see what was right under her nose.

"What about Daniel?" No one wanted my brother and Charlotte together more than our spunky ginger best friend; Noelle was constantly nudging Char about him.

Unfortunately, so far, our efforts had proved futile, and even though it was weird to think about one of my best friends marrying my brother one day, I had to admit I didn't really mind the idea. For all of Gabbi's jokes about marrying one of our siblings, I understood what she meant. We were bonded, the four of us, and being connected with a different kind of bond didn't sound bad at all.

I wanted these girls to stay in my life forever. I wanted us to be thirty, forty, fifty, still sitting around a table drinking coffee or wine and talking about books. I couldn't imagine my life without them.

"Daniel and I are just friends," Charlotte insisted once again. "Besides. We're firmly in the friend zone. If he liked me like that, he would have made a move in college." She shrugged. "I've just accepted that I'm going to be alone forever."

"Char," Noelle groaned. "You're not going to be alone forever. None of you girls are. You're all going to meet the right person, I swear. Maybe you already have," she added, looking pointedly at me.

"Don't look at me," I said. "We're barely even at the friends level! I'm not falling in love with the guy."

"You sure about that?" Gabbi asked.

"Yes."

CHAPTER 26
Benjamin

"Hey, little bro," Hunter said, ruffling my hair as if I was still a kid and he was still the big older brother I looked up to.

In some ways, he was. He'd always had everything together, been our parents' favorite, the one who followed in their footsteps. Maybe that's why it'd been so hard for me to maintain my relationship with him for so long. Because I resented the fact that my parents loved him most.

But it wasn't really true, was it? They loved us all in different ways, and it only took me thirty years to realize that. It wasn't that they weren't supportive of my dream—they simply didn't understand it. Hunter, the perfect son and protégé who had gone to medical school and gotten into a great residency program? They understood him.

"Hey," I grinned, holding up a beer. "I got you one already."

"IPA?"

"Yeah." He nodded in thanks, taking a big sip. "How's work?"

"Fine," he grunted. "The usual. You?"

"You know, it's not bad." I thought about lunch breaks with Angelina, about the times I'd catch a glimpse of her at work and she'd give me one of those small, rare smiles; no matter how tedious or awful work was on any given day, I still wouldn't hate it, because it brought me to her.

Shit. Who was I and what had I done with the man who didn't want a relationship? Then again, maybe I'd never been that man at all.

"So... You going home for Thanksgiving this year?" I asked him, not wanting to sound too hopeful—but he knew what the occasion was.

"Yeah. Mom said she'd kill me if I didn't show up. It's a big one, huh? You bringing your girl?"

"She's not my girl."

He scoffed. "Sure."

"But yeah," I mumbled, "I was going to ask her." I squeezed my eyes shut. After all the time we'd been spending together, it wouldn't feel right not to have her with me. And even though things were better with Hunter, I still wanted her there when I was around my parents. Sometimes things were tense, and Angelina always seemed to know how to soothe me.

Hunter sighed, and I nudged him in the ribs. "What's up with you?"

"Nothing." But he seemed especially grouchy tonight, and when he dragged a hand down his face, covering his eyes, I knew it was serious. "We, uh... I lost a patient. It happens, you know? But it's always hard because they're just kids, and it's not fair." He exhaled shakily, running a hand through his curly brown hair. It reminded me of Dad's hair: short and lighter than mine.

I gripped his shoulder. "I'm sorry."

Hunter shrugged. "I don't know if I could have kids and go through all of that with my own. Mom keeps pressuring me to settle down, have a family... I know she wants grandkids, but I just—"

"Yeah. I understand. Mom's relentless, huh?"

"That she is," he chuckled. "Did you tell her about Angelina?"

"Not yet. Then I'd have to explain the fact that we're together, but... not together."

He glanced at me. "But you want to be, right?"

"Yeah." And it surprised me how easily the words slipped out of my mouth. "Yeah, I do. But Angelina... I don't know. I'm not sure she wants that."

"I think you should get your head out of your ass and tell her how you feel. Don't be a fucking idiot." He slapped me on the back before downing the rest of his beer.

"One day when you're having women problems, I can't wait to give you grief about this."

"You wish. I don't get into situations where I could come across women problems. One night. That's it. No chance of them getting attached to you that way."

"But what if *you* got attached to her."

Hunter snorted, then stared at me. "You think I have time to get attached to a woman? Ha. Fat chance. I barely have time to get attached to a TV show. Or a pet. Can you imagine me with a dog? I can't even take care of a houseplant. I'm almost thirty-two, and I can't keep a fucking plant alive."

I chuckled, patting him on the shoulder. "Don't tell Mom that. She'll be determined to find you one you can't kill."

"She's already tried. Air plants. You know those things you're not supposed to be able to kill? Still killed one of those." He rubbed his temples. "Too much shit and not enough time, man."

"That's what happens when you spend ninety percent of your waking hours at work. When was the last time you even took time off? And I don't mean a long weekend to go home. I mean a real, actual vacation."

Hunter shrugged. "I don't know. College?"

I shook my head. "You're hopeless."

"No more than you are." He bumped his shoulder against mine.

"Well, you may be right about that."

We ordered another round of drinks, and by the time we said

goodbye, I might not have felt any better about where I was at with Angelina, but I was happy to have gotten to spend time with my brother. He was back in my life and for that, I was grateful.

∽

"Hey, Benjamin."

I looked up from my desk, only a little surprised to see the tall, lanky blonde man standing there, leaning against the door frame. "Hi. What can I do for you, Nicolas?" I said politely, straightening up the pile of papers I'd been working on to give him my full attention—after all, he was my boss.

"How's Angelina?"

"She's good," I answered, before I could realize my mistake. *Shit.*

Nicolas smirked. "Don't think you've been so sneaky that I didn't notice there was something going on between the two of you."

"We're not—" I started, but I wasn't sure what we were and were not anymore. "We're just friends," I finished, lamely.

"Yeah, yeah." He waved me off. "Sure. Anyways, listen, I don't know if you've heard the rumors, but I do have something I need to talk to you about." Nicolas plopped in one of the cushy chairs across my desk, making himself at home.

"You do?"

He nodded. "He's not ready to announce it yet, but my dad's stepping down at the end of the year and leaving the company to me. It's why I've been running around like a chicken with its head cut off for the last few months." Nicolas winced. "I miss getting eight hours of sleep a night. Anyways, as I'm sure you know, you're our best candidate for taking over for me as CFO."

"Yes," I nodded slowly. I didn't care if it made me sound conceited, because I was the best candidate—no one else understood this business as backwards and forwards as I did. The only other option was bringing someone in from outside, which would take a lot more time because we'd have to train them.

"I had my reservations about you, you know." Nicolas inspected his fingernails like I wasn't sitting in front of him. I waited for him to continue, knowing he would without an input from me. "But I've been watching you ever since the retreat. I've seen you change. You and Angelina both. Do you know how much more she smiles now?"

"Yeah." I did. I liked to think it was because of me.

"You're easier to be around too. Less of a sarcastic asshole."

"Do you have a point, or are you just going to sit there and insult me all day?"

"Yeah, yeah, I'm getting there. Anyway, my point is, when I stuck you two together for the retreat, I didn't think this would happen. That you two would hit it off and actually, you know... make a go of it."

A beat passed. "That was *you*? You were the one who put us in the same group?" I was so mad about it back then—Angelina hated me with a passion, and I couldn't stand her watching me with her irritated (albeit beautiful) face.

Nicolas scratched his head. "Well, Gabbi too. We both thought you needed to get those weird emails out of your systems. The sexual tension was..." He grimaced, trailing off. "See, I just thought the two of you would fuck and move on. But Gabbi could see the real long game there. That's why she played along."

This was way too much information to process. "And you're telling me all of this now? Why?"

"Because we're going to announce you as my successor at the board meeting next month, and I want you to be fully prepared to take over at the first of the year. So, we have a lot of work to get done."

Wow. "Alright. That's—Thank you." I'd spent so much time dreaming about this and doing everything I could to get this promotion, and now it was really happening. "Can I just ask you something?"

"Yeah, of course. What is it?"

"Can you not tell Angelina about the retreat or... any of this?"

I didn't think she'd take it well, since Nicolas and Gabbi basically manipulated us; but I also had a feeling she'd find some way to turn this on me and take it out on me, and everything was delicate enough as it was.

It wouldn't hurt her if she didn't find out, right?

"Sure, man. That's fine. Anyway, I'll have Zo set up a weekly meeting from now on so we can work on stuff. Sounds good with you?"

"Yeah, sure."

"Oh, and I feel the need to specify here—the assistant does not come with the job. You gotta hire your own."

It was my turn to smirk. "Someone sounds attached to their assistant, Mr. Larsen."

"I think I'd lose my head without her." Nicolas's smile was playful, but there was genuine fondness in his eyes. "She's the best."

We shook on it, and that was that. Everything I'd been working for was finally coming true.

So what was this sinking feeling at the bottom of my stomach?

CHAPTER 27
Angelina

November brought with it one of my favorite events of the year: Willamette Tech's annual charity gala. Call me a princess all you want, but I liked dressing up and feeling fancy in an evening gown. And this year, well...

"Damn, Angel," Benjamin whistled as I stepped out of the bathroom, wearing a tight-fitting red dress that hugged my hips perfectly. I'd felt like a siren when I tried it out at the boutique. I chose well apparently. "You look—Wow."

"That good, huh?" I smirked, doing a little twirl for him. I couldn't quite explain why I was over at his place to get ready, only it was closer to the event and... I liked spending time with him.

"So, are we going to attend this thing together?" I watched him put on his shoes, tying the laces over a pair of black socks with little grey Batman logos on them. They made me smile.

"Are you asking if you're my *date*, Sullivan?"

He shrugged. "No, because that goes against your rules."

Right. My rules, which we'd been good at following for so long... until we weren't. No sleepovers, no dates—those were long out the window. All we had left were no expectations for each other. Funny, I thought to myself. Expectations were what most people wanted from a relationship, any kind of relationship really. The no-expectations rule was my last stronghold, yet this thing between us still felt like more. I felt more with him. As much as I didn't hate Benjamin anymore, I hated how he'd slid into my life so quickly, like this was so simple and easy.

My life was anything but simple and easy.

"I just meant, did you want to drive together or separately?"

"You can drive and drop me at the dor."

"Oh, it's like that, is it?" He pulled me closer, eliciting a little shriek from me, and put his mouth on my ear. "I don't know how I'm going to be able to keep my hands off of you tonight."

I gave him a playful little shove. "Well, you're gonna have to. Because *this*," I said, gesturing to myself, not missing the heat in his eyes, "is off limits, Sullivan. I might be okay with you kissing me in front of my friends, but our coworkers are a different story."

He grunted. "Noted. Unfortunately."

I put my earrings on—a long, dangly silver pair—then I applied a last coat of red lipstick.

"Let me," Benjamin murmured as I was grabbing my heels, and I couldn't bring myself to deny him. Sitting on the edge of the bed, I held my breath when his hand wrapped around my ankle and delicately slipped my toes through the black straps.

The moment felt more intimate than most times we were naked together. He was on his knee, deftly buckling my shoes.

I was rapt by the way he was touching my skin. His eyes found mine, and my breath hitched.

"You're beautiful," he whispered, cupping my cheek.

"We should go," I said, fighting the urge to lean on his palm and ignoring the emotions in his gaze.

He blinked them away and stood, offering me his hand. "Your chariot awaits, Princess."

THIS YEAR'S gala was astonishing. They'd really outdone themselves. It was the twenty-fifth anniversary of Willamette Tech, and if Nicolas's tuxedo had any significance, a very important celebration for the company. The ceiling was blanketed in twinkling lights and a soft tulle that left a heavenly glow over the hall. It was elegant, classy, and beautiful. A Night Under the Stars, indeed.

The kind of thing I'd like to have at my wedding one day. *My wedding?* Where had that come from? The last time I dreamed about getting married was years ago. A decade, maybe. I shook off the thought.

Every year we hosted a charity gala, donating all the proceeds from a silent auction to a non-profit of the company's choosing. This year was to a childhood cancer organization, and I couldn't help but wonder if Benjamin was involved with the recommendation, given that his brother worked with kids at OHSU.

I was trying to keep my thoughts about Benjamin and how good he looked in his tux at bay, but my eyes kept straying to the door. So, I was relieved when I found my friends—they'd be a good distraction from this weird feeling I'd had in my chest for days.

"Angelina!" Harper called from the high-top table where she was gathered with Gabbi and another girl from her department.

"Hey!" I grinned, hugging them both. Gabbi's dress was a deep purple, sweetheart neckline with an A-line shape that trailed to the floor with a long slit up her leg. With how many neutrals were in her closet, it was funny to see her in such a vibrant color, but it suited her beautifully.

"I was surprised you didn't come with Gabrielle," Harper remarked, looking between us with a quizzical expression on her face. She was in a gown of baby blue, a structured corset top, and chiffon that fell down her legs in pretty waves.

Harper didn't know about Benjamin. I was all too aware of what she thought of his reputation as a player. But Gabbi knew, and if she speculated that I was spending more time with him than seemed necessary, well... she would never comment on it to the rest of them.

"Oh, yeah," I said. "Something came up, so we came separately."

Gabbi looked at me, the smirk on her face saying, *oh, yes, something came up alright, and that thing is Benjamin's d*—which I promptly ignored. Sure, I was getting laid regularly now, but that was the only thing that was going on between us. Even if Gabrielle thought differently.

"Oh, sure. Makes sense." Harper nodded as she picked up her glass, and I wondered if she didn't believe me like I didn't believe myself.

"Has anyone seen Zofia yet tonight? I saw Nic when I first got here, but no sign of her." I'd catch glimpses of her at work, but between my work project and everything Nicolas had her doing, it felt like there was hardly enough time in the day anymore.

It may or may not have been also due to my turning down the last few invitations to get drinks with coworkers to spend time with Benjamin. We'd started watching all the Batman movies, and even though it was sort of terrible, I liked to tell him *Batman and Robin* (yes, the one from 1997 with George Clooney) was my favorite just to fuck with him. He'd get annoyed, but it was fun.

"I think she's running around trying to make sure everything is going smoothly," Gabbi said.

"That girl sure has been working her ass off," Harper muttered, shaking her head. But a few moments later, I finally spotted her, looking gorgeous in a pale green formal sari, embellished in gold. She was glowing.

"Zo!" I waved her over, and she gave us a smile as she approached our table.

"Hey, Ang," she said, exhaling like she could dispel all the tension in her body that way.

"Everything good?" Gabbi asked.

Zofia nodded. "Finally! I thought I was going to go crazy with all the things Mr. Larsen kept tacking on for me to do."

"Nicolas or his father?" I laughed.

"Both." She rolled her eyes lightheartedly.

"Well, it's done now. Want to get something to drink?"

"*Please.*"

We moved towards the bar, and even with the girls at my side, I couldn't miss his presence. Benjamin and I in the same room were like two magnets that couldn't help but be drawn together. It'd been that way ever since the first day at the lodge, and since then it was all I could do to fight the attraction. I'd realized it was better to give into that magnetism than to keep resisting it.

It was crazy how finely tuned my body was to notice his presence. How my breathing picked up just slightly when he was nearby. How quickly he could completely divert my attention from whatever I was doing and pull me out of my brain. I loved and hated it at the same time.

Because why did it have to be him who could command my body like that? Why was he the one who knew how to coax me out of my hiding spot like a scared kitten? I wasn't a little frightened animal afraid of the world, anyway. I was a jungle cat. A black panther, fierce and bold enough to show my teeth. *Except with him.*

"Well, well. Doesn't he clean up nice?" Harper let out a low noise of appreciation, and I braced myself for impact.

Benjamin's eyes locked with mine as soon as I turned my head. It hadn't even been thirty minutes since we last spoke, yet all I wanted to do was go over to him, let him pull me into his arms, and dance like we did that night on the dock.

Why did everything seem so much easier at the retreat? Sure, there were less eyes on us, but also… everything was simple. It was just *us.*

I averted my eyes, ignoring the question in his gaze, and turned back to Harper. "Does he? I hadn't noticed."

Liar. Filthy, filthy liar.

I noticed the moment he walked out of the bedroom with the tux shirt on. I noticed as he affixed the cufflinks to his perfectly ironed shirt. I noticed as he put on the bow tie and then the jacket. I hadn't been able to *stop* noticing. And maybe that was the problem.

He was beautiful. His hair was perfectly styled with gel, those dark strands I loved to run my fingers through pushed back; and even though he was freshly shaven, he looked every bit the confident businessman that he was.

That strong, cocky smile that hid insecurities and vulnerability. And every time he let me in, let me see the boy inside the man, I knew he'd been making true to his promise: he was wearing me down, bit by bit.

Because I liked him. More than I should. More than I ever should have allowed myself to. And it was too late now to go back.

∽

Benjamin

I'D NEVER LIKED Willamette Tech's annual charity gala in years past. I avoided it last year entirely. Too many women were on the lookout for a rich, attractive man in a suit.

This year was different.

Angelina was absolutely *resplendent* in her gown of red silk that seemed to hug every curve on her body before spilling onto the floor in ripples. And watching her float around, mingling with people from the charity we were raising money for, I couldn't help the itch to be at her side.

When she stepped out of the bathroom earlier, it took my breath away. My brain emptied of all thoughts. All I could see and hear and breathe was her. Angelina was gorgeous. And when I saw the low-cut back, I'd almost spun her around and pinned her to the wall to have my way with her. I couldn't keep my eyes off her, even now at the gala.

Which we were intentionally not attending together. Even if we came together and we would leave together. And I'd peel that dress from her body and put my mouth on every inch of her skin. God. I was out of my mind, because that was the only thing I could think about as I watched her. She was captivating, mesmerizing—for so many reasons besides just how beautiful she was.

"Sullivan!" A voice came from my right, and I turned to find Nicolas Larsen, looking perfectly polished in his tux, not a blonde hair out of place. "Fancy seeing you here, man."

"Of course," I said. "Gotta do my part." My eyes were still lingering on Angelina across the room, talking to one of the marketing girls on her team.

Nicolas was quick to track my gaze, and he gave me one of those smiles that aggravated me to no end because it reminded me how freaking perfect he was. If someone could have Nicolas Larsen, why would they bother with anyone else?

"She looks beautiful, doesn't she?"

"What?" I said, willing the ground to open up and swallow me. No matter what we'd talked about in his office last week, I still couldn't bring myself to admit the true nature of our relationship to him.

"Angelina. You were looking at her." My only response was a guttural noise that escaped my lips.

We weren't together, in any capacity, and this seemed like something that she'd get pissed about if she found out I was talking about her. With a friend of hers, moreover. "There are lots of beautiful women here tonight."

Nicolas nodded his head, a faint blush creeping over his cheeks. "So there are." Zofia stood in the corner of the room sipping on what looked like water in her glass, looking like she wasn't quite taking part in the activities and more like observing that everything was going well. This time, Nicolas wasn't quick enough to avert his eyes from her.

I went back to sipping my drink, wishing I could escape this conversation. Nicolas and I had never been close, despite our working relationship, and this little chat was already too awkward for my liking.

"Come on, though," he nudged me. "I can see the way you look at her. Something *is* going on between the two of you, isn't it?"

I shook my head, trying to scowl my expression in a neutral one. "No, nothing there. We can't stand each other." I wished. It would make it that much easier to deny all this affection I had for her.

"I saw how cozy you two were during the retreat. You're telling me that was nothing?"

"Eh. We just bickered more than anything." That was true at least—no matter what Angelina and I did, we spent most of our time locked in a verbal battle. It was as much of a turn-on at this point as she was.

Couples had started moving towards the wooden dance floor, and the live band was playing a particularly sappy song. I didn't want to look for Angelina again, but this time, out of fear that I'd find her dancing with someone else.

She wasn't mine, but I knew myself enough that I could admit it would make me crazy to see her giving the smiles that were supposed to be mine to a stranger, letting another man hold her the way I craved.

"Zofia looks lonely," I said, hoping this would finally get Nicolas to leave me alone.

He gave me a glare followed by a pointed look, before heading towards Zofia, who looked instantly happier to have her boss by her side. Huh. Interesting.

"Hey, Boy Scout." I fought back a grin before turning toward her voice.

"Princess," I purred, because no one else was around and I needed to let out the tension somehow.

"Do you want to dance?" she asked, holding a hand out to me.

I raised an eyebrow. "Dance?"

"Come on. It's not a proposal. Friends dance. You know, since we are friends." She narrowed her eyes when seconds passed without a response. "Take it or leave it, Sullivan."

I quickly swallowed the rest of my drink before taking her hand, letting her lead me to the dance floor, where plenty of other people were swaying to the music. Keeping our hands together, I wrapped the other one around her waist as she placed hers on my shoulder.

"This is nice," I mused out loud. "Reminds me of another dance we shared. Back when we were not friends."

Angelina rolled her eyes. "I still can't stand you."

"Eh, but you've admitted that you like me, so who's winning in this scenario?"

"Still me, because you, sir, are delusional."

"And you're the hottest goddamn woman in this ballroom."

She snorted. "Hardly."

"You don't believe me?" I said, subtly pressing my hips against hers. "Maybe I'll have to show you later."

"Benjamin..." she whispered, and I was taken aback by the expression on her face. She looked at me like she was enchanted. Like she wanted nothing more than for me to kiss her.

Instead, I did what any good dance partner would do: I made her twirl before dipping her. No matter how much I wanted it, this *wasn't* a relationship, and our jobs came before our desires. Always. That's why we made this agreement in the first place.

A new song started, and neither of us made a move to go.

"Mind if I cut in?" A voice interrupted our little bubble, and I was surprised to find Liam next to us. With a grin on his face that told me he had some sort of strange pleasure in doing this to me.

"Yes." I narrowed my eyes, holding Angelina tighter, which prompted a glare from her.

"I'm perfectly capable of making my own decisions, Sullivan," she said, before looking up at my friend. "Hi, Liam. I'm actually okay here but thank you for the offer. It turns out Benjamin is a pretty good dance partner, after all."

Oh. Well, that was unexpected. My chest swelled with affection. I knew I was a goner as soon the thought formed in my mind, but it felt like she was picking me, and that made me stupidly happy.

Liam left us with a goodbye and a promise for a drink later. I looked back at Angelina, and I wasn't sure what my eyes were saying, but she gave me one of her rare, brilliant smiles that made me weak in the knees. I brushed my lips to her forehead, and she leaned her cheek against my chest, swaying quietly.

"After the auction is over, do you want to get out of here?" I murmured against her hair.

"I'd like nothing more, Ben."

And that's when I knew—I failed at my plan of not catching feelings for her.

CHAPTER 28
Benjamin

"Hey, sleepyhead," I said, shaking her shoulder lightly. "We're here."

We left after the auction ended and the night died down, slipping out before anyone could notice we were missing. Angelina fell asleep on the car ride home.

"Hmm?" She blinked a few times, looking up at me groggily. I'd given her my suit jacket as we walked out, and she looked so cute all cuddled up in it.

"We gotta go upstairs, Princess." I gave her a little smile, and she frowned, still half asleep.

When she kept looking up at me a little disoriented, I decided to scoop her up in my arms, one hand supporting her back and the other under her legs.

"No one's ever carried me before," she sighed, nuzzling against my shirt as I headed towards the elevator.

"How so?"

"Too tall," she mumbled, then yawned, closing her eyes. "Intimidated."

I liked how tall she was. I liked that when she wore a pair of heels, I could stare directly into her eyes. I could still rest my chin on top of her head when she was barefoot, so it was the best of both worlds, really. To think that other guys had made her feel like less because of something as irrelevant as height? Morons.

"They were stupid," I grunted, entering my apartment and carrying Angelina to the bedroom. She barely murmured back an agreement, and when I set her down, her eyes drifted open. "Let's get this off of you, huh?" Angelina nodded, turning away so I could slide the zipper down on the back of the dress, baring her skin. She'd begun to lose her summer glow, her complexion going back to a beautiful creamy white.

Not that I minded what she looked like. Short or tall, tanned or pale—none of that mattered, because what drew me to her in the first place, and what still made my heart race, was her sparkly personality, her wit, her intelligence.

I hung the dress in my closet, and Angelina gave a little sigh of relief as she stretched on the bed, which made me do a double take.

"You're not wearing panties."

"Uh-uh. Lines would have shown."

"You're telling me," I said, my voice dropping, "that you were next to me all night, wearing absolutely nothing down there, and I was none the wiser?" She gave me a wicked little grin, although it was a bit crooked from her sleepiness, and I laughed. "Damn, Angel. If I'd known..."

She undid her bra and slipped under the covers, waiting for me to join her. "Benjamin."

"Yeah?"

"What are we doing?"

"Right now, I'm getting you ready for bed."

"No. I mean... What are we doing? What's this?" She reached out and trailed a finger along my cheek. "It doesn't feel like we're just sleeping together anymore."

"I don't know, Angel, but I do know that I like spending time with you. And I don't want this to end. We don't have to define it any more than you're comfortable, alright?"

"Right, because even if I like you, there are so many reasons we wouldn't work together long term and—what?"

"You like me?" I couldn't contain my grin. "*Like* like me?"

"What are you, five?" She scoffed, crossing her arms. "This isn't elementary school. Keep up. I'm saying we wouldn't work in a relationship."

"Why?"

"Because I don't have time for one, and you've said a thousand times that you're not good at them."

I did, didn't I? But somewhere along the line, that changed. I changed. We changed, and those reasons didn't feel true anymore. Every girl I'd been with told me I wasn't a good boyfriend, yes, but I realized now that it wasn't entirely because of me. It was simply because we weren't a good match. But with Angelina... Fuck. I'd do anything to make her happy, to keep her happy.

"Maybe I could be."

"What?"

I looked at her, feeling the seriousness of the conversation for the first time. "Maybe I could be. For you."

"Benjamin..." Angelina sat up. "That's crazy. This is crazy. You know this wouldn't work. We can't stand each other, right? We fight all the time. We just don't work together."

"Do we?" I asked, and it didn't matter what I was responding to. It wasn't a simple matter of tolerating each other, not anymore. We didn't fight, not really. Bantering was our own form of communication, with all the teasing and the prodding, but it'd never felt like fighting. It was just us. And we did work. With our stubbornness and our fragilities, *we* worked together.

I hesitated before bringing my hand up to stroke her hair. Then, slowly, I started pulling out the bobby pins she'd used to keep the hairdo in place.

Our bodies had gotten so used to being in close proximity that sometimes I wondered if our hearts beat to the same tune. If they understood each other on a fundamental level that even we, rationally, did not.

"Sullivan—"

"No. We're not doing this last name thing. Not right now. I'm serious. What's so wrong with me that you won't even consider it?" It took everything in me to ask that question, because I knew what was wrong with me, but if Angelina just said the word...

She bit her lip, and I could see the wheels turning in her head. I always liked to watch her like this, as if I could imagine the gears turning, her spinning something around like a notch she was determined to fit into its slot. Angelina was a logical thinker—except, apparently, when it came to us. Because she was settling for this, this nonsensical friends-with-benefits, I-get-some-of-you-but-not-all-of-you relationship, only because she was scared. And I needed her to know that she could be scared with me. We could be terrified about this together.

Because I did want it all. I wanted to spend every minute of my free time with her. I wanted to take her on dates, to hold her hand when we walked down the street, to know that she was always by my side, and to have her know that I would always have her back. She didn't need it—she didn't need me, but I wanted her to count on that.

I needed her to see that I could be the man that she *wanted*.

No sarcasm, no pretenses, no hiding behind the humor because of undealt with insecurities. Just Benjamin. Angelina had slowly but surely worn away at my armor, making me see what I was missing out on—who I was missing out on. The real me.

"We said no feelings," she whispered, eyes wide and glassy.

"We said a lot of things, sweetheart." I brushed my thumb on her cheek. "We've kind of broken all of your rules, haven't we?" She shook her head vehemently, pulling away, and I frowned. "Angelina—"

"I just—I can't. And you need to respect that." Her tone was final, and I wondered, if this had been another girl, another life, if she would've broken down in tears. But this was Angelina, my strong, stubborn, opinionated girl, who wore her own suit of armor and hardly ever let anyone see her without it.

She was focused. Disciplined. I'd almost say she was a freak about it, but the truth was, I liked her exactly the way she was. I liked her independence. The fact that she didn't need me but allowed me to be so close to her was one of the many reasons I grew fond of her.

Although sometimes it was too much, even for her. She'd built her walls so high she could barely see over them. She'd perfected herself so the world would see her as strong and whole and beautiful. But she had feelings too. Her heart was big, and it pained me to see her repress herself so much.

I tilted up her chin to make her look at me. "Angel. Breathe."

"I'm just... I'm scared."

"Can I tell you something?" I waited for her nod to continue. "I'm scared too."

By now I knew this wasn't the right time to convince her of giving us a chance, but I hoped my words would stay with her and make her see how we didn't need to be or feel perfect to build something together. We just needed to *be*, fears and all.

When she calmed down a little, I took her hand in mine and kissed her. Slowly, just a peck. She sighed against my mouth and wrapped her arms around my neck. She was tired, so I let her set the pace, to touch me however she liked. She deepened the kiss, her hands stroking and tugging and undoing. Once I was left in my briefs, I pulled away to grab an oversized T-shirt from my drawer and handed it to her.

Angelina stilled, frowning at the garment. "You don't want to..."

Shit. Of course, she'd think I was rejecting her because she told me she was scared. I shook my head and kissed her forehead. "I want to. I always want to, baby. But you're tired, and you've been working yourself too hard lately."

Her shoulders relaxed imperceptibly. "Oh."

"And we have all day tomorrow, Angel."

"Okay," she said, letting me put the T-shirt over her body.

I quickly went to the bathroom, then turned the lights off and joined her under the covers. She was already fast asleep when I kissed her forehead with a whispered, "Goodnight."

∼

Angelina

Something felt irreversibly changed between us after the night of the gala. I'd woken up the next morning with my head on Benjamin's chest, sleeping in his T-shirt with nothing underneath, and all I wanted was to stay like that—no complications, no intrusive thoughts.

"Morning," I mumbled when I looked up at him and saw him already awake. I wondered how long he'd been watching me sleep.

"Hey." He kissed the top of my head. "Want breakfast? I could make something."

"Yes, but... Can we stay like this for a moment?" I snuggled in closer to him, closing my eyes. Benjamin's nose buried in my hair, like he was trying to inhale the scent.

"You know you're my best friend?" he said after a minute. My breath hitched. "Sometimes, I think you're the best friend I've ever had."

And with the back of his hand slowly caressing my arm, I think I did. I did know, because he'd become one of my best friends too.

I opened my eyes and found him looking at me with an intensity that almost made me gasp.

"Listen," he said, grabbing my hand and tracing circles on my palm. "I have a question, but I don't want you to freak out about it. It doesn't have to mean anything."

"O-okay."

"I'm going home for Thanksgiving. For my birthday." I didn't know his birthday was so close, but before I could ask him about it, he closed his eyes, took a breath, and said, "Would you come with me?" It took a long moment for his words to sink in, but watching him prepare himself for a rejection broke my heart. I reached up to touch his face, brushing my fingers over his cheek, which gave him the courage to open his eyes and continue. "It's hard, going back, trying to live up to my parents' expectations. I know it's a lot to ask, but I would really love to have you there with me." I could feel it, sitting there underneath: *I need you.*

I didn't know what we were anymore. I stopped knowing a long time ago, if I was being honest. After our conversation last night, I was forced to confront the feelings I'd been ignoring for far too long. I couldn't pinpoint the exact moment it stopped feeling like this—*us*—was just casual. But maybe... maybe I needed him the same way he needed me.

Benjamin felt like my lifeline, something I could cling to when everything else was falling apart, when nothing else made sense, because he'd be there for me. Of that, I was sure.

And I wanted to be there for him, too.

Did that mean we could be together? I didn't know. I told him the truth when I said I was scared. And I liked to think that he was telling the truth when he said that he could be a good boyfriend, for me. But could I be a good girlfriend to him?

"Okay," I finally said, and I let him pull me onto his lap. "But what are we going to tell your family? Because we're not dating..."

"We'll tell them the truth. That we're friends." He locked eyes with me, and I could feel it, simmering there. So many feelings bubbling under the surface. *Sometimes, I think you're the best friend I've ever had.* No one had ever said something like that to me before, so reverently. I felt the corner of my lips tipping up in a smile. "What?"

"It's just... I can't believe that I went from hating you to this."

"What is *this*, Angelina?" he whispered, and I gulped. I hid my face in his neck, leaving a soft kiss there hoping he could forgive me that I couldn't articulate it. That I couldn't put into words what I felt for him. It was this giant something, that much I knew, but every time I thought about it, the answer slipped away. The very words wouldn't stick to my tongue, like they hadn't settled into my bones yet. "So you'll come?" he asked eventually, and I surrendered to the hope in his voice.

"If you want me there," I said, "then I'll be there." He nodded, squeezing me tight. "Do you think your sister will to hate me? And is your brother going to be there? Because I feel like I still need to interrogate him about the Halloween Party."

"What about the Halloween Party?"

"Didn't you see him flirting with Gabbi?"

Benjamin blinked. "You mean when they were talking and we snuck off to make out in a closet?"

"Well, yeah."

He tilted his head. "I would hardly define that flirting. Sure, Hunter didn't stomp away grunting, but I don't think there's any more to that."

"There is totally more to that. He got under her skin like no one I've ever seen before."

"Like I do with you?" Benjamin puffed up his chest, reminding me of a preening bird, but I just laughed.

"Down, boy. And no. We taunt each other. That was..." I paused, thinking back to the first day Gabrielle and I met. "I don't think she's ever been so effortlessly frustrated by a man without walking away with a roll of her eyes."

Benjamin chuckled. "There's a good guy underneath all of that grump, I promise. But yeah, he's supposed to be there. I asked him last week. And don't worry, Emily will love you, I promise." He squeezed my hand, knowing exactly what kind of reassurance I needed. "And she'll probably talk your ear off about fashion once she realizes how much you love clothes and shoes. It's a wonder she's not already stalking your Instagram account. She'd love all of those photos you post."

I raised an eyebrow. "Been stalking my Insta, have you, Sullivan?"

"Hell yeah, I have, Princess. You're gorgeous. Sorry if sometimes I stare at your photos because I'm missing you." He smacked a kiss on my cheek.

"You know, there's an easy solution to that," I said, giving him a sly grin.

"Oh?"

"Mm-hmm. I could send you your own."

"Are we talking like... outfit of the day photos? Because while I really like those—" I shook my head, biting my lip. "Oh. *Oh.* Well. Maybe I'd like that."

"Maybe?"

"Uh-huh."

I laced my fingers with his. "So, are we flying to your parents, or..."

"I thought we'd drive. It's about two days if we break it up, and then we have an excuse to get out of there if they pull any crazy cards."

"Do they do that often?"

Benjamin grimaced. "Sometimes. But it's my birthday. And Thanksgiving. Which means they'll have to be on their best behavior." There was a frowning line between his eyebrows that I wanted to smooth over. "Plus, when I tell them I'm bringing you..."

"Oh," I laughed. "So that's what I'm supposed to be? The parent buffer?"

"No. But I do think they're going to love you." He kissed my knuckles, and I hoped in my heart that it was true. That they wouldn't judge who I was or what I wanted out of my life.

Meeting Benjamin's parents... Regardless of what he said, this was big. Huge, even. And I didn't completely hate it. The importance of it all. What it clearly meant for him.

Fuck, I was so in over my head here.

CHAPTER 29
Angelina

That was how I found myself driving to Montana with Benjamin, not only to celebrate his birthday and Thanksgiving but also to meet his parents. And although we kept saying we weren't in a relationship, this certainly felt like girlfriend territory to me. To say I was terrified was an understatement.

We hadn't finished our conversation from the other night, but I knew we were going to have to tackle it sooner or later. Our feelings had grown too big to pretend they weren't there.

I was scrolling through emails on my phone, catching up on what I'd missed taking the extra day off work for the drive, when Benjamin turned onto a gravel road.

"Welcome to my childhood home," he said as we pulled into a large driveway.

"Wow." My face was glued to the window. "You grew up here?" Holy shit. My parents were well-off, but this house... It must be worth millions. It was a gorgeous mansion—a huge craftsman-style one built on several acres on the outskirts of Benjamin's hometown.

"Two doctors, remember?" He shrugged, but I could tell it made him uncomfortable. "Plus, they both came from family money." It was a reminder that he did too. Not that I cared—I never really had. Money was money, and I had enough of my own that it didn't matter. But Benjamin's feelings, they mattered. "Hunter's supposed to get in tonight, I think, but Emily's already here. I told them I was bringing you and it's... Well, Mom wanted to make a bigger deal of it, but I asked her not to."

He looked off into the distance, deep in thought. Where was my teasing, sarcastic man? The one sitting next to me now was withdrawn, quiet, wary almost.

I tugged on his arm, bringing his attention back to me. "Hey. I'm here. Whatever you need, okay?" Benjamin took a few deep breaths before I brushed his hair off his forehead and kissed his cheek.

"This isn't too much, right? Meeting my parents and coming home with me? Because if it is, I can—"

"Ben, it's not. It's not too much." It had freaked me out at first, but now I was happy to be here. *I'd do anything for you.* I blinked the thought away as soon as it came to me. Rein it in, Angelina.

We walked hand in hand to the door, and I gave him a little nod and a reassuring smile when he looked at me before ringing the doorbell. I didn't drop his hand, didn't dare lose that connection to him, much less when I knew he needed it.

A middle-aged woman opened the door, a big smile on her face and an apron tied around her waist, covered in flour. "Benjamin!" She pulled him into a tight hug, then turned to me. "You must be Angelina. I'm so happy to meet you, honey. I'm Molly, Benjamin's mom." She hugged me too, and, surprisingly, I didn't mind.

"Hello, Mrs. Sullivan." I pulled the flowers we'd picked up in town from behind my back and presented them to her. "These are for you."

"Oh, dear, you didn't have to."

"Of course we did, Mom. Now, are you going to let us in or do we have to stand out here in the cold all day?" Benjamin gave her a little smirk, and I kept in my giggle over this grown man sassing his own mother.

"Yes, yes, come in." She ushered us in, and we stopped in the foyer.

"I'll get the bags out of the car," Benjamin said. "Don't let her interrogate you too much." And with a wink, he was out the door.

I gave his mom a small smile. "Your home is lovely." It really was. The ceilings were high, with exposed wooden beams, and I was in awe over the level of detail it contained. The foyer opened into a large entryway with a giant staircase up to the second floor, and in front of it stood a twenty-foot Christmas tree, perfectly decorated in garlands and ornaments.

"Thank you. We've certainly gotten a lot more out of it over the past few years since John and I took a step back at work."

"Oh. Benjamin told me you were both doctors. I figured..."

"That we'd keep working until the day we died?" She laughed. "Me too. Well, we're still working, just cut back on the hours, and John stepped back as Chief of Surgery. We wanted to travel and see the world before we were too old. Now, take your shoes off and come into the kitchen. I made fresh cookies, and I need someone to try them."

As I followed her through the house, I admired my surroundings. This place looked so homey—quite different from Benjamin's descriptions of his childhood. He had good memories and it was clear that his parents loved him, but I hadn't expected such a domestic sight. I thought his mother would be the kind of woman who had a cook and never touched her own kitchen.

I was happy to be proved wrong.

"What's that smell?" Benjamin asked as he joined us.

"I made cookies. I was just asking Angelina to taste test for me."

"Oh, the ever-present quest to find the perfect recipe continues, hm?" He laughed, sneaking a cookie off the tray and popping it in his mouth. After complimenting his mom, he leaned over to speak quietly in my ear: "I put your bags in my room. Is that okay with you?"

I nodded as I took a bite myself. "These are good!" The cookies were like spice cake with cream cheese icing drizzled on top. I gave a thumbs up to Mrs. Sullivan as I bit into the other half. "My friend Noelle would be obsessed with these."

Benjamin smiled at me as he ate another one.

"Why don't you two get settled in before dinner? And Benjamin, you can give Angelina a tour of the house."

He nodded, grabbing my hand and pulling me out of the kitchen.

"House?" I snorted. "This place is a freaking palace." Benjamin led me up the stairs towards the bedrooms, and I was pretty sure this place was twice as big as any house my parents had ever owned. Maybe that's why I was so determined to make my own successes—I wanted a giant house like this, and to know I'd earned it.

"Just wait until you see the pool."

"There's a pool?" I squealed, but then frowned. "Oh. I didn't bring a suit. That sucks."

"I'm sure Emily has one you can borrow. Now, do you want to change before the tour?" He eyed the skinny jeans and black and white striped sweater I'd chosen for the drive. November in Portland was cold enough, but November in Montana? I needed every layer I could get for when we'd get out at the rest stops. But it was warm and toasty here, and I had something more comfortable I could throw on packed in my very stuffed bag.

Had I overpacked for a four-day trip to his parents' house? Maybe. But you couldn't say I wasn't prepared for literally anything. Except, of course, a freaking pool.

"Here we are," Benjamin said, pulling me to a stop in front of a large room.

I didn't know what I was expecting from his childhood bedroom, but it was not... this. "Where's all your nerd memorabilia? I expected more," I pouted.

"I took it all with me when I moved," he laughed, wrapping his arms around me. "And then Mom hired an interior decorator a few years ago and prettied it up."

It looked like a guest room, devoid of most personal touches—except a photo of Benjamin and Hunter as kids on the desk, wearing their Boy Scout Uniforms, and his Eagle Scout Certificate framed over that.

"Cute." I grinned at him.

"I'm gonna go change. Let me know if you need anything." He padded into the bathroom, giving me a few minutes to myself to gather my thoughts.

After I pulled on a hoodie and a fuzzy pair of socks, Benjamin came out with only a pair of sweatpants on, hung low around his waist. "That's not fair" I whined.

"What?"

"At least put on a T-shirt or something, I don't think I can look at you like that all night."

"Relax, Princess. I know how hard it is for you to control yourself around me, don't worry."

"As if," I scoffed.

Benjamin pressed a kiss to my forehead before digging around in his bag and putting on a T-shirt. "Better?"

"Yes. Now come on, let's go see this mansion."

∽

THE POOL WAS in fact a heated indoor pool, complete with a hot tub, and there was no way I was passing up the opportunity to use it. Even more impressive, somehow, was Benjamin's sister's setup in the basement.

"Oh my god," I said, staring at the full-blown studio. "This is incredible."

"Benjamin?" A female voice called from the open door in the corner of the room.

"Hey, Em!" And out came his sister, carrying a giant stack of clothes. She was much shorter than him—and a few shorter than me—but looked just like him, despite her lighter brown hair and adorable button nose. Benjamin walked over, took the bundle from her arms, and pulled her into a bear hug.

"*Ohmygod!*" Emily squealed. "Is this her?" She gave me a huge smile and then hit her brother on his chest. "You didn't tell me she was so pretty."

"Ow! As if you didn't stalk her social media the moment I said she was coming," he grumbled.

I cleared my throat. "Hi. I'm Angelina. This is quite the set-up you have here." Emily ignored my outstretched hand and pulled me into a hug. Oh. Okay. I guess that's how Emily Olivia Sullivan had so quickly amassed thousands of followers on social media: she was as sweet as she was effortlessly gorgeous. Her hair was held back in a big claw clip, and the desk in the room was currently scattered with various makeup products.

"I have a shoot in town," she explained as my eyes lingered over the table. "No rest in this line of business," Emily laughed.

"What's all this?" I asked, looking over the bags and boxes stacked in a corner.

She sighed. "Those are all of the sponsored products I still have to shoot and create content for."

"Wow." I rustled through the bags. There was quite an array, from skincare products to clothes. "And you get paid for all of this? Benjamin told me you dropped out of college."

"Yeah. My parents were sort of pissed at first, but then they realized how much I was making from every campaign. This is all pennies compared to that." She shrugged. "Also, Benjamin's right. I totally did stalk your Instagram."

He smirked at me and mouthed, "Told you so."

"Want to come with me to take some photos today?" She eyed me appraisingly. "I probably have some stuff you could wear."

I looked at Benjamin, who raised an eyebrow. I liked to think I understood Benjamin's little facial expressions by now, so I took that to mean, "Do you want to go?" As much as I wanted to sit and cuddle on the couch with him, it did sound like fun—and Emily had this energy to her which made me want to say yes to whatever she asked.

"That sounds great," I said, smiling at her.

"While you guys are off, I'm going to go help Mom. Angel, text me if you need anything, okay?" Benjamin gave me a kiss on the forehead.

As soon as he was gone, Emily turned to me with a wicked grin. "I thought he'd never leave." She cleared off the couch and patted the space next to her. "Now, tell me *everything*."

"Everything?" I repeated, like this wasn't the most loaded question she could possibly ask. "Um."

She gave me a sly smile. "My brother has never brought a girl home before, so this must be serious. How long have you been dating?"

What had he told them? "Well... We're not technically dating," I said with a wince.

Emily widened her eyes. "You're kidding, right?" She stood up. "Hold on. Stay here." She looked at my feet. "What size of shoes do you wear?"

"Um. Ten."

"Thought so. Be right back." She left with a wink, and started digging through several closets, dressers, and drawers, throwing pieces of clothes on the floor every so often. "This job never ends!" she shouted from the walk-in closet.

I laughed, watching her work. I honestly had no idea what was happening, other than the pile of clothes and accessories on the floor was growing. Finally, she stopped by the couch, chucked a few garments at me, and said, "Get changed. But don't think I'm letting you off the hook. We'll talk in the car."

Oh, goodie. I kept on my jeans, pulling on the chunky rose-colored cable knit sweater and white fuzzy jacket, as well as the black boots she had miraculously found. I was starting to suspect this woman was some kind of clothing guru. That was the only explanation for how quickly she'd put together an outfit for me.

Never mind that I dressed myself with the same finesse at home.

"Ready?" she asked, standing in front of me dressed in all white with tan boots, an outfit that made her brown hair and red lipstick pop beautifully.

"I guess?"

Emily grabbed her purse, and I followed her out of the house and into the little Subaru parked in the garage. It seemed... decidedly normal for a girl who had an entire room full of glammed up stuff.

"Okay. I drive, you talk."

"This feels like an interrogation," I muttered under my breath. "Where do I even start?"

"At the beginning."

So, I did. I told her all about our emails, how I refused to meet with Benjamin in person out of spite, how we'd met at the retreat and been paired together for the week's activities, and how he'd slowly pestered me to hang out with him until I realized he wasn't such a bad guy. I left out the night of passionate sex in his cabin. And the one in mine. I didn't need to share those details with his sister. All the countless other nights ever since. I finished my tale by telling her that Benjamin and I were now very good friends.

"So, let me get this straight. You're spending all your time together, sleeping together," she looked pointedly at me, "and you're *not* together?"

"Yup. That about sums it up." It did sound kind of ridiculous when you put it like that.

"My brother is an idiot."

I laughed. "Now, on that front, we agree." But he was my idiot. And I liked him way too much for what we were doing all the same.

Because we were supposed to be just casual, and there was nothing casual about what I felt for him.

CHAPTER 30
Benjamin

Angelina was in the living room with Emily as we cleaned up after dinner. She'd gotten back from their little trip with her cheeks flushed from the cold, but she seemed happy. Which made me happy.

Mom had made lasagna, my childhood favorite, and I was sure there was an Oreo dessert in the fridge that she made to surprise me. She could be intense, and she had worked a lot when I was a kid, but I could never doubt her love for all of us. It was just a little misplaced sometimes.

"You love her, don't you?" Mom interrupted my thoughts, looking up at me from the sink while she washed the dishes and I dried them.

"I—"

"Don't even try to tell me no, Ben. I can see it in your eyes."

"We're just friends, Mom." Good friends, maybe even best friends, and friends with a lot of benefits, sure, but still, *friends*. "We're not in a relationship."

"But you could be?" she asked, hopefully.

"Mom." I sighed, shaking my head. "I don't know. We just..." How did I explain to my mother that I would do anything for Angelina but I didn't want to lose her by pushing her too much?

If I could have her, like this, forever, would that be enough? "We haven't even talked about it." Us.

We'd been dancing around the conversation ever since the night of the gala. I knew we needed to talk, but I was worried it would ruin everything. At least now I had her. She was mine, albeit not completely.

"Well, you know how to fix that, right?" I stared blankly at my mom. "Talk to her, silly!"

"It's not that simple."

Mom turned off the faucet to glare at me. "Benjamin William Sullivan. What is with you men these days? I didn't think I raised you like this." She smacked me with a dry towel. "How am I ever going to end up with grandkids between you and your brother?"

"What about Em?"

"She's still young. She has time to sort herself out before I'm going to pressure her. Unlike you."

"I don't think Angelina even wants that."

"What? Marriage?"

"No. Kids."

Her voice softened. "But you do, don't you?"

I blinked. "Yeah. I do." It was the first time I said it out loud, and it felt good. Because it was true. I could imagine myself with kids—reading to them at night, making sure they always knew how loved they were. A little boy with Angelina's eyes and my brown hair. A little girl with the stubbornness and intelligence of her mother. The two of us sneaking away to get a moment of peace. "But I care about her more than that." I wanted kids, but I didn't care if we didn't have any, as long as we were together.

My mom rubbed my back like she used to when I was a kid, and when she said, "That's love, Benjamin," I knew, in the deepest depths of my heart, that she was right.

"Happy Birthday." Her smile was radiant as Angelina looked up at me from her place on my chest. She kissed my shoulder, and I pulled her closer.

How long had it been since I woke up on my birthday and felt this happy? Curled up together in my childhood's bed, I didn't want anything to pull us out of this moment. Waking up next to Angelina was always like this, but spending my birthday with the girl I was hopelessly falling for? It was pure bliss.

"What's on the agenda for the day, Birthday Boy?"

"Hm. I was thinking maybe we could go to the hot springs and wander around town before dinner."

I was used to my birthday falling on Thanksgiving since it happened every few years, but I didn't mind too much this year. Things really seemed good again with my parents now that they had both semi-retired from the hospital, and my relationship with Hunter was better than ever. Angelina by my side was the cherry on top. She made today perfect.

"That sounds nice."

I laughed at that, thinking about our first few days together, when I had to practically force her to go for a hike with me. "Remember when you used to tell me no whenever I tried to get you to do something with me?"

"Yeah." She smirked. "Want me to start again?"

"No." I sat up and pulled her into my lap. "I like *this* Angelina better."

She batted her eyelashes. "The one you abandoned to let your sister interrogate yesterday, or the one whose pants you want to get into?"

"Abandoned seems like a strong word. Besides, you guys were laughing when you got back. Was it that bad?"

"No. I'm just teasing you. She did demand all the details about us, though."

I raised an eyebrow. "What did you tell her?"

"The truth. Minus the boring sex stuff."

"Mmm, boring, huh?" I said, pressing my erection against her core.

"Benjamin!" she shrieked. "I wasn't going to tell your *little sister* about our sex life."

I flipped her over, pinning her down against the pillows. "That's good. I like having you all to myself like this."

She laughed as I peppered her face with kisses, trailing down to her neck and collarbone before she finally pushed me off. "Down, boy. We need to shower or we're never going to leave this bedroom."

"You say it like it's a bad thing."

"Did turning thirty make you even more insatiable?"

"No, that's just you." Her fierce spirit turned me on all the time, and I loved it.

Goddamn, I was so in love with her.

∼

THE HOT SPRINGS were a beautiful facility with multiple pools and saunas, and I took a moment to take in the sight for the first time in years. Some kids had local pools growing up—we had this.

"It's f-f-freezing," Angelina said as she got out of the car, wrapping the scarf my sister gave her yesterday tighter around her neck.

I pulled her hat down further around her ears, blinking at her. "It won't be soon."

"Bastard," she muttered under her breath, and I squeezed her hand.

The employee gave us a quick tour of the facilities. We wouldn't be using the outdoor pools, but it didn't matter. Angelina didn't know that I'd called in a favor.

"See you on the other side," she said, giving me a fake salute before going into the women's changing area. I went to the men's changing room, eagerly stripping out my clothes to pull my bathing suit on, excited to sit in the warm hot springs water with her.

Once I'd stored all my stuff and padded outside, there she was, clad in a tiny white bikini that screamed at me to be ripped off, her long hair secured up in a clip instead of her usual high bun or ponytail.

"Wow." That's all I could say, really.

Angelina grinned, doing a little hip roll. "Thank God your sister had something I could borrow."

I plucked at the strings before nipping at her neck. "I'll remember to thank her later. Best birthday present ever." I took her hand, guiding her towards one of the empty hot tubs. The whole place was empty, actually. And she was now starting to realize too.

"Benjamin? Why are we the only ones here?"

"Oh, that?" I smirked. "I called in an old favor. Hunter saved the owner's daughter's life. They were all too happy to oblige my request when I called and asked for a few hours alone here."

"So..." Angelina gave me that look as she played with the tiny strap of her top, which barely contained her tits as it was. God, they were glorious. "We're completely alone?" Her finger trailed across my collarbone, over my chest and stomach.

"Don't be getting any ideas," I said into her ear. "There are still security cameras." Angelina deflated instantly. "Sorry, baby. I know how much you love to sit on my dick, but—mph." She covered my mouth to silence me.

I led her over to the hot tub, getting in first, and extending my hand to her as she inched inside the steaming water.

She moaned happily once she was fully in. "That's more like it."

"Did I do good?" I said, sitting on the stone bench.

"You did great." But Angelina didn't sit next to me. She waded into the pool, the top half of her body covered in little droplets of water, enticing as fuck, just staring at me.

"C'mere, Angel." I watched her like a man starved: the curve of her neck, the dip of her hips, and those tiny triangles that kept me from what I wanted most. She swayed over to me, and then straddled my waist before sitting on top of me, perfectly aligning her center over my rapidly hardening dick. "You little tease," I muttered into her ear. "Doing that where you know I can't act on it."

"Why can't you?" she breathed, tracing circles over my chest, her fingers appreciating each of my abs.

I brushed a loose lock of hair back from her face while I gripped her waist. "Fuck, I like you in white," I said with a smile as she wrapped her arms around my neck. "It looks good on you."

She nestled against me, and I couldn't help it. I needed to kiss her. I didn't even care if we were in a public place, or if someone looked at the video footage. I captured her mouth in a rough kiss, biting her lip and sucking it before soothing it with my tongue. Angelina gasped, but I kept going, touching her through that damn bikini as we kissed and kissed and kissed.

"Benjamin," she moaned, eyes lidded, and I was so very aware of how she was pressed against me, how her hips rocked against mine, how desperate she was for a release.

"Does my good girl need to come?" I said against her ear, voice so low that I knew no one would have heard even if we weren't alone.

Angelina groaned, rubbing against me, her motions speeding up. "Yes, *please*." I wondered if she could get herself off like this with enough friction. I moved one of those white triangles aside, exposing her beautiful breast to me. I sucked her nipple into my mouth before worshiping the hardened peak with my tongue. "Oh, Benjamin," she cried. "Don't stop."

I freed the other breast too, fondling and kneading, rolling her nipples between my fingers and toying with her until she was panting and mewling. I began to move my hips then, thrusting up in short, shallow motions, just enough that I knew I was hitting her sweet spot. Angelina cried out and her head rolled back. Eyes squeezed shut, her whole body shuddered as she came, her thighs quivering around me. Once she caught her breath, she slumped against my body, and I held her close.

"Oh my god. I've never..." Her face was beautifully flushed, from the hot water or her orgasm, I wasn't sure. "That's never happened to me before. Without..." She shook her head, laughing incredulously.

I kissed her, and then I nuzzled against her neck as she righted her bikini, covering up her delectable tits. I supposed it was a good thing, because if she'd kept them out like that, I wouldn't have been able to help myself from continuing what we started.

After a long soak—and more fondling and kissing—and a steamy session in the sauna, we got out and quickly put our warm clothes back on. I wasn't surprised with how much my body ached for her; my cock was left unattended as I'd focused entirely on her pleasure. I could take care of myself later, but getting Angelina off? That was always my priority.

~

"Thank you, Mom," I smiled, giving her a quick peck on the cheek as I helped Hunter clear the table. "Dinner was great."

We had our traditional Thanksgiving dinner, the five of us and Angelina piled around the giant feast my mom had created. Normally, I helped her and Hunter cook, while Em made desserts, but this year I'd been too busy showing Angelina around town. I showed her my elementary school, my high school, and the store where I bought my first comic book. The park where I decided I wanted to go into accounting and not follow in my parents' footsteps as a doctor. It was a town with a lot of memories for me, but I was glad to be making new ones with her.

After stuffing ourselves full of turkey, mashed potatoes, stuffing, and a whole lot of gravy, we moved into the living room, flopping down on the giant sectional couch. Angelina sat next to me —close enough that our thighs touched, but not on top of me as she did at home. I had to remind myself that my apartment wasn't *her* home, even though it felt more like mine just by having her there.

My gifts from my family included a new Nintendo Switch game from Em, a new watch from Hunter, a fancy portfolio from my mom, and a brand-new fountain pen from my dad. Thankfully, we kept birthdays small in my family, because Mom had always gone a little overboard for Christmas. Angelina surprised me by pulling out a small, thin box.

"You didn't have to get me anything."

"I know. But I wanted to."

Inside was a black satin tie, with dark patterns printed onto it. I looked closer and realized they were little bat symbols. The box also had a little batman tie clip.

"You know, to match your socks," she said, looking up and batting her eyelashes at me, which made me laugh.

"Thank you. It's great." It was subtle enough that I could wear it to work, but also the most thoughtful gesture a girl had ever given me. Angelina had thought about me and what I liked, and that mattered more than I could ever put into words.

She leaned in to whisper in my ear. "I have something else upstairs, too." Oh? She smirked. *Oh.*

"Well, come on then, time for dessert!" Mom ushered us all to the kitchen, and anticipation grew in me. I couldn't wait to get Angelina alone in my room. But that would have to wait until after the pie.

∽

SHE ASKED me to give her a ten-minute head start, so I finished the dishes as my mom just looked at me, sighing deeply every other minute.

"Whatever you're doing isn't going to change the way things are between us, Mom," I said, glaring at her. I couldn't make Angelina want to be with me or love me. But I loved her enough that if this was the only way I could have her, then I would take it. She might not love me, but it would be okay. It would have to be.

Finally, I made my way upstairs, and when I knocked on my bedroom door, Angelina told me to close my eyes. I did, and she pulled me into the room a moment later.

"Aaand open."

My jaw dropped and my breath caught as my eyes trailed down the length of her body. Lacy black bra, too meager to fully contain her breasts. Strappy lacy panties that were connected to long, black stockings. My eyes focused on those thin garter straps, and I felt a low rumble in my chest. I wanted to break those little clips with my teeth. She had those damn black heels on that she knew I loved. Fuck.

"I have one last birthday gift for you," she said, grinning, but I only heard it from her tone because I couldn't keep my eyes off of her body and that beautiful, indecent getup she was wearing.

"I thought *you* were my gift."

She placed a kiss on my cheek before giving me a sly smile. "I am." Angelina grabbed a small package, placing it in front of me. "I couldn't give you this one in front of your family for, well... obvious reasons."

I quirked an eyebrow, wondering what the hell she bought me that my parents couldn't see. I unwrapped the box, pulling out something wrapped in tissue. And I couldn't help but chuckle, even more than I did with her sock comment earlier. I knew she liked my Batman socks, she just wouldn't admit it. I liked wearing them with my suit, just to see the little twinkle in her eyes when she'd notice them. "Oh." My eyes met hers for a scorching moment before focusing back on the contents of the box. "Are these what I think they are?" I picked them up, twirling them around a finger.

"Batcuffs, Batboy," Angelina purred.

"You're the most ridiculous and wonderful person in the world." My gift was a pair of Batman logo-shaped handcuffs, and though I had absolutely no idea how one was supposed to use them, they made me smile. Because she'd put so much time and thought into everything she'd given me today—down to the batcuffs. Seriously, they were the most bizarre and impractical things I'd ever seen in my life.

I set down the box and the gift, then bent down to murmur in her ear, "How attached are you to this little thing, Angel?" while toying with the strap of her bra. It barely deserved to be called one, anyway, since you could see her pebbled pink nipples through them.

She flicked her eyes up to me, unhooking the lace garment herself. I pulled her against me and kissed her, slow and deep. I couldn't express my feelings with words, but I could show her. I tore the underwear off her body, leaving her in just those damn black nylons, and when Angelina frowned in dismay against my lips, I said, "I'll buy you new ones. A hundred pairs."

I wanted to take my sweet time with her, trailing my mouth all over her body, drawing patterns with my tongue, but I was already rock solid. I went to pull my shirt off, but Angelina made a little tsk sound.

"My treat," she said, that little twinkle of mischief in her eyes, and she went to work undressing me herself. First my shirt, as she licked down my chest and happy trail. Then my pants, which I assisted her by kicking off the rest of the way.

One hand slid inside my boxers as the other pushed them down my legs. She pumped my length once, and I groaned. I wasn't going to last long, not after our little trip to the hot springs. I hadn't been able to take care of myself yet.

"I want you," I panted against her mouth. "Need to feel you."

We tumbled in bed seconds later, me on top of her, and when her hips rolled against mine, I knew she felt the same urgency. I cupped her pussy, feeling her juices already dripping on my hand, and I gently pushed two fingers inside, making sure she was ready.

"I'm on the pill," she said, each sentence punctuated by little pants. "And I'm clean. There hasn't been anyone else."

"Me too." Not in a very long time. Not since I'd first seen her.

I couldn't describe what it was exactly, but there was something different with how we were touching each other this time. More delicate, almost reverent. This wasn't just about her pleasure or mine—it was about us, together.

I nudged my tip against her entrance, running it along her slit back and forth until Angelina was begging for more. When neither of us could take it any longer, I pushed into her, slow and steady, sliding home. If I thought being inside her with a condom on was perfect, this was unbelievable.

"You're so perfect, Angel," I breathed, leaning my forehead against hers. Nuzzling her nose. My arms were wrapped around her back as she took all of me, and there weren't enough words for what I felt, having her like this. Being fully sheathed inside of her, feeling every inch of her around me.

She gasped as I pulled out, slowly, before plunging back in. This wasn't a race to the finish line. This wasn't some fast thing because we needed our release. We weren't simply getting each other off. It was more than that—so much more.

I kissed her as she wiggled further down onto me, rubbing back and forth as my hips rocked against her. Every little moan she gave me was the best sound I'd ever heard.

"Benjamin…" She cupped my face, stroking my cheek, and I closed my eyes at her touch before kissing her palm.

"I know," I said. We didn't need words. We both felt every bit of this moment in the way we held each other, fingers intertwined on the pillow over her head, bodies moving as one. And as we slowly reached that final peak, the words bubbled up in my throat.

I love you, I thought, as I pushed into her.

I love you, as she cried out.

I love you, as I felt her clenching around me.

I love you, I marveled, as I came inside of her, painting her walls, thinking that in all my thirty years of life, I'd never experienced something where I felt so much and said so little. I'd never had sex without a condom before, and I'd certainly never had sex like this. With my heart, as much as with my body.

∼

"I KNOW I said it already, but one last time before it's over. Happy Birthday, old man." Angelina kissed me on the cheek when I laid down next to her, pulling up the comforter.

"You do know I'm only a few years older than you?" I huffed. Who did she think she was, calling me old?

"I'm twenty-six. You're *thirty*. That makes you ancient compared to me. You're basically robbing the cradle here."

"Whatever you say, Angel. As long as I get to keep you, I don't care what people say about us."

As soon as it was out of my mouth, I wondered if it was the wrong thing to say. But Angelina didn't seem to react one way or another, and I suspected she did it on purpose. It was all I wanted, though, wasn't it? To keep her.

I watched her as she fell asleep, arms around my body, her head nuzzled against my chest. My Angelina. The woman who, for all I had tried to resist, I fell for.

But I couldn't bring myself to tell her yet. I couldn't ask her if she wanted something more. I was paralyzed with fear, worried that one wrong word would ruin everything. I placed a light kiss on her forehead. Being here, home, with her, it had all hit me like a load of bricks. I'd known it before my mom said the words, but when she asked me, point blank, I had to come to terms with it. With my feelings. I was a grown man, after all. Yet Angelina couldn't know, not now. Maybe not ever.

Because I couldn't afford to lose her. She was ingrained in my veins, in the fiber of my being. She was the water and the sun to an otherwise withering plant. I needed her warmth, her passion, and her fiery spirit. I needed her love for romance books and old movies, I needed her glares, her quips, her "I hate you" followed by a searing kiss.

I needed the peace that came from being with her—the trust that only came when two people understood each other as we did.

So, I murmured the words against her hair, low, like a secret, hoping that it would be enough. "I love you."

☙

I WOKE up before the sun on the second day of my thirtieth year. Admittedly, I'd been dreading turning thirty—it'd been looming there, like a reminder that I hadn't accomplished anything substantial yet, and I was still alone. But now, it didn't seem so bad. Especially with Angelina at my side.

She roused slowly when I kissed her shoulder and blinked at me.

"Good morning, Angel," I said, smoothing her tangled hair off of her face. She normally slept in a bun, and every time I saw her like this, I was reminded why. It made me smile, though, seeing her less-than-perfect. A state that only I got to enjoy: the Angelina with no makeup, no hair done, no perfectly polished clothes—and who didn't care about it.

"Morning." She yawned and snuggled in closer to me. "Do we really have to go back today?"

I chuckled. "I wish we could stay here forever, but I think my parents would have something to say about that." I kissed her forehead, disentangling myself from the sheets and her legs. "I'm going to shower."

"Can I join you?" she asked coyly, tugging at the collar of the shirt she'd worn to bed. My shirt. It reached the top of her thighs, so when she stood and slowly walked towards me, hips swaying exaggeratedly, her panties peeked out, and I groaned at the sight.

"You're going to kill me, woman."

"That was the idea."

"I suppose it wouldn't hurt. There are much worse ways to die."

We didn't get an early head start back to Portland like I'd

planned, because we couldn't keep our hands off of each other in the shower. We fooled around, taking our time, neither of us daring to broach the subject hanging over our heads like the sword of Damocles.

We were happy in our little bubble, and we both wanted to preserve it for a while longer.

Finally, once we'd said goodbye to my family, we loaded our bags in the car and began the road trip back to Portland. The plan was to stop in Spokane for the night, so we could divide up the drive in two days, and I intended to make full use of our time together since the time alone at my parents' house had been scarce. I had half a mind to pull over right here on this quiet stretch of road and pull Angelina on top of me, to sink into her and drive her wild till she came.

But no—I was trying to be a gentleman.

"Next time we go to your parents', we're getting a hotel."

"Next time, huh?" I smirked at her, but I felt my heart drop at her words. Was she implying that there would be a next time? Did she… see a future with me?

She playfully pushed at my shoulder. "I'm just teasing you, Benjamin." I swallowed, trying not to show my disappointment. Of course she was joking. "But I did love your family. I'd be happy to come back with you any time."

That filled my chest with warmth. I was glad she'd enjoyed herself. Angelina read a book for the rest of the drive, and I kept my eyes focused on the road—knowing if I let them linger, I'd be pulling off much sooner than our halfway point, and I wanted nothing more than a private room to ourselves tonight. So, no distractions.

The next day, after an eventful night and not quite enough sleep, Gabbi was home when I dropped Angelina off, and she gave me a shit-eating grin as I carried Angelina's bag inside.

"Karma is going to bite you in the ass one day," I grumbled under my breath when Angelina slipped by to put her things in her room. I went to the kitchen to prepare some coffee.

"What was that?" Gabbi's smile was sickeningly sweet.

"Everyone underestimates you, don't they?"

"Not everyone."

"Nicolas told me about the retreat." I got straight to the point.

"Yeah, well." She shrugged. "I didn't do that much."

"I assume you haven't told Angelina?"

"No. I don't..." She glanced towards the hall and lowered her voice. "I don't know how she'll react."

"Why?"

"If she finds out I was the one who helped you with all the little things you didn't know about her, she'll be pissed. I really don't want to ruin my friendship over you."

"It was just a few little favors, Gabrielle. I'm sure she'll understand if I explained that I literally begged for your help."

"Yeah, well, now I'm begging you—please. She's like my sister. She's my person, you know?"

I *did* know, because she was my person too. "Yeah," I said. "I do. But I still think you should tell her what you and Nicolas did. Because I didn't ask for this, and—" I cut myself off when I heard footsteps.

"What are you two talking about?" Angelina came into the kitchen and wrapped her arm around my back when I handed her a mug.

"Oh, nothing," Gabbi said, blowing us a kiss and retreating to the living room. "See you, Benjamin!"

"That was weird," Angelina muttered, sipping her coffee.

"You're telling me," I laughed, hoping my light tone would cover up the amount of tension in the air.

Gabbi wanted me to keep this from Angelina—my girl. Her best friend. But how could I? Some things shouldn't be kept a secret from people you love. But this one wasn't mine to tell.

I just hoped it wouldn't come back to bite me in the ass.

CHAPTER 31
Angelina

The idea of waking up in bed alone after spending a long weekend with Benjamin was strange. It felt cold and distant. Like I didn't belong. The opposite of us sleeping in his childhood bedroom together.

And it wasn't even about sex anymore, but somehow it still surprised me how little that mattered compared to just being with him. To fall asleep in his arms and wake up with my head on his chest. I thought I could get used to good morning kisses and the way my heart fluttered a little bit every time his lips brushed my forehead.

Between his sister asking about our relationship and the rest of his family being so warm and welcoming, I couldn't help but wonder if maybe there was a future for us. If there was something here that I didn't want to give up.

He was my best friend, there was no denying that anymore. The girls would always be my sisters, the people I couldn't live without, the people I'd do anything for, but Benjamin was my person. And it felt right. Which didn't mean we weren't still enjoying tormenting the shit out of each other. I hoped that would never stop, actually, because I loved it more than I wanted to admit.

It was hard to remember what made me so resistant to the idea in the first place.

When we got home, Benjamin carried my duffel bag inside—now even more stuffed after Emily had insisted on sending me home with some of her influencer gifts she claimed to never wear—and I had the strangest sensation of wanting to ask him not to leave. To stay with me.

But I couldn't, and I knew I was going to have to redraw the line between us soon. Because he'd made love to me on his birthday, and now I wanted it again and again—I wanted *him*. I couldn't keep doing this casual-with-no-complications thing much longer because I wanted more, but I was scared and I would fuck it up and Benjamin would leave me and I was going to do the one thing I'd always vowed not to do.

Let a man break my heart.

I hated watching my mom struggle after the divorce. There were so many nights where she'd cried herself to sleep on the couch or hidden in the car inside the garage. Dad hadn't cheated, and Mom still loved him. But somewhere along the way, the people they were when they got married and the people they were after having me and Daniel had changed.

It was hard to watch them both struggle to stay together for our sakes, but it was even harder after they divorced. Watching them both try to move on, while the only person I felt like I truly had anymore was Daniel. I'd vowed then, after seeing what the divorce left in its wake, the way it split our family apart, that I'd never let myself be in a situation like that. Where I loved somebody, but it wasn't enough. If I wasn't enough for them, couldn't be enough for them, I didn't need them in my life. It was why I'd stopped dating. Because men always wanted more than I could give.

Gabbi smirked at me as I plopped on the couch after Benjamin left. "So. How was it? Benjamin's Birthday?"

I'd told her all about it before leaving, since I was going to be gone for almost a week, and I'd known right away that it was all bullshit when she gave me a look that said, *going with him to his parents' house? For his Birthday? With no feelings involved. Sure.* But I apparently liked lying to myself, so I just shrugged.

"It was nice. His sister is fun."

"That's it? That's all you're giving me. *Nice?* Come on, I want to know the nitty-gritty! Give a girl something!"

I shook my head at her puppy dog eyes. "I'm still not sharing details of my intimate life with you—and no, I'm not telling you whether or not there *was* any sex."

"You're no fun," she whined. "I can get more out of Charlotte, and she hasn't had sex yet. I swear."

"Yeah, well," I laughed. "She also turns beet red when you talk about sex, so I think she's still got a long way to go on that front."

"Eh. So, what's going on with you?" Her expression turned serious, almost worried. "I hardly ever see you home anymore."

It was my turn to blush, thinking about what I was doing those nights, and I gave her a sheepish, guilty smile. Gabbi was right, I'd spent more nights at Benjamin's lately than here, even before the trip. I was saved from finding a good enough answer by a chiming sound. Toothless padded over to me, the bell on her collar jingling with each step, and she meowed, pawing at my feet and nuzzling against me.

"Well, hello to you too, sweetie," I said, petting the cat's soft head, making her purr.

"You know you can bring him over more often, right? I don't mind."

"I just... I didn't want you to feel like I was pushing my not-boyfriend slash hookup slash friend-with-benefits on you. I've tried to only have him over when you're not home." When I glanced at her, Gabbi had a weird look on her face—one that had been there for longer than the last few months. "What?"

"Huh?" She blinked, then waved me off. "Oh. It's nothing."

"You're being weird."

She nudged me with her shoulder. "Nah. Just thinking."

"About what?" I tried prodding her, but she changed the subject, and I let her.

"Want to watch a movie?"

We spread a blanket over our laps, enjoying some quality time with each other as Toothless curled up between us. I snuggled close to her. I may never have a man love me, but I'd always have my best friend by my side.

∼

THE NEXT TWO weeks passed quickly. Benjamin and I were both swamped with work before the holidays, and it felt like the only time I saw him was when we'd brush past each other in the hallways. I'd get home late at night, collapse into bed, and I'd be fast asleep in a matter of seconds. I didn't even have time to turn on my Kindle, let alone spend time with Benjamin.

This forced time apart was making me question everything, and I didn't like it. I'd always been the kind of person with straight ideas in mind, never vacillating, someone whose actions were rational and based on logic. What was wrong with me now that I'd become this mess of emotions? Not to mention the fact that I felt an inescapable draw to Benjamin, like he'd become essential to my day-to-day life.

There wasn't a specific reason my feet brought me to his office, but here I was. I stood in front of the door, ready to knock, when I heard voices inside. Is that…?

"Nicolas. Hi." I shouldn't have been surprised to see my friend coming out of Benjamin's office. He was his superior, after all. But he looked too chummy to be leaving a business meeting. Nicolas used to tell me how stubborn Benjamin was, how much of a pain in the ass he could be. I wondered if that was half of the reason I'd started being a bitch to him in the first place—because Nicolas hadn't cared for him. But this? Nicolas looked *joyful*. Which was weird, to say the least.

"Hello, Angelina. Wish I could stay and chat, but I have a

meeting with Zo in a few minutes. Good to see you!" And then he was gone, and I had this strange feeling in my gut that maybe I didn't understand anything at all.

I knocked on the door lightly before walking in. Benjamin looked happy to see me, but also... anxious? I wasn't sure what that was about, either.

"Hey. What were you talking to Nicolas about?"

"What?" He looked over at the door, as if he could still see Nicolas standing there. "Oh. Nothing important."

"Are you two actually friends now?"

He shrugged. "I guess." Huh. That was definitely weird.

"Do you want to get lunch?" I asked him, biting my lip.

"I'm sorry, Angel. I have a lot to do and..."

"No, no. I get it. It's fine."

"I'll make it up to you tonight?" he said, giving me a grin that didn't reach his eyes.

I nodded, still perplexed. "Sure. That's fine." What else could I say? I didn't know where my sweet, playful man had gone. The one who brought me ice cream when I wasn't feeling good or threatened to tie me up just because he knew it turned me on. But no matter what was on his mind, I thought he trusted me enough to share it, whatever was troubling him, regardless of the status of our relationship.

"I'll see you tonight," I said, and I had to swallow the lump in my throat when I left his office without another word from him. Memories of our time together flashed through my mind. Sneaking away during lunch breaks to fool around. Late nights spent working on the small couch in his office, laptop on my lap and feet on his. Shoulder massages when he saw me stressed from all the work I'd been doing on my ad campaign in order to secure my promotion. He'd been there every step of the way for me, so why wasn't he including me in this?

The rest of the day was spent with a bitter feeling in my chest—something that felt a whole lot like heartache.

It was two weeks until Christmas when Alexander Larsen called for a company-wide meeting, causing everyone to be crammed in our biggest conference room.

"Fancy seeing you here," came a smooth voice that I recognized by now. I turned, and grinning at me in all his ginger glory was Benjamin's friend, Liam.

"Hello, Liam," I said, giving him a small smile.

"So, you heard, huh? Can't believe the two of you at that retreat led to this."

"Hm? What are you talking about?"

"About Benjamin? He did tell you the news, right?" The answer must have been apparent on my face because Liam grimaced. "Oh, shit. He hasn't talked to you? I just assumed—"

"Liam." I cut him off, feeling more agitated by the minute. "What do you mean? What's going on?"

But before he could respond, Nicolas's father was on the stage, greeting the employees. "I will keep this brief. As you know, I've been waiting for the right moment to step down and turn the company over to my son, Nicolas." That was a known fact. Mr. Larsen had wanted to set the company up to be in a good place for his son. Someone may think he was a fool to leave the tech company he'd built from the ground up to his twenty-seven-year-old son, but I thought it was smart. Nicolas was intelligent, curious, and passionate, which will make him a great leader when the time comes. He already had big plans to keep the business growing.

I looked around for Benjamin, but I didn't see him. I hadn't seen him at all, actually, ever since I'd left his apartment this morning. Things had gone back to normal after that day in his office—as normal as they could be with our not-relationship—but I still had this nagging feeling in my stomach that something was wrong. That there was something he wasn't telling me.

Gabbi slid into the empty seat next to me, and I leaned over to ask about Benjamin, but she hadn't seen him either. What was going on? I felt an ominous feeling wrapping around my lungs like there was something I was missing. Then I finally spotted Benjamin near the stage, and I could breathe a little easier. He was... laughing with Nicolas? As the latter patted him on the back. They seemed so buddy-buddy, so different from a few months ago when Benjamin used to resent Nicolas for his position in the company. I still hadn't figured out what had changed between them to make them now on such good terms.

"After a lot of deliberation and encouragement from my darling wife," Mr. Larsen continued, "I've decided to retire, effective January 1st of next year." A stunned gasp rippled through the room, and then there was Nicolas joining his father on stage, his bright blonde hair standing out under the harsh lights. That was sooner than any of us expected. "I know he'll do a great job carrying on my legacy, and I'm excited to witness all of the new changes and practices he's going to implement—some of which from the comfort of my private plane, of course." Everyone laughed around me, but the knot in my stomach wouldn't go away. "Take it away, son."

"Liam," I hissed under my breath. "What were you going to tell me?"

He looked at me like he'd seen a ghost. "He didn't tell you about why he and Nicolas had been meeting for weeks?"

"Weeks? But Nicolas and Benjamin didn't get along until after..."

"Along with other staff changes that will be announced in the next few weeks," Nicolas said from the stage, "I'm pleased to announce my successor as CFO will be none other than Benjamin Sullivan. He's worked under me diligently for the last two years, and I am confident he's going to be an excellent addition to the team."

There were more words and clapping and laughter, but I didn't hear any of it. My head was spinning and my heart was ringing in my ears.

I could have seen this coming. I should have seen this coming, and yet—yet nothing seemed to make sense. Or maybe everything did. Finally. The reason Benjamin had wanted to get close to me in the first place at the retreat. The reason he'd insisted he wasn't such a bad guy and that if I just gave him a chance, I would see…

He was after the promotion. He knew Mr. Larsen would make the announcement soon and if I, Nicolas's best friend at the company, was persuaded he was a good person, Nicolas would trust my judgment and entrust Benjamin with the role of CFO.

Don't jump to conclusions, Angelina. It was my brother's voice in my head. But Daniel wasn't here, was he? And he didn't have to stare at the face of the man he loved—loved, dammit, because I was stupid enough to go and fall for him—as he stood on stage looking overjoyed while he shook hands with Nicolas's father.

I looked up at both of them, the man who was supposed to be my friend and the man I was in love with, and I realized I didn't know anything. Not at all.

CHAPTER 32
Angelina

I had to get out of there before I spiraled. I could pull myself together. I could go back to being the cool, calm, and collected Angelina. I just needed a minute. Because I had no intention of letting any of these people see me break.

Unfortunately, my best friend was on my heels, shouting my name in the hallway, and I spun around. "Gabrielle." She stopped and stood straight when I addressed her by her full name, something I never did. "What's going on? I need you to tell me the truth because Benjamin and Nicolas—"

"Oh, God." Gabbi looked sick. "He told you."

"Told me what?" My voice sounded dangerously close to shrill, but I needed someone to make all this make sense. "What's going on?"

She stumbled upon her words. "Wait. What did you mean?"

"Liam told me that Benjamin and Nicolas have been having meetings for weeks. Did you know?"

She frowned. "Not about that, just—I knew Nicolas was planning on giving Benjamin the promotion because they'd worked out their issues and gotten closer over the last few months, but I didn't know specifically..."

"Why." One word—not a question.

"Why what?" she whispered.

"Nicolas must have told you. What happened? What changed?"

I watched her as she considered whether to tell me something or not, until she made up her mind and said, "You did."

"Me? I don't understand. It wasn't like we hung out with him together. I..." I inhaled deeply before I felt a pang in my chest. "Wait. Did he—Benjamin, he was—he was using me to get closer to Nicolas. And you... you knew?"

"No! Ang, no."

I turned away, confused by all the emotions bubbling up inside of me. This is what happens when you ignore them, thinking they'd just go away somehow. Your carefully built facade cracks, until they burst out of you in the worst way possible. In a way you can't control.

"Angelina, please. It wasn't like that. I don't think it was like that for him, either."

"How do you know?"

There was a pause before Gabbi sighed. "This is why I told him that I didn't want to tell you—"

"What, Gabbi? Tell me *what*!" She was like a deer in the headlights when I snapped, and I had a sinking feeling in my gut. "Tell me what? What are you saying right now? Were you..." I had to stop and take a breath, feeling my voice wobbling. "Have you been keeping something from me too?"

"Angelina..." She took a step towards me, her voice low and pleading. "It's not like that. Please, just let me explain. Nicolas and I, we—"

"I-I can't believe you. You're supposed to be my best friend. How could you let him use me like this? And help him get closer to me?"

"It wasn't like that! You don't understand. I would never—"

"Gabs, I love you, but I *can't* do this right now. I just..." I shook my head, stepping away from her. "I don't understand how this happened. How I let this happen."

I turned to walk away, to get back to my office, to be anywhere but here, but Gabbi grabbed my wrist. "Please, just listen to me. You're in your own way, Ang, and you need to get out of it if you want to be happy. You've always gone on about how you are okay being alone, and I know you are, but with Benjamin? I've never seen you so happy. I just want you to live, because you're my best friend and I love you."

"No matter how you felt," I said, dreading the sting in my eyes. "You had no right." I tore my wrist from her grip, storming away.

∽

WHAT WAS REAL, and what was so he could get close to me for this promotion? That was the one question occupying my mind. I was going over every moment we'd spent together, every word, every gesture.

He used to hate me. That much I was sure of. The moment we crashed into each other at the retreat, he knew who I was, and I was sure he wasn't happy to see me. He'd been a jerk, like he always was. But then, what changed? Had he seen me talking to Nicolas and realized that we were close friends? Thought perhaps he could exploit our friendship to get what he wanted? I'd gotten the feeling from Nicolas that Benjamin resented working under someone younger than him, but in the entire time we'd been together... No, not *together*, I had to remind myself.

It didn't matter that he'd taken me to his parents' house. It didn't matter that we'd made love as if we were in love. I'd never slept with someone without a condom before, and yet I did with him. Let him have a final piece of myself that I hadn't even realized I was giving over.

But I'd given him my heart long before, willingly or not.

I went back to the conference room after getting some air, and I was standing right at the entrance, on the furthest side from the stage. Frozen, watching the scene of Benjamin shaking hands with

Mr. Larsen and Nicolas for the pictures. It was a blur of flashes, voices, and small talk with colleagues, until Benjamin's face was suddenly in front of me, and he was smiling at me, and I couldn't for the life of me figure out what I'd done to him to make him want to do something like this to me in the first place.

To make me fall in love with him just to break my heart.

"I couldn't have done it without you," he said, squeezing my hand. I let him hold onto it and steer me to an empty hallway, away from prying eyes. I kept thinking about all the little things he said and did that had never quite added up. Couldn't have done it without me? All those times I'd seen him talk to Nicolas at work events, even during the retreat... He'd just been using me to suck up to my friend all along.

As soon as we were alone, Benjamin leaned in to kiss me, but I backed away. Turned away from him and steeled myself.

"Was this a game to you?" My voice was cold, hostile. Nothing like the warmth I'd given him before. He didn't deserve my smiles anymore.

"What?"

"Us," I said, turning around. "Was it all just a game to you? A ruse to get yourself the promotion?"

It seemed to dawn on him then. "No. Angelina, no—" He reached for my hand, but I took a step back. He would not comfort me this time.

"Tell me the truth. Please." I took a shaky breath. "Did you befriend me with the intention of getting in my good graces so you could look better to Nicolas Larsen, my friend and CFO of the company?" A long moment passed. "Yes or no, Benjamin."

He hung his head, and I knew then. "Yes."

Crack.

"And did you plot with Gabbi on ways to make me like you using information only she would know as my best friend?"

"Angelina—"

"Answer. The. Question." I quickly wiped my eyes. I wouldn't let him see me like that.

"Yes."

Crack.

"So what? You were using me, the whole time?" I didn't cry. I never cried. But *dammit*.

"I never intended—"

"For me to find out?" I laughed, but it was bitter and wobbly. "It's a little late for that, isn't it? Was I just some sort of challenge for you? Some sort of epic conquest? A dare from your buddies? 'Can I get the ice bitch to sleep with me?' Well, congratulations. I hope you got what you wanted." The next words scraped at my throat when I forced them out. "Because you've lost me."

"Angel, baby, no." Benjamin halted, wide-eyed, when I put a hand between us. He wanted to touch me and I just couldn't let him. "You've got it all wrong. It wasn't like that. Not for me. You're the one who said you wanted to keep things casual. Just sex."

I gaped at him. "Because we're both bad at relationships! We both said that."

"Then what have we been doing the last two months? Because that sure as hell felt like a relationship to me."

"This is why we were supposed to have rules! So no one got hurt!"

"Don't put this on me like I was the one who threw them out. We both did. Together. And don't tell me that you would've rather we kept it cold, impersonal sex."

"But those rules were there for a reason, weren't they?" I whispered, so low I could barely hear myself.

He stood there, looking at me like I held the answer to the universe, like I could give him everything or take it away. Like one word from me would've wiped the pain from his eyes, that same pain that was spearing right through my soul.

"So neither of us would fall in love."

I shrugged my shoulders, sniffling a bit. "Because we're not together."

"Aren't we?"

"No, Ben. We agreed it was just sex. And no matter how great it was, you were just using me to get your promotion. None of it was real." This conversation didn't feel real to me. It was making me question everything about who I was and that was exactly why I only had flings—because feelings were complicated, and I didn't want that. I didn't *need* that.

"Angelina…" Benjamin's hands twitched by his sides and he closed them into fists. I knew he wanted to wipe away the tears that I was trying to hold in, and a sob almost broke out of me.

I would not cry in front of him.

"This—whatever it was—it's over." I swallowed. "I don't want to see you again. Don't talk to me if you see me around the office."

"Please," he whispered, "just hear me out. Let me explain."

"Congratulations again," I said, my voice devoid of any emotion. "I hope you have everything you wanted now." I turned around to leave but spun on my heels when Benjamin's loud voice made me flinch.

"God! You don't even know."

"Know what?! Know how betrayed I felt when I found out about Nicolas? About how Gabbi has been helping you win me over behind my back? That you have—"

"That I love you!" The words erupted from him like a volcano that's been inactive for centuries and its sudden blast left nothing but agony and destruction in its wake. "You don't know that I've been in love with you from the first time I saw you on my first day at the company. I asked Gabbi for your name, I begged her to help me because I couldn't get you out of my damn mind. All those emails, every stupid excuse, were just me trying to get to know you. All I wanted was a chance." He huffed, breathless from his outburst. "And then you literally fell into my arms, but you hated me. Of course you hated me. And it felt like nothing I did was enough."

"But you *had* me," I whispered, trying to reconcile his words with everything that happened. "I was yours."

"Not completely. You wanted something casual. And maybe at first, that was enough. Just to have you at all, but then it wasn't. Because I loved you, and you looked at me like there was no way I could ever love you back."

"I told you I'm not good at relationships," I said, like that statement was the only thing keeping me upright.

"I don't think that's true," Benjamin said, taking a tentative step towards me. "Your relationships may have never worked out, but you're perfect with me. You're perfect to me, Angel. You're scared to let someone love you, and I think I get it now. But I'm not going to leave. I'm going to fight for you, show you that I can be everything you need. That I can be someone you want.

"A life without you in it isn't a life that I want. I like it when you yell at me. When we bicker, and there's that little spark of fire in your eyes. Some people might call you cold, but that's because they don't know you like I do. You're full of fire, Angel, you burn inside and I want to burn with you. And you don't even know. You don't even *know*."

Minutes or hours passed in which time was suspended and I couldn't feel myself blinking, thinking, breathing.

"Angelina. Look at me." Suddenly, Benjamin was right in front of me and grabbed my hand. "Look me in the eyes and tell me you don't have feelings for me. Tell me you don't care about me. Tell me you don't want to be with me."

I inhaled, ready to say the words. Ready to put an end to this madness. But couldn't.

My traitor, traitor heart.

"Why can't you accept that someone could love you? That—I could love you?" His touch across my skin was so gentle and caring, reminding me how he'd always gone out of his way for me, even when I hated him. Even when I thought he hated me. But everything I knew, everything I thought I knew, none of it had been real, and my mind was reeling all over again.

Do you really? I wanted to ask him, but shook my head instead. "I don't know," I whispered back. How long had I felt unlovable, without even realizing it? Did I even know where the feeling stemmed from?

"I just want to *try*, Angelina. It's a leap of faith. You fall, I'll catch you." He tucked a loose strand of hair from my ponytail behind my ear. "There's no one I want more than you. Nothing I want more than to make you happy. To see you smile."

"I..." And until the words came out, I wasn't sure what I would say. "I can't." My throat was tightening, and I didn't know what to do. All I knew was I didn't want to cry—not here, not in front of him. "I can't do this. I have to go. I'm sorry. I'm so—I just—" I turned and ran down the hall.

It was over. We were over.

We weren't supposed to fall for each other, and we weren't supposed to get attached. That was our agreement. That was my most important rule.

But I broke it. I fell in love with Benjamin Sullivan. And he lied to me from the very beginning.

CHAPTER 33
Benjamin

"What happened?" Gabbi came straight to my office once everyone returned to work. I wanted to follow Angelina, but I knew that would only make it worse.

"She found out."

"I gathered that much. But how? I didn't say anything to her, and Liam—"

"Liam?" I frowned. "What did he tell her?"

"Enough. Benjamin, she thinks you've been using her. You gotta tell her the truth."

"I *tried*. And you were the one who didn't want to tell her anything in the first place. About you and Nicolas and your schemes."

"But it's not true, right? You didn't..."

I wished I could say no, that the thought never even crossed my mind. But... I pinched the top of my nose. "She thinks I went after her at the retreat just to get in Nicolas's good graces."

"And you told her it's not true, right?" Shame filled me as I looked at her. "Right?" Gabbi said again, begging me to tell her what she needed to hear.

"I..." I couldn't tell her it wasn't true. Because, at first, I did want to befriend Angelina to make sure she didn't fuck up my chances for the promotion. It was wrong, I manipulated her, and, fuck, I was an asshole for it. But I didn't sleep with her to get on her good side. It took me a very short time—spending the day together, doing all the activities—to realize how much I genuinely liked her. And I couldn't help that I'd always been attracted to her, since the very first time I saw her.

Everything I ever told Angelina was real, but there was so much more she didn't know.

"I never meant for this to happen. I never meant to hurt her. You have to believe me. I'd never..." My voice broke, and I had to clear my throat. "I need your help, Gabrielle. Please."

She let out a deep sigh, pondering her options. Finally, she cursed under her breath. "She seems equally pissed at me right now, so I'm not sure how much help I can be."

"You don't understand." I sucked in a breath. "I can't lose her. I can't."

"Just... give her some time and space. She needs to process this on her own before she's going to talk to either of us."

I didn't want to give her space; I didn't want to go days without talking to her. But I told her I loved her, and she didn't say it back. Didn't even acknowledge it.

Gabbi was right, though. I tried calling Angelina over the weekend, but she sent me straight to voicemail. And my texts were all unread.

On Monday, Liam sat across from me in my office, shoulders hunched and sounding regretful as he told me what he'd said to Angelina. I'd never told him that Angelina and I were sleeping together, or about our relationship, but I found myself sharing the full story, how it began and where we were now.

"I'm sorry, man. I didn't know."

"You couldn't have. It's fine." I sighed. "You can go, no sense in both of us sitting around miserable."

"You sure you're okay?" he asked, and I didn't know what to say.

No, I'm not okay. I love her, and she won't talk to me. "I gotta go," I muttered after a moment. I took the elevator to head down to the Marketing floor, but her desk was empty.

"Is Angelina not in today?" I asked Harper, whose desk was next to her. Harper had always liked flirting with me, but we both knew it was harmless; she was one of the few colleagues I chatted with every now and then.

"No, she called and said she wasn't feeling well. She'll be working from home this week. Send her an email if you need something."

I wanted to laugh at the hilarity of the situation. Not because it was funny, but because she'd just reduced our entire relationship—its importance—down to sending an email. I thought about all of those emails Angelina and I exchanged over the past year.

The ones she'd send first thing in the morning when she was so polite, almost warm. Like maybe, after a good night's sleep, she forgot why she hated me so much. The ones she'd send me in the late afternoon, after a tiring day. Concise and professional, but slightly less considerate and a lot more explicit in showing her frustration with my quips and not-as-necessary corrections.

And then there were the few ones she'd send me at night, long after she was clocked out of work, full of misspellings where she'd tell me off, clearly emboldened by some amount of alcohol. Those were the ones I'd never forget. I'd printed out one where she'd signed off with *Disrespectfully Yours*, followed by her name.

What was I supposed to do now? Send her an email, begging her to talk to me? It was pathetic, but desperate times call for desperate measures.

From: b.sullivan@willamettetech.com
Date: December 12, 2022 at 11:13 AM
To: a.bradford@willamettetech.com
Subject: Please

Angelina,
I know I don't deserve for you to hear me out, but I'm a selfish bastard and can't go another day without talking to you. Regardless of the means.
Liam told me what he said at the announcement, and I need you to know, it wasn't true. Not all of it, at least. I never meant to hurt you, and I never meant for any of this to happen.
At the retreat, I was trying to get on your good side so that we could be friends. I won't lie about that. And if I originally believed that maybe getting closer to you meant I had more chances with Nicolas, that thought was out of my mind as soon as I got to know you. It took me just a few days, that was enough for you to bewitch me.
I never intended on falling in love with you, but I did. It was real for me, all of it. I agreed to being friends with benefits because I was lying to myself, telling myself I didn't want all of you. And when I finally got my head out of my ass, I was terrified of scaring you away. You said you wanted to be just friends, that you didn't want a commitment, and I was trying to respect that.
If you believe anything I say, believe this: I would have never done anything to intentionally cause you harm or hurt you. You mean too much to me.
Nicolas was the one who put us together for the activities at the company retreat, because he and Gabbi thought that maybe we'd be able to get over our emails feud if we worked it out in person. Joke's on them, huh?
I did ask Gabbi for help getting to know you better. (She told me your shoe size. And your favorite snack.) Don't be mad at her. She loves you. She was one of the first people I met when joining the company, and when I asked her about you, her face lit up and she told me that you were her best friend. I never meant to manipulate you by asking her for help. I know it's not enough, and I know intentions don't always matter when you end up hurting someone you care about. So, I'm sorry.
I miss you.

It's barely been four days and I'm going out of my mind. What spell did you use on me, Bradford? Please, yell at me. Please, tell me you (don't) hate me.

Always Yours,
Benjamin Sullivan

I NEEDED to fix what I broke, and I needed to do it now, before any more time slipped past. It'd been a week, and as I feared, Angelina never responded. So, I called for all hands-on deck.

There were only four people who knew exactly how to get through to her, so I'd sent an SOS text to Gabbi, asking her to assemble the girls and Daniel. It was Saturday, which means I had only two days to figure out a way to win her back before she returned to the office on Monday.

"I'll tell you exactly what you need," Noelle said, looking around the table. "Big. Romantic. Gesture."

"For Angelina?" I asked, skeptical. "Would that work? Isn't she anti-romance in real life?" I smiled to myself, because I'd said something similar to her when we started watching romcoms together. But I'd always suspected, deep down, that wasn't true. Angelina craved romance; she was just scared to admit it to herself.

"She's got a tough shell," Gabbi mused. "Because she's been afraid of letting someone in for so long that she forgot how to love. But all she really needs is someone to fight for her. Someone to show her that no matter what, through thick and thin, they're going to be there for her."

Noelle agreed, bobbing her head. "She's never tried to be in a relationship because she saw her parents' marriage fall apart, and I think she worries if that ever happened to her, it would be game over. How do you come back from that?" The redhead looked at her boyfriend, Matthew, sitting beside her. "How do you go from loving someone with your whole heart to losing them? It's scary."

"I know firsthand how hard it was for her to watch our parents' divorce," Daniel sighed. "It changed her, in so many ways. Ways I'm not even sure she's fully accepted. But I do know one thing." He looked at me and paused before saying, "She cares about you. More than that, she has feelings for you."

My first instinct was to deny it. Deny that Angelina could ever love me, especially after I messed everything up. But then I thought about my birthday. About her gifts. We made love, and she let me be intimate with her in a way I suspected she never had before. Was it really that crazy? To think that she fell for me too?

"Did you tell her you love her? That you want to be with her?" Charlotte asked, happily sipping on a milkshake even during an emergency meeting.

"No," I said. Not before all of this. "Angelina has never wanted serious. I was still—I was trying to figure out how to ask her to forget the rules and be in a relationship with me. It was too soon to talk about feelings."

"You do, though, don't you," Charlotte said sweetly. "Love her."

My mom had asked me the same question at Thanksgiving, and if I hadn't been certain at that moment, I was after, when I held Angelina in my arms in my childhood bed. "Yeah. I do. I love her."

There was a moment of silence full of tension. The truth was out, and we were all coming to terms with it.

"Okay," Gabbi said eventually. The girls seemed to have a silent conversation among them before finally nodding their heads.

"So, you'll help me?" I would beg and plead if I had to. I needed the woman I loved back.

"You have a plan?" Gabbi crossed her arms over the table as she stared at me.

"I do. And I need you guys to get her there, so she'll hear me out."

"We can do that." Charlotte smiled at me, and Noelle squeezed my arm.

"I'm going to fight for her. And then I'm going to prove to her that I'm here for the long haul."

Angelina needed to know that I wasn't going to leave. I loved her, and I wanted her and her glares, her snarky remarks, her grumpy attitude, and I wanted it all. Forever.

I was going to convince her that I was here to stay.

CHAPTER 34
Angelina

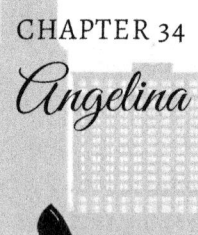

I wish I could say that after leaving work that day, I went home and carried on with life as usual. Held my head high, went to the gym, and ran until my legs hurt on the treadmill and my heart put itself back together.

Instead, I was a coward. I called in sick and asked to work from home the next week. I ignored texts and calls. I shut myself in my room and stared at the blank canvas in front of me—a life that I'd always been too busy to fully paint in. I'd given it little details, here and there, some spots of color, but there had never been a fully formed, painted picture. Not until Benjamin came into my life and made me slow down and appreciate the little things.

What was left of that? I felt hollow inside, and I ached in a way I'd never experienced before.

All my life, I'd never felt good enough. It was hard to explain exactly where this deep-rooted fear came from. It wasn't like I hadn't gotten enough love as a child or lacked good friends. But I'd always had this gut feeling that everyone I loved would leave me. Why would they stay? I was quick-tempered, prone to irritation, cold, and no matter how nicely I dressed or how much makeup I wore, my armor couldn't hide the terrible facets of my personality.

Sometimes, I liked to think about fifteen-year-old Angelina. The one who naively believed that everything in the world was magical, and that people were inherently good. I liked to think of her as nice Angelina. The Angelina of before. There was a before and an after—after I learned the world was a cruel place, after the joyful laughter and the family days and the carefree spirit.

High school was rough. I retreated into myself. I stopped opening up to people. I stopped being friendly to guys because I realized that if you were too nice to them, they would think you were interested. I alienated my friends, afraid that they were talking bad about me behind my back.

College was like when you looked out the window during a storm, and there was that one little sliver of glass with no rain running down on it. I found Gabbi, Noelle, and Charlotte, who didn't care that sometimes I was moody or grumpy or not quite easy to be around.

They didn't know that sometimes I would lock myself in my room and scream into a pillow until there was nothing left. But I didn't cry. When was the last time I cried?

I hated the person I'd become—the cold shell of a person who never stepped outside her comfort zone, who was so terrified of personal failure that she put everything she had, heart and soul, into her job because that was the easiest thing. I'd never tried dating seriously because I was *so* sure it wouldn't end well.

I didn't allow myself to love, because I didn't want to give them an opportunity to break me any more than I already was. I knew I wasn't good enough—why would I let anyone else realize that as well? I was too smart, too logical, too intimidating. Too cold, too focused, too closed off. I was everything, and I was nothing. I was carrying around years of feeling inadequate, and still, I never cried.

Sometimes I wanted to scream at the world and ask what I'd done to deserve this. To deserve feeling like if I disappeared tomorrow, no one would care. It was like navigating inside a dark storm cloud, and I kept forgetting that people were standing right outside of it, waiting to comfort me, to care for me, to love me.

And now I'd shut out the only person I had ever let in, the one person who might care about me as much as I cared about him, and why? Because I was scared. I was scared to let him love me.

It wasn't fair. It wasn't fair to him that I was a giant mess bundled up in pretty packaging. Benjamin deserved someone who could love him with every piece of their being, and who he could love right back. But could that be me?

I didn't know how long I sat there, staring at the window, wrapped in my own agony. It felt suffocating, like if I just dove a little deeper, maybe I'd drown under its weight.

Who was I?

I kept asking myself the same question, over and over. Who was I? I hated him because I hated myself. I hated him because his emails hit every insecurity I had and worked their way into my mind, like a poisonous snake coiled in the bushes, ready to strike, and he didn't even know. I hated him because he was perfect, and no matter how much I worked on it, I wasn't, and that wasn't fair. I hated him because how could someone that perfect love a broken thing like me?

He couldn't. But who was I? Maybe I wasn't asking the right question. Who did I want to be? Who was I going to choose to be? Maybe those were the questions I'd been avoiding answering all along.

I wanted to be the kind of woman who could love with all her heart. The one who could tip her head back and smile simply because the sun was shining on her face. The one who didn't let a single moment in life pass by and captured all the memories, good and bad, because that's what life was. The one who, no matter how much life kicked her down, always got up again. A little bit insecure, and a little bit bruised, but happy and proud to have made it.

I wanted to be the person the people I loved believed I could be. No more fake it till you make it bullshit. I'd made it anyway, hadn't I? The promotion was mine. I knew as soon as I went back to work, it'd be mine. Funny. It was the one thing I'd been working towards all this time, but now that I had it... it didn't make me as happy as I thought it would.

I didn't even care anymore, because everything I'd been working towards—none of it made me happy anymore.

What made me happy? Benjamin Sullivan.

When he smiled at me as we played video games together on his couch. The dumb Batman socks he'd wear with his suit. The way he'd gotten me a copy of his favorite Batman and Catwoman comic, even though it was almost impossible to find and couldn't have been cheap. The way he'd take care of me even when I didn't ask for it. Even when I said no.

How could I let someone like that into my life and not fall in love with them? Impossible. I fell, and I fell hard. Foolishly. Inexorably. There wasn't a single moment I could pinpoint where I thought, "This is it. It's happening." I'd been falling in love with him for so long that he had a permanent spot in my heart now. Which, again. Funny. Because he didn't know. Because I pushed him away.

The rules. Those stupid rules had one goal, one purpose, and I went and completely missed it. I did the opposite of what the rules were about, really.

I fell in love with the best man I'd ever known, and at the first complication, I turned my back on him. I jumped to conclusions, I refused to listen. He told me he loved me, and I walked away.

And my best friend had known all along, hadn't she? Gabrielle had been there for every moment. The stupid email feud. The constant complaining. The lying to myself and trying to convince myself there was nothing more to it than sex. But she'd known. And she'd given Benjamin the littlest things, just some hints—not the full picture. That was for him to find out.

To slowly peel off the layers and reach the core of who I was. And he did that. Patiently, so patiently.

It was never about Gabbi helping him woo me. It was him asking for help.

Something I desperately needed to do now, if I was going to clean up the mess I'd made and tell him the truth.

Tomorrow. I'd sort myself out tomorrow, I promised myself after I finished screaming into my pillow. It was surprisingly therapeutic. I closed my eyes and hugged the pillow to my abdomen, enjoying the quiet that came from being home alone.

For about .5 seconds, until the door to my bedroom was thrown open.

"We're going out," Gabbi said after bursting in, staring down at me with her hands on her hips and a determined expression on her face. "I'm tired of seeing you mope over a guy."

"I'm not moping."

"Then what do you call this?" She gestured around the room—which was, frankly, a bit of a mess—and my sweatpants. The horror: I only owned one pair, and they were generally buried deep in the recesses of my closet. A messy room and sweatpants weren't like me. *But maybe*, a voice in my head said, *maybe it could be the new you.*

At least I wasn't crying. I was just wallowing in my stupidity. I was brooding over the fact that I let myself fall in love with someone just to push them away, afraid to find out that they weren't in it for the right reasons in the first place. But I owed it to myself, and to Benjamin, to hear him out. To let him tell me the real story. The full story.

"This," I said, "is called me being a normal human being. You know. I thought I'd try it from time to time."

"Huh." A beat. "Well, are you done then?"

I knew none of this was Gabbi's fault, but I still couldn't help being the teensy bit upset with her that she hadn't told me any of it from the beginning. "Five more minutes," I requested, pulling the blankets over my body.

"Nope. Time to get up," she said, pulling the covers off of me. "I called in reinforcements."

I groaned, throwing the pillow over my head. "I just want to stay home. It's the weekend anyway, can't I be lazy for no reason?"

Gabbi yanked it out of my hands, glaring at me. "No."

"Oh, cool, thanks," I glared right back. "What a great best friend you are."

"Look. I'm sorry I didn't tell you about helping Benjamin. I really thought you'd be happy with him, okay? And I didn't want to be the one to burst that bubble when you finally seemed to be enjoying yourself for the first time in your life."

"Gabs, I just..." I sighed. "I'm not mad at you, okay? I'm not even mad at him."

"Then what's wrong?"

"I'm an idiot."

"No news there."

"Hey!" I threw the pillow at her, and she threw it right back.

"What's wrong with you?"

"What's wrong with me," I said, on the verge of screaming, "is that he told me he loved me, and I'm a coward! A big, fat, scaredy cat who ran away when things got difficult. He told me he loved me and I. Walked. Away." I punched the pillow. "What am I supposed to do with that?!"

"That's why you're going to get your ass out of bed, shower, and then we're all going to get dressed up and go out for dinner."

I sighed dejectedly. "Just the four of us?"

"Yup," she nodded. "Like old times. Best Friends Book Club and all that." She waved her hand with a little smile. "Noelle told me to say that. Don't tell her, but it's growing on me."

"Okay, I surrender." I wished I had a little white flag to wave, but when it came to arguing with Gabbi, there was no point. Yes, I was stubborn, but she was even more so.

"Good." She flashed a grin as she pushed me into the bathroom, and I took the time to clear my head.

I might lose Benjamin—I wasn't sure he'd want to talk to me

again which caused my heart to shrink on itself—but I had my friends, and damn if I didn't love them more than anything else. They were my constant, my rock. My lighthouse in the stormy sea that was life.

When I got out of the shower, I found Noelle and Charlotte had joined Gabbi and the three of them were all going through my closet.

"I can pick out my own clothes, you know."

Noelle tilted her head. "Oh, we know. Don't worry."

Gabbi placed a hanger into my hands: my favorite red satin dress. Charlotte handed me my favorite heels and Noelle revealed my favorite diamond pendant.

"You guys..." I didn't know how they could manage to make me feel so loved with such small things, but I was grateful to have them.

The girls took charge then, sitting me down at my vanity so they could do my hair and makeup to perfection. My armor, I thought, looking at myself in the mirror as I applied a last swipe of red lipstick; and also, my very sense of being. The core of who I was.

Until now. I didn't want to hide behind my fears anymore. Maybe it would take more than welcoming love into my life to do it, to really accept myself with all my flaws and vulnerabilities, but I had to try. I owed it to myself.

"Thank you," I said to my girls, my best friends, as they crowded around me. "I really do love you all so much."

"Don't cry," Gabbi said, tipping up my chin as I stared at all three of them. "It'll ruin your makeup."

I laughed. "As if."

Now wasn't the time for crying. Now was the time for loving. Loving my friends. Loving the life I wanted to lead from now on. Hopefully, loving the man who, very unwisely, chose me.

And tomorrow... tomorrow would be the time for honesty, and maybe, hopefully, for forgiveness and new beginnings.

CHAPTER 35
Angelina

"What's going on?"

The restaurant was completely empty and dim, which was so unlike an ordinary weekend night. It was a fancy place Benjamin and I had talked about trying, but never had the chance to—partially because I'd insisted on no dates, but we were also so busy with work that we normally ended up with takeout on his couch. The thought made my heart clench painfully. How many things had we wanted to do together? And I'd pulled back so much.

I blinked, shoving my feelings in a far recess of my mind to put in a nice box that I could deal with later. "Why is no one here?" I asked, only to find my friends weren't behind me, and before I could start panicking, the lights came on—but not the overhead lighting, no. A thousand twinkle lights, threaded throughout the ceiling, and in the middle of all of that was... Benjamin.

Dressed to the nines, holding a bouquet of roses, looking as handsome as ever. My heart started hammering in my chest and my lungs felt suddenly too small to properly do their job.

"What are you doing here?" I whispered, my throat too tight to let out anything else.

"I'm getting you back," he said, taking a step forward and handing me the roses.

"How can you get me back if we were never together?"

Benjamin smirked, giving me that cocky look I'd grown to love. Dammit, how was I supposed to remain strong when he looked at me like that? "If that's what you're calling it, Angel."

"Benjamin, I..." There were so many things swirling in my head that I needed to say, but I wasn't ready yet. He'd managed to one-up me once again.

He shook his head as I stared down at the beautiful red roses. Sure, they were cliché, but they were also my favorite. My girls, always coming to the rescue.

"Please, let me explain," he said. "And don't say it's over just yet. Have dinner with me."

I took a deep breath. "You don't have to explain," I said. I'd read his email before going out tonight, and all the text messages he'd sent over the last week. I didn't need him to say everything all over again. I trusted that what he said was true. There were other things that were much more important right now.

"What do you mean?"

"You remember what you told me? That I was your best friend?" I bit my lip, watching an array of emotions flashing in his eyes. Confusion. Regret. Hurt. Tentative hope. "I think you're my best friend too. And more. I don't know how it happened, how you wormed your way in, but I can't imagine..." I left the rest unsaid: *I can't imagine being with anyone else.*

I meant it. If this ended, I wasn't sure I'd ever find someone else I wanted to spend time with as much as I did with Benjamin; someone that I liked everything about. Someone who liked me, on the good days and on the bad days.

"How do you feel now?" I said in a small voice. "Do you still want to be with me?"

"There's only you, Angel. There's no one else for me. There's been no one else since the first time I saw you." There was a resigned sort of smile on his face when Benjamin shook his head.

Like he'd accepted that I would take longer to catch up with him. "I told you, right after I first started with the company, I saw you. And I haven't been able to get you out of my mind ever since."

I finally let my mind process all the things I'd been ignoring for the last week. It took me a while, but...

Oh.

Oh.

"I thought you hated me."

"No. Never. I loved teasing you and imagining you scowling and huffing through your emails. You definitely hated me, though," he added with a smirk

"No way," I scowled. "I hated you because I thought you hated me. Why else would you send all those emails?"

"I was just trying to get close to you, the only way I could think of to not seem like a creepy stalker." He rubbed the back of his head, embarrassed by his confession. "Haven't we gone over this already? I started being kind of an asshole to you—which I apologize for—because you hated me. And the angry emails made me smile."

"All those times you asked to meet in person..." He'd liked me all along. Even when I hated him, he was attracted to me. Wanted to get to know me. "This is crazy."

"Maybe," he said, shrugging. "Or maybe it's just meant to be."

My heart was screaming at me that maybe he was right, but... "I just—I don't know..."

"Please don't hate me," he whispered.

"I don't."

A beat. "You don't?"

"No," I said, sighing and squeezing my eyes shut. "I don't think I ever did." I opened them to the feeling of Benjamin cupping my face, cradling me like I was something sacred, something revered and loved. "I was scared," I admitted quietly. "So scared to let you in, to love you, because loving you meant I could lose you, and if I hated you, that couldn't happen. But I know now that I don't need to be scared of loving you, Benjamin. That's not how I want to live my life, not anymore. And maybe—maybe I masked my feelings with hate because I never thought you could feel the same way. I thought you were like every other man who just wanted me for my body and thought I was a stuck-up bitch behind my back."

"Never. Fuck, Angelina, I'd never do that to a woman, let alone to you. You..." Benjamin leaned in, his eyes fierce with determination. "You thought I hated you, but hate was the furthest thing from my mind when it came to you. All our fighting and bickering and tormenting each other, first through emails and then in person, has been the best part of my day for the longest time. You have been the best part of my life since you walked into that lodge." He swallowed. "You carved your place into my heart, and I can't get you out. I don't want to get you out. I want to love you for the rest of my life, because loving you is like breathing fresh mountain air for me."

A small gasp sounded between us, and I didn't know who was more shocked by those words.

"I'm so in love with you, Angelina Bradford. So, if you wanna leave for good, please tell me now and I promise I won't ever bother you again. But if you want to stay," his voice broke, and I had to fight back tears. "If you want to stay and do this with me, I swear I'm never letting you go. I'm in this for the long haul, Angel. I'll fight tooth and nail for you. And I know that whatever happens, we'll get through it together. Okay?" He wiped his thumbs under my eyes, and I knew I'd lost my battle.

"Okay," I said, and I was crying and smiling, and he picked me up and the sound of my laugh was almost foreign to my ears when he twirled me around.

"Say it again," he breathed against my lips after putting me down.

"Okay. Okay, okay, *okay*—" And it was the only truth that could come from my lips, because I wanted him more than anything. Benjamin knew and kissed me until I was out of breath.

I took the leap, plunged feet first into the cold water of the lake, dove into the shallow pool of uncertainty with the one man I was certain about. He was fighting for me, but I wanted to fight for him too. For us. "I love you, Benjamin Sullivan."

"You're aware you're crying, right?" he responded, and I laughed.

"Shut up."

"Never," Benjamin grinned, then grew serious and leaned his forehead against mine. "I love you. So fucking much."

I sighed happily. "You're still an ass."

"Yeah, but you love me."

"I do. Very much, unfortunately."

"You know, now we really have broken all of your rules."

I didn't feel anything except wild joy at that. Yes, we did. And it felt incredible. I curled into him, burying my face against his chest as he wrapped his arms around me. *My safe place*, I thought, and for once it didn't scare me. "Maybe they were stupid rules," I said.

"Nah. You just hated me then."

Maybe. Or maybe, deep down I knew that I was risking my heart with him and there would be no going back from it. I huffed anyway. "I told you I only hated you because you were an asshole to me first."

"I'm sorry."

"Says the person who literally just told me that he had fun tormenting me."

"You're going to hold this against me for the rest of my life, aren't you?"

"Yup. Speaking of, remember that email where you—" He cut me off with a kiss. Like I said, ass.

"No takebacks, Angel," and he peppered kisses all over my face, making me laugh. Making me feel alive. For the first time in my life, I wasn't just existing. I was thriving, blooming under Benjamin's touch. I'd painted a canvas with all our memories, and now I wanted to live in that world—a world that was so full of color. A world that was *us*.

"Now, Boy Scout," I said, wrapping my arms around his neck. "Will you take me home?"

"You don't want to join the girls?"

I shook my head. "Tomorrow. Now I want to go home."

"With me?"

"It doesn't feel like home without you."

I let him hold me tight as we left the restaurant. Slipped my hand in his, kept them intertwined as he drove. He pulled me into his body as we waited for the elevator up to his apartment, kept his mouth on my head for the ride. I wanted his touch more than anything. Wanted his arms around me, his body all over me.

I wanted him, forever.

∼

AFTER AN ENTIRE WEEK APART, I never wanted to feel like that again. Lost. Helpless. Desperate. I needed Benjamin, and I wasn't afraid of it anymore.

I needed him to remind me that I was strong, and I was lovable, and that it was okay for me to fall apart sometimes, not because he would put me back together, but because he'd be there to let me cry, and then he'd hold my hand as I got back up. I didn't need him, inherently, but I wanted him—to walk side by side with me in life.

Our hands were still clasped together when he opened the front door.

"Benjamin, I—" I started, but he silenced me with a soft kiss.

"I need you," he said, so quietly I almost didn't hear him, but there it was. His vulnerability for me to welcome and care for. I made a promise to myself that I always would.

"Me too," I said, squeezing his hand.

He gave me another quick kiss before he tucked an arm under

my legs, lifting me effortlessly and carrying me like a bride over the threshold and into his room.

"I missed you so much, Angel." He dropped his head to mine. "I was scared you'd never talk to me again."

"Ben..." My heart soared with love for this man. "I just needed you to suffer a little like I was," I said, giving him a little wink. "I never would've shut you out forever, believe me. Even if the girls hadn't kidnapped me, I was going to come find you tomorrow."

His grin radiated warmth and happiness and love, and he took my hand to kiss my palm. "I can't believe you love me."

"Well, get used to it. Cause you're stuck with me now."

"That was the idea." His lips stopped near my ear. "Now, I need to get you naked because I'm going to fuck you until you cry my name, okay, Angel?"

Chills ran down my spine. I nodded enthusiastically—who would say no to that? He put me down and stripped me of my dress and underwear. I fisted his hair, pulling his lips to mine to claim in a searing kiss.

And then I was desperate to get him naked too, bare in front of him, my nipples rubbing against his chest as I kicked my heels off. I tugged off his tie, fumbling with the belt of his dress pants, and happily discarding his suit right in the middle of the floor before I dragged him on the bed.

It felt like it'd been longer than a week when he finally sank into me. My hair was fanned out over the pillows, my cheeks felt bright and warm, and I'd never felt more beautiful, more venerated as Benjamin stared down at me like I was something sacred.

"Come here," I said, pulling him down to kiss him.

We were both crazy with want, and yet none of it was frantic or hard. It was slow, steady. Intentional. Meaningful. *We made it,* it felt like we said. *Now we have each other. It's us and it's real.*

"Angel..." Benjamin moaned, pulling back and thrusting in again. "How do you always feel so good? Fuck. Like you were made for me."

"Maybe I was," I said breathlessly.

He increased the tempo with a groan, gripping my waist tightly while reaching between my thighs with his other hand. I felt a sting on my clit, and I realized he'd spanked me only when he said, "And whose pussy is this?"

"Yours," I cried out as he did it again.

"Who's the only man who gets to see you like this?" He rubbed my folds before pinching my clit lightly.

"Y-you."

"Good girl." He leaned down, taking one of my nipples in his mouth. "I love you," he said against my chest as he plunged deeper inside of me. I threw my head back, unable to hold back my cries. "I love you," he said into my neck, and I held onto his shoulders to stare into his eyes. They were hooded with lust and darker than usual. He wanted me. He loved me. And I could see it all in the burning intensity of his gaze. And *oh God*, I was so close, if he continued hitting that spot that he knew made me wild—

"Benjamin!" I gasped, arching my back, and toppled over the edge. Nothing had ever felt as right as it felt to be with him, and the way he told me he loved me as he kept pushing into me made me come harder than usual. Spent and still panting, feeling his seed inside me, I rested my forehead against his. "I love you."

"You're mine," he said, breathing me in like he couldn't believe it still.

"I'm yours. And you're mine too."

We slept like that, nestled in each other's arms, a reminder that this was real, we were here, and everything was going to be okay.

I didn't stir until late in the morning, to an empty bed and the smell of sizzling bacon. I beamed at the ceiling. I felt like a fool in love, and it was great. I pulled myself out of bed, threw on one of Benjamin's shirts, and went to meet the man I loved for the first of many mornings together.

Maybe I was a hopeless romantic after all.

CHAPTER 36
Benjamin

I'm not saying that I never liked Christmas; I wasn't a *Scrooge*. But this one felt extra special. Being with Angelina was a Christmas worthy of remembering; one of a long series for as long as she was by my side. And my new plan—designed with and approved by her this time—was to keep her forever.

Considering she lived in the Pacific Northwest, her hate for the cold was ironic. The Montana cold was different from the Portland cold, probably because it wasn't as damp, but still, I was always surprised when I caught her all bundled up in layers of multiple fabrics. I loved her grumpy little moods when she complained about things. The way her nose would turn red when she was cold, and I'd offer to kiss it to make it better, and she'd growl at me.

I was especially thankful for the time we had off work for the holidays because I'd never needed a vacation as badly as I did after the events of last week. The days I spent without Angelina had been awful, but as miserable as I was, I knew she'd been suffering too.

Now, finally, everything was perfect.

We went to my parents' house on Thursday after work so we

could spend time with my family—and some alone time together, of course. Angelina packed her own swimsuit for the hot tub this time, but I'd sneakily packed in that tiny white bikini she'd borrowed from my sister. I was obsessed with her body in it, sue me.

"What do you want to do today?" I kissed the top of her head, enjoying watching her pretend to be asleep so she could stay under the covers longer.

Waking up with a smile on my face was becoming a constant, along with my girl in my arms. Being with Angelina felt right, like the final piece of a puzzle slotting into place. Everything in my life made sense again. I had the woman I loved, my family, and the job I'd always dreamed of. Nothing else mattered.

She sighed contentedly, faking a yawn.

"My mom was talking about baking cookies, or we could go into town. Maybe build a gingerbread house while sipping on hot chocolate?"

Angelina snorted. "Dear, I think those are the most domestic words you've ever said to me." Dear. Huh.

"Darling," I said back, placing a small kiss on her lips, "I will be domestic as fuck for you because it means making you happy, and making you happy means seeing you smile, and your smiles are the best part of my day." I flicked her nose. "Second only to your little grumpy faces." She frowned at me, and I smoothed out the wrinkles above her brows. "See?"

"You're the wooorst," she whined, getting out of bed—completely, gloriously naked. I'd stripped her clothes off her last night to eat her out and she'd fallen asleep after she came on my tongue. Twice.

I watched her sway her hips, bare little ass swinging enticingly while she walked into the en suite bathroom and turned the shower water on. "You coming?" she smirked at me over her shoulder, and I was next to her in an instant.

After a very long, steamy shower session, we finally made it downstairs to the kitchen, where my mom was making cookies.

"Need any help, Mom?"

"Want to decorate? The first batch is all cooled and ready for it."

I looked at Angelina and she was already smiling. "Let's do it!" We gathered the supplies and got ourselves situated at the table. Mom had made all sorts of shapes, and we had a variety of colors of frosting and toppings in our arsenal, so we went to town. I started with a tree-shaped cookie and Angelina with a candy cane. Mom turning up the Christmas music playing in the living room was the icing on the cake.

"So, do you two have any plans for the day?" she asked.

Angelina sat her cookie and icing bag down to look at her, licking a spare bit of frosting off her finger before answering. "Benjamin was telling me about the Christmas Market in town, so we were thinking about going there later. I could use picking up a few last-minute gifts." She felt bad because she hadn't really had time to get my family anything, and I knew she'd have fun going through the stalls. She'd pulled me along to the mall in Portland several times for shopping trips, and her enthusiasm was contagious. I still had a few things I wanted to get, too, if I was being honest.

"Oh, that'll be nice," Mom said. "You have to take her by Sally's bakery, get some of that hot chocolate you always liked as a kid."

I smiled. "Okay, Mom."

We finished decorating the rest of the cookies, washing our hands a few times in between so they didn't get too sticky. We kept up idle chatter with my mom, talking about the holidays, Mom asking Angelina about her family traditions, her talking about all the things she'd done with her brother or her friends over the last few years. If my mom thought it was weird that Angelina didn't mention plans with her parents for the holidays, she didn't say anything.

At some point, Angelina reached over, a glob of frosting on her finger, and rubbed it on my nose, which caused a battle of who could get the other stickier. When there was a little bit too much frosting everywhere, I kissed it off her lips.

"We should probably clean up now, Princess." My mom just laughed at us, mumbling something under her breath before walking away. "Come on," I said, looking at our finished pile of cookies. "Let's get ready for the Christmas Market."

Angelina nodded, wiping a little frosting off my cheek. "Lead the way."

∽

Holding Angelina's hand as we walked through town, sipping on the best hot chocolate ever as little snowflakes fell from a white sky, might be my favorite Christmas activity of all time. We wandered the market for a while, collecting more and more bags, most of which I insisted on carrying.

She was wearing one of my sister's beanies that had a big pompom on top, wrapped up in a thick wool coat and scarf. She'd also borrowed a pair of mittens from my mom—something I'd never thought I'd see.

"You're so cute," I said, looking at her. I was always looking at her.

"Yeah, I am," she beamed.

"And humble, too."

She locked her arms around my neck. "I think you're cute too, Boy Scout. And very handsome." She buried her face in my neck so she could whisper in my ear. "And very good with your—"

"Angel!" I couldn't help laughing at her expression. "We're in public."

"What?" She shrugged. "I was just going to say your hands. I saw those cookies earlier, sir. Very good piping skills."

"You're really gonna get it later," I murmured, and she gave me a flirty stare.

"Looking forward to it."

"Come on, let's get home," I said, looking at the sky. It was starting to snow harder, and I didn't want to stay out much longer in case it accumulated any more thickness. Driving in deep powder wasn't much fun. "We're decorating the tree tonight."

"Really?" she squealed, and her excitement made me delirious with joy.

"Angel," I squeezed her hand, "I'm so happy you're here with me. It wouldn't be the same without you."

"I wouldn't have missed being here with you for the world."

Angelina

I ROLLED over from my position nestled against Benjamin, reveling in the way his cock was pressed against my back when he spooned me. I was trying to decide if there was a better way to wake up on Christmas morning when my boyfriend stirred, bringing his arms over my belly to pull me in tighter.

"Merry Christmas, Angel," Benjamin said, kissing the top of my head.

"Merry Christmas, Benjamin." I snuggled closer, happy to be spending our first holiday together as a real couple.

I hadn't celebrated with my parents in years, since I graduated from college and got my own place, but when Benjamin asked me if I wanted to go with him to his parents' house for Christmas this year, I accepted right away. Even if it meant staying in his childhood bedroom. This room held good memories, after all.

Happy didn't even begin to describe us now. We'd fought these feelings for so long, this connection between us. Now that we were together, I could finally say with certainty how stupid we both had been. I was happier than ever, and I knew he was too. I could feel it, in his kisses, his hugs, in the way he looked at me like he couldn't believe I was real.

It turned out I could have it all—the job, the best friends a girl could ask for, the man who loved me for exactly who I was, and the life I'd always wanted to live but was scared to open my heart to for the longest time.

We spent the first week after the night at the restaurant working through a lot of things. We were both getting promoted, which was fantastic, but a little less so from our relationship's point of view. We talked with Nicolas and with the board of directors, who had approved our promotions, and it was agreed that the two of us both serving as executives of the company would be fine as long as our relationship didn't affect our work. We would be extra transparent, and any decision either of us would make that would affect the company would also include the CEO. Besides that, we just had to figure *us* out, and we were. Every day, patiently, happily.

"Do you want to go downstairs and see what's for breakfast?" Benjamin murmured, but I shook my head, interlacing my fingers with his over my chest.

"Wanna stay here for now. In our little bubble."

He chuckled. "You remember what we said the last time we were here? That we," he placed a kiss on my neck, "would get a hotel."

"Mmm. Right. Because we couldn't have sex in your childhood bedroom... again," I giggled. "Aren't you glad we threw that rule out the window too?"

"It's still kinda weird. I don't like having my family in the same house and risking them walking in on us."

"Babe." I turned around and gave him a look. "I think your parents respect our privacy enough not to enter your room without knocking."

"You've met them, right?" He raised an eyebrow. "But anyway, I'm glad I changed my mind."

"Oh, you are?" I grinned. "What tipped the scale for you? When I rode you in the hot tub or when I gave you a blowjob in the shower? Or was it when—"

He cut me off with a kiss. "You're insatiable. Come sit on my face and let me give you your Christmas present."

I laughed. "It better not be the only one, Sullivan." Though I couldn't say I wasn't looking forward to him eating me out. His tongue did feel like heaven.

"Oh, this is just the beginning, sweetheart." He rolled onto his back, and I straddled his chest; I hadn't bothered to put panties on after last night's adventures. "Hold on to the headboard," Benjamin smirked, and then he very much did use his tongue till I was squirming and moaning for him. Merry Christmas to me indeed.

∽

WHEN WE FINALLY STUMBLED OUT OF bed, all cleaned up and sated, we found a giant breakfast buffet set up at the table in the dining room and a heap of presents gathered beneath the Christmas tree.

"Wow. This is incredible." I piled some crepes onto my plate and slathered them full of Nutella and strawberries. "How do you get the presents to look so wonderful, Mrs. Sullivan?" I asked as we all sat around the table. We'd decorated it the other night all together, Benjamin, his family, and I. We had hot apple cider, popcorn, and the cookies Benjamin and I had iced that day, plus a lot more his mom had baked, and it was the perfect evening. I felt like a heroine in a Hallmark movie, and I wasn't ashamed of it.

Mrs. Sullivan smiled. "The trick is to wrap really big boxes, even if the gift is small."

Benjamin rolled his eyes affectionately. "Do you know how many times she's given me a gift card inside a giant box?"

Hunter huffed at that. "At least she didn't wrap it in multiple boxes and make you keep opening wrapping paper until you thought you were going crazy."

"That was one time," she laughed. "And to be fair, Emily wrapped that one."

"Mom!" Emily protested. "You weren't supposed to tell them that."

"Sorry, sweetie. Cat's out of the bag now."

Meals with Benjamin's family were becoming one of my favorite things. Emily was still the craziest ball of energy and fun and style I'd ever met, wrapped up in one person. She'd sent me dozens of photos over the last week for social media. The candid of Benjamin and I cuddled up on the couch, his arms around my middle as I sat in his lap, almost made me tear up.

We were all wearing different Christmas pajamas. My and Benjamin's, much to my delight, were matching. He'd surprised me this morning, saying it was tradition to spend Christmas Day at the Sullivans in a new pair of PJs. Ours were green and red with tiny reindeer all over them, and I loved them because he picked them out himself. Hunter's pajamas consisted of a plaid, forest green Henley and bottoms with snowflakes all over them. Emily wore a green elf onesie, complete with a hood, making her look extremely cute.

"Is everyone ready for presents?" John, their dad, asked as we all helped clear the table. They tended to do this, always helping each other with tasks, whether it was Benjamin helping his mom do the dishes or Hunter helping her cook—I told him I was pretty sure if medical school hadn't worked out for him, he would've made a great chef. The sight made my heart full of warm fuzzies. It was so homey here that sometimes my heart felt like it could burst with joy.

Benjamin's parents were so proud of him for becoming CFO. They had a long conversation the other day, where Benjamin shared how he'd always felt like he was never good enough for them, and that they were disappointed in his career choice. They were surprised but apologized to him. Benjamin's eyes were red when he came upstairs after, but he was happy. It was obvious, watching the way his parents were with him, that they loved him so much. I was just glad that he felt close to his family again. He'd been calling Emily more since his birthday too, and she even texted me sometimes, so I knew how much her brother meant to her.

Once we were all gathered on the couch and armchairs, we started passing out gifts. Emily was the designated present-hander-outer, and they all took the time to open each one individually instead of just ripping into the pile.

I'd managed to get a little something for everyone, and I was genuinely surprised to find that they'd gotten me something, too.

"We knew you two would make it," Mrs. Sullivan had told me at one point yesterday when I was helping her in the kitchen. "It was obvious how much Ben loved you last time you were here." I didn't blush easily, but those words had made my cheeks flush instantly and my heart swell.

Finally, the stack of presents dwindled, and we were down to only a few left under the tree. Benjamin pulled one out of his pocket, handing it to me, and I looked down at the small package with a smile before opening it carefully. Inside a black box was a little heart necklace with a gem that fluttered. A little gasp escaped my lips.

"It's beautiful. When did you get this?"

"You remember when we got back from Thanksgiving?" I nodded. Right before the conference at the company and the mess that followed. "It was that week."

"Oh." He'd held onto it all this time. Even though we weren't together. Even though I'd ended things. I fought back the tears that threatened to well up in my eyes. Was it possible to cry out of sheer happiness? "Thank you," I said, kissing his cheek as I settled back between his legs. "I love it."

"You're welcome." Then he whispered in my ear: "I have one more thing for you, but that's strictly for my eyes only, so I'll give it to you later."

"Okay," I giggled.

Emily opened the cashmere scarf I got her, and Benjamin had helped me pick out a new compass for Hunter—the brothers said they wanted to get back into hiking, and as long as they didn't force me along every time, I was happy to encourage the habit.

I didn't know how I could possibly top his birthday present, but I'd managed to find some comics Benjamin didn't have for his collection and more nerdy socks he could wear with his suits. I was especially pleased, looking down at our feet, with our matching pair of Batman and Catwoman socks. I'd had to custom order them, and he was so excited when he opened them that he insisted we had to put them on immediately.

I might not have hope for my own parents, given my mom's imminent remarriage and my dad's perpetual absence in my life, but I was learning to let that go. I had two families now: the one I'd built with my best friends, and this one that I was building with Benjamin. I had so many people who loved me and cared for me, and I knew I'd never feel lonely or unwanted ever again.

As I sat there, Benjamin's arms around me, a cup of hot chocolate in my hands, surrounded my laughter and joy, I knew this was what life was all about.

~

MRS. SULLIVAN and I were sitting on the couch as the guys were outside shoveling snow off the driveway. It was a beautiful white Christmas, something I loved more than I could explain. I had my newest romance book in my lap while she thumbed through a cooking magazine next to me.

"So, what do you think about kids?"

I almost spit out my apple cider. *Kids?* Benjamin and I had talked about kids before, but only briefly and jokingly—certainly not since we'd gotten together for real. Did I want kids? My job had always been my priority and success all I could think about. I'd never actually thought about kids, not for me at least. But now...

I chuckled, hoping I didn't sound too nervous. "Maybe we should see about marriage first."

Mrs. Sullivan's eyes twinkled with excitement, and she gave me a little wink. "I don't think it'll be too long."

"Mrs. Sullivan…"

"Please, sweetie. Call me Molly."

"Well, Molly," I said, looked across the room at my boyfriend through the large windows, and my heart fluttered at seeing him laughing with his dad and brother. "We've only been officially together for a few weeks, so I don't know what our future is going to look like yet, but I can tell you one thing." I turned to her. "I do, very much, love your son."

"I know," she beamed. "I'm so glad to have you. Goodness knows Hunter hasn't brought anyone home yet, and he's already thirty-two," she tsked. "I know Ben's younger, but he's also the most sensitive one, the quiet one. He always preferred to stay in and play video games instead of going out. I used to think he was lazy or scared, but now I know the truth."

"What's that?" I was distracted by the guys hollering outside in the snow, throwing snowballs at each other. We were planning on going into town for some of the Christmas festivities—the perks of spending Christmas in a small town, I was told—but it looked like it'd be a while before they cleared off the freshly fallen snow.

"He just hadn't met you yet."

"Oh," I looked up, finding Molly giving me a warm smile as she held my gaze, and I dipped my head. "I'm sure Hunter will find the right person, too," I reassured her by patting her hand. She squeezed it, and then we went back to our respective readings. But one thought lingered in my mind, about Hunter and Gabbi at the Halloween party, and I wondered if something could really happen from there. Today wasn't the day to ponder that, though.

Benjamin came back inside, cheeks red from the cold and eyelashes wet with snowflakes, but with the happiest smile on his face as he came over to me and scooped me up. His mom clearly took that as a sign because she made herself scarce, and I couldn't find it in me to feel sorry or embarrassed.

"Hey!" I shrieked. "You're all wet! Get off!"

He pulled me in for a kiss. "Nope. I'm afraid I can't do that."

"Why not?" I pouted. My pajamas were already starting to get soaked, and then I'd need to change and... Oh. Maybe that wasn't so bad. I wrapped my arms around his neck, leaning up to give him the smallest whisper of a kiss. "If you're going to get me wet, you better take care of it."

"Oh, baby, I plan on it." He winked.

Benjamin shrugged off his coat and snow pants, leaving a big pile of wet clothes on the floor, and then snuggled up with me on the couch. He played with my hair as I read my book, and when I finished the chapter, I let my head fall back against his chest.

"Hi," I whispered, tilting up my chin to find him looking at me.

"Hi," he said back, kissing me lightly. "I can't wait for a hundred more Christmases like today."

I nodded dreamily. "If this is what life will be like together..."

"Every moment with you is going to be perfect, Angel. Because it's us."

"You're a sap."

"You love me."

I hummed and kissed him.

Even though I was a little sad not to spend this Christmas with my brother, it felt good to be with a family that cared about me. And a man that really, truly loved me. One who had a surprise for me upstairs. I couldn't wait, because I had one for him too.

The rest of our lives couldn't come fast enough.

CHAPTER 37
Benjamin

"5, 4, 3, 2, 1... Happy New Year!" The room erupted in a boisterous scream as everyone cheered and exchanged hugs with their loved ones. I pulled Angelina in and kissed her deeply.

"Happy New Year, my love."

Her blue eyes, full and sparkling, looked up at me as she smiled. "Happy New Year, Benjamin."

I grabbed two champagne flutes from a waiter and handed her one before clinking our glasses together. "To many more years together."

"All of them, I hope," she said. "Now, come on, let's go find our friends."

The rest of our crew had wandered out onto the patio of the hotel we'd chosen to spend New Year's at. It was cold and chilly, but it was a beautiful night. I draped my suit jacket over Angelina's shoulders, so we didn't have to go find her wrap, and steered her outside.

Noelle and Matthew were curled up on a tiny loveseat near the space heater—the two biggest people in our group sharing the smallest chair was always funny to see. Gabbi and Charlotte were sitting on a nearby couch talking with Hunter and Daniel.

"Hey gang," Angelina said with a smile, plopping down between her two friends, leaving me to join the guys on the couch across from them.

"How's it going out here?" I asked, taking another sip of champagne before setting the glass on the coffee table.

"It's cold," Charlotte shivered, even under her blanket. I wondered who she bribed to get it. The girl was always cold, no matter her attire, and it certainly didn't help that it was December—well, January now—and in the middle of Portland winter. Adding the fact that she was dressed up for the New Year's Eve party? She was doomed from the start. "And we had to watch these two make out while you were gone."

"Hey!" Noelle protested, her boyfriend turning bright red. "We weren't making out. It was one midnight kiss!"

Gabrielle rolled her eyes. "It's official. This group has been infected by the love disease. I'm going to go vomit in the trash can now."

"Oh, shut up," Charlotte laughed. "Say that to the book you've been reading on your phone all night."

Gabbi gasped, pretending to be offended, and I couldn't keep in my laugh. Angelina and her friends and their romance novels were adorable. Even if my girl read the least out of all of them. But she was so proud when she'd held up the cover of Noelle's first self-published book to me, showing me the artwork she'd done for the cover.

"You two are the worst," Angelina chuckled, but hugged her two friends tightly. "Who thought this was a good idea to spend New Year's here, again? We could have been all warm and cozy at Matthew and Noelle's."

"Yeah, and I could be reading a book with zero judgment," Gabrielle huffed at her side.

Sitting next to Hunter, I couldn't help but notice how his eyes were on Gabrielle, warily watching her movements. He looked half irritated, half amused. I didn't know what to make of it, to be honest. Maybe it was a little bit like me and Angelina at first. I hoped Gabbi wouldn't have any reason to hate Hunter, though. He may be a grump, but he was a good man.

"Noted, Angel," I said. "No rooftop bars for New Year's."

"Not unless we're somewhere warm and sunny," Charlotte chimed in.

I looked around us, at our little group. It was only the second time after Halloween that we hung out like this—the girls, Matthew, Angelina's brother, and my brother, but I kind of liked it. It was fun when all eight of us got together. Even if half of it consisted of listening to the girls talk about books.

"Warm and sunny sounds nice," Angelina agreed.

The two weeks since that night at the restaurant had been amazing. We were together, *really* together, and I liked calling her my girlfriend more than I could have ever imagined. I liked waking her up with toe-curling orgasms even more.

I was looking forward to the next year together, thinking about all the things I wanted to do for her, all of the places I wanted to take her. We weren't living together yet, since Angelina didn't want to leave Gabbi alone in their apartment, but I had plans to woo her over on that front.

Starting with a list of houses that were in my saved bookmarks on my laptop. I wouldn't buy one without her, and while it wouldn't be anything like my parents' house in Montana, I wanted her to have a place that she loved, where she felt at *home*. Was it too soon to buy a house together? Probably. Did I care? Absolutely fucking not. We'd already messed up the order of everything anyway. What were a few more unconventional decisions? I was thirty, madly in love with my girl, and I had my dream job. Life was good. More than. It was great.

"That can be arranged," I grinned, staring at the woman I'd do anything to make happy. The one whose picture was now my lock screen and home screen. We'd taken so many photos since that first one on the waterfall hike, but I liked to look at it sometimes and marvel at how far we'd come.

"Take me too, please," Gabbi begged. "I'm dying to go somewhere. See the world. Travel."

Angelina rolled her eyes at her best friend as she leaned her head on her shoulder. "He's not a billionaire, you know. He doesn't have endless pockets."

Gabbi pouted. "Can't he just send us on a girls trip? You know, to make you happy?"

"Maybe we can all go somewhere this summer?" I said, and Noelle perked up.

"Yes! Let's do it! I'd love to go somewhere before classes are back in session."

Matthew groaned at that. "Don't remind me that spring semester is starting soon and I won't be able to keep you all to myself anymore."

Noelle planted a kiss on his forehead, and then leaned in to whisper something in his ear, which must have been fairly suggestive because his cheeks flushed bright red. "You little fox," he scolded, tickling her sides. "You're gonna pay for that comment later."

"Oh, I hope so," she said, batting her lashes.

Gabbi threw her hands over her eyes. "Gross! Come on! See what I mean? Can't a single girl have one moment of peace around here?"

Hunter looked straight at her, smirked, and said, "I might know where you can get some peace," and then took a long sip of his beer as they held eye contact. I almost held my breath wondering who would look away first. It was like a train wreck you couldn't look away from.

Gabbi blinked, then narrowed her eyes. "I don't need that sort of peace, thank you."

"Oh, my god," Charlotte guffawed. "That was so good. Gabbi, you should have seen your face."

It was good indeed, because even from across the table, the glow on her face was unmistakable as she continued staring down my brother, ignoring his insinuation that they could get out of here and... do whatever it was my brother did with his one-night stands. That was something I did not want to picture. Hunter having sex? Ew. Add in Angelina's best friend? Double ew. My eyebrow twitched as I picked up my drink, quickly draining it.

"Well, on that note, who wants to call it a night?" It was almost one AM, and we'd been out here for a while. Even with the space heaters and the lack of drizzle for once, it was still pretty cold.

Angelina yawned, stretching her arms up. "Sounds like a plan, babe. But only if you carry me." The others snickered, but I wasn't one to tell her no. I turned around and bent my knees, letting her climb on my back in a piggyback ride. We said goodnight to our friends, and she relaxed against my shoulders; I could see her eyes fluttering shut as I carried her out and to my car.

"Did you have fun tonight?"

"Mm-hmm."

"Do you think Noelle and Matthew are going to go home and have as freaky of sex as we will?"

"Benjamin!" That got her to wake up. Her cheeks were red, and I wasn't sure which part embarrassed her more—me talking about sex so freely or the idea of her friends doing it. Although she'd gotten more open and honest about her feelings with me lately, and I would never take it for granted. There'd always been a solid foundation of trust that we'd built upon, but now it was different. Now I felt like I could tell her anything, and I knew she felt the same with me.

"I did mean what I said, you know. That I'd take you somewhere warm and sunny. I'll take you anywhere you want to go, my angel."

"I like the sound of that," she hummed. I let her slide off my back to climb into the car, and as I drove home, my hand around hers on her lap, I thought to myself, does life get any more perfect than this?

Angelina

"*I want your midnights but I'll be cleaning up bottles with you on New Year's Day...*"

The speakers in Benjamin's apartment—soon to be *our* apartment if I got my way—played as we swayed in the kitchen at nine AM on January 1st. It was a quiet sort of peace; one I wasn't sure I'd ever really enjoyed before he came into my life. I wanted this—him, all his midnights, and all the time in between.

"So, Princess, what do you think?"

"About what?"

"About our next year together."

"Hmm, I'm considering it."

"I'll take as many as you'll give me."

I laid my head on his shoulder. "I feel greedy."

"Why?"

"Because I want them all."

He kissed the top of my head. "You and I both, Angel."

"Good," I said, squeezing him. "Hopefully there's a lot more adventures to come."

"I can think of a few," he grinned mischievously.

"Please tell me that they don't involve hiking. Or bugs. Or dirt."

Benjamin laughed. "Maybe not. But there are so many places I'd like to go with you. I want to see the world together."

"That does sound nice. Where shall we start?"

"Where do you want to go? I know you've always said Paris is your favorite, but if you want to go somewhere else—"

"Paris is perfect," I said. "Besides, you know what they call it, right?"

"The City of Lights?"

"No." I beamed up at him. "The City of Love. And I can think of nothing I'd rather do than go there with the man I love."

Benjamin kissed my lips, once, twice, before nuzzling my nose. "I don't think I'm ever going to get used to you calling me that."

"Well, you better. Because you're stuck with me."

"Oh, that's where you're wrong. Because you, my beautiful angel, are stuck with *me*."

"Speaking of being stuck with me," I said, biting my lip, "I was thinking, you know, my lease with Gabbi expires in a few months, and then... What if we moved in together? I spend almost all my time here anyway. It would only make sense," I rushed in to add.

"It would make sense, yes. Except my lease is expiring in a few months too."

"What?" I frowned. "You're not going to renew? But this place is incredible." I loved the floor to ceiling windows and the spacious kitchen with the beautiful island. I couldn't imagine him not living here.

"You see," he said, steering me over to the table where his open laptop was. He plopped me into a chair in front of it. "I had a better idea."

The webpage in front of me had a house listing, and I blinked up at him in surprise. "You're going to buy a house?"

"No, Angel. We are going to buy a house." I gaped at him, and he cleared his throat. "If you want, of course. I was thinking we could start looking together. No rush. We could do new construction if you want, that way you could design your dream house. One we could live in. Together."

I felt the telltale sting in my eyes, but I wasn't going to cry. Absolutely not. But I was floored that he'd even considered this. I jumped up and wrapped my arms around his waist. "I would love that. Let's do it."

"Yeah?" He cupped my cheeks in his hands.

"Yeah," I answered with a kiss. "I want to do everything as long as it's with you."

"Everything? Does that include being the future Mrs. Sullivan?"

My heart threatened to explode inside my chest. "You better buy me one big rock, Mr. Sullivan." My voice was wobbly, but I didn't care.

"Oh, I wouldn't do anything less."

I considered whether telling him or not, but I quickly made up my mind. "Did you know your mom asked me about grandchildren when we were there for Christmas? We'd been officially dating for like, a minute, and it kind of caught me off guard."

His face grew serious, and his hand went to my arm, stroking it up and down in a soothing motion. "I'm sorry. I'll tell her to leave it alone." I smiled in gratitude, and after a moment he asked, "How do you feel about kids?"

"I don't want them now, but maybe someday, when I'm, y'know, thirty-something and I've accomplished all my goals, maybe we can sit down and think about having one."

He hummed. "Thirty."

"What?"

"Let's have one when you're thirty."

I laughed. "You make it sound so easy."

"I'll do everything I can to make it as easy as possible for you. There's no one else I want to do this with, Angel."

"Alright, that's enough sweetness for the day, mister. Now get out of my hair before I claw your eyes out." I waved my nails in front of his face.

He grinned but pulled me closer, making me moan when I felt him against my lower belly. "You say that as if I didn't like it when you scratched me last night."

"Is that a challenge, Sullivan?"

"Always, with you."

And so, our morning turned into a long afternoon in bed, as Benjamin showed me just how much he enjoyed it when I got my claws on him. Several times.

To think that, just a few months ago, I'd been opposed to this. To fall in love, to accept that someone could love me for who I was, that I could find happiness with a man by my side.

I'd never been so happy to be completely, irremediably wrong.

Epilogue
ANGELINA

Three Months Later...

"Where are we going?" I looked out the window of the private jet Benjamin had somehow convinced Nicolas to let him borrow for the weekend. Which was madness.

"You'll see," my boyfriend said with a smug grin.

In the almost four months that we'd been together—about six when you included our we're-not-together, friends-with-benefits period—this may be the craziest thing Benjamin had done for me. Second only to falling in love with me.

I used to believe that love wasn't something I had time for, something that was worth making space for in my life. I used to think most men wouldn't want a career-oriented woman, a woman who was focused on herself and couldn't put a relationship first. And maybe I was right about most men, but not about him.

Benjamin was proving to me, day after day, that he loved all of me—even the part of me that spent too many hours in the office. If I wasn't home for dinner? He'd bring it to me at work. If I was tired and couldn't stay awake at night? He'd rub my back before sending me to bed. I didn't know how good it would be to love someone until I had him.

"I can't believe you planned this without me knowing." I also couldn't believe we were flying on a private plane, fully equipped with a bedroom that I intended to make use of later.

"Gabbi thought I was crazy trying to pack for you without telling you."

"Yeah? Well, she's right."

"I know," he said, kissing my hand. "That's why I asked for her help."

"Oh. Well." I gave him that look—the one that said, *you're totally getting laid later*. Joining the mile high club sounded like fun to me. "We'll see how you did when we unpack."

"You're beautiful no matter what you wear, Angelina." Benjamin brushed a strand of hair behind my ear. I'd come to love wearing it down; I enjoyed when he played with my hair. "Or better yet, he added, "nothing at all." At that, I looked around and then thought, *fuck it*. I unbuckled my seatbelt and climbed on top of him, straddling his lap. "What are you doing?"

I leaned down to kiss his neck. "You can't just say things like that, Sullivan."

"Is that so?"

"Not without making me want to climb you like a tree."

He grinned, then stood from his seat, carrying me with him as I wrapped my legs around his waist. "You know that's one of my favorite positions, darling, but I have a better idea right now."

"Yeah?" I said, breathless already. If I shifted just a little lower, he'd be pressed against me in all his glory. I tried to wiggle myself down, desperate to feel him, but he held me in place.

"Not yet, Princess. I have plans for you." He proceeded to spend the next few hours showing me just how detailed those plans were.

∽

AFTER PULLING ourselves out of the bedroom and the orgasm-filled haze, we were once again seated in the main cabin of the plane, champagne glasses and a plate of chocolate-covered strawberries sitting in front of us.

"This is lovely," I sighed. "You probably could have won me over a lot faster if you started with this."

"Nah, I like our path to get here just the way it was." Benjamin kissed my forehead. "And now I have one more surprise for you."

I raised my eyebrows. Between this trip, plane sex, and everything else, this man was off the hook for presents for a year. And more. Not that I would ever complain about him buying me things. I knew how satisfying it was for him to see me wearing his well-thought-out presents.

Benjamin took a small box out of his pocket, and my breath caught in my throat. Was he—*No*. A beautiful necklace pendant was sitting in the middle of the black velvet. A little silver charm shining brightly.

My eyes welled up with tears. He knew how much this meant to me. He'd listened to me, and remembered, and I loved him so much more than I could ever express in words. "Benjamin," I said in an awed whisper, looking at the tiny Eiffel Tower charm.

"I told you I'd take you to Paris, Angel. This is me fulfilling my promise."

"But all this... You did all this for me? Just for the weekend?"

"We have a lot to jam in, but I promise I will make it the best weekend of your life."

"It already is." I sniffled.

"Want me to put it on you?" I nodded, then took off the pendant I was wearing: a charm with my name initial. He reached around my neck, sweeping my hair to the side, and clasped the ends of the necklace together, letting the little Eiffel Tower rest against my breastbone. "Beautiful," he murmured, eyes full of love.

I touched the pendant for a moment, but before I could say anything, the flight attendant came into the cabin. "Mr. Sullivan, we just wanted to let you know that we'll be dimming the cabin lights shortly for the night. We still have a few hours before we land."

Benjamin thanked him, then took my hand and we headed back to the bedroom. We barely got any sleep, though—I was too busy showing my boyfriend exactly how much I loved him.

∼

Benjamin

Admittedly, this plan of mine was a little insane, but when Nicolas told me I could borrow his jet, I hadn't been able to resist. Who knew there were so many perks to being friends with a millionaire's son.

The day Angelina told me that she'd always loved France and Paris specifically, I knew that I had to take her one day. I wanted to make her happy in her favorite place in the world. I wanted to make her happy everywhere, really, but this was a start.

"Okay," she said, coming out of the bathroom wearing a white robe. "This is the most over the top hotel I've ever stayed in. Like, seriously. Feel this robe." I rubbed a hand over it just to appease her, but she was right. It was luxuriously soft. Angelina flopped onto the bed, her curls spilling wildly over the comforter. "What's the plan for tonight?"

I looked at my watch. We'd landed mid-morning, and by the time we got to our hotel, it was early afternoon. Plenty of time to go out and do something—my big plans weren't till tomorrow anyway. "Hmm," I thought out loud. "What would you like to do? Besides kissing your wonderful boyfriend who brought you here, of course."

"Wonderful might be a bit of an understatement," she said, pulling me onto the bed with her to give me a kiss.

"Wow, a rare compliment from Angelina Bradford. What will I do with myself?"

She rolled her eyes. "Don't let it go to your head."

"Too late."

"Anyway, I thought you would've already made plans. Isn't there anything you want to do? We could go up the Eiffel Tower if you haven't before. Or we could go find a little place to get dinner."

"Whatever you want. All my plans are for tomorrow."

"Alright, I've got it!" She snapped her fingers. "Dinner, Eiffel Tower, and crepes. In that order."

"Let's do it."

Hours later, once we were stuffed with a delicious dinner of French delicacies, we watched the Eiffel Tower light up before taking the elevator to the top. The view of the city, with all the twinkling lights and the Seine below us, was breathtaking. But Angelina's eyes as she leaned on the metal railing, wrapping her coat around her tighter as the wind blew in her hair—that was my favorite sight of all. Seeing the wonder and happiness on her face.

We set off towards the Seine and found a small patisserie along the way where we stopped for crepes. I preferred savory dishes, but even I had to admit the strawberry crepe I ordered was incredible.

"So good," Angelina moaned in between bites with her mouth full. She insisted we couldn't share, because of all the desserts she'd in her life, she claimed this one took the top spot. She'd never been like her friend Noelle, who loved sweets of all kinds, and normally stuck to either dark chocolate or coffee flavored things. But watching Angelina eat her Nutella crepe with so much enthusiasm made the whole weekend worth it.

"Are you excited for tomorrow?"

"Always," she smiled, and I wiped a little bit of chocolate from her cheek.

We ended the night by strolling down the river, hand in hand, relishing the beauty of Paris.

∼

It turned out, when it came to planning, Angelina was the expert, but I had still put together what I thought was a great itinerary for the day: visiting some of her favorite spots and sneaking in some other things I thought she'd love.

By the last stop on our day's agenda, we were both exhausted, so we got back to the hotel. But I had one more trick up my sleeve. "What do you think about one more surprise?"

Angelina's lazy form was sprawled out on the bed, trying to prolong her late-afternoon nap. "I think if you give me any more surprises, I'm going to expect this treatment on a regular basis."

I laughed. "Get dressed. Wear something nice. We're going to dinner."

"Don't I always dress nice?" she glared at me with only one eye open.

"You're not trapping me with that. You know I think you look beautiful in anything. Or nothing. But you'll want to dress up particularly nice for where we're going." And for what I was planning to do. Because I knew her, and if her nails weren't perfect and her hair and makeup wasn't done, she'd be annoyed with me forever. This was an important memory for her, for us, and I wanted it to be one she would always look back on fondly. That's why I'd gotten Gabbi's help on picking out a few of her favorite dresses to pack.

After styling her hair in a fancy updo, Angelina wore my favorite of her dresses. It was white, and more feminine and pretty than anything else I'd seen in her closet; it complemented her complexion beautifully, and I loved the full skirt. She did look beautiful in everything, but *damn*.

"Ready?" she asked after putting her earrings on.

"You look stunning." She sat down to put her heels on, and I —as per my routine, because I gained immense satisfaction from doing things for her—kneeled to buckle them for her.

"Thank you."

"You never have to thank me for taking care of you, Princess," I said with a kiss on her ankle.

She rolled her eyes lightheartedly. "You are the most ridiculous man."

Our driver awaited us downstairs, and after a twenty-minute drive we got the restaurant where we had the best French food and wine of my life. Dessert, too, was amazing; or should I say desserts, because Angelina couldn't decide so we ordered a taste of each one.

"Want to walk?" I said after paying the bill. She nodded and slipped her hand into mind. Luckily, we didn't have too far to go, but even in her three-inch heels she didn't look like she minded.

Angelina sighed happily as the view came into sight. "This has been the perfect day," she said with a smile, leaning her head on my shoulder as we stood holding hands, staring at the Eiffel Tower from the concrete platform that overlooked it.

"Are you happy?"

"So happy. But you know I didn't need any of this. I love it, don't get me wrong, but—"

"You know, I don't think I like calling you my girlfriend anymore."

"What?" Confused, she wrinkled her nose, then dropped my hand and scowled at me. "You brought me to Paris just to say *that*?"

I chuckled. "No, Angel. I didn't bring you to Paris just to say that." She huffed and turned away, grumbling under her breath. Cursing me and my teasing, most likely. Except I wasn't teasing, not this time. "Angelina." She crossed her arms and kept stubbornly looking at the Eiffel Tower in front of her.

I cleared my throat and said, "Babe." And she must have heard something in my voice because she finally turned around, gasping loudly. "I have a better title in mind."

"Oh my god." Her hands flew to her mouth when she saw me down on one knee before her.

"A way better title."

"Oh my god. *Shut up.*"

I grinned and took her hand in mine. "Angelina Rose Bradford, from the very first moment you walked into my life, you captivated me. Then you frustrated me endlessly, made me chase after you, and I've never regretted one single moment. I never will. I love you when you roll your eyes at me, when you glare at me, when you challenge me; I love you when you listen to me talk about my favorite comics and I love you when you cuddle with me on the couch and we watch another romcom that we both know will end the same, but we watch it anyway because it makes you happy." A little sob escaped her, and I fought against my own tears. "I want to spend the rest my life teaching you how to play video games so you can kick my ass, I want to wake up every morning and kiss you, and maybe have a kid or two that we'll spoil like crazy and I'll stay home with them so that you can keep being a corporate badass. I want to do everything with you because you're my best friend and the love of my life."

"Oh," she said, barely above a whisper. Her free hand was clasped over her chest. I'd stunned her into silence.

"Will you marry me, Angel? Be my wife?"

A moment passed in which she blinked back the tears. Then, "Nope," she said. It was my turn to glare at her as her lips spread into the biggest grin. "Yes, Benjamin. I'd love to marry you."

"I told you I didn't want to call you my girlfriend anymore. Fiancée might be temporary, but it has a nice ring to it. Although I cannot wait to call you my wife."

I slid the ring onto her finger before standing up and pulling her into my arms. Dipping her, and I didn't care if anyone was watching us when I kissed the love of my life with the biggest grin on my face. She giggled as I kissed her nose, her cheek, her forehead, and when we finally pulled apart, she held up her hand, admiring the ring on her left ring finger.

"You, Mr. Sullivan, are a romantic at heart."

"That I might be, future Mrs. Sullivan."

A little glint flickered in her eyes. "And what if I wanted to keep my last name?"

"Then I'd take yours."

"I think Angelina Bradford Sullivan has a nice ring to it."

"Agreed." I sealed it with a kiss.

I'd arranged for a photographer to take photos, and after that, we went to sit on the lawn, looking at the Eiffel Tower as we waited for it to sparkle on the top of the hour. We took a selfie, just like that first one at the waterfall. I liked this one even better. There was a ring in it.

"Who would have thought," Angelina said, "that we'd end up like this?"

I wrapped my arms around her middle, her back to my chest. "Together? In Paris?"

"Mm-hmm. And getting married. Remember when I hated you?"

"You only remind me of it every other day."

"I can't help it if you're the most infuriating man on the planet."

"But you love me."

"I do." She grinned. "And I hope you know I'm going to be stealing the covers *and* your shirts for the rest of our lives."

"I'm counting on it." I cupped her cheek and kissed her, and then we stayed like that, with Angelina cocooned in my arms, until the Eiffel Tower did its thing and glimmered.

Before the night was over, I took her on a last little Parisian adventure: a cruise down the Seine. It was nice that we were alone here, just the two of us, with no rush to call our families or friends. I liked that we could keep this moment, this new beginning, to ourselves for now. There would be time for Instagram posts and Facebook status updates later, but right now, I just wanted to be here. Holding the love of my life as we swayed slowly on the little bateau.

"Isn't it beautiful?" Angelina said.

"Yes," I responded, but I wasn't looking at the view around us. I was looking at her, wearing my ring on her finger, lit up with joy as she looked at the city that she loved so much. "Yes, it is." I stroked her hair and kissed her temple. "But not as beautiful as you."

"Are you happy?"

"The happiest."

She squeezed me tight and placed a soft kiss on my cheek. "I never knew I could be this happy."

"I plan to make you this happy, and more, for the rest of our lives."

"You better," she said, looking up at me from under her lashes. "Or I'll divorce you and keep the cat."

I frowned. "We don't have a cat."

My lovely bride-to-be smirked. "Not yet."

"Hmm. We'll see."

She narrowed her eyes. "Benjamin."

"Angelina." She huffed and I kissed her. "I love you."

"I know." She sighed happily and wrapped her arms around me. If forever looked like this, I couldn't wait to get started.

"What do you think about a summer wedding?"

Angelina's eyes sparkled brighter than Paris. "What do you think about here?"

"I'll be the one at the end of the aisle."

"And I'll be the one saying yes."

Extended Epilogue
ANGELINA

One Year Later...

"Oh my god," I laughed. "*You didn't!*"

My husband looked at me with a cocky smile as we stood before a familiar lodge. "I did."

"Hmm," I looked around, pretending I was seeing the place for the first time. "The lake looks very nice."

Benjamin hugged me from behind. "I've heard it's good for midnight swims."

"Oh? What else have you heard?"

"That if you get really lucky, the girl of your dreams will fall in love with you here."

"That seems unlikely."

"It does, doesn't it." He placed a kiss on the crown of my head. "But sometimes dreams come true."

"I can't believe you really did this."

"You should know me well enough by now. I like spoiling you. And even more than that, I like taking you away."

Hence the weekend getaway. It'd been six months since our wedding—since we exchanged vows in my favorite city in the world. And now here we were, at the place where we first met, only this time it was covered in snow, and we'd be sharing a cabin. I doubted we'd want to leave, but even I had to admit that the snow-clad landscape was beautiful. I'd go on a run with Benjamin before curling up with a book at the big ski lodge at the bottom of the mountain, and once he was done with his exercises and we had a cup of hot chocolate to warm up, well, then he could take me back to the cabin and warm me up in a different (and better) way.

Except, "Oh. Where are we going?" We passed the cabins where we'd stayed last year, and Benjamin kept walking.

"You didn't think I'd let my wife stay in one of those tiny little cabins, did you?"

I shrugged. "Figured it'd be for old time's sake."

He gave me a little grin. "Nah. Come on." We trudged through more snow before stopping in front of a much larger wooden structure. "It's the Honeymoon Suite, I'm told."

"Benjamin! You didn't have to do all of this, really."

He pulled me against his chest. "You know I'd do anything for you. Plus, this one has a jacuzzi tub inside. I thought you might like that to help those muscles of yours that are about to be very sore."

"I don't think skiing will be that—"

"Oh, you misunderstand me, Angel," he said, and my body lit up under his stare.

"Insatiable."

"Only for you," he muttered, and steered me inside.

The Suite was gorgeous, so much more spacious than the ordinary cabins, complete with a small kitchen, a king-sized bed, and of course the giant tub in the bathroom. It also had a couch and a little round table and chairs. Benjamin was right: this was way better.

"I know it's not Paris, but..."

"I don't need Paris," I said. "Not when I'm with you."

He let out a fake gasp. "Who are you and what have you done with my wife? She's never this sweet to me."

I smacked him in the chest. "Let me say thank you, husband, and then I'll go back to telling you that you're the worst, okay?"

He leaned down, pulling me into his arms once again, and placed a kiss on my lips. "You can tell me how terrible I am any day of the week, as long as I get to have you like this."

"You know," I said, bringing my arms around his neck. "I'm very glad we eloped."

"Sometimes I worry you'll regret giving up the big fancy wedding that you deserved."

Our wedding was a whirlwind—we'd decided to elope, and we brought our best friends and closest family with us to Paris for the wedding of my dreams. "I'm happy with every single choice I've made when it comes to you, Ben. I don't regret a single thing."

"Even when you pushed me away and rejected my love?"

I tugged on his hair. "You deserved that, you jerk."

"Ouch. You wound me."

"You're a big, strong man, I think you can handle it."

"Hmm, your big, strong man would like to show you just how much he can handle—" I cut him off with a kiss. "Such an effective way of getting me to shut up, Mrs. Bradford Sullivan."

I hummed and stood on my tiptoes to deepen the kiss. He pulled me closer, tightening his embrace. "I can think of even better ways, Mr. Sullivan. Though they involve a little less snow and a lot less clothes."

"I do like the sound of that."

"Good. Because I can't wait to show you *my* special surprise. But you'll have to feed me first."

"What if I eat you instead?" His voice got husky as his hands fondled my ass.

"Uh-uh." I took his hands in mine. "We're going skiing, getting hot chocolate and cookies, and then you get your gift."

Benjamin pouted. "No fair."

"Appease me," I laughed. "But you're holding my hand on the chair lift."

"Always."

We'd gone on a ski trip last month with our friends, so we had brand new snow clothes and equipment and didn't need to rent anything. I'd forgotten how much I loved rushing down the mountain with the wind and snowflakes in my face. As much as I loved relaxing in the lounge by the big fireplace and reading a book while I let Benjamin run out some of his excess energy. Not too much, though—he had to save some for keeping up with me in the bedroom.

For some people, the passion waned after being together for long enough. Maybe it was routine or maybe that was simply how it worked for them. Benjamin and I had been together for over a year now, and I wanted him more today than our first night together. And I would want him more tomorrow. And the day after that. And the day after that.

"How do you think our babies are doing?" I asked him as we snuggled on the couch after a long day of skiing. I'd wimped out around mid-afternoon and went back to the cabin to take a nice long bath in that glorious hot tub.

"I still can't believe I let you talk me into that," Benjamin grumbled.

Much to his dismay, we got not one, but two cats. When we went to the shelter, there was a bonded pair of little black kittens; we took one look at them and knew we couldn't separate them.

Bruce and Selina were currently six months old, and we adopted them after getting back from our very lavish Honeymoon—two weeks in Greece, enjoying the warm beaches of the Mediterranean, and another two weeks of traveling around Europe. It was fantastic, and I'd gotten the best tan (and sex) of my life. So, when we got back home, it seemed like the perfect time to expand our family. I wasn't ready to have kids yet, but I knew Benjamin was going to make an excellent stay-at-home Dad one day.

"You love them."

He sighed, kissing the top of my head. "I love you. And I love them." Benjamin was a dog person, but it was hard for him to convince me that he only *tolerated* our kittens when I found him curled up on the couch with them all the time—one on his lap, the other by his legs—or when he'd carry them around the house like babies. Once I even found him working in his home office with Bruce on his lap and Selina on his shoulder. I almost cried.

"You know, I love it here, but..." He ran his fingers through my hair, distracting me for a moment. "I think I like our house more. Do you think we could install a hot tub at home?"

We bought a new construction house in Beaverton. It was further away from work, but a lot of people in the office were going remote anyways, and Benjamin didn't mind the drive. The neighborhood was new, quiet, and gated. Plus, the house was beautiful, and even if it wasn't a mansion like his parents' house, it was still two floors and thousands of square feet more than I'd ever had growing up. We were working on convincing our friends to buy houses and move onto our street. I couldn't think of anything better than having the family we'd built right next door.

"Anything for you, Angel."

"Good," I smirked.

"Is there anything you can't get away with?"

I straddled his lap. "I don't know," I said, raising an eyebrow. "Want to find out?"

"Oh yes." His lips were on mine in an instant, catching me off guard. Every time Benjamin kissed me, even after all this time, it was like this. Full of fire, longing, and so much love. I gave it all back to him, every piece of my heart he'd conquered. They were all his anyway. I didn't want them back.

"You know the problem with a hot tub?" he mused, running his thumb over my lips. "I won't be able to control myself."

"Hmm, I think I like you uncontrolled," I said, and then his mouth was back on me, and he picked me up from the couch, wrapped my legs around his waist, and pushed me against the wooden wall.

"You haven't seen anything yet, Angel." A shiver went down

my spine and my breath itched. He always got this reaction out of me when he acted like this, wild and close to losing control for me.

"Ben!" I squealed, trying to wriggle away as he planted kisses all over my neck, tickling me.

"Sorry, you're just too tempting. I can't help myself."

"I hate you."

He smirked. "No, you don't."

I narrowed my eyes at him. Damn him and his stupidly attractive—*everything*. I wanted him so much, and from the arrogant smug look on his face, he knew it all too well. Whenever I tried to look pissed off, it was no use, really. I hoped to never stop feeling this way.

"How do you want me?" he asked, already tugging my leggings down. "Like this, against the wall, or on the bed?" He nipped at my neck, causing me to moan, and then licked over the spot to soothe it. When his erection pressed against me, my eyes rolled back. His fingers made their way into my panties, and I gasped, rocking against him.

"You're so wet," he groaned. "How do you want me, baby? Use your words."

"Wall," I panted, shimmying out of my underwear and fumbling with Benjamin's sweats.

"Good girl."

Thank God for birth control, I thought as his cock sprang free. I aligned myself and pushed down onto him, crying out as he bottomed out. I'd never get used to how incredible he felt.

"Fuck, baby. You feel amazing." I held onto his shoulders, my nails digging into the fabric of his T-shirt as he started moving, picking up the tempo and pounding into me. "Such a good girl. Look how well you take me, Angel. Fuck."

"Benjamin?" I panted against his mouth.

"Yeah?" He gripped my ass and squeezed tightly, surely leaving bruises. It made me delirious to know he loved to leave marks on my body.

"Shut up and fuck me. Hard." He complied. I gasped as he drilled into me, faster and rougher, until he sent me over the edge. I clung to him as waves of pleasure slammed into me, making me shudder, and moments later I felt Benjamin found his own release. Warmth spilled into me, and I let out a satisfied sigh. As much as I loved it, he had a secret obsession with painting me with his come, inside or out. Once we stopped using condoms, he started pushing it back into my body or watching as his come dripped down my thighs with a reverent look on his face. It's safe to say he was going to be obsessed with getting me pregnant whenever I let him.

When our breaths finally evened out, Benjamin brought me over to the hot tub. We stripped the rest of our clothes off and got inside.

It took just a few minutes of kissing in the hot water for us to become desperate again. I rode him as he guided my hips up and down, thrusting in and out with his eyes fixed on me.

"You look like a goddess when you fuck me like this, baby," he panted. Those words, paired with him biting and licking my breasts, were like a drug to me, making me come on the spot. Benjamin wasn't too far behind me.

In my pleasure-hazed state, I hoped our lives would always be like this. That we would always love each other like this. I thought about our journey, how we started and what we'd overcome to be here, together. No matter what would happen in the future, I knew I'd always have him by my side, and that was all that mattered. Because Benjamin Sullivan was my home. And that was enough.

"Angelina?"

"Hmm?"

"Let's get the damn hot tub."

The End

Acknowledgments

Sometimes it's still hard to believe I wrote one complete book, let alone two. I was lucky enough to be able to quit my job to pursue writing full time, and I have loved how much I've learned over the last six months during this journey. I'm so glad to be able to tell stories that I love. I hope you love them too and will stick around with me for many more books to come.

To Gabbi, my best friend, my person: Thank you for not telling me to shut up as I tell you about my writing for the hundredth time. I swear, I've texted you six billion times with things about Gabbi (since you are her namesake, after all). Thank you for always brainstorming with me, giving me new ideas, and in general, just being my sounding board. I cannot wait to write your book next, and I'm absolutely going to cry over it with you. I know I say it all the time, but you are so important to me, and I love you so much. You are one person I don't know what I would do without, and I'm so grateful to have you in my life. Love you!

To Al, who drew the beautiful art that graces this cover: What would I do without you?? Thank you for letting me go on and on about Angelina and Benjamin dressing up as Batman and Catwoman, and for all of our crazy insane conversations. I am so grateful to have someone like you to turn my characters into a reality. I cannot wait for the rest!

To Arzum, the captain of my hype squad: Truly, I am so *so* grateful for you! You have been cheering me on from the moment you read my first book, and we've become such good friends. Our daily conversations bring me so much joy, as does constantly teasing you with this story before it was finished. You are literally a ray of sunshine, and I cannot wait for you to freak out over Benjamin and Angelina as much as I am sure you will. I love you!

To my friends and my beta readers—you know who you are, I appreciate you and your thoughts so much! I am so grateful to have such a great support system in all of you.

To my Parents: I love you. I am so grateful for your support and cheering me on. Please *never* ever read my books. Thanks.

Also by Jennifer Chipman

Best Friends Book Club
Academically Yours - Noelle & Matthew
Disrespectfully Yours - Angelina & Benjamin
Fearlessly Yours - Gabrielle & Hunter
Gracefully Yours - Charlotte & Daniel
Contractually Yours - Nicolas & Zofia (coming soon)

Castleton University
A Not-So Prince Charming - Ella & Cameron
Once Upon A Fake Date - Audrey & Parker (late 2024)

Witches of Pleasant Grove
Spookily Yours - Willow & Damien
Wickedly Yours - Luna & Zain (coming Fall 2024)

About the Author

Originally from the Portland area, Jennifer now lives in Orlando with her dog, Walter and cat, Max. She always has her nose in a book and loves going to the Disney Parks in her free time.

Website: www.jennchipman.com

- amazon.com/author/jenniferchipman
- goodreads.com/jennchipman
- instagram.com/jennchipmanauthor
- x.com/jennchipman
- tiktok.com/@jennchipmanauthor
- pinterest.com/jennchipmanauthor

Printed in Great Britain
by Amazon